THE HOLLOWS

TOM HORN

Published by Purple Parrot Publishing

Printed in the United Kingdom

First Printing, 2020

ISBN: Print: 978-1-912677-58-0

Ebook: 978-1-912677-59-7

Purple Parrot Publishing

www.purpleparrotpublishing.co.uk

Edited by Viv Ainslie

ACKNOWLEDGEMENTS

Much like my first novel *The Chosen: The Chronicles of Vespia Book 1*, this second novel, *The Hollows*, could not have been possible without the help of those close to me; friends and family alike. Countless hours have been spent reading, editing and developing the manuscript to the point that the book could be placed in your hands. I have a small circle of *beta readers* that endure *every* draft along the way. To all involved you have my gratitude and love.

As always, Dorian, my darling wife of 38 years has been a tremendous force in getting this book *just so*. She has guided me with her love and support through each step of the process. And admittedly she is responsible for several chapters being written—vital information that I had neglected that *needed* to be included (but I had been *too lazy* to actually write). She cracked her whip and steadfastly demanded they be written. Honestly the book is much better for it. And in my *haste* to finish the book I rushed its completion—but she didn't like the way I ended it. (Nor did I, if I'm being honest.) She put her foot down and *demanded* it be changed. Knowing all along that she was right, I altered the ending to our *mutual* satisfaction. (*Thank you for keeping me honest with myself!*) NNCH!

When my Editor first read the completed manuscript, it wasn't her *cup of tea*. But as we delved through the book during the editing process, she came to love it. The complex characters drew her into *The Hollows* and she began to get excited about the novel. Her efforts have continued to strengthen the book, making it better and better. Vivienne puts in an extraordinary amount of time and work into each book she publishes under the *Purple Parrot* banner and it shows! I will forever be thankful that she has invited me into the *Parrot Cage*. I couldn't be in better company, and I feel truly blessed.

Thank you all!

—TH

January 2020

DEDICATION

For Jayne and Katy...

CONTENTS

PROLOGUE
THE ACCIDENT

"Clear!"

They tried again to revive my mother but it wasn't working. I stood motionless beside the window staring at the medical staff trying vainly to restore life to the woman that I knew was already gone. They were so busy trying to save her that they didn't seem to notice that my brother and I were standing there. I kept Bobby pressed against me wishing that neither of us had entered our mother's hospital room. I vaguely heard the doctor ordering the nurse to recharge the paddles but my whole brain seemed muddled in a thick fog of grief and utter panic. I turned from their futile efforts and stared down at my brother—he was staring transfixed out the window—I wasn't even sure he was breathing. A single tear fell from my eye, rolled down my cheek and struck his brunette curls. I followed his spellbound gaze and frowned in disbelief.

Just beyond the parking lot I could see a gray wolf sitting upon its haunches. Curiously it seemed to be bathed in a ghostly bluish-white light. It lifted its head and howled a mournful plea to the silvery ball of the moon; which hung in a cloudless sky thick with a smattering of sparkling stars that were like diamonds set against a sea of black velvet.

In the heavy fog of numbness that surrounded my six-year-old brother and me, I could hear the doctor cite the time of our mother's passing. It was 7:57pm. I could faintly detect his cold hand upon my shoulder in his clinical attempt to offer me comfort. His other hand tousled my brother's hair. *"I'm sorry,"* I think he said, but I couldn't be certain. I couldn't take my eyes from what I was witnessing outside the hospital.

A white wolf bathed in the same ghostly light as the gray, loped across the parking lot toward the other. As the white reached the grassy knoll where the gray waited, they greeted one another playfully. After a moment they turned and seemed to stare right at my brother and I. The white barked twice and lifted a solitary paw before both wolves slipped off into the night. A moment later the gray returned and seemed to lock his gaze with mine. I felt oddly comforted. Bobby looked up at me and asked, "Was that Mom and Dad?"

The realization struck me like a bolt of lightning out of the blue, clear sky. My gaze was immediately pulled back to the spot where the wolves had been. I shook my head. *"How can it be?"* My words sounded hollow and unconvincing even to me. I truly wanted to believe that they weren't really gone. That they had transformed somehow, defying all logic and reason. Crazy right? But I could hope. Hope was all that I had left. That wasn't true. I still had Bobbybear.

Only hours before I had gotten the call that Mom and Dad had been in a horrible collision with a semi-truck on the Interstate. Dad had been killed instantly but Mom was barely hanging on by a thread. We had taken a taxi to the hospital so that we could be with her when she woke. Her condition had stabilized and the doctors had moved her to a private room. They said she was going to be fine. But she wasn't. She died never knowing that we were there for her.

We have no family in the city. It has always just been the four of us. Now it was just going to be Bobby and me. I didn't really have a clue what our next step should be. I knew Mom and Dad had family in a tiny mountain community upstate known as *The Hollows*. But I had no idea who they are or how I could contact them.

I know it sounds strange, but my parents never really talked about their family—at least not in front of us kids. They never talked about where they were from either. My relatives are just as much a mystery to me as The Hollows. All I really knew for certain was that my Mom had a sister by the name of Abigail Wellington.

Aunt Abigail had sent me the charm I wore around my neck as a present for my thirteenth birthday. I've worn it for almost three years straight without ever taking it off. It is a white-gold pentagram within a circle. There are even those that believe it is a talisman... said to ward off the mystical pull of the moon and prevent lycanthropy. On the back of the charm is etched a simple phrase in Latin: *Cave Canem* which translates to '*Beware of the dog*' if you can believe it.

I always thought that the whole thing was a load of crap. In the days ahead I was going to find out just how wrong a girl could be...

CHAPTER 1
ABIGAIL WELLINGTON

I turned from the window and blinked twice trying to force my mind back to the present. The doctor had spoken to me and I hadn't heard a word he said. I stared at him blankly. He smiled as he straightened his posture. His demeanor was cold. Professional. Detached. He glanced at the attending nurse and gave her a curt nod before he turned and walked briskly out of the room. He couldn't leave fast enough.

The nurse's bedside manner was one of comfort and caring—the exact opposite of the doctor's. She placed a gentle hand upon my shoulder and looked at me with sad, compassion filled eyes. "Do you need a moment alone with your mommy?"

It was like a bucket of ice cold water had been poured over me forcing me back to the reality that I couldn't face on my own. I couldn't bring myself to look at my mom. I shook my head and turned to the window but the wolves were gone. Their ghostly light had faded into the deepening shadows of the night. No proof remained that they had been there at all. I sighed heavily wishing that this were all just a dream. I wanted desperately to get home and hop into bed pulling the sheets up under my chin and drift off to dreamless sleep; so that I could awaken and find things back to normal. I would wake up to the sounds of my mother moving about the kitchen as she set the breakfast table—I wanted to hear my dad rustle the pages of the newspaper as he read the day's news. But now those things would forever be lost to me. I felt empty inside. I was a fifteen-year-old orphan. My whole world had changed in the blink of an eye and I was left feeling frightened and insecure.

But somehow, I had to pull myself together. If it were just me, I'd find a dark corner and slide down the wall hugging my knees close to my chest and cry my eyes out giving into my grief. But I had Bobby to think about. Poor kid must be devastated. I was all he had. I needed to be his strength—his Rock of Gibraltar.

But who would be mine?

The nurse squeezed my shoulder as she cocked her head to one side. "You gonna be okay, sweetie?"

I could feel the tears welling up inside me and I was helpless to stop them. The nurse with the cheery disposition wrapped her strong arms around me and hugged me close. I immediately felt both safe and comforted in her embrace; but despite the sense of security that flooded over me I couldn't stop my body's shuddering and wracking sobs. My shoulders shook with my bereavement and overwhelming sense of loss. Both of my parents were gone. I was alone, except for Bobbybear. We were all that was left of our happy little family of four.

Nurse Chapel kissed the top of my head and squeezed me tightly. "You hush now. Don't you fret, everything is going to be all right. Take all the time you need sweetie. I'll stay right here. I'm not going anywhere."

I lost all track of time. I don't know whether seconds or minutes passed before the other nurse appeared in the doorway. She cleared her throat softly and seemed to shrink under Nurse Chapel's harsh glare. She spoke timidly, "They have family outside."

Her words struck a chord within me. I pushed away from the larger woman and wiped the tears from my eyes wondering who it could be. I had just lost both my parents in a terrible car accident. I had no other relatives in the city. I was still shrouded in a thick fog of grief that seemed to be weighing heavily upon my fragile shoulders. I couldn't think clearly.

Nurse Chapel eyed me critically. "You see? You aren't alone

in this. You have kin just waiting to help you get through this."

"Who?" I somehow managed to ask, bewildered. I looked down at my brother. He didn't have answers either.

Bobby blinked up at me with wide, dry eyes.

The nurse offered me a kind smile. "There is only one way to find out. You have to place one foot in front of the other and go out there. See what the future holds. You can't hide from it. It's gonna come at you whether you're ready or not. You might as well square your shoulders and face it."

I took a deep breath and exhaled slowly as I wiped more tears and mascara from my eyes. I was a complete mess, I knew. Nurse Chapel seemed to understand me on a level that no one else ever had—had she truly been exposed to so much tragedy that she was now the consummate professional in handling heartache and despair?

With a nod of her head she indicated the bathroom door. "Go and compose yourself. When you are ready, we will go out together."

I was deeply touched by the woman's kindness and generosity. She seemed to know exactly what I was in need of. I had no doubt that she was an absolute professional—seasoned with years of experience dealing with grief, suffering and distress. She was acting as my guide gently prodding me in the direction in which I needed to go if I were to make it through this ordeal. And I had to for Bobbybear's sake. We had lost too much already. I had to pull myself together. Take charge. Be responsible. Be the adult.

I closed the bathroom door behind me and pressed my back upon its smooth surface. As the tears assailed me I slid down the length of the door and sobbed uncontrollably. My shoulders shook with sorrow and gut-wrenching pain. I was completely lost—a ship without a captain sailing upon a turbulent sea in the midst of a violent storm. I felt as though I were sinking into the cold depths that raged all around me.

I couldn't understand why God had forsaken me. Didn't He know how much I still needed my parents—*both of them*? How could He take them from me like this? Didn't what I want count for anything? I slammed my fists upon the bathroom tiled flooring *twice* in rapid succession. I needed the pain in the heels of my hands to help me regain control of what little composure I could muster.

I simply refused to meet my family as a distraught mess. That would not happen. I may have lost just about everything else, but I refused to let go of my pride. I reached up and grabbed the edge of the porcelain sink and pulled myself up. I hardly recognized the mascara-streaked girl reflecting back at me in the pristine mirror. I twisted the cold-water tap and cupped my hands beneath the stream of water. My hands were trembling. I sighed heavily and then splashed my face. The water was cold and *very* refreshing. It was just what I needed.

As I stepped back into the hospital room Nurse Chapel gave me an approving smile. "Are you ready sweetheart?" she asked in a soft and friendly voice. She was holding Bobby by the hand as she reached out her other for me.

I nodded.

But I had no idea what waited for me outside my mother's room... I glanced at Bobby and offered him a weak smile. I so wanted to cry my eyes out again but I couldn't. He gave me a confident smile in return. "Everything's going to be all right, Kat. You'll see." He seemed so much older than he was. I guess that it was a by-product of our home schooling and being around adults more than kids our own age. Bobbybear was strong, perhaps even stronger than I was. I couldn't help but think that I needed him more than he needed me. He was *my* strength. If I were going to get through this ordeal, I would have to lean on him. He took my hand and squeezed it firmly. "Trust me." He laughed giving my hand another squeeze. "You looked like a big raccoon."

I laughed as I tousled his hair and then hugged him close. He was going to be fine. His toughness was going to see us both through. I had found my rock—though I had thought it was the tiniest of pebbles. I glanced up at the nurse; she had been so kind, so understanding. "Could you give us a minute?"

She nodded with a sweet smile curving her lips pleasantly. "Sure thing, sweetie."

I looked back at Bobby and squeezed his arm. "Do you trust me, Bobbybear?" I asked. Something inside me—almost *a primal instinct*—was telling me to run. I could feel a tingling sensation stirring deep within me. It was as though *something* inside me was trying to warn me of impending danger. Crazy, I know, but I couldn't shake the feeling.

Bobbybear's brow furrowed as he slowly nodded.

I took his hand firmly in my own and we stepped to the door. Nurse Chapel had her back to us. She was paying attention to a conversation between the doctor and whomever it was that had come for Bobby and I. We slipped out of the room and began to move swiftly in the opposite direction. Bobbybear's forceful tugging at my hand brought us to a halt.

"Bobby!" I whispered harshly in his ear, "We need to move! *Now!*"

He didn't budge. He was pointing back in the direction from which we had come, his mouth agape, his eyes wide with dismay. Glancing back, I was totally unprepared for what waited outside the hospital room. Or rather *who* waited for us. My mom stood in the hallway by the nurse's station talking to the doctor who had just failed to save her life. I could feel Bobby's grip on my hand tighten, his small voice penetrating my shock. "*Is that Mom?*" he asked.

I blinked unsure of what to say or do. I turned my attention to Nurse Chapel who was stepping toward us. "What is going on?" I somehow managed. I felt as though I had entered the *Twilight Zone*.

The sweet nurse seemed to blush. Her eyes growing slightly wide, she said softly, "I thought you knew. That is Abigail Wellington. Your mother's twin sister."

Of course, it was. It all made sense now. Aunt Abigail was the spitting image of our mom. The only difference was the strands of white near the front of her jet-black hair. Otherwise it was mom brought back from the dead, alive, in the flesh. But sadly that was impossible

Aunt Abigail glanced our way and then nodded at the doctor. She touched his arm as she handed him a long envelope, and then quickly walked to where Bobby and I stood with Nurse Chapel. She smiled at the nurse and then knelt so that her eyes were even with my brother's. "You must be Bobby." She ran a hand through his dark curls, and then touched his cheek. "You have your father's hair... and his eyes."

Bobby nodded as a slow smile turned the corners of his mouth. "Are you my mommy?"

Her eyes grew wide and filled with compassionate tears. She hugged Bobby close and kissed the top of his head. "No sweetheart. I'm your mother's twin sister. I'm Aunt Abby."

"Oh," Bobbybear said softly. I could hear the hope die in his small voice and I wanted to cry for him because somehow, I knew that he couldn't. My heart was breaking for him.

Aunt Abigail stood and smiled at me. "I've looked forward to meeting you for a very long time. You've grown into a very beautiful young lady Kat."

Nurse Chapel gave my arm a tender squeeze. "Well, I'll leave you all to get better acquainted. If you need anything just give me a call."

I gave the big woman a warm hug. "Thank you so much!"

Tears formed in her dark eyes as she only nodded before walking to the nurse's station. I smiled shyly at my aunt. "She was such a sweet lady. Not like that doctor at all."

"A cold fish," my aunt said with a knowing nod. "No compassion for the dead, only the living—but only if they can line his pockets; pay for his summer house in Maine, his estate in Florida. I know the type. He has no use for those that are healthy."

She touched Bobby's shoulder and smiled. "I bet the two of you are ready to get out of this place. I know you're tired and probably hungry. We can stop at your place and pack a couple of bags and then grab a bite somewhere before we head out."

"Where are we going?" I asked, suddenly apprehensive.

She seemed to study me for a brief minute before answering. "Upstate. Your grandmother is expecting you."

"The Hollows?"

She nodded. "That's where she lives."

Bobby gave her a curious look as he glanced up at her. "Will we be living with you too?"

Aunt Abigail laughed suddenly. "No. I haven't lived in Wellington House for several years. I live in a cottage nearby, though. It's just a bit deeper in the woods."

Bobbybear seemed disappointed and she tousled his hair. "But you can visit any time you want."

He smiled. "I think that I'd like that."

She gave me a long steady look. "Your grandmother can be difficult at times. Just remember to tread lightly around her. She dislikes disobedience. Her house. Her rules. Keep that in mind and you shouldn't have any problems. She demands respect and absolutely will not tolerate anything less. She will not want to call you by anything less than your given names. And she will insist that you call her Grandmother—never Grandma."

I swallowed. Aunt Abigail made it sound as though we were in for a grand time. I really knew nothing about Grandmother. Mom never talked about her family in front of us. I remember hearing only snippets of conversation between her and dad. Her comments about her mother were never very flattering—at least they never seemed to be. Already I was beginning to dread moving to The Hollows.

"It's really not so bad. Your grandmother is a very influential person in The Hollows and that certainly has its advantages. She keeps a tight rein on all that she believes is hers." A sad look crossed her face, but it was only a glimmer of an expression and it quickly faded. "Sometimes too tightly I think." She smiled as though she were suddenly embarrassed. Her gaze flickered to the chain around my neck and the medallion that it held. She smiled as she reached out and lifted the talisman. "I see you are wearing my gift."

I nodded with only a moment's hesitation. "Always. I never take it off. I haven't since you sent it to me."

Her eyes met mine. There was *something* there, but it was fleeting, and I failed to grasp it's meaning. "Good," she said.

"Mom said that it was special and that I should always wear it for protection. It would keep me safe. When I asked her about it, she'd just laugh and say that you believed it would prevent lycanthropy. When I pressed her about it, she'd just change the subject, muttering something about her *crazy* sister."

Aunt Abigail chuckled softly. "That is so like your mother. She was always good about skirting the subject. She was a master at it in fact. She used to drive our mother nuts!" She studied me for a minute. "You know, you seem pretty mature for your age. Both of you do."

"We've spent more time around adults than with kids our own age. Mom said that she didn't have any faith in the public-school system. I always wondered about that." I glanced down at the talisman that I held in my fingers. "I almost think that it had something to do with this." I was hoping my aunt would say *something* about it. Give me something, *anything*.

She gave Bobby's hand a squeeze, "You know what I'm in the mood for?" She didn't wait for a response. "Ice Cream!"

"Yeah!" Bobby said enthusiastically. "Me too!"

It would seem that Mom wasn't the only member of the Wellington clan that was good at avoiding topics that they didn't want to discuss.

"We haven't eaten dinner," I said, "we probably shouldn't start with dessert." I couldn't believe it. I was sounding just like Mom already.

Aunt Abby laughed it off as though she hadn't noticed. "Oh, I don't think it will hurt just this once." She glanced back down at Bobby her eyes sparkling with her radiant smile lighting her face. "What's your favorite flavor?"

"Chocolate!" Bobby declared enthusiastically.

"Mine too!" she said. She returned her gaze to me. "What about you Kat? What's your favorite flavor?"

"Dad says she's a plain Jane, just like mom." Bobby supplied before I could answer.

Aunt Abby rolled her eyes. "Ah, another vanilla enthusiast, eh?"

"That's all she ever eats!" Bobby said smiling.

"I happen to *like* vanilla." I said in my defense.

"That's quite all right," Aunt Abby said as she tickled Bobbybear on the stomach, "that leaves more chocolate and strawberry for us!"

"Yeah!" he giggled enthusiastically.

I looked across the table and couldn't help but smile. Bobby had a melted ring of chocolate ice cream all around his mouth. There was even some on his forehead. How it got there I had no idea. It was almost as if he had fallen in. I turned my gaze to our aunt and was startled to see that she was staring at me. I blinked.

"You've won him over with the ice cream," I said with a nod toward my brother.

She smiled. "But not you."

"He's just a kid," I said with a shrug. "I'm not."

Abigail leaned forward, her elbows on the table. She rested her chin on her intertwined fingers. "I'm not trying to step on your toes Kat. Nor am I trying to usurp your authority in any way. You're his big sister. I understand that. I'm only here to help the two of you. It's going to take time to adjust. If I can make that adjustment any easier, then that's what I want to do." She stretched a hand across the table toward me. "All I want to do is help, if you'll let me."

I crossed my arms over my chest not wanting to give in so easily. I stared at Bobby. He was still tackling the last of his ice cream. "He looks at you and he sees Mom." I narrowed my eyes and stared across the table at her. I couldn't disguise the anger that put a sharp edge to my words. "He doesn't see *you*, he sees our *dead mother*."

A flicker of pain darted through Aunt Abby's eyes as she nodded. "I see. Maybe this wasn't such a good idea after all. I should've let mother handle matters. She could have sent someone else instead."

I was sorry that I had caused her pain, but I was *angry* that she looked so much like Mom. I reached across the table to take her hand and offer my apology, but she withdrew hers, giving me a taste of my own medicine.

"We should go."

I nodded. "What's the plan?"

"I need to take you back to your place so you can grab the essentials. Then we have to get to the train station."

"What about the rest of our stuff?" I said. "We can't just leave it all behind."

"Your grandmother has made all the arrangements for your things to be brought to The Hollows. We just need to gather the necessities."

"What about our neighbors? Don't we even get to say goodbye to any of them?"

Aunt Abigail gave me a steady look. "I'm afraid there's no time for that, Kat. Our train leaves at eleven."

"This is a load of crap!"

She leaned across the table her jaw tightening, "This is how it is going to be. We leave at eleven and will arrive in The Hollows early tomorrow morning. A car will then take us to Wellington House where your grandmother is waiting. I suggest you use the time that you have here wisely." She smiled. "I'd lose that attitude and the foul language rather quickly. You don't want to *piss* your grandmother off, believe me."

I continued to study her, my eyes burning behind narrowed slits. I was angry, but there seemed to be very little that I could do about it. I wished that Bobby and I had managed to flee the hospital without getting stopped. I sighed. There was nothing I could do about that, either. "I saw you hand an envelope to that doctor. What was that all about?" I tried to keep my tone civil, but I was nonetheless curious.

Aunt Abigail batted a hand in the air. "Nothing that you should be concerned about."

I reached across the table and touched her arm. "Please, stop treating me like a child."

She eyed me critically for a moment, as though sizing me up. "Very well. It was the arrangements that are in place to have your parent's bodies shipped to The Hollows for burial." Her eyes seemed to soften. "I thought it was time that your parents came home."

I felt the tears welling up in my eyes. There it was, coldly stated. My parents' remains were to be sent to The Hollows like cargo.

CHAPTER 2
WELLINGTON HOUSE

I stepped off the train onto the wooden platform and yawned as I rubbed the sleep from my eyes. It was pitch black outside except for a light that flickered from the lamppost that hung above the small depot landing. It was doing little good to dispel the darkness. A thick fog was all around enveloping us with chilled wet air. The porter placed our baggage at our feet and Aunt Abby thanked him as she handed him a generous tip. "What time is it?" I asked still trying to awaken.

We were the only passengers to disembark from the train. It made a hissing sound and blew off steam as it started rolling with a jerk leaving The Hollows behind. The chug-chug-chug of the steam engine increased as the train picked up speed. It seemed in a hurry to depart the sleepy mountain town.

Aunt Abigail growled under her breath as she began to pace the platform in growing agitation. "Harrison where are you?"

"Who's that?" I asked, curious.

"Harrison Beckett is your grandmother's man-servant. He does whatever she desires him to do."

"You're joking right ? Grandmother has a butler?"

Aunt Abigail shook her head. "Oh he is much more than a mere butler, that one. He is your Grandmother's *lackey*. She blushed as she caught me staring at her. "You'll be able to form your own opinion of him if he ever shows up. Don't let me influence you in any way."

"I take it you don't like him very much!" I said.

Her eyes met mine briefly, but she quickly glanced away, searching the darkness. Finally, she spoke. "Harrison and I have never gotten along very well. He is steadfastly loyal to my mother—which I suppose is a good thing—but there has always been *something* about him that..." she sighed heavily, "...I don't know." She gave a slight shake of her head. "He makes my skin crawl."

We all nearly jumped out of our skins as suddenly, there he was, standing only a few feet away. It was almost as if he had just appeared on the platform out of nowhere. I guess it was the fog. "Good evening Miss Abigail," he said stoically. "I trust your trip was pleasant?" The look on his face said quite clearly that he couldn't care less.

"Jesus Harrison!" Aunt Abby said breathlessly causing Bobby to chuckle.

Bobbybear seemed to be the only one that hadn't been surprised by the sudden appearance of the tall, thin man. I could still feel my heart racing inside my chest and the fine hairs on my arms were prickling from the fright.

"I left the engine running on the car and the heat is on. Might I suggest the three of you make yourselves comfortable? I'll see to the bags." With that, Harrison Beckett turned and started gathering our belongings.

Aunt Abby took my brother and I by the hand and we headed off toward the headlights of the car; they seemed to waver in the slowly swirling mist. The shiny black exterior of the Bentley Mark VI glistened in the thick gray fog as we approached. The low purr of the engine promised refuge and comfort from the biting cold. Our pace quickened with eager anticipation.

Aunt Abby and I slid into the back seat with Bobby between us. Harrison had thought ahead and put a blanket in the car for us to snuggle up in. I gave my aunt a telling look. He *couldn't* be all that bad. She practically snorted as she rolled her eyes. "Are you kidding me?" she asked. "Mother must have told him to bring the blanket. Harrison would *never* think of the comfort of others without her orders."

Bobbybear nuzzled up against her body and she wrapped her arm around him and held him close. "Trust me, Kat. You haven't had the chance to get to know him yet. Give it time. You'll see for yourself. He will reveal his true nature and then there will be no doubting what I've told you."

I leaned back as much as the leather seat would allow, which wasn't that much. I closed my eyes still hoping this wasn't real. I didn't want it to be. Bobby and I needed our parents. He was still so young, and I was going to have to grow up fast. I opened my eyes as Harrison slid behind the wheel. "Home James," I spoke louder than I had intended. He glared at me through the rearview mirror; his eyes were icy blue and menacing. I felt a sudden chill run down my spine. Maybe Aunt Abby was right after all.

We slowly pulled out of the train station and headed off into the darkness. I sat up and peered out the window as we drove through the sleepy town known as The Hollows. All of the businesses were closed due to the lateness of the hour, and I couldn't tell much about them. It seemed nothing more than a quaint little burg nestled away in the mountains; utterly drab and boring. I already missed life in the city.

I couldn't stop the unexpected tears that rolled down my cheeks. Aunt Abigail must have noticed; she reached out and gave my arm a loving squeeze. When she spoke her voice was soft and tender. "Are you okay?"

I shook my head in despair, certain that my life was over. "I hate it here," I said flatly. I stared out the window gloomily. Everything was *so* dark. I missed the lights of the city. The traffic. The people. "There's nothing to do here."

I could hear her gentle sigh over Bobbybear's deep, sleep-filled breaths. At least one of us was at peace. "It'll be alright, Kat. You'll make new friends soon enough."

I whirled around to face her, suddenly angry. "I don't *want* new friends! I want my old friends. *I want to go home!*" Not that I had many friends my own age, but the few that I had I already missed dearly.

I could see her nod in the shadows that filled the car. "This is your home now. The sooner you accept it, the quicker things will get back to normal."

"*Normal?*" I lashed out at her. "Are you *kidding* me? There's nothing normal about any of this! My life has been turned completely upside down! My parents are dead, nothing will *ever* be normal again!"

She placed a soothing hand on Bobby who was stirring against her. My outburst was clearly disturbing him. "You're not the only one who has lost them, Kat. We all have. I know it hurts, but it *will* get better. I *promise* it will."

She sounded so like my mother that I almost believed that it was *her* sitting in the shadows, but I knew she wasn't. My mom was dead. I crossed my arms tightly over my chest and closed my eyes, seeking comfort in my own embrace. I had never felt so completely alone.

I knew it was wrong to blame Aunt Abby for any of this; it wasn't her fault. The simple fact that she *looked* and *sounded* so much like my mother was making things extremely difficult. I wanted to *hate* her for all the similarities that she shared with mom, but deep down I knew I couldn't. That would be too much like hating my mother. Though I was very angry with my parents for leaving us, I could never hate them. But I could be angry. Bobby and I had that right.

"I'm sorry," I said quietly. I needed to apologize for being so snippy with my aunt.

"I know, sweetie. It's okay to be angry. I completely get it. You can rant and rave at me all you want if it'll help. Just try to control yourself around your grandmother. I promise you, she will not understand."

"Is she really that cold?" I found it difficult to believe that anyone could actually be the way that she was being depicted, especially my own grandmother.

"Stoic. Icy." She sighed heavily. "I'm sure she's not as bad as I make her out to be. But she has *always* been overly strict. I guess that makes her seem frozen. She'd had a hard life. Surrounded by brothers. Her own mother died bringing her into the world. There were no aunts or girl cousins. She grew to adulthood in a man's world. It made her tougher than she had to be, I suppose. She had to assert her will to get whatever she wanted."

"She sounds like a remarkable woman." I couldn't help but

admire her a little. She sounded an awful lot like my mom. I wonder if that was where my mother got her strength? Had I inherited any of these same Wellington genes? Did I have the inner capacity to survive the obstacles that stood in my way? I could only hope so. I'd like to think that I did, anyway.

As though suddenly coming to the realization that her own mother was exceptional, Aunt Abigail chuckled softly. "I guess she is."

I saw the look that she exchanged with Harrison in the rearview mirror and had to turn toward the window to hide my smile. It was like they had come to a mutual understanding about the matriarch of Wellington House. I saw the last of the town slip by the glass as we continued the drive. Pretty soon tall Eastern White Pines surrounded both sides of the narrow two-lane road. I could see occasional clumps of what looked like Speckled Alder here and there. I nearly jumped out of my skin a moment later. I gasped sharply.

Aunt Abigail stared at me as though suddenly afraid. "What is it?" She sounded breathless. I had obviously startled her.

I turned and looked out of the back window of the Bentley, but I could no longer see what had alarmed me. "That poor deer!" I said feeling helpless. "I just saw a pack of wolves kill a deer!"

Aunt Abby settled back in her seat. I saw her exchange another knowing look with Harrison. "These woods are full of wild animals. It could've been anything."

I gave her an incredulous look. "Are you seriously kidding me? I *know* what I saw! It was a pack of wolves! They were huge! There's no way I mistook them for something else!" I shook my head. "Why would you even suggest that I had?"

She leaned back and closed her eyes. "Don't wake your brother." She was obviously going to ignore me.

I wasn't going to give in quite that easily. "I'm just trying to understand what's going on. Why would you say I didn't see the wolves when I know that I did?"

I was greeted by her silence. Her deep breathing clearly said she was asleep. Could anyone fall to sleep so quickly? Either she had, or she was a really great faker. I shook my head and turned back to the window. "Unbelievable."

It had begun to rain lightly. Tiny drops splattered against the glass and ran sideways in tiny rivulets. The window had fogged up making it impossible to see anything outside the car clearly. With nothing else to do, I allowed myself to drift off to a restless slumber.

I don't know how long I had been asleep but I woke up with a start. We had turned onto a single lane dirt road that was in bad need of grading. I thought I was going to crack a tooth as the vibrations caused my teeth to bounce together. I was lucky I hadn't bitten my tongue. I leaned forward in my seat, hoping for a better look. I could see the trees beginning to part on the right side of the muddy road. A lush green, well-manicured lawn came into view. Up ahead I could see a stone structure with wood trim rising out of the gloom. It was absolutely huge.

Wellington House was dark. Not a single light shone in any of the windows. It seemed cold and unwelcoming, almost brooding and sinister in the gray mist that clung to the ground. I sat back startled, seeing a thin white-haired woman on the second floor staring out the window, watching as we approached.

The Bentley came to a stop in front of gray stone steps that led up to the huge arched double doors of the mansion, they were barely visible in the swirling fog. Aunt Abigail slid out of the car and hefted Bobbybear up into her arms. Awake now, he rested his sleepy head upon her shoulder and watched me exit the car with droopy eyes. "Don't worry about the bags. Harrison will see them to your rooms."

I glanced toward Harrison for confirmation and he nodded curtly but said nothing. He disappeared toward the rear of the car and I heard the popping of the trunk a moment later. With nothing else to do, I followed Aunt Abigail up the steps and into the house.

We had just entered the massive foyer when we heard my grandmother's voice greet us from the top of the staircase that took up most of the entry. "What is the matter with the boy?" she said. "Can he not walk?"

"Of course he can walk. He's tired, Mother. It was a long, exhausting trip." Aunt Abby said curtly.

"Do not use that tone with me, Abigail. It will not be tolerated under my own roof." She glanced briefly at me, as though sending fair warning. "If the boy can walk, he can stand." The commanding tone of her voice left no room for defiance. Aunt Abigail had little choice but to put Bobbybear down. My grandmother nodded once. "That will be all Abigail."

Dismissed, Aunt Abigail offered Bobby and me a stiff smile. "I'll see you both later." She tousled my brother's curly hair. "Sweet dreams." She turned and glanced up the stairs. "Mother."

"Breakfast will be served promptly at 7 am. I'll have a setting for you."

Aunt Abigail shook her head slowly, a smile curving the corner of her mouth. "That won't be necessary Mother. I'm going to sleep in."

Even from here I could see my grandmother clench her jaw in annoyance. Tension sizzled in the air; it was almost touchable. Aunt Abby gave me a wink, then turned and left through the front door. Bobby must've felt it too. He reached up and took my hand. I smiled and gave his hand a reassuring squeeze.

"Well," Grandmother said, "do not just stand there. Come up here so that I can get a good look at you." She tapped her cane repeatedly upon the floor—I was certain it would splinter at any second. "I am *not* getting any younger you know."

I was beginning to understand why our parents left The Hollows behind all those years ago. Bobby and I started up the stairs taking two at a time, fearing the wrath of our grandmother. We weren't sure what to expect from her, but neither of us wanted to anger her further.

Both Bobby and I were breathing hard by the time we reached the landing where Grandmother waited. She gave us a hard look as she walked around us giving us a military-type inspection. She swung her cane up and struck my bottom. "You are slouching! A young lady does not slouch."

"I'm tired," I offered in my defense.

"Excuses will not be tolerated here at Wellington House!" she snapped, rapping the point of her cane upon the flagstones for added emphasis. She completed her inspection and stood in front of us. She glared down her nose at Bobby. "What is that all over your face, young man?"

Bobbybear shrugged. "Ice cream, maybe?"

"Ice cream?" She sounded appalled.

Bobby nodded with a huge smile, "Aunt Abby bought it for us. I had chocolate!"

"You mean Abigail bought it for you," she corrected.

Bobbybear nodded. "Uh-huh."

"Yes ma'am," she corrected again.

He frowned. "You mean yes sir. You called me a ma'am."

She seemed flabbergasted for a second. "No, I did not! I was merely correcting your grammar."

Bobby shook his head. "I dunno..."

Grandmother slammed the point of her cane against the floor. "Enough of this nonsense!" She turned her attention to me. "What is that you are wearing?" She pointed a bent finger at my pants.

They were my favorite jeans. They sported a gaping hole across the left thigh, but they were extremely comfortable. "You mean my Levi's?"

She *tsked* loudly. "A young woman should wear a nice dress, not worn-out jeans." She narrowed her eyes at me. "Are you wearing makeup?"

I swallowed. "A little," I said meekly.

She shook her head as though not satisfied with what she saw before her. "Well, we have certainly got our work cut out for us." She sighed. "How are you both doing in your schooling?"

"Mom homeschooled us. We have already completed all the requirements for this year."

Grandmother arched a brow. "Have you now? And I trust that you are both performing to the highest standards?"

I nodded, my chin rising with pride. "Mom and Dad were very adamant about our studies. Both Bobby and I are exceeding the standards set forth by the State."

"I see. Well, at least they managed to do *that* right."

I wasn't sure if she was trying to provoke a response from me, but it took all I had to keep silent. I hoped she hadn't noticed that my jaw was clenched in anger. My hands were fisted tightly at my sides.

"School is still in session here in The Hollows. I do not suppose it would do either of you any good to repeat what the remainder of the school year has to offer. It would likely be a waste of time." She looked us over, as though sizing us up. "Perhaps your time would be better spent performing chores around the Manor. I believe one should earn one's keep. Do you not agree?"

I nodded. "Of course Grandmother."

She pointed her cane at a door off the corridor to her right. "That is your room, Robert." She swung the cane to the corridor on the left. "The one at the end of the hallway is yours, Katherine." She raised her chin as she looked down upon us. "You will find the bathrooms fully stocked. Harrison has already placed your luggage in your rooms. Should you require anything during what remains of the night, simply pick up the phone. It will automatically ring Margaret. She will attend you."

She gave us one last look. "Questions?"

I shook my head quickly. I was eager to get away. To my surprise, Bobbybear stepped forward and wrapped his arms around our grandmother and gave her a quick hug. "Goodnight, Grandma."

I saw her stiffen at his words. She patted the top of his head as though she didn't quite know what else to do. "I would prefer it if you would call me *Grandmother*."

Bobby smiled. "Okay, Grandmother." He paused. "I think that I would prefer you called me *Bobby*. Everyone does. Don't they Kat?"

I could only nod in stunned silence. I couldn't be more proud of Bobbybear's bravado. He had more nerve than I did.

To my surprise Grandmother smiled. Until that point I wasn't sure she knew how to smile. It's amazing how such a simple act can transform a face, melt away a cold, stuffy disposition and resolve it into a pleasing sight to behold. It certainly worked wonders for Grandmother – it made her look more human.

"Remember," her voice was amiable, "breakfast is served promptly at 7 am." She turned toward me. "Make certain you are suitably attired." The Ice-maiden had returned. "Now off with you both."

Bobby rushed over and gave me a quick hug. I kissed the top of his head and patted his bottom. "If you need *anything* I'll be right down the hallway."

He smiled brightly. "And if *you* need anything, you know where I'll be!"

I couldn't help but chuckle. "G'night Bobbybear."

"Goodnight Kat." He turned and walked down the hall as though he hadn't a care in the world. He was much stronger than I was.

I smiled at Grandmother. "Goodnight."

She said nothing and nodded only once. Taking my cue, I turned and started down the hallway. With each step I took, the shadows seemed to jump out at me, swallowing me whole. Finally, after what seemed like an eternity, I stood in front of the huge double doors of my bedroom. I guess I should have known that the room would be huge. Why else would it have tall double doors for an entrance? And it was! Huge, I mean. It was what you'd expect from a grand old house where royalty lived. A king-sized four-poster bed was along one wall. There was a writing desk fully stocked with paper, pens and pencils. Another doorway was opened to the left. This led into a spacious bathroom where a white porcelain tub, with polished brass claw feet, was the main feature.

I gave a low whistle. "I've died and gone to heaven!"

It didn't take me long to decide that a nice soothing bath was in order to help me de-stress from the day's events. I put the plug in the tub and started running water. A bottle of Rose water was on the shelf near the tub, and without a second's thought, I poured some into the bath. While the tub was filling I returned to the bedroom and began to unpack my bags.

With the tub waiting, it didn't take me long to put my things away. I turned off the water and quickly undressed, tossing my clothes into a haphazard pile. I slipped into the tub, relishing the heat of the water. The smell of roses made me think of Mom and I smiled. I totally immersed myself and then reemerged with my eyes closed and a contented smile on my face. "Heaven indeed!" I whispered softly to myself as I rested my arms along the side of the tub. I had always dreamed of having my own bathroom where I could spend hours soaking in a tub like this.

CHAPTER 3
MAGIC

I awoke just before dawn. It was pitch black in the room. For a moment I didn't know where I was, but I was certain that I wasn't home. I panicked. *"Mom?"* I called out in the darkness, and then remembered: *She can never again answer my call...*

I reached for the dainty Timex watch that lay on the nightstand next to the bed. My dad had given it to my mom on her last birthday. It was just after five. I needed to get up and make sure that Bobby was ready to go down for breakfast. I didn't want either of us to be late. I wanted our first full day at Wellington House to go smoothly. I knew in order for that to happen, we had to start out on the right foot. And that meant getting to breakfast on time. *Properly dressed.*

Finishing up in the bathroom I quickly dressed in a dark blue pair of Jordache jeans—they were the best that I owned. I finished the ensemble with a red button-up blouse. This old house seemed drafty, so I pulled on a cardigan for added warmth. After slipping into my white sneakers I gave the bedroom a last look over. The bed was made and everything was put away properly. I was certain that Grandmother would have no complaints. I glanced at my watch, it was 6.15 am, there was still time to get Bobby ready and head downstairs to greet the day.

As I walked down the long hallway I couldn't help but think about how far apart our rooms were. What if Bobbybear needed me during the night? I was so far away that I might not be able to hear him if he called out for me. I wonder why Grandmother had given us the rooms she had. It almost seemed as if she were *trying* to separate us. I chided myself for being so silly. What possible motive could she have for that? None that I could readily think of, she had probably given us those rooms to give us more privacy. After all, I was almost sixteen and Bobby was only six. Back home our rooms were right next door to one another and we shared a bathroom.

I softly knocked on my brother's door and waited. When Bobby didn't answer I knocked again as I opened the door. Expecting to see him still in bed I said, "Time to rise and shine Bobbybear!"

To my surprise his bed was empty. His room was practically a twin to the one I had been given, so I checked the bathroom. He wasn't there either. His pajamas were hung on the doorknob; he couldn't quite reach the hook on the back of the door. Evidently, Bobby was already dressed and somewhere in the house. I just hoped that he wasn't up to some form of mischief. He had an innate sense of curiosity that could easily lead him astray and get him into trouble. I just prayed that he didn't break anything while he was exploring the grand old house that we now lived in. When we arrived I had noticed several antiques that looked both fragile and expensive. I had the feeling that our grandmother wouldn't like having them broken into a million tiny pieces and scattered upon the floor.

I had no idea where to begin looking for Bobby. He could be anywhere. I decided to start downstairs first, thinking that if he had gotten hungry he might look for the kitchen. I took a step and then heard Bobby's unmistakable giggle coming from my right. It sounded as though he were *above* me. Turning, I saw a stairwell heading up into the darkness. "Bobby?" My voice was scarcely more than a whisper.

I started up the stairs slowly at first. I could hear my brother talking to someone and there was another voice intertwining with his. "Bobbybear?" I called out again, this time a little louder than before. He still didn't answer. It wasn't like Bobby to ignore me. Feeling slightly agitated that he wasn't responding to my call, I took the steps two at a time, my anger only rising with each step. As I climbed upward I could feel the air growing colder. *Had he opened a window?*

I stood on the top landing and faced a closed door. Catching my breath, I tried the doorknob. It was locked and it was ice-cold. I could hear Bobby on the other side of the door speaking in muffled tones. I knocked on the door, suddenly filled with a dreaded sense of unexplainable fear. "*Bobby?*" I swallowed the lump in my throat. "Bobby, it's me, Kat. Open the door."

The whispers stopped. Silence greeted me. I could feel the hairs on the back of my neck begin to prickle. I reached for the doorknob but before I could close my hand around it, the door was yanked open. I stumbled back in surprise and felt my foot slip on the edge of the landing. Flailing my arms wildly in the air, I knew it was no use; I couldn't regain my balance – I was going to fall!

"*Kat!*" Bobby reached out and somehow managed to grab my wrist. It was enough to allow me to steady myself long enough to clutch the handrail and keep from falling.

Catching my breath I hugged Bobby close. I could feel my heart pounding inside my chest. He had saved me from a terrible fall. I could have easily broken my neck, and then poor Bobbybear would be left all alone. I couldn't bear the thought of him being stuck here in Wellington House without me.

Bobby giggled, oblivious to how close misfortune had actually come. "Your eyes were so wide! You should've seen them!"

I couldn't help but chuckle. "I bet they were. I thought I was going to fall for a second but you saved me, kiddo." I tried looking past him to see who he'd been talking to, but I didn't see anyone.

I took a step closer. "Were you talking to someone?" I tried to look in the room, but he reached out and closed the door.

"I wasn't talking to anyone. I was just playing by myself."

"Bobby, I heard someone in the room with you."

He frowned. "I wasn't with anyone. It was only me."

"Then why was the door locked, Bobby?"

"It wasn't locked, Kat." He looked at me with wide innocent eyes. I couldn't tell if he was lying or not.

"It was locked, Bobby." I could feel my anger starting to return. "I tried to get in and I couldn't."

He shrugged. "Maybe it was just stuck then."

I reached around him and tried the knob. It wouldn't turn.

"See?" Bobby said. "I went into the room and the door closed behind me. I couldn't get out cause it was stuck."

I looked into his blue eyes searchingly. I knew there was something that he wasn't telling me but I didn't have a clue as to what it might be. It wasn't like Bobbybear to lie to me.

"It's an old house Kat. Doors probably get stuck a lot if they don't get much use."

I just stared at him, dumbfounded. Bobby sounded much older than his six years. He shrugged as he stepped past me and started down the stairs. "Is it time to eat yet? I'm starving."

I turned back to the closed door, almost certain that I had just heard the muffled laughter of a small girl. I got that funny, strange feeling stealing over me. The light hairs on my arms stood on end. I didn't like this place. Something about Wellington House gave me the willies.

"Kat, are you coming?" Bobby sounded impatient.

I forced my eyes from the door and started down the steps with Bobby descending ahead of me. Halfway down I turned and looked back at the door. A chill swept through me like a jolt of electricity.

The door was ajar...

Bobby and I were already sitting at the dining table when Grandmother entered the room. She arched a brow in surprise; clearly she hadn't expected that we would be on time, let alone that we would be early. I couldn't tell if she were pleased or if it had been a momentary flicker of shock that I had seen in her eyes. Whatever it was, Grandmother was expert at hiding it quickly. Had I not been studying her for a response, it might have gone unnoticed entirely and I would have been none the wiser.

She sat with an elegant grace that seemed to come naturally to her. It struck me then how beautiful my grandmother truly was. I had no doubt that she turned heads when she was a young woman. I could only hope that I aged as well she had.

She glanced from Bobby to me before she spoke. "I trust you slept well?"

I could feel myself straightening my own posture, as I smiled pleasantly. "I can't believe how soundly I slept." It was true. The mattress was very comfortable and the pillows were just the way I liked them; firm but with just the right amount of fluff to keep them from being overly hard.

She turned her attention to my brother. "And how did you sleep, Robert?" She blinked for a second. "I mean, Bobby." Her eyes sparkled in the morning light; a small smile threatened the corner of her mouth.

His face contorted into a frown. "I kept hearing things."

Grandmother arched her brow. "Perhaps it was only the wind you heard. This is a very old house. It tends to make noises when it is stormy outside."

Bobby scrunched his face. "I heard whispers." He looked at Grandmother curiously. "Does your house talk?"

"Don't be silly Rob... uh, Bobby. Of course the house doesn't speak." She reached out and squeezed his hand warmly. "But wouldn't it be nice if it did? Wellington House is over a hundred and seventy years old, just imagine the stories it could tell!" She had a far away look in her eyes as though recalling fond memories from long ago.

Grandmother looked absolutely radiant. The sunlight crept through the tall windows and caressed her hair, causing the silver highlights to almost glow. Her blue eyes sparkled, warm and inviting. She looked nothing like the stern, unapproachably cold woman we had first met. Perhaps I had misjudged her. She looked almost angelic surrounded by the golden luminescence of the sunlight. But the moment was fleeting.

A dark cloud slowly floated in and blocked the rays of the morning sun just as Harrison Beckett entered the room carrying a large tray. Grandmother's mood seemed to change with this new turn of events. Grandmother stiffened and her charming smile vanished, replaced by a thin line. The sparkle that had lit her eyes with warmth was gone as well; they now were icy blue pools that you could very easily drown in. She had transformed.

I watched Harrison Beckett as he poured a cup of hot coffee for my grandmother. I could only wonder if his presence had triggered the change in her demeanor. He added a small amount of sugar to the cup and then whispered softly in her ear. She nodded once, but remained silent.

We spent the rest of breakfast eating quietly. Afterwards, Grandmother excused herself saying she had matters to attend to in the village and would be gone most of the day. Bobby and I would be left to entertain ourselves. I could tell by the look in my brother's eyes that he already had a plan forming. I was almost certain that it involved the room at the top of the stairs. That thought alone was enough to send chills through me.

As Bobby and I left the dining room I put a hand on his shoulder, giving it a loving squeeze. "How would you like to do a little exploring outside?"

He shrugged. "Sure. Why not? Do you think we might see a deer?" His face brightened as another thought occurred to him. "Or maybe a bear or a wolf? That would be so cool!" He jumped up and down excitedly.

I could only think of what I'd seen on our drive up to Wellington House—how that pack of wolves had taken down that helpless deer. Aunt Abby had said that the woods were full of wild animals. Maybe exploring outside wasn't such a good idea after all. I quickly looked back at Bobby and said, "Or maybe we could continue to explore the house. There's still a lot that we haven't seen. Besides," I added, "it looks as though it's fixing to storm. I don't think Grandmother would be too happy with us if we trailed mud through Wellington House."

He shook his head slowly as he seemed to consider this. Then he looked at me with his eyes full of curiosity. "Why do you suppose they named this house? It seems a silly thing to do, I mean, we never named ours."

Good question. It was one that I didn't readily have an answer to. I knelt down beside my brother so that our eyes could be on the same level. "I'm not sure, Bobbybear. People used to name houses for a lot of different reasons."

"Like what?" He asked, not yet willing to let it go.

I smiled. "Well, they were named after the people who first lived in them, I guess. Or for the person who built them. Some are named for historical reasons or important events that occurred nearby. It could be for any number of other reasons too, I suppose."

"Hmm." He said with a thoughtful frown.

I tousled his hair. "I wouldn't worry too much about it Bobbybear. People do a lot of silly things for reasons all their own."

His face brightened as he reached up and messed up my hair. "I'm not worried about it, Kat. I was just curious."

I quickly grabbed him in a tight embrace and tickled his stomach. He knew I didn't like my hair being messed with, yet he enjoyed doing it anyway. "You little booger!" Bobby squirmed in an attempt to get away, but I maintained my hold on him. Soon we were both giggling uncontrollably.

Aunt Abby called out to us. "Hello! Is anybody home?" Her voice seemed to echo in the grand entrance of Wellington House. It's cheery sound and our own laughter seemed oddly out of place in the drab manor.

"Aunt Abby!" Bobby squealed in delight as he managed to break from my grasp and run to her. His boundless energy made her smile. I could feel the pull on my heartstrings. In the dimly lit foyer she looked so much like my mother.

I felt my eyes beginning to tear, and quickly gave my head a little shake. I silently scolded myself, of course she looked like Mom, they were twins after all. "Good morning Aunt Abby," I said with a smile.

She scooped Bobby up into her arms giving him a hug and a kiss on the cheek before setting him back down. "Good morning, Kat. I trust you both slept well?"

I couldn't help but smile. I'd slept better than I had in weeks, despite the events of the last couple of days. "Our rooms are huge! And we each have our own bathroom!" I was shocked at how pleased I sounded. I immediately felt guilty. I had no right to feel this amount of joy—I had just lost *both* of my parents. *Wasn't this some sort of a betrayal of their memories?*

Aunt Abby seemed to sense how I was feeling and she gave me a tender embrace. She kissed me on the temple. "I'm glad you find the room to your liking. You both so desperately needed a change of atmosphere; the city can be so claustrophobic!"

I smiled weakly. "This place certainly has a lot of atmosphere." I said. "It's huge compared to what we're used to. It's a wonder we didn't get lost on our way down to breakfast."

Aunt Abby had a horror-stricken look on her face. "You weren't late were you?"

"Nope!" Bobby chimed in. "We were the first ones there!"

Aunt Abby chuckled and shook her head. "Mother must have been in total shock! No one ever gets to the table ahead of her—and she never hesitates to let you know that you allowed her meal to grow cold while she waited for you to arrive." She smiled at us both. "Good for you!" She seemed genuinely pleased that we had started out on the right footing.

She tousled Bobby's hair and smiled as she looked at me. "So, what plans have you made for the day? Anything exciting planned for your first full day in The Hollows?"

I almost laughed. We were so new to this place that we really had no idea where to even start. "We figured that we'd look around outside a bit. Bobby's already explored inside the house, so we thought we'd take a look in the forest."

I was surprised by the look that appeared on Aunt Abby's face. I couldn't tell whether it was fear or just surprise. "Is there something wrong?"

She quickly recovered and shook her head. "No, not really. But you need to be careful traipsing through these woods until you know your way around. It is very easy to lose your way and get hopelessly lost. With all the wildlife that inhabits this neck of the forest it might even be a bit dangerous."

"We weren't going to wander far." I said. Something about her change of manner left me feeling a little miffed. We weren't *completely* helpless.

She returned my stare. "Trust me Kat. You don't have to go far to lose your way."

Were we still talking about the woods? With all the events of the last couple of days I wasn't certain about anything anymore. Was there a hidden message in what she was telling me? I searched her face—*my mother's face*—for a clue... Maybe Aunt Abby was right; I was already beginning to feel lost.

With the death of my parents still so new I felt raw and insecure. They had been the glue that held our family together, but now they were gone—ripped from us in a flash. Our family had been shattered, and Bobby and I were left alone to pick up the pieces.

I needed to show Bobby that everything was going to be all

right despite the tragedy that had wrecked our lives like a raging storm; that we were going to be okay. But first I had to believe it.

I still needed to come to terms with all that was happening. I was almost sixteen and my whole world had been turned completely upside down. I had been thrust into a new life—one that seemed so different from the one I had grown accustomed to. Bobby and I were being forced to start our lives over. The only familiar things we had were each other, and what few belongings we had been allowed to pack in a whirlwind assault on our house. We had left so much behind. Possessions, photos, even our friends. *Everything*.

I blinked. Somehow, I had gotten lost in my thoughts and became completely oblivious to everything around me. Aunt Abby and Bobby were in the middle of a conversation and I had no idea what they were talking about. I wasn't even sure how much time had passed.

I vaguely heard Bobby speaking. "She's been doing that a lot lately." He giggled as he and Aunt Abby both looked in my direction. "Sometimes she'll even speak to you but she doesn't really make any sense."

Aunt Abigail rubbed my arm lovingly. She smiled sweetly as she came to my defense. "Your sister has got a lot on her mind." She gave Bobby's hair a quick tousle. "She'll be back to normal before you know it."

Bobbybear giggled again. "I hope not! She's funny when she gets that look in her eyes. It's like she's someplace else!"

I reached out and tickled Bobby's sides. "You little stinker!"

Aunt Abby and I followed behind Bobby as he walked along the trail through the woods; he was kicking a stone as he went and slashing at the shrubbery with a twisted stick he had found. We had left Wellington House and were on our way to the cottage where she lived. Though Aunt Abigail said we were following a path, I couldn't see it—I was already hopelessly lost.

"So, what do you do?" I asked. "Do you have a job?" I really knew nothing about my aunt.

Aunt Abigail chuckled softly. "I wasn't expecting that!"

There was a long pause as though she were trying to consider exactly *how* to answer my question. Finally, she responded, "Yes, I have a job, but not in the conventional sense."

I looked at her quizzically. "I'm not sure what you even mean by that." She was *so* like my mom! Speaking in ways that could be easily misinterpreted. You *had* to stay on your toes when having a simple conversation with either of them.

We walked along in silence. I kept waiting for Aunt Abigail to explain her comment, but she seemed to be content to leave it at that. "Well?" I pressed, raising my brows.

A small smile curved the corner of her mouth. "I guess you could say that I'm something of a healer. But really, that is only a small part of what I do."

I looked at her in astonishment. I reached out and took her arm as we both came to a stop. "You mean like a doctor?"

Again, she laughed. It was such a delightful sound coming from her; both lighthearted and uplifting at the same time. It reminded me so much of my mom. "I use herbs and what-not to help both people and animals." She gave me a long look, as though trying to decide *how much* to tell me. "There are a lot of people in these parts that can't afford to see a physician. And there are those that simply do not trust modern medicine. I offer them another choice. A more natural way of healing."

I was intrigued. "What do you mean by *herbs* and *what-not*?" There was something that I just wasn't getting. She could be so frustrating at times with her vague generalities! Come to think of it, my mom was the *exact* same way!

Before she could respond, Bobbybear rejoined us. "She's a witch," he said simply. It was almost as if he'd known it all along. There was no doubt in his voice whatsoever; nothing but conviction.

Aunt Abigail didn't even try to deny it. She gave a little smile and confirmed it by stating with a slight shrug, "I'm a witch."

My jaw dropped clear to the forest ground. I was so stunned that I couldn't even speak. I could vaguely hear some strange sounds *trying* to come out of my mouth, but it *certainly* wasn't anything intelligible.

Aunt Abby leaned toward Bobby. "Is she often like this?"

The little traitor nodded vigorously with a wide grin and a chuckle. "Yep! That's Kat!"

I swatted a hand in Bobby's direction, but he artfully dodged the halfhearted blow. He just giggled as he stepped aside. "You guys are *terrible*!" I shook my head as I stared at my aunt in disbelief. "I didn't think witches were even real."

She reached out and tousled *my* hair. I vowed never to do that to Bobby *ever* again! It was absolutely infuriating! Aunt Abigail must've seen the burning look in my eyes and she quickly apologized. "I'm so sorry, Kat. I don't know what came over me." She nodded, sobering. "Yes. Witches *are* real. As a matter of fact, you'll discover that life in The Hollows is far different than life anywhere else you may have been."

Bobby had turned away and was swinging his stick in a side-to-side arc in front of him as he walked along the narrow pathway that I could barely even see. Aunt Abby inclined her head in his direction. "We'd better not let him get too far ahead."

I laughed. "He's making enough noise to scare anything off. I don't think he's in any real danger."

"Don't be so naïve. I told you The Hollows isn't like anyplace you're accustomed to. Remember that pack of wolves you saw take down that deer? They could easily be attracted by the noise that Bobby is making."

"Bobbybear! Throw that stick away. *NOW!*" I yelled after him; suddenly terrified of what might be lurking, unseen in the woods around us.

Aunt Abigail's cottage wasn't at all what I had expected it to be. For some reason I had figured it was going to be a rickety old log cabin. But it wasn't. It reminded me of the cottage that Snow White shared with the Seven Dwarfs. It gave the woods surrounding the cottage that fairytale feeling. I half expected the dwarves singing "Hi ho, hi ho."

Various brightly colored flowers sat in boxes hung along the windowsills on either side of the doorway. Two white rocking chairs and a table sat on the covered front porch. I could see Aunt Abby's herb garden to the right of the cottage though most of it was still hidden from view. An old-fashioned water well was centered in her front yard; tangled vines clung to the rough-hewn stone. Faded red brick pavers led from her porch and circled the well. Sprigs of untended grass pushed up between the brick here and there.

Bobby looked up at Aunt Abby with a furrowed brow. "Is that a Wishing Well?" he asked curiously.

She smiled slyly and gave him a secretive wink. I could feel a sudden rise of anger within me. Bobbybear didn't need any encouragement. I knew he'd simply wish for the impossible, only to be horribly disappointed. I was about to voice my objections when she added, "It very well could be. Why don't you give it a try?"

Bobby's face brightened as he dropped his stick and shoved his hands deep into his pockets. He frowned darkly as he came up empty. "I don't have any coins." The disappointment in his voice was heartbreaking.

Aunt Abby knelt down and smiled at him brightly. "Sure, you do Bobby!" She reached out and pulled a shiny quarter from behind his left ear. "See?"

"Oh wow!" Bobby yelled in excitement. "How'd you do that?"

She straightened up and touched a bent finger to his chin. "Magic!"

CHAPTER 4
WOLVES IN THE WOODS

Aunt Abigail turned Bobby around to face the well. She rested her hands on his small shoulders and spoke softly in his right ear. "Close your eyes tightly and think about your wish. When you know what you want, kiss the coin and then toss it into the Wishing Well."

Bobby nodded his understanding. After a moment of silence, he brought the coin to his lips and kissed it. A small smile curved the corners of his mouth; he nodded once and cast the quarter into the well.

Together we all watched the shiny quarter tumble down into the darkening depths of the well. When we could no longer see it, we waited, holding our breath. After a moment we could hear the soft *plunk!* of the coin as it hit the water.

"There you go." Aunt Abby said giving his shoulders a loving squeeze.

He looked up at her with a hopeful expression in his eyes. "When will I know if I get my wish?"

Aunt Abigail completely ignored the warning look I tried to convey to her. "Oh, I don't know. It's hard to say. Some wishes are harder to grant than others. Some are granted right away." She leveled her eyes at me. "And some are never granted at all."

Bobby frowned, trying hard to understand. "Who decides?"

Aunt Abby shook her head. "I don't have an answer for that."

"Why not? I thought witches were supposed to know everything." Bobby said innocently.

She laughed. "That would certainly be nice, wouldn't it?" She poked him in the stomach. "Are you sure you are only six years old?"

He grinned. "I'll be seven in almost nine months!"

Aunt Abby laughed again. "I think I have some cookies inside; would you like some?"

His face brightened. "Yeah!"

She placed a loving hand on his shoulder. "They're on the counter in the kitchen. Go help yourself." As Bobby took off at a run, Aunt Abigail turned her attention to me. She eyed me critically as she crossed her arms over her chest. "You don't approve?"

I shook my head. "How could you do that?" I waved a hand at the well. "You *know* what he wished for!"

She arched a brow. "How would I know?"

I was furious! I decided not to bother trying to reel my anger in. She needed to understand that her actions had consequences. She couldn't continue to be so carefree. "We just lost our parents! You know what Bobbybear wished for! He wants them back!" I ran a hand through my hair as I shoved the other into my pocket. Tears stung at my eyes. I was still so angry with her. "Now thanks to you, he believes they're both gonna walk back into our lives because of a stupid wish he made!"

"I wouldn't be so sure, Kat."

"How can you say that?" I couldn't believe her. "Now who's being naïve?"

"Kat, your brother has already come to terms with your parents' passing; but I think that you haven't." She reached out and touched my arm in a vain attempt to offer me some form of comfort.

But I wasn't having it. As tears rolled down my cheeks, I managed to slip away from her outstretched hand. "You don't know what you're talking about. You don't know anything about me." I was bitter. I turned from her and ran into the woods; bleary eyed from the tears, I was almost blind, but there was nothing wrong with my hearing.

"Kat!" Aunt Abigail called after me, but I ignored her. Fortunately, Bobby called to her from the front door of the cabin asking something about milk. The distraction allowed me to escape and prevented her from following.

I had to zig and zag my way through the thick forest and in a matter of seconds I was disoriented. Turning, I could no longer tell from which direction I had come. Everything looked the same. I knew that I was completely lost, but I was too proud to call out for help.

I shrugged. Not yet willing to admit defeat, I pushed onward. I figured that if I could at least get within sight of the cottage all would be fine. Problem was, I had no idea *where* I was, let alone my aunt's cabin. Not only was I lost, but I wasn't even certain how much time had gone by. The *good* thing about being alone was it gave me time to think. Problem was, I couldn't really think about anything else other than just being lost.

If I was being honest with myself, I had to admit that Aunt Abby might be on to something. Maybe I hadn't yet come to terms with the loss of my parents. I had been so worried about Bobbybear that I hadn't taken time for myself. I hadn't even really stopped to consider my own needs. Bobbybear was so young, so fragile. *But was he really?*

Turns out Aunt Abby might actually be right. Bobby may have come to terms with all that had happened. The little booger was stronger than I gave him credit for. Guess he could teach me a thing or two. He *had* handled everything in the hospital far better than I had expected him to.

I stopped walking and looked around me. I had absolutely no clue where I was. I could see moss growing on one side of the trees and knew that meant either *that* side was north, or possibly south—I just couldn't remember which. It really didn't matter; I really didn't know in *which* direction Aunt Abby's cottage was from where I was right now. All I really knew was that I had changed directions so many times that I was probably going around in circles.

I saw a fallen log and decided to stop and rest. I desperately needed to come up with a plan. I couldn't just continue to wander aimlessly through the woods. Surely Aunt Abigail would grow concerned about my wellbeing when I didn't return. She would eventually start looking for me. I *had* to keep telling myself that or else I knew I'd panic and make things even worse. I needed to stay put so that she could find me. She knew this forest and could probably track me down with very little effort. At least I hoped that she could.

It was growing colder, and I was getting thirsty *and* hungry. I didn't know how long I'd been sitting there oblivious to my surroundings but I was certain that at least an hour had passed. I looked up toward the sky but it was hard to see anything through the overhanging branches of the towering trees. I could only see small patches of gray that were probably storm clouds mixed with the browns and deep greens of the forest.

Then I heard a rustling among the brush and shrubbery. I stiffened in alarm. *Was that a growl?* I couldn't be sure, but it sounded like an animal, probably a dog. *Or maybe a wolf!* Off to my left I heard another guttural snarl.

I jumped up terrified, knowing I was in serious trouble. I couldn't hope to outrun a pack of wild wolves. They'd take me down quicker than they had that poor defenseless deer. I frantically searched the forest ground hoping to find a large rock or even a hefty stick... anything that I might use to defend myself. There wasn't anything that I could see.

I swallowed the lump of fear that lodged in my throat. My mouth was incredibly dry; and I was breathing hard, so that wasn't helping matters. I was about to die a horrible death. *'Poor Bobbybear!'* I thought to myself. He'd be left all alone if he lost me too... I could only hope that when they found my body there'd be enough left over to identify. I wanted Bobby to know that I was gone. I didn't want him to be left to always wonder what had happened to me. And I certainly didn't want him thinking that I had just abandoned him completely...

The realization that I was about to be ripped to shreds by a pack of hungry wolves sent a chill to spread through me. There was nothing that I could do. I was at the mercy of wild animals. I wondered how long I might be able to fight them off? Could I hold out until help arrived? I seriously doubted it.

It grew deathly quiet all of a sudden. I tried to swallow, but even that wasn't easy. This was it! They were fixing to attack! But they didn't. Had the wolves somehow been frightened away? That thought was almost enough to make me laugh; I think I did. I could feel the rapid beating of my heart pounding inside my chest. I half expected it to burst through my skin at any second. I had to calm myself down.

I blew out a slow, steady breath. My knees felt weak and my hands were still trembling with my fright, but it was working. I was beginning to feel less afraid. The brush in front of me began to move and the fear immediately returned. *This was it! The wolves were attacking!*

To my surprise it wasn't a pack of hungry wolves that stepped out to greet me—but two shirtless teenage boys. I could see two more coming up behind them. The first to emerge from the brush had a dark, shaggy head of hair. I have to admit, his disheveled appearance made him look totally *hot!* He had blue eyes and dimples and a clearly defined cleft in his chin. He had a surprised look on his face when he saw me. "What are *you* doing out here?" he asked, his brow began to furrow as he scrutinized me. His friends were beginning to slip back into their shirts.

I could see that they were all close to my age, maybe a year older. Every single one of them was fit and well-muscled. I was no longer frightened. Maybe the boys' presence had chased the wolves off. I was curious though. "Isn't it a little chilly to be running around half dressed?"

I tried to peek past them, my brow arching curiously. "What were you guys doing back there, anyway?" I quickly spread my hands in the air, fingers wide. "Never mind! I *don't* want to know!"

"Funny!" He said, clearly *not* amused by my lame attempt at humor.

"Then what were *you* guys doing together... half dressed?" I couldn't keep the amusement off my face or out of my voice.

He was getting so mad! He shook his head. "We were just out for a morning run, if you must know. We're on the football team and need to stay in shape." He had a fiery look of anger in his eyes. His teeth were tightly clenched. *Way to make friends, Kat!*

"Oh." I said feeling like a foolish schoolgirl. I wasn't very adept at flirting, obviously.

"You're new around here, aren't you?" A red-haired boy

with long lashes and freckles asked. His smile was friendly, encouraging.

I pulled my eyes away from his friend and nodded. "Yeah. My little brother and I just moved in with our grandmother. We'll be starting school in The Hollows next year."

"Sweet!" he said. Sticking out his hand toward me, he added, "I'm Silas Monaghan."

I shook his hand. "Katherine St. Claire. But please, call me Kat."

Silas grinned. "Okay, Kat it is." He pointed to a dark-skinned oriental looking boy with broad shoulders and thick arms, "That's Cho Ming—we like to call him Chow Mein—he's *always* hungry."

Cho had a friendly smile as he patted his flat stomach. "You got anything to eat?" I shook my head and he looked suddenly sad and disappointed. "Ah, no worries!"

Standing next to Cho was a muscular dark-skinned black guy. He too had a friendly disposition. "That's Tucker Morrison."

Tucker was the smallest of the gang, but his body seemed more toned and muscular than the rest. "Nice to meet you, Kat." He had a nice, wide smile, with perfect teeth.

"Nice to meet you too, Tucker."

"And the guy with the stick up his arse," Silas indicated the last of them, "is Brock Jacobins."

He snubbed me completely by shoving his hands into his back pockets. Clearly, he wasn't interested in making a new friend or welcoming me to The Hollows. Fine by me, if that was how he wanted to play it. His companions seemed nice enough.

Silas rolled his eyes. "Why are you waiting to start school next year? Why not start now, it'd be a shame to lose the last few months of this year."

I smiled. "My mom homeschooled my brother and I. We've already completed all the State requirements for this year."

Brock snorted with a shake of his head. "So, you *think* that you're better than us?"

My eyes grew wide at his cutting remark. I hadn't expected his attack on me. "No. I *never* said that!"

Tucker slapped Brock on the shoulder. "Damn bro!" He shook his head and gave me a friendly wink. "Don't worry about him. He's just upset that his exercise got interrupted. He's really pretty cool."

"These woods aren't that safe to wander around alone in," Cho said as he tucked his shirt into his pants.

"He's right," Silas added with a nod. "Who did you say your grandmother was?"

I panicked. I didn't really know her first name. "Wellington," I said simply.

They all looked startled. Silas touched my sleeve. "Your grandmother is Elizabeth Wellington? You're staying at Wellington House?"

I nodded. "That's right."

"Whoa!" Silas said.

They all exchanged looks and then turned toward Brock. He spat upon the ground. "Your aunt is Abigail Wellington?"

I crossed my arms over my chest. I was *still* a little miffed at him. "Is that a problem?"

His face softened slightly and he might have even smiled - I couldn't be sure. I could feel my anger starting to rise. "Nope. No problem." He reached out and took my elbow, "But we'd better see you safely to her place."

I pulled out of his grasp. "I can get back without your help!" I insisted. Something about Brock Jacobins infuriated me.

He raised his hands in the air. "Hey, fine by me."

I started off and then stopped when I heard their snickers. I glared at them. "What?"

Silas silently mouthed the words, 'Wrong way.'

I growled in embarrassment. Turning. I set out in a new direction. This time I was greeted by their howls of laughter. I faced them knowing that I had turned a bright red. I could feel the heat under my skin. Chuckling softly, I said, "Okay, so I'm lost! I don't know how to get back." I kicked at the ground with the toe of my sneakers. "Will you help me? *Please?*"

Brock chuckled. "We'd be delighted to."

CHAPTER 5
AN ISSUE OF TRUST

I walked along beside Brock while the others roughhoused behind us. He looked over at me and smiled. "I'm sorry about how I acted earlier. I guess it was kind of rude of me."

I nodded in agreement. I sighed, deciding to let him off easy. He was just too good looking to stay mad at. And I *liked* the way that he smiled at me. "Forgiven!" I said with a beaming smile of my own, and another nod for emphasis.

He chuckled softly. "So, what brings you to The Hollows to live with your grandmother? What's the deal with your folks?"

Being lost in the woods had given me the opportunity to face facts and deal with the loss of my parents. I accepted it—I didn't *like* it, but I was ready to handle it though I still felt raw inside. I couldn't look at Brock. I kept my eyes fixed upon the ground in front of us. I could already feel the tears forming in my eyes and I knew if I looked at him I'd turn into a blubbering mess. There was *no way* I wanted him seeing me like that. "They were killed in a car accident just the other day."

He stopped and surprised me by wrapping his arms around me. I tried to push away but his grip only tightened. In seconds I was giving way to my grief. My whole body trembled against him. My sobs threatened the quiet that had descended upon us. Through my grief I could feel him kiss the top of my head. Still crying, I started to laugh as I felt the others close in for a group hug.

We walked up to the cottage in time to see Aunt Abigail and Bobby coming out of the front door. She had a strange look on her face as she looked from me to my companions. "Is everything alright?" she asked, her voice sounded guarded.

Brock quickly nodded, "Yes ma'am. We were out for our morning run and we found her deep in the woods up near Valen's Ridge. We figured that we'd see her safely back to you."

Aunt Abby thanked them again and then Bobby and I were ushered into the cottage. She gave me a good looking over and studied my face. "You're not hurt? Everything's okay?"

I nodded. "Yeah. I'm... I'm fine. A little tired, maybe. And *very* thirsty." My stomach growled, demanding that it not be left out. I smiled. "Guess I'm a little hungry as well."

Aunt Abby opened the refrigerator and pulled out the fixings for sandwiches. She started making us all lunch. I couldn't help but notice that her hands were shaking. I felt horrible. My prolonged absence must have frightened her—I *had* been gone quite a while.

I rubbed her back. "I'm sorry Aunt Abby. For everything. You were right about me. I see that now."

She wiped a single tear from her eye and nodded. "You must promise me that you'll never again go off alone like that. My God, Kat! Valen's Ridge? What on earth made you go so far?"

I shrugged. "I didn't mean to. I got so lost and I just kept going. I really thought I was heading back, but everything looks the same out there!"

She gave me a hard look. "The woods out there are *very* dangerous, especially so early in the day." She chuckled. "All the time, really. It's just not safe. Promise me you won't go off like that again."

I nodded. "Don't worry, I won't. I almost got attacked by wolves."

"Cool!" Bobby said sounding excited. "Were you scared?"

Aunt Abby had gone pale. I really hadn't meant to say anything about the wolves—it just kinda slipped out. She seemed frozen in place, unable to move.

"How big were they?" Bobby continued. "How many were there?" He kinda took my arm and tried to twist me about. "How come you don't look like you're hurt anywhere?" He sounded a little disappointed to discover that I wasn't bleeding all over the place.

"You saw them?" Aunt Abby asked in a whisper.

I shook my head. "No. I didn't actually *see* the wolves."

"Aaw man!" Bobbybear howled dejectedly.

I rolled my eyes and crossed my arms over my chest. "I guess the guys scared them off when they showed up. They probably saved my life."

Aunt Abby nodded. "Yeah, I'm sure that must've been what happened. Still, you were very lucky. The wolves could've easily torn you apart."

"*Cool!*" Bobby said with renewed vigor.

"*Bobby!*" Aunt Abby and I said in unison.

He ducked like we had thrown something at him. "Sorry," he said covering up his head with his arms. He began to giggle.

Aunt Abby and I exchanged looks. Somehow, it was like we were now of one mind. Crazy right? Together we pounced on Bobbybear and began tickling him unmercifully. His face turned bright red and he could scarcely breathe through his constant giggles. In seconds we were all laughing so hard that we were giddy and crying uncontrollably.

Bobby was sound asleep on Aunt Abby's overstuffed sofa. She had built a fire and a nice orange glow was coming from the hearth, filling the room with warmth. She was sipping a glass of wine as we lounged in matching recliners. I noticed that she was studying me intently over the rim of her glass.

"Something on your mind?" I asked with narrowing eyes. Sooner or later she was going to have to come clean with me. I could sense that there was something she wanted to say, but for some reason she was holding back. I wasn't sure how I could get her to open up to me.

She lowered her footrest and leaned forward, holding her glass of merlot in both hands. "What do you know about The

Hollows? What have your parents told you of this place?"

I lowered my footrest and leaned toward her. Our faces were less than a foot apart. I shook my head. "Nothing. Mom and Dad never discussed where they were from with me." I glanced at my brother who was still sleeping peacefully, completely oblivious to everything. I almost envied him. So sweet, still so innocent.

"Did they ever tell you about that talisman? Why it was so important that you always wear it? Never take it off?" Her eyes drifted over the amulet and then locked with mine. Her eyes had an intensity that made me a little uncomfortable.

I couldn't help but feel that I was on the verge of learning something truly important. I couldn't even speak—I was afraid to say anything. I didn't want to give my aunt *any* reason to clam up. Finally, I couldn't help myself. The anticipation was *killing* me. "I know the inscription on the back, *'Cave Canem'* means *'Beware the dog'* but other than that, I don't really know much more than what Mom told me. I have always been curious. It seems such an odd phrase to inscribe upon a piece of jewelry intended for somebody's niece."

She smiled slyly. "It has been for your protection as much as anyone else's."

I frowned. "I... I don't understand. I'm not following you."

She sighed heavily as she drained the rest of the merlot from the glass. "How could you possibly?"

I wasn't getting anywhere like this. I slid off the chair and plopped in front of her on the floor. I took the empty glass from her hands and sat it on the coffee table. I took her hands in mine and squeezed them firmly. "Please, Aunt Abby. Explain this madness to me before I really do go crazy."

She took a deep breath and stared at me intently, not saying anything. Finally, she nodded. "Okay." She ran her hands through her hair and sighed wearily, trying to decide just where to begin. After a minute she exhaled slowly. She said, "Your parents weren't normal. They were... *different.*"

Bobby stirred upon the sofa and sat up looking bleary eyed. "What's going on?" He still sounded half asleep.

"Aunt Abby and I are having a little talk, that's all." I so wanted him to go back to sleep, but deep down I knew that wasn't going to happen.

Aunt Abby stood up and stretched. "We ought to take him home. You and I can talk another time."

"No, Aunt Abby! Please..."

She shook her head. "He doesn't need to hear all this. It would be best if we took him back to Wellington House." She gave me a knowing look. "Perhaps Mother would allow you to spend the night here with me. Then we can finish our talk."

I stood up and nodded. "I think I'd like that."

She laughed. "I wouldn't be so sure of that, Kat. Not until you've heard all that I have to tell you."

Surprisingly, I think, to both Aunt Abigail and I, Grandmother didn't object with me returning to the cottage for the night. She even expressed an interest in 'getting to know her grandson better.'

I hated feeling like I was abandoning Bobbybear, but I felt I needed to know what Aunt Abigail was talking about. I was tired of her cryptic clues—they were making my head hurt. Besides, I seriously doubted that what she had to tell me was worth such secrecy. I knew my parents. They were *perfectly* normal. I really didn't think she could tell me anything that I didn't already know.

The front doors of Wellington House seemed to close with an eerie sense of finality. I had to fight the urge to fling the doors open and run to Bobby. But I swallowed and took a slow, steady breath.

Aunt Abigail seemed to sense my uncertainty. She offered a small smile and a narrow gaze. "It isn't too late to turn back, you know. Sometimes it's better to keep the memories that you have rather than to trade them for something you're not sure of. Especially when what you discover could very well change the perception you have of your parents. The choice is entirely yours to make Kat. I'll not try to persuade you either way."

I raised my chin slightly and shook my head. I was determined to know what secrets she held concerning my parents. "There's no way that I'm turning back now. I need to find out what you *think* you know about my mom and dad. It's been a long time since they were last in The Hollows; people do change. You might not know them as well as you think."

Aunt Abby laughed. "Ah, you have much to learn, Kat. People

can change but there are some things that are likely to *always* remain the same. No matter how much you try to manipulate matters to suit your needs, some things simply *are*." She gave me a knowing smile. "Your parents were like that. They hoped that life would be different for them once they left The Hollows behind."

She glanced away, scanning the forest before continuing, "I hoped that it would for them too. But I think that deep down we all knew that it wouldn't. Some things in life are inevitable. You can't outrun your destiny. You can certainly try, but sooner or later it will catch up with you. It always does."

"You sound like you're speaking from experience." I said.

She nodded her head; it was *barely* perceptible. "Maybe I am."

We walked along in silence for a while longer, my thoughts a jumbled mess. What were my parents running from? Had they broken some law that had forced them to flee their home? The thought that my parents could be wanted fugitives was unlikely, but it left me feeling unsettled nonetheless. My parents were *good* people; to think otherwise was a betrayal to their memories. Had they somehow made an enemy that threatened them in some way? What could it possibly be? I didn't know. But I was determined to find out.

I grasped my aunt by the arm and forced her to stop and face me. "What were my parents running from? You *still* haven't told me anything, not really."

She studied me silently as a slow smile crept on her face. "You really need to learn patience Kat." She wrapped her arm around me and forced me to walk with her. "Relax. I'm getting to it, I promise. When I'm done, I'll answer all of your questions."

I sighed. There was no rushing her. She was going to take her own sweet time telling me what I wanted to know. I decided that I would listen intently and not interrupt. The sooner I got through this, the better. Afterwards she had promised that she would answer anything. I just hoped she'd stop rambling and get to the point.

"Your parents were madly in love with each other and wanted to get married, but your grandmother refused to allow it."

"Why?" I couldn't help myself. I had to ask.

Aunt Abby smiled. "My mother did not feel that your father was good enough to marry a Wellington. His family wasn't amongst those that first settled in The Hollows; nor were they well connected. In fact, they came to work for one of the original Founders as indentured servants. Mother could not allow one of her daughters to marry so far below her station. She felt that it would reflect badly upon her. It didn't matter that your father's family had risen above their former social ranking over the years. Mother couldn't get over their humble beginnings. In her eyes, it just wouldn't be proper."

"Wow." I hadn't any idea.

"Your grandmother forbade your mother from seeing your father. But they were determined. No matter how difficult my mother made things, my sister always found a way to see the love of her life." Aunt Abby smiled. There was a hint of pride in her voice. She turned and looked at me. Her eyes were bright and full of moisture. "They finally decided that the only way that they could win our mother's approval was to settle things once and for all. They eloped. When your grandmother found out, she was absolutely furious. She threatened to have their marriage annulled and the minister who had wed them, defrocked." The smile left her face. "She had that kind of power."

I was unprepared for my aunt's sudden laughter. "But your mother was a smart one, to be sure. She was *very* determined. She knew what our mother was capable of." Her eyes sparkled in the dying light of the day. "She knew that the *only* way to stop our mother's interference once and for all, was to become pregnant."

My jaw dropped open. "*What?*"

"Your father objected at first. He wanted to plead his case with your grandmother, convince her somehow that she was wrong to keep them apart. But my sister knew our mother would chew him up and destroy him. So, she persuaded him that her solution was the only viable alternative."

"Didn't that make Grandmother angry?"

"Oh definitely!" Aunt Abby nodded vigorously. "I had never seen my mother so furious. It was frightening. She disowned your mother on the spot. She even went as far as getting your dad fired from his job. She had so much influence in the area that he couldn't get work anywhere. But he had to support a new wife with a baby on the way." She shrugged. "So, they moved away. They headed south, to the City, where our mother had absolutely no power over them or what they did."

She grew strangely silent. It was almost as if she were struggling with what she wanted to say next. Finally, I watched as a single tear fell from both eyes; her bottom lip quivered. "I never saw either of them alive again."

I didn't know what to say. I reached out and rubbed her arm with a tender caress.

"I don't have a phone—hardly anyone does here in The Hollows; so we never talked. We corresponded, but rarely. They seemed to want to leave it all behind... friends, family... The Hollows... everything."

My heart ached for my aunt. She had been *so* close to my mom, and then *suddenly* all contact had been severed. It must have been difficult for her... it *still* must be. I gave her a loving embrace and kissed the side of her head. Her entire body shook with her grief. I was unprepared for it, and it overwhelmed me. In seconds we were holding each other and crying.

"You must understand how hard moving from The Hollows had to be for your parents. As I said, they were not *normal*. They were as *far* from normal as you can possibly get."

"How?"

We had reached the cottage. The sky above the trees was turning a beautiful shade of blue and orange. Soon night would fall and claim the forest. Already a few stars were appearing in the darkening sky, sparkling like diamonds. The great silvery ball of the moon was rising beyond the trees.

"You would *never* believe me if I told you. You'd think that I was stark raving mad. Certifiable even. So," she smiled, "you'll have to trust me, and I'll *show* you." The look in her eyes had turned steely as she gazed upon me. She was deadly serious. Unwavering. "Do you trust me Kat?"

CHAPTER 6
PROOF POSITIVE

Aunt Abigail opened the cellar door and hit the switch located on the wall to the right of the doorway. After a second's hesitation the light flickered and then shone brightly. The hum of the electric current was noticeable as we descended the stairs.

The room was empty except for some thick, heavy chains attached to the floor in the center of the basement, and a video recorder mounted on a tripod. I was suddenly suspicious. I had no clue what was fixing to happen. Aunt Abigail mentioned something about *trust* but I was starting to feel increasingly uncomfortable.

"What's this about?" I asked waving a hand toward the center of the room.

"I need you to trust me," she said again.

To say that I was confused would be a gross understatement. I decided to try my attempt at humor—despite knowing that I am *never* as funny as I *think* I am, or hardly ever, anyway. "Jeez, Aunt Abigail," I stooped to pick up the chain. *It was very heavy!* "I didn't know you were into this sort of kinky stuff!" I gave her my best *'Aren't I hilariously witty?'* look.

She gave me a thin smile and narrowed her eyes at me. Her

voice had a hint of humor; she seemed to be enjoying my discomfort. "Oh, these aren't for me, they're all for my favorite niece."

Before I could react, Aunt Abigail stepped forward and took the chain out of my hand. She allowed the chain to slip through her hands until she was holding up the shackle. "If you want to learn anything more from me about your parents, then you have to do it *my* way. Refuse, and I take you back to Wellington House without another word."

I guess that she could still see the uncertainty that lingered in my eyes. "You *can* trust me Kat. This is as much for your protection as it is my own."

Suddenly I was transported almost three years into the past. I was sitting with my parents in our living room. I had just opened up a package that Aunt Abigail had sent me from The Hollows; inside was the talisman. Mom had placed the chain around my neck and said, "Your Aunt Abigail said that you need to wear this at all times. You can trust her, Kat. She would never do anything to harm you."

Mom's voice sounded *so* clearly in my head. Seeing Aunt Abby in front of me, it was almost like I was standing beside my mother. Tears sprang to my eyes, and I nodded my acceptance, they rolled down my cheeks and dripped off my chin. "I trust you Aunt Abby—with my life."

"Good." She said as she locked the shackles around my wrists. I was completely at her mercy now. I stood there trembling as she removed my sneakers and started to unfasten my jeans.

I twisted my body away from her, I no longer wanted to continue with this insanity. "What *are* you doing?" I asked pointedly.

She smiled. "I thought you might not want to ruin your jeans, that's all."

"What are you talking about?" I really was thinking that I'd made a *huge* mistake.

"Trust me, Kat. If I don't take your jeans off, they will be completely ruined." She looked into my eyes. "Trust me."

The tears continued to fall from my eyes. I closed them tightly, but the waterworks persisted. I nodded silently. I had no idea what I had gotten myself into, but I needed to know this *secret* about my parents that she was keeping from me. And this was the *only* way I was going to find out what it was. All I could think of was how *this* had better be worth it. But right now, I really couldn't see it.

Aunt Abigail tugged my jeans down my legs and I did little to assist her other than stepping out of them in the end. I couldn't help but think that I should've shaved my legs this morning. She placed the other two shackles around my ankles and stood up. The steel was cold and heavy. She folded my jeans neatly and placed them near the tripod.

My lip quivered as I watched her in silence. She turned on the video recorder and then said softly, "Okay. Here we go." She stepped toward me and placed her arms around my shoulders. Her fingers found the clasp on my talisman's chain. A second later, the amulet was in her hands.

I stared at it as she stepped away from me. I had worn that piece of jewelry constantly for three years. I had been told never to take it off, yet now I had. I had *never* been so frightened in all my life. Aunt Abby watched in silence, her eyes wide and expectant. I was going to hyperventilate. *Now I felt naked!*

Without warning I felt a stab of sharp pain in my abdomen. It caused me to gasp and double over, clutching my stomach. I was terrified. "What's happening to me?" New waves of excruciating pain seized my body in several places all at once. It felt like the bones in my shoulders, arms and legs were snapping apart, threatening to tear through my skin at any second. Even my face hurt.

"Please Aunt Abby... make it stop!" I was breathing heavily and crying in huge sobs all at the same time. I could feel my heart pounding inside my chest, battering my sore ribs unmercifully. My pulse raced in my temples. My vision began to blur. I was being torn apart from the *inside*! I could hear the ripping fabric of what few clothes I had still been wearing as they were stretched beyond their limits. I knew I was dying.

The pain was excruciating!

Dropping to my knees I screamed in agony. I felt both dizzy and nauseous. I was vaguely aware that my screams had turned to an unfamiliar *howling...*

I sat upon the sofa in my aunt's living room with a blanket wrapped around me. I couldn't stop shivering. The morning rays of golden sunlight streamed through the open curtains but they offered no warmth. I think I was still in shock. I felt incredibly weak.

This was the third time that I had viewed the video recording. It was still an unbelievable nightmare. It was like watching a horror movie with me as the star. *"Please Aunt Abby... make it stop!"* The girl in the movie pleaded for mercy as her bones and cartilage snapped and reformed along with the impossible reshaping of her muscles. I saw the poor girl drop—*or rather I saw myself drop*—to the floor, begging the camera for my life to be spared. I watched, horrified, as I saw my clothes rip apart at the seams and fall away from my misshapen body. Hair began to sprout where none had been a moment before. I heard my chilling scream turn to an animalistic howl. *I* was gone, replaced by a large, angry and snarling wolf that was chained before me. Its eyes glowing red with hungered fury.

"Drink this!" Aunt Abby shoved a glass into my hands as she snatched the remote away from me and turned off the VCR. "It'll help get you back to normal."

I drained the whiskey in one huge gulp and relished the way it burned all the way down to my gut. I coughed, unable to catch my breath. She took the glass from me and poured another. "Take it slowly," she cautioned.

I waved the glass toward the television. "Why? What's the point? I mean, seriously?" I looked at her incredulously.

"We still need to talk, Kat. It would be best if you were sober."

I gave her a look that I hoped told her quite plainly, that I *didn't* care. I tossed the whiskey down, my eyes tearing at the burn. "Whoa!" I said breathlessly exhaling.

She shook her head in resignation and drained her own glass before refilling both. She set the empty bottle onto the coffee table. Now I was forced to drink more slowly if I wanted it to last. And I did. Though I hate the taste of the whiskey, I had a feeling that I was going to need the whiskey to get through this extraordinary event.

We sat in silence, just staring at each other. Finally, I gave my head a slight shake. "So... I'm a monster." I said flatly. My life was over and I knew it.

"No," she said smiling slowly. "You're a girl who can *turn* into a wolf."

"There's a difference?" I asked in disbelief.

She placed her glass on the table and took my knee in both of her hands, giving it a firm squeeze and a shake. "Absolutely there is!"

"What do you mean? Please explain *this* to me!"

She sighed. "Well, you are only a monster if you choose to be."

I slammed my glass down onto the coffee table with such force that caused some of the amber liquid to spill from my glass. *"I didn't choose any of this!"* I was starting to feel a little heady. I was done with the whiskey—I didn't want to start slurring my words. I'd never really drank any alcohol before other than a bit of champagne on special occasions.

She raised her hands placatingly. "I know. I know. Bad choice of words. Sorry." She took a deep breath. "All I meant to say was that this *doesn't* make you a monster. If you stay true to who you are, then you'll be fine. Granted, it's going to take some getting used to; but you can control it. Your parents did, and so have others."

"You mean that there are *others* like me?" I couldn't believe it.

Aunt Abigail laughed. "Remember those boys you met in the woods yesterday morning? They're the *same* wolf pack that took down that deer you saw when we first got here."

I know my eyes had grown incredibly large at this piece of information. I would never have guessed that about those guys. Silas had seemed so sweet. So had Tucker, Cho and even Brock in the end. I would never have believed they could be *monsters!* They seemed like all the other boys I knew back in the city.

"The difference between them and you is that they can control when they change. But they had to *learn* how—just as you will. Once you've gotten control over your wolf, you'll be able to master the metamorphosis."

"Are you telling me that I'll be able to change into a wolf at *will?* Why on earth would anyone want to do that?" I couldn't believe it. I had *never* been in so much pain in my entire life. I just couldn't imagine anyone being *willing* to go through that agony on purpose.

"I know that transforming hurts like Hell," Aunt Abby said sympathetically, "but the more you do it, the easier and less painful it becomes."

"Are you a wolf?" I asked her.

She shook her head. "No. I told you. I'm a witch. But enough have told me that it gets easier with time. The guys you met yesterday, your mom and your dad."

"What about Bobbybear? Is he a wolf too?" I couldn't bear the thought of him suffering through the metamorphosis as I had. I wanted to protect him from harm; not see him hurt.

Aunt Abby picked up her glass of whiskey and took a sip. "He'll be fine until he turns thirteen, just like you were."

I played with the talisman that was back safely around my neck; where it belonged. "So, if I wear this *thing* I won't turn again?"

She nodded. "That's right. It keeps your inner wolf repressed. I'll make one for your brother when he's of age. It's only fair that you both have the right to choose. The talisman gives you that choice."

I nodded thoughtfully. This was a *lot* to take in. I looked at her and frowned. "I always thought you had to be in the moonlight to change into a werewolf."

"Not necessarily," Abigail replied, "you feel the pull of the moon wherever you are."

"Is Grandmother a wolf?" I asked.

Aunt Abby practically snorted. "Oh heavens no." She shook her head as she chuckled. "Your grandmother would rather *die* than be a wolf! She is a powerful witch though. A *priestess* if you can believe it. Her *coven* is one of the most revered in the area. They are *very* anti-wolf!"

I crinkled my brow, trying to get a better picture of everything. "So, are you a member of her coven?"

Aunt Abby shook her head. "No, I am not. I was brought up to be—just as your mom was—but we chose different paths. Your grandmother was never very happy with our decision, but there was little she could do about it once we'd made up our minds. She never quite forgave us, I don't think. She took it as a personal slight against her. She felt that it weakened her position." Aunt Abigail shook her head. "She worries how *everything* affects her." She sighed. "It's always about *her.*"

"When I was the wolf," I began slowly, "I had no conscious thought. It's like Katherine St. Claire didn't even exist anymore. It was *only* the wolf."

"It won't always be that way, Kat," she assured me. "You and the wolf will become *one*. It'll just take time."

I tossed the blanket aside and stood. "I don't know if I *want* to become *one* with the wolf!" The experience had been incredibly painful and parts of my body were *still* aching. I looked at her pleadingly. "Can't I just be me without all this... this *other* crap?"

She hugged me close and kissed the side of my head. "I'm afraid not, kiddo. The wolf is part of you. It *always* has been, and so shall it forever be. Now that she has been released, she'll *want* her freedom. You'll find that she can be *very* demanding. The wolf doesn't like to be contained."

"But it *shouldn't* be about what the wolf wants. It should be about what *I* want!"

Aunt Abby nodded. "That is precisely why you need to train. You need to be the mistress of all that you are—including the wolf. At first, she may seem more dominant, but you'll *have* to learn to suppress her desires. If you give in, you could lose yourself completely."

CHAPTER 7
THE FUNERAL

The day was dark and dreary, almost a perfect match for my mood. The morning sun refused to shine, opting to remain hidden behind dark clouds, thick with the promise of rain. As Bobby and I made our way down the stairs he stuck a finger in his collar and pulled against it. "I can't breathe," he complained, scowling.

I could see Grandmother and Aunt Abby waiting for us in the foyer, both were wearing dark dresses and thin veils of lacy black. My dress was similar to theirs, extending to just below the knees. Grandmother was wearing heels, Aunt Abby and I were both in flats—thank God for small favors. Aunt Abby was pacing restlessly, the fingers of her hands seemed in constant motion. No one was comfortable.

Grandmother slapped at Bobby's hand as his fingers made their way to his collar once again. "Stop that!" she said, sounding annoyed.

He sighed heavily. "But it's too tight!" he moaned. "I can't breathe!"

"Of course you can," she said gruffly. She glanced at my aunt.

"Abigail, will you please stop that pacing and check on the car. What is keeping that man?"

Aunt Abigail practically snorted. "You're talking about Harrison Beckett, Mother. The man is a complete imbi—"

Grandmother rapped the end of her cane sharply against the smooth flagstones of the foyer. "Enough! Now is *not* the time for this nonsense."

Without another word, Aunt Abby opened the front door and stuck her head outside. I could hear the heavy roll of thunder echoing through the forest, the smell of rain thickly tainted the air as a gust of wind tore through the Manor.

Today was a *perfect* day for a funeral...

Aunt Abby leaned back inside. "He's pulling the car up now."

Bobbybear sat between Grandmother and I in the back seat of the Bentley, Aunt Abby was forced to ride up front with Harrison Beckett; she looked less than thrilled. As rain began to spatter down upon us I gazed out of the window. A dense fog drifted through the tall pines that lined the road as we turned onto the main road, heading toward the cemetery just outside of The Hollows. I was finding it difficult to concentrate on anything other than what was about to happen. Today we were putting our parents into the ground. It made this nightmare all the more real. It was not just a dream from which I could awaken. I felt my eyes beginning to water. I wiped away at my tears as they slid down my cheeks, with the white handkerchief that I gripped ever so tightly in my left hand. I sniffled, wishing that I could control my emotions, but it was a lost cause.

Bobbybear coughed beside me. He too, was struggling with his feelings.

I took his tiny hand in my right and gave it a reassuring squeeze, letting him know that we were going to get through this thing together. He continued to look straight ahead, and I could see that his blue eyes were swimming in tears of his own. He gave his head an almost imperceptible nod.

I understood. Completely.

We stood at the double gravesite as the rain continued to pelt us relentlessly. Aunt Abby held up a large black umbrella that sheltered Bobbybear, her and me from most of the deluge. Harrison Beckett had an apathetic expression on his face as he held a smaller umbrella above Grandmother; he, however, was getting drenched.

The minister had a young man standing at his side holding an umbrella for him, keeping both he and the Bible he read from as dry as possible. There were no others in attendance. It was sad, really. Mom and Dad had no friends here in The Hollows to mourn their passing. It occurred to me that things would have been far different had they been buried in the City.

After the service had ended, we made our way back to the Bentley. Grandmother and Harrison were already there, waiting. I opened the door for Bobbybear and he slid in quickly out of the rain. I noticed that Aunt Abby was looking back at the gravesite, a small, sad smile curving the corners of her mouth. I glanced back and saw a lone figure, a man, standing over the graves.

I looked at my aunt and said, "Who is that man?"

She blinked, a blush rising to her cheeks. "What man?" she asked.

I turned back toward the gravesite, but no one was standing there. *Had I simply imagined it?* I would have thought that likely had I not seen the color rise to Aunt Abigail's face. She had seen the mysterious figure too. Of that, I was certain.

As we headed back toward Wellington House, I stared out of the passenger window. The drizzling rain had slowed to a light sprinkle and much of the fog had dissipated. My mind kept wandering back to the lone figure that I had seen standing over my parents' graves. Who was he? Why had he waited until everyone had left the service? Was he a friend of my parents, some old acquaintance paying his last respects? I would probably never know.

I glanced at Aunt Abigail as she sat in the passenger seat, her jaw set firmly as she stared out of the windshield. She *knew* who the man was. Why had she bothered denying it?

I turned my attention back to my window and my eyes grew suddenly wide with surprise. I saw the pack of wolves at the forest's edge, their heads tilted upwards as they howled mournfully as we passed, almost as though in some form of tribute. Deeper in the scattered pines I thought I saw two wolves bathed in a glowing aura of bluish-white light. As the Bentley rounded a bend in the road, I lost sight of them altogether.

CHAPTER 8
ACCEPTANCE

Deep down I knew that Aunt Abigail had been right. The wolf had *always* been a part of me. Understanding that was helping me to deal with it on a whole other level. I started spending more and more time at the cottage, and Grandmother seemed pleased to have the time alone with Bobbybear. *That* should've made me curious enough to question things, but it didn't. I was so wrapped up in my own problems that I never thought to check and see how Bobby was doing. He *seemed* fine. I *trusted* that Grandmother would keep him safe and out of mischief.

I'd find out later that I *still* had much to learn...

But for now, I was learning to deal with the beast lurking beneath my skin. It always seemed to be hovering close to the surface, eagerly awaiting its release. The wolf *wanted* to run free.

Aunt Abby continued to utilize the chains in the basement for about a week. I readily agreed with her reasoning. Safety was paramount—both hers, and my own. Until I could control the wolf, to *tame* her to a degree so that I could keep her from becoming a dangerously wild animal, the chains *were* necessary. The primal instincts of the wolf were demanding satisfaction.

The beast wanted to stalk prey, and that frightened me no end. Yet, I knew, deep down there was a part of me that was looking forward to it with anticipation. And I found that really scary.

We were both satisfied with the progress that I had made. In the basement I could call the wolf forth and send her away on demand—even in the midst of transitioning. It was time to release the wolf into the woods. There would be no chains to hold her back. The wolf wanted to run, *and I was gonna let her...*

Aunt Abby and I walked through the woods bundled in jackets and scarves to keep out the cold. It was late afternoon and the sun would be setting within the hour. To say that I was insanely nervous would be an understatement. This was the first time that we were allowing the wolf to run freely.

Finally, we stopped in a small clearing. A ring of stones circled a stack of dry wood. Aunt Abigail quickly went to work getting a fire started for warmth as I began undressing.

Bathed in the warm glow of the dancing flames Aunt Abigail smiled, her eyes sparkling in the firelight. I could tell that she was nervous. I was too. "I will be here waiting for you to return," she said softly.

I crossed my arms over my chest, more for warmth than modesty. My teeth chattered. I nodded, unable to speak. I turned in the direction that Aunt Abby pointed, took a long, deep breath. I nodded once more and then I began to run. I could feel the adrenaline pumping through me as I went faster and faster.

The wolf was eager to run. I could feel the beast tugging at me, demanding to be set free. A fallen tree lay across the path in front of me. As I leapt into the air to hurdle the log, I released the animal within.

After hours of practice my bones and muscles were used to the transformation, and it was smooth and relatively pain free. By the time I cleared the rotting log and landed back on the path I was the wolf. I shared my mind with the beast and pushed back when the wolf tried to fully take over. The wolf snarled in protest. She wanted to be the boss while in this form.

Somehow, I could sense that the wolf was holding back, as though she resented my presence. I eased up on my control somewhat and was *immediately* rewarded with greater speed. The wolf was far faster than I could ever hope to be even with years of training. It was an exhilarating run; dodging rocks, thick brush and clumps of trees. I let her have a little more freedom...

I knew *instantly* that I had made a mistake, but there was nothing that I could do. The wolf pushed hard against me and I was not prepared for the mental assault. In a matter of seconds the wolf had established control and I was a helpless captive of her whims. It was all that I could do to just hang on. I was afraid that I'd be lost forever if I slipped any further.

At first I was terrified; I became completely overwhelmed by new sounds, smells and sights assailing me all at once. The forest sprang to life around me like *never* before. I could hear twittering in the trees and the sway of the grass in the gentle breeze. My eyes were sharper than they'd ever been, allowing me to see in greater detail. The wolf *improved* me.

Far off to my right I heard the slight bending of a branch. Somehow, I *knew* it was a deer passing by. I wanted to see if I was right. The wolf responded, sensing my need it loped off through the trees. The wolf stopped abruptly as it - *we* came face-to-face with a doe. I tried to shout, hoping to scare the deer off, but a vicious snarl escaped instead. *I realized that I was the wolf, but I still had no control.*

The deer bolted to the left, absolute fear in its wide, brown eyes. The wolf anticipated the move as it sprang up; its powerful jaw clamping down upon the doe's soft, sinewy neck. The struggle was over in an instant. The wolf had won. She tore at the carcass and I relished in the warm taste of blood. *It was invigorating!*

My belly was full, but the blood that clung to and matted my fur, had done little to quench my thirst. I trotted through the forest toward the stream that I could hear lapping against large rocks. It was cold and refreshing; just what I needed. I froze suddenly. Unnerved. I was staring at the wolf's reflection, seeing it through my own eyes. It was oddly disturbing coming to the realization that I was the wolf. I *willed* the wolf away, and I saw myself transition back into human form. I gasped at the sight of my blood-covered chin and the splatter of so much blood that covered my bare chest and arms. Startled by what I saw, I very nearly fell into the stream. I hadn't been prepared for *this* reality. For a minute I thought that I was going to pass out.

I cupped my hands and plunged them into the stream and closing my eyes I splashed water on my face. It immediately helped to alleviate the wave of nausea that swept over me. I could *still* taste the coppery tang of the deer's blood in my mouth. I bent my mouth to the stream and gulped down the cold water as fast as I could.

After drinking my fill, I heard a wolf howl at the rising moon. Another soon joined it. The howls sounded close. On the other side of the stream, not twenty yards away, a brown wolf tinged with reddish fur watched me intently. Noticing that I had discovered its presence, the wolf eased closer to the far bank. It barked twice, and I could see the fanning of the shrubbery with each wag of its tail. The wolf seemed to shimmer slightly and then it was gone. A human boy stood in his place. I recognized him almost immediately—Silas Monaghan! I panicked. I transformed back into the wolf and bared my fangs in warning.

I could hear two more wolves howling on my side of the stream. Looking up toward the silver sphere that was rising up above the forest, I saw two wolves on a rocky outcrop further upstream. One white, one gray. Both seemed to be bathed in a ghostly light. I was immediately reminded of the two wolves that Bobbybear and I had seen outside the hospital. Was this merely a trick of the moonlight or something else entirely? I couldn't be sure. I glanced back to where I had seen Silas, hoping that maybe he had seen them too, but he was gone. He had slipped back into the forest.

I looked up at the wolves silhouetted against the moon and howled. It sounded mournful and heartbreaking even to me. I watched as the two turned in my direction, and then left the outcropping and disappeared into the trees. Without thinking I plunged through the forest and raced uphill and soon found myself on the barren rock where they had been.

Looking around I saw the two wolves on the bank of the stream where I had been moments before. I howled in anger and frustration. I leapt headlong into the forest, racing back the way I had come. As I stood beside the stream I quickly glanced around, fearing that I had been abandoned. But the white and the gray were still nearby, only deeper in the woods. They seemed to be waiting for me to join them.

As I started to trot toward them, the wolves turned and ran. I barked once, and then sprinted after them. No matter how hard I tried to catch them, they continued to stay ahead of me. I was more than a little aggravated at them. I needed to know more about them, but they seemed intent on keeping their distance and their secrets from me.

The smell of woodsmoke filled the night air. The flickering glow of firelight was visible through the trees just up ahead. I slid to a halt, kicking up clouds of dust. The two wolves had vanished. I searched around for their scent but I couldn't detect either of them. It was like they had never been there. I snarled angrily.

"Kat? Is that you?" I heard Aunt Abigail call out timidly. She sounded frightened, yet hopeful. I could see her through the trees and undergrowth. She was standing near the campfire shining a flashlight into the forest, searching.

I morphed back into human form and immediately felt the cold slap of the night air upon my bare skin. I stepped into the clearing and must've been a Hell of a sight, because Aunt Abby gasped in surprise, her eyes growing wide. Despite my best efforts I was *still* a bloody mess.

She quickly wrapped a blanket around me and guided me to the fire. "Let's get you warm and then we'll clean you up." I could only nod in response; I could feel the wolf receding from my mind; satiated but never really gone.

After sitting me down on a fallen log beside the campfire, Aunt Abby took a damp cloth and began to wipe the drying blood from the sides of my face. Seeing the bloodstained cloth jolted me out of my stupor. I vividly recalled brutally taking the doe down. I began to sob uncontrollably.

Aunt Abigail wrapped her arms around me and held me close. She kissed the side of my head as she tried to offer me comfort. "Ssh! It's going to be all right my darling. Everything's going to be just fine."

I shook my head and slipped out of her arms. I made my way to the edge of the clearing and dropped to my knees. I could *still* taste the raw flesh and blood of the poor animal that I had killed. I wretched violently for several minutes. Every time I thought I was through, another wave hit me.

Aunt Abigail poured water over the dying embers of the fire. She turned to me and smiled as a thin column of twisting smoke rose in the air in futile protest. "Let's get back to the cottage. It's been a long night for you, and we're both tired."

"How long was I gone?" I asked, having no idea. The wolf seemed to have no sense of time whatsoever.

She smiled slowly. "It'll be dawn in a few hours. We'll be lucky to get back to the cottage before the sun rises."

I looked at her in disbelief. I had spent nearly the *entire* night as the wolf. Though to me, it had only seemed an hour or two at best.

I was all dressed and had the blanket wrapped around me, and I was still shivering. What I really needed was a nice long, hot bath. A *really* good cleansing! I sighed lazily. "I saw one of the guys out there, hunting."

"Oh?" she said. "Did he see you?"

I chuckled softly, my own eyes growing wide beneath raised brows. "Oh yeah. He saw far more of me than I'm really comfortable with."

She gave me a questioning look, so I continued. "It was just after I had killed the doe. I was thirsty despite all the blood I'd drank. I was getting a drink from the stream and I got kinda freaked out seeing the wolf's reflection stare back at me, so I transformed back to being a human. That was when I saw Silas on the other side of the stream. At first he was in wolf form with reddish-brown fur, but when he saw me, he switched to his true self." I couldn't keep the small smile from curving the corner of my mouth as I recalled him standing on the bank, naked. "I saw pretty much *all* of him too."

"I see." Aunt Abby said. "At least it was Silas and not one of the others. He's always been really sweet. Still," she paused, seeming to consider it further, "he is a teenage boy."

I shrugged. "We're both practically adults, it's *not* a big deal."

We got to the cottage just as the first rays of the morning sunlight broke through the trees. "You up for a hot breakfast?" Aunt Abby asked as she stepped on the front porch. "I know I'm starving! And a hot cup of coffee sounds absolutely divine!"

The thought of eating sent a chill through me. I closed my eyes and shook my head. "All I want is a scalding cup of coffee and a nice, relaxing bath."

She chuckled as she opened the door. "Okay my love. You get started on that bath, and I'll get a pot of coffee brewing. It'll be ready in just a few minutes."

I climbed out of the cold bath water and dried off with a

towel. I ran it over my head and then wrapped my hair up in the towel. I took another from the shelf and draped it around my body. I *desperately* needed that cup of coffee.

Despite my objection to eating, Aunt Abby had prepared bacon and eggs. I still felt a little unsettled, but my stomach growled hungrily. I plopped down across from my aunt and eagerly attacked the food on my plate. I felt ravenous—but I *knew* it wasn't really me it was due to the wolf. I could only hope it would get the taste of the deer out of my mouth.

Aunt Abby arched a brow as she watched me in amusement. I could see the smile tugging at the corner of her mouth above her strategically placed coffee cup. She asked me about my experience as the wolf and I answered truthfully, leaving nothing out. I told her about the wolves that had led me back to her, and about the wolves that Bobbybear and I had seen outside the hospital after our mom had died. "Do you think that Bobby could be right? Was that *really* Mom and Dad? Is that even possible? I mean, how could it be?"

I shook my head not waiting for a response. "How is *any* of this even real?"

She sipped her coffee before answering. Finally she said, "In all honesty, I really don't know. It could all just be coincidental, but I somehow doubt that. Your parents were killed while in human form. Maybe their wolf spirits somehow survived." She shook her head much the same way I had just done. "I really don't know."

I don't know why, but somehow I think she may have nailed it. Maybe what Bobbybear and I saw was their wolf spirits. That would definitely explain their ghostly aura. And they had led me back to where Aunt Abigail was waiting for me. They had seen me to safety. I couldn't help but think that Mom and Dad were still watching over us. It left me with a nice, warm feeling inside.

CHAPTER 9
ISSUES OF TRUST, AGAIN

I entered Wellington House well after lunch and headed straight upstairs. I was feeling like the absolute *worst* sister ever. I had been completely ignoring Bobbybear lately and was feeling rotten about it. It had been selfish of me to think only of myself. I wasn't the only one who had lost our parents; Bobby had too. He was probably feeling like he'd lost his sister as well, and who could blame him? As I took the stairs two at a time, I vowed to make it up to him.

As I reached the second-floor landing, I heard Grandmother call out to me from downstairs. I couldn't just pretend I hadn't heard her or ignore her completely. Bobbybear would have to wait a bit longer. I stepped to the railing and peered over, forcing a smile to my face. "Yes, Grandmother?"

"I would like to speak with you for a moment, Katherine." I knew that it wasn't an invitation. Grandmother seldom *asked* for anything. It was just her way of demanding your obedience, simply telling you what she wanted.

"I was just going to check on Bobby." I said sounding hopeful.

"Robert is fine, I assure you." Her voice was unwavering; as cold as frost covered steel left outside on a winter's eve—*that* cold. "You can see to him later—after our talk."

I swallowed the lump in my throat. The woman scared me. "Very well, Grandmother. May I wash up first? I was helping Aunt Abigail in her garden."

She repeatedly tapped her cane upon the stone floor. I could detect a slight rise to her brow. "If you must. But make it quick, I'm not getting any younger."

I pushed away from the railing. "I won't be but a minute!" I turned and ran to my room and washed my hands and face with warm tap water. I quickly brushed my teeth, patted my mouth dry with a face towel, and then headed to the stairs. I desperately needed to pee but I didn't want to keep Grandmother waiting any longer than I already had. I just hoped that I wouldn't regret *that* decision.

The massive double door leading to the drawing room was closed. I wasn't sure what protocol demanded of me, so I knocked lightly. "Grandmother?" Even I could detect the fear in my voice.

"Come in, Katherine." I found Grandmother sitting regally in a high-backed chair. One hand was placed demurely in her lap the other clutched her ever present cane. "Close the door behind you my dear, so that we may have some privacy."

I nodded turning back to the door and closing it securely. It gave me a chance to compose myself. For that I was truly grateful. I smiled as I faced her. "You wanted to see me Grandmother?" My voice sounded pleasant and unwavering.

She pointed a finger at the plush eighteenth-century sofa across from her. "Have a seat Katherine. If I have to look up to you any longer it'll put a strain on my neck."

She studied me with a shrewd eye as I sat down, only renewing my discomfort. I placed my sweaty palms on my knees and gave her my best smile. God, I hoped this didn't take long! I *really* had to pee! I sat with my back straight, mindful *not* to slouch. If she had to reprimand me for my inadequate posture it would only prolong our conversation.

"So," her chin rose slightly, "what have you and your Aunt Abigail been doing with your time?" She was prying, that much was obvious.

I swallowed. "Uh... talking, mostly."

"Oh?" Her grip seemed to tighten on the hilt of her cane.

Was she nervous? "What have you been talking about?" She had already recovered sufficiently enough to leave me wondering if I had only imagined it all.

I shrugged and attempted to laugh. "Oh, this and that. You know, *girl talk.*" Her left brow shot up into an impossible arch. My fingers fidgeted in my lap. "I've just been all out of sorts since my parents died. Aunt Abigail has been kinda helping me deal with everything. We've been talking a lot about Mom and Dad."

"I see." Her tone seemed on edge, guarded.

"I've been talking about how Mom and Dad were since moving to the City. She had really no idea because they hadn't kept in touch. Just talking about them, my memories of them, seems to help. You know?"

I couldn't help but smile as tears formed in my eyes. "I loved hearing about my mom and Aunt Abigail when they were young. It made Mom seem closer somehow."

"Well, your Aunt Abigail lives in a fantasy world of her own design. You cannot always believe the things that come out of that girl's mouth. Oh, I'm certain she means well enough, but she has a very *wild* imagination. Folks around these parts refer to her as *'Crazy Abby'* when they think I'm not listening. I guess they try their best to spare me, but I know the truth of the matter. Abigail has never been fully right in the head."

She smiled at me after a moment. "But that is a mother's cross to bear and no other's, I suppose. That is why your folks truly left The Hollows all those years ago. It hurt them deeply to see Abigail and the way she'd become. They were both terribly fond of her."

Grandmother had a sad look in her eyes. "If you ever want to know the truth of things, you can always come to me. I will not lie to you Katherine." She leaned forward and gave my knee a reassuring squeeze.

She must have detected the confusion I felt, or maybe it was written all over my face. "What is it dear?" she asked. "What's troubling you?"

I shrugged. "Everything. I guess. Aunt Abigail said that my parents left The Hollows because of *you.*"

To my surprise Grandmother burst into a fit of laughter. I never would've believed it was even possible. "You see?" She said,

"Of course she would say that! Anything to remove all blame from herself! It's total nonsense, I assure you! Your aunt tried to come between your parents. She had convinced herself that she was in love with your father. She even posed as your mother to try and seduce the poor man. Had I not intervened she might have even succeeded with her bizarre plans. It could have ruined everything. I made the suggestion to your parents that they move away. In the end they agreed that it would be best. Abigail needed time to get over her feelings for your father. She'd never be able to do that while he was still here."

Grandmother shook her head. "I hated seeing them go. Especially since your mother was expecting. But I could not take the chance that you would be harmed. There is no telling what Abigail might have done in her state of mind."

She touched her lips with a dainty white handkerchief and waved a hand at the decanter on a shelf to her right. "Pour me a sherry if you would be so kind?"

I got up and poured half a glass for her. I half expected her to demand it be filled completely, but she accepted it graciously. "Thank you, my dear. I'll not keep you any longer. You've enough to think about for one afternoon. Just close the door on your way out."

"Of course. Then there'll be nothing else?" I asked.

"I'll see you at dinner *darling*." She waved at the door. "Go find your brother."

I closed the door and leaned against it. My mind was so confused that I was actually starting to make my head hurt; I was getting a migraine. I now had two scenarios that conflicted greatly. Each of them was plausible. I didn't know *who* to believe. Did I trust my aunt who was helping me come to terms with the wolf inside me? Or trust my grandmother?

Aunt Abigail had always seemed sane enough. But her claims of being a witch could easily contradict that notion. But she *had* crafted the Talisman that allowed me to keep the wolf at bay. Who could do that, but a witch?

Still, Grandmother had definitely given me something to consider. Was it possible that Aunt Abigail had posed as my mom to seduce my dad? *Eew!* Had she been infatuated with my father? If so, did she *resent* my mom?

I had *a lot* to think about...

CHAPTER 10

BOBBYBEAR

I took the stairs slowly, my mind still a jumbled mess. All thoughts of finding Bobbybear were pushed aside. Who knew that living in The Hollows could be so utterly complicated and confusing all at the same time? I needed another nice hot bath to remove the tension that I felt creeping back into my muscles. My head and my neck ached unmercifully, and now I was beginning to feel it in both of my shoulders too. But first things first! I still had to pee!

I eased my body into the hot tub water slowly. I had it hotter than I normally cared for but the tenseness I felt more than warranted the extra heat. I just hoped it wasn't too hot. I didn't want it scalding. To top things off, I had used the last of my Calgon Bubble Bath. I could only hope that this backwater town had at *least* this simple luxury on hand. I so needed my bubble baths! Life was going to be unbearable if I couldn't resupply a *much-needed* necessity! Knowing my luck, I'd have to settle for Mr. Bubble! But even *that* would be better than dish soap!

I began to relax as the aches in my body began to ease away. I closed my eyes and sighed. I wondered what had happened between my grandmother and my aunt to cause them to become so estranged. It was unfortunate, really. Neither seemed able to get past their differences. They were family. Nothing in the world could ever change that. You'd think after the death of my mom they'd be able to see how important family really was. It was profoundly sad. Before I knew it, I had drifted off...

...I was the wolf. I was running through the woods, but I was not alone. A big reddish-brown wolf accompanied me. He nuzzled me playfully as we ran through the forest undergrowth. It was a cloudless night. A smattering of bright stars could be seen above the treetops, sharing the heavens with a huge, silvery moon.

We found ourselves at the edge of a secluded pond. The red wolf nuzzled me again, and then he transitioned into his human form. Silas dove into the pond. When he surfaced, he grinned back at me. "Come on!" he urged mischievously.

I didn't hesitate. I transformed as I leapt toward him. When I surfaced, I looked around for him, but I didn't see him anywhere. A second later he was there, beside me, water dripping from his head. Silas pulled me against him and kissed me passionately, his tongue darting past my parted lips to find my own.

I awoke with a start, almost splashing water over the side of the tub. *Where did that come from?* I could feel the heat rising on my face. I had no earthly idea what time it was. The bath water was cold; so I knew I had been soaking for quite a while. I studied my hand and frowned; my fingers were wrinkled. I lifted a foot out of the water and noticed the same affliction on my toes and heel. I had been in the water far too long. As I climbed from the tub I noticed a chill in the air. Goosebumps were forming on my exposed flesh—which happened to be *all* of me.

I grabbed a bath towel from the rack and covered my head, rubbing my hair vigorously. I twisted the towel up on my head, tucking a few errant strands of my hair under the towel and grabbed another to dry my body. Wrapping the towel around me I stepped into the bedroom and froze in place. *Someone* had been *in* my room. They were just now closing the door on their way out!

I raced to the door and grabbed the knob; fully intent on catching whomever had been snooping around in my room—or worse yet, *spying on me while I bathed!* The doorknob was *ice cold.* So cold that it almost burned. And it was locked! How could that even be possible? The lock was on *my side* of the door! "Bobby?" I shouted. "Open the door!"

Only silence greeted me.

I tried the doorknob again. This time it turned freely. I yanked the door open expecting to see Bobbybear standing there with a guilty expression on his face and offering a lame excuse. But no one was there. I could see light around the cracked doorway of Bobby's room at the far end of the hallway. A second later his door closed.

I started down the corridor, unconcerned that I still only had a towel wrapped around me. I didn't even stop to consider the impossibility of Bobby racing down the hallway so quickly. There was no way he could've run so fast without me seeing him. I hadn't paused *that* long behind my own door. These thoughts never entered my head. No one else was around; who else could it have been but Bobbybear?

The thought that Bobby had been watching me bathe was appalling. It made my skin crawl. *He was only six!* Where had his innocence gone? What had happened to my dear sweet baby brother? Wellington House was making monsters of us both or so it seemed.

A cold draft blew up the stairs from the foyer causing me to shiver. Only now was I fully aware that I had very little on; yet I pressed on. As I neared Bobbybear's room I heard girlish laughter coming from the stairwell leading up to the locked door. For some inexplicable reason I felt drawn to the sound. Before I even realized what I was doing, I turned from Bobby's room and started ascending the narrow stairs.

The air was cold. It grew even colder as I climbed. My pulse raced; my heart thudded inside my chest with each upward step that I took. As I reached the top landing, I could see my breath before me. My breathing had become labored with the climb. I could hear my pulse pounding thunderously in my ears.

As I reached for the doorknob, I could see the slight tremor in my fingers and hand. Why was I so frightened? I didn't really think I had much cause for alarm. I guess I'd watched too many scary movies about old houses growing up, and now they were coming back to haunt me. Mom had always said they'd give me nightmares. I was just being silly, surely. I flexed my fingers and gave my hand a quick shake, hoping to relieve some of the anxiety that I felt.

It didn't help. My hand was still shaking when I reached out again. Like my own doorknob had been, this one was also freezing cold. It almost seemed to burn causing me to draw my hand away from the cold metal, yet I pressed on. I expected it to be locked, but much to my surprise it wasn't. It turned easily.

I thought I could hear whispering on the other side of the door. I tried to open the door quietly and as slowly as I could. It made a loud creaking sound and the low voices inside the room quieted immediately. I flung the door open and stepped inside bravely, almost losing my towel in the process.

It was dimly lit by the fading sunlight that streamed through a shuttered window at the front of the house. It smelled heavily of dust. I could still faintly make out Bobby's footprints. Already they were thinly coated with a new layer of dust. It didn't look like he'd been up here recently. I saw no sign that anyone else had been in here either. But I had heard laughter *and* whispering—I was sure of it. But no one was here that I could see.

Bobbybear's tracks led to a portrait of a little girl close to Bobby's age. A dingy canvas lay crumpled on the floor at the base of the easel holding the painting. The girl was dressed in old clothes, probably from the Victorian era. In the portrait she was holding a wooden figure. I had to lean closer to see that it was a soldier. The girl's eyes seemed to bore into me, leaving me with a sense of unease.

There was really very little of real interest in this attic-like room. I could see stacked boxes here and there, and furniture draped with canvas drop cloths or dingy white sheets. I saw little reason to disturb anything—Bobby hadn't. His dusty footprints led to the portrait and then back to the door.

I decided to leave and go back downstairs. It had to be getting close to dinnertime and I still wasn't dressed. I glanced once more at the painting of the little girl. I gasped in shock. To my complete surprise she was no longer holding the toy soldier... *Had it been only my imagination?* That was silly. Why would my imagination conjure up the image of her holding a boy's toy - why not a doll instead?

The air had suddenly grown much colder. I could once again see my breath hanging in the air in front of me. As I opened the door, I *distinctly* heard a little girl whisper harshly over my shoulder, *"He's mine!"*

I whirled around, forgetting about the towel and almost losing it in the process once again. No one was standing there. I could see no one lurking about in the shadows, either. Soft, girlish laughter seemed to be emanating *from* the portrait. I could feel the hairs on my arms begin to prickle. My breath caught in my throat.

I quickly stepped out of the storage room and went to close the door behind me. It slammed forcefully as I reached for the doorknob. I jerked my hand back just barely in time to keep from jamming my fingers. I almost lost my balance. I had to grasp the handrail frantically with both hands to keep from falling down the stairs.

I entered the dining room just as Grandmother was taking her seat. She glanced at me with a raised brow. "So nice of you to join us, Katherine."

I could feel the heat of embarrassment rising to my cheeks as I pulled out my chair and sat down. "I'm sorry, Grandmother. I must've fallen asleep in the bath." I said apologetically.

"You must take care, Katherine. That can be dangerous." She turned her attention to Bobby. "You're not to bring toys to the table, Bobby."

He had placed a toy soldier beside his plate; he quickly snatched it away, a flash of red and black cupped in his hand. He placed it in his lap. I gasped sharply. The toy looked oddly like the one I had *thought* the girl in the portrait had been holding. I couldn't wait for dinner to be over so that I could ask him about it.

Grandmother had a keen eye, of that there was never any doubt. She could tell that I was anxious about something. "Is there something on your mind, Katherine?" You seem a bit preoccupied."

I shook my head and chewed my mouthful of peas longer than necessary, but it gave me time to think. Swallowing, I said, "I've just been thinking a lot more about what you said earlier."

She looked as though she didn't quite believe me. "And that is all? You seem a trifle apprehensive."

I met her gaze head on. Two could play this game, I decided. "I would think that'd be enough to make anyone a bit disquieted, wouldn't you? After all, that *was* quite the bombshell you dropped on me."

I could tell by the flash in her eyes that I had angered her. "I don't want to sound so flippant, Grandmother, but it is an awful lot to take in. I mean, I certainly had no idea that Aunt Abigail was..." I glanced at Bobbybear, " ...well, you know." Grandmother smiled. I could tell that I had pleased her with my discretion.

The remainder of the meal passed relatively quietly. Afterwards Grandmother excused herself saying that she had business to attend to in The Hollows and wouldn't be back until much later. So we said our 'goodnights' early. For that I was thankful. Grandmother wouldn't want me to join her in the parlor afterwards.

Bobby was halfway up the stairs before I could catch up with him. "What's the big rush, Bobbybear?"

He shoved the wooden soldier into a deep pocket of his cargo shorts and shrugged. "I was just going up to my room to play, that's all."

I indicated his pocket with an inclination of my head. "Where did you get your new toy?"

He squinted and cocked his head to the side. "What toy?" He was *so not* a good liar.

I couldn't help but laugh. "The one you had out at the dinner table." I pointed. "The one in your pocket."

Color brightened his face. "Oh." He frowned. "Well he isn't a *new* toy. I've had him for a while."

I sat down on the steps so that we could be at eye level with each other. "Really? I don't recall ever seeing him before."

He fidgeted. "That's because you've been gone a lot lately."

I felt a tug at my heartstrings. This kid was good! He knew how to turn the tables on me so effortlessly. Now it was *my* fault that we hadn't been spending time together like we used to. I hugged him close, pulling him onto my lap. I kissed the side of his head. "I know, Bobbybear, and I'm sorry that I've been neglecting you so much lately. Really I am. Can you *ever* forgive me?"

I could feel him nod against me. "Yeah," he said in a tiny voice that threatened to break my heart in two. He wrapped his arms around me and hugged me tightly. "I love you Kat," he said softly.

"I love you too, Bobbybear! More than anything else!"

He slid off my lap and looked at me with big, puppy dog eyes. His lips were firmly in a pout. He was a professional pouter. "You mean it Kat?"

I smiled at him. "Of course I do Bobbybear."

He grinned and stretched his arms up above his head, yawning. "I've had a long day and I'm tired. I think I'm gonna go to my room and get ready for bed." He leaned in and kissed me on the cheek. "G'night Kat."

I kissed him on the forehead. "Goodnight Bobbybear. Sweet dreams." His yawn seemed a bit forced and I doubted its validity. But I decided to let him off the hook. I could always find out the story of the little wooden soldier another day. Right now it really just didn't seem all that important.

We climbed the last few stairs to the second floor, and then went our separate ways. I watched Bobby from my doorway. His strides were shorter than mine. I don't know what I was expecting him to do—I guess I was afraid he might venture up to the storage room; but he didn't. He went to his room and closed the door behind him without even a backward glance in my direction. It left me feeling kinda sad.

I closed my door and leaned against it with my back. I wept softly, not really knowing why. It dawned on me that I missed my old life in the city and the close friends that I had. I missed my parents. I *hated* the fact that Bobbybear and I seemed to be growing apart. I wish that we'd never come to The Hollows.

CHAPTER 11
SARA ROBINSON

I lay in bed unable to sleep. I was too hot with the blankets up, and too cold with them down. I couldn't get my pillows to lay right. I was horribly uncomfortable. I was doomed to a sleepless night from the start; my mind was a jumbled mess. Both Grandmother and Aunt Abigail were telling me conflicting stories, each one making the other out to be the bad guy. I honestly didn't know who to believe. I wished my parents had been more forthcoming with information about their families *and* their reasons for leaving The Hollows behind. Either would've made my life *so* much simpler.

My thoughts returned to the portrait of the little girl in the attic storage room. Surely there was some way to find out exactly *who* she was. Maybe there was something written on the back of the canvas. It never occurred to me to check earlier. It may not even matter. But something was telling me that the girl in the painting was somehow important. As to what it could all mean, I didn't have a clue. Not yet, anyway. But I fully intended to solve this particular mystery.

I was sure that I had heard a little girl's laughter coming from that room. I was fairly certain that she had held the toy soldier in the portrait, and then when I looked again, her hands were empty. What did it mean? I remember the hostility in her voice telling me that *he belonged to her*. But what had she been referring to? The toy soldier? Or had her meaning been more *sinister*? Had she been letting me know that Bobby was hers?

A chill swept over me.

I sat up and cast my coverings aside. I had to check on my brother. There was *no way* it could wait until morning. I *had* to know that he was alright. Initially I had thought that the little girl was referring to the toy soldier when she harshly whispered, *'He's mine!'* but now I couldn't be certain. I'd never forgive myself if I allowed something to happen to Bobbybear—especially if I could have prevented it.

I put on my slippers and grabbed my robe from the foot of my bed. I tied it at the waist as I opened my bedroom door. The house was dark and quiet. Outside a storm was brewing. A sudden flash of lightning momentarily illuminated the hallway, driving back the shadows to where the light couldn't reach. But as the thunder rumbled ominously, the darkness claimed Wellington House once again. The rain wasn't far off.

I hurried down the long hallway as fast as I could. I *hated* thunderstorms with a passion. I was seeing *all kinds* of menacing monsters lurking in the dark shadows; all of which were products of my imagination—or so I hoped.

Finally reaching my destination, I was breathing hard. I tried to calm myself by taking a few deep, long breaths and blowing them out slowly. Sufficiently calmed, I opened Bobbybear's door and stepped inside his room. Another flash of lightning followed immediately by a growl of angry thunder that caused me to jump and shut his door with a resounding *THUD!*

I glanced at the bed and Bobby sat up rubbing his eyes sleepily. "Kat? Is that you?"

I hurried to his side and slipped beneath the covers, snuggling him close to me. "I was worried you might be frightened by the storm."

He chuckled against me. "You're the one that gets scared, not me!"

I nuzzled my chin against his neck. "I know! Can I sleep with you tonight?"

He squirmed and giggled. My chin always tickled him this way. "Yes! I was *hoping* that you'd come!"

I kissed the back of his neck as I wrapped my arms around him and pulled him against me. "Thank you Bobbybear. I love you!"

He bent his head and kissed the back of my hand. "I love you too, Kat!"

With Bobbybear snuggled firmly against me, I could finally begin to relax. He began to breathe heavily and I knew he was sound asleep. It had been a long time since our last snuggle session. I had missed it. I bent my knees and tucked him closer to me, wanting as much contact with him as possible. It wasn't long before I began to drift.

I awoke with a start. The air in the room was ice-cold; I could see my breath forming clouds as I exhaled. The faint scent of lilacs seemed to permeate the air. A glance at my brother confirmed he was still soundly sleeping.

The bedroom door was open a crack, which I found odd. *I know* that it had been securely closed. Had someone been in the room while we slept? That would certainly explain the perfume. I searched my memory but could come up with no one in the manor that wore the scent of lilacs

I eased out of bed, careful not to disturb Bobbybear. I tiptoed to the door and opened it. Peering into the darkness, I could see a rectangular section of yellow light reflected upon the floor at the foot of the staircase going up to the attic storage room. Someone was up there!

I hurried to the stairs and glanced upward. The door was open, and light was coming from the room. Without hesitating I started up the steps. At the last second I managed to avoid the creaking step—I didn't want to alert anyone to my presence.

I paused at the doorway on the top of the landing to catch my breath. My heart was pounding inside my chest with nervous anxiety. Finally, steeling my nerves, I forced myself into the room. No one was there. A single bulb was illuminated above the portrait. I could see something shiny glowing at the base of the frame.

Attracted to the gleam like a moth to an open flame, I found myself in front of the painting. There was a small brass tag attached to the bottom of the portrait that I hadn't noticed before. It was inscribed with ornate script that I had difficulty making out. Years of grime had caked upon the tag.

I wiped it with a dampened thumb; two words and a date were revealed:

Sara Robinson, 1884

I stared at the little girl in the portrait. I now had a name. But what did it all really mean? Who was Sara Robinson, and what was her connection with Bobbybear? The toy soldier was the *only* common factor between the two of them that I could see. At least I now had something to go on. I was determined to find out more...

Grandmother said little at breakfast. She was obviously preoccupied with matters of her own concern. When Bobbybear tried to engage her in conversation, she simply smiled and said, "Not now, dear."

It really wasn't *that* unusual. Grandmother was so not a morning person. I smiled and looked at Bobby. "Aunt Abigail and I are going to do a little shopping in The Hollows today, would you care to join us?"

He shook his head. "No way! I already got plans of my own!"

"Oh?" I was genuinely curious as to what they might be. Bobby wasn't very forthcoming however. I knew that he had been doing a fair amount of exploration of Wellington House on his own. Who knew what mysteries he had already uncovered? Somehow he had come into possession of the toy soldier. "Are you sure you don't want to come along?"

He spooned some cereal into his mouth and then wiped his lips with the back of his hand. "Nope. I'm good."

"You sure?" I asked. "There might be candy involved." I tempted with a smile. I knew Bobby had a sweet tooth.

He hesitated slightly. "You could always bring me back something." He sounded hopeful. A sweet treat was *always* hard for him to resist.

I laughed. "I suppose I could. But you have to promise to behave and not get into any trouble while we're gone."

He shrugged. "I'll be good."

I smiled at him, waiting for more.

Bobbybear rolled his eyes and grinned. "Promise," he said.

There was absolutely no love lost between Aunt Abigail and Harrison Beckett; that much was clearly evident. She slid into the back seat of the Bentley without so much as a word to him as he held the door. He stared ahead with a look that resembled disinterest tempered with disgust. I almost laughed out loud, but somehow managed to control myself.

As I slid in beside Aunt Abby, he closed the door firmly. "Is he *always* this warm and cheery?" I asked with an amused smile.

Aunt Abigail practically snorted. "Are you kidding? He absolutely *hates* having to play chauffeur to me. If you weren't coming along, he would've found some way to weasel out of going altogether. Mother is *making* him take us into town. It is the *only* way she can find out what we've been up to. He's her little spy!"

I couldn't help but roll my eyes. Whatever was going on between Grandmother and Aunt Abigail I wanted no part of. I figured that it was best if I simply stayed clear of it all.

"What can you tell me of a Sara Robinson?" I asked, staring directly at her. I knew it would make it harder for her to lie to me.

Aunt Abigail shook her head. "Who? I don't believe that I know a Sara Robinson. Who is she? A friend of yours?"

"I found her portrait up in the attic storage room along with a bunch of boxes and old furniture. It was a very old painting. It had her name with the date of 1884 on it. I was doing a bit of exploring and I found it. I was just curious."

She shook her head. "I don't think that I've *ever* seen it."

I could tell she was lying. She seemed suddenly very uncomfortable. She knew more than she was letting on. I was certain of it. I guess I was going to have to find out about Sara on my own.

Harrison Beckett pulled the Bentley to a stop in front of the Benning's Auto-body shop. He opened the door and offered a brief explanation. "The car needs a tuning."

"Really?" Aunt Abigail said heatedly. "You couldn't drop us off first?"

His eyes sparkled. "It's such a nice day. I figured you could use the walk." The smirk on his face really said it all. He knew that he had angered Aunt Abigail, and it was obvious that he didn't care. He had accomplished what he had set out to do. He was quite pleased with himself.

Aunt Abby was livid. The fire burned hot in her eyes, but it chilled me to the bone. "I see," she said simply. "Have it your way, you little toad." Her eyes narrowed, causing the chauffeur to take a step back. "Just remember you started this. I hope that you are prepared for the consequences."

Harrison Beckett glanced briefly at me, and then returned his attention to my aunt. "I'm not afraid of your idle threats, Abigail. Witch or no!"

Aunt Abigail laughed. "Then you are a bigger fool than even I gave you credit for!" She pointed a finger in his face. "This isn't over!"

He shrank back, stumbling against the Bentley and almost falling completely over. I could tell that she had indeed frightened him. He was no longer the stuffy, arrogant man that he had been a moment ago. He was something else entirely. Something *smaller*.

Aunt Abigail took my hand and smiled. "Come along, Kat. We've got a lot to do."

We walked away from Benning's leaving poor Mr. Beckett to compose himself. After a moment, we stopped. "Is something wrong?" I asked. Aunt Abigail seemed distant. Though she was standing beside me she seemed far away. I touched her arm. "Aunt Abby?"

She blinked and a slow, tentative smile appeared on her face. "I'm sorry, Kat. There's something that I need to attend to. Why don't you go on without me, and I'll catch up with you."

I looked around, trying to get my bearings. I had spotted a public library as we drove through town. Maybe I could find out about Sara Robinson there. "I want to pick up something to read. I think I'll wait for you in the library."

She nodded. "That's nice. Just up the street." She glanced back at Benning's and her face seemed to harden. "I'll meet you there in about an hour."

I followed her gaze to the Auto-body shop and was suddenly very fearful for Mr. Beckett. Was she capable of harming him in some way? He had called her a *'witch'* and she had admitted to me that she *was one—but more of a 'healer'*. Was it possible she was *more* than that? I wasn't overly fond of Harrison Beckett myself, but I certainly didn't wish him harm. I could only wonder what she had in mind. I couldn't really be sure that she had anything planned against my grandmother's chauffeur, but her sudden change of plans definitely had me suspicious.

The Hollows Public Library smelled of old books and newspapers. It brought a smile to my face; I could get lost in here for hours. Easily. I stepped up to the counter and rang the bell for service. A moment later a plump girl with brown curls and huge round-lensed glasses stepped out of a room in the back. She was about my age. Upon seeing me she smiled brightly, accenting the dimples in her cheeks. "Hello there! Welcome to The Hollows Public Library! Is there something that I can help you with?" She wiped her hands upon the dark blue apron that she was wearing.

"I certainly hope so," I said. I wasn't entirely sure how to proceed.

The girl stuck her head out toward me like a turtle would coming out of its shell. She smiled sweetly. "Well?" she prompted, eyebrows raised expectantly.

I chuckled nervously. "This may be stupid, really. I'm not sure that you can help me, honestly."

She reached across the counter and patted the back of my hand. "We have some of the classic literary works and also newspapers dating clear back to when The Hollows was first established. If it is in one of these books or in a newspaper, I can certainly do my best to help you."

"I hope so," I grinned. Her good nature was contagious.

"My name's Millie Bradford." She looked me over. "You just passing through?" She laughed as though she had just told a joke. "Who am I kidding? No one *ever* passes through The Hollows! So, you *must* be new!"

I laughed. "Your powers of deduction are amazing!"

She beamed at me proudly. "Why thank you so very much for noticing!" She did the turtle thing with her head again. "And you are?"

"Oh!" I felt myself blush. "I'm Kat St. Claire. Pleased to meet you, Millie." I extended my hand.

She shook my hand. "Likewise." She frowned and touched her finger to her lips. "St. Claire you said? Hmm... any relation to Samuel St. Claire?" She rolled her eyes and waved a hand in the air before I could answer. "That would be silly! He's just an old hermit!"

"There's a St. Claire living in The Hollows?" I asked; my interest suddenly piqued.

She nodded. "Well, I guess he doesn't actually live in The Hollows. He has a rickety old shack somewhere deep in the woods. Prefers his solitude I guess. *Hates* people from what I understand."

"Hmm..." I said more to myself. Could this hermit be some relation to Bobby and me? It might be worth checking into. But first things first. *Sara Robinson...*

"Any-hoo!" Millie said raising her brows. "What can I help you find?" She drummed her fingertips upon the countertop.

"Well, I was going through my grandmother's attic and I stumbled across an old portrait of a little girl. The brass tag on the painting had a name and a date. I was hoping to learn more."

"The name?" she asked.

"Elizabeth Wellington."

Millie froze in place. Her jaw dropped. "Uh... you're kidding, right?"

I blushed again. "No, I mean, Elizabeth Wellington is my grandmother. I found the painting in *her* attic." I couldn't believe that I had made that mistake.

"Wow!" Millie said. "Elizabeth Wellington is *your* grandmother? That's amazing. She's like *the* richest person in The Hollows!" She chuckled and put a hand to her chest. "Oh my!"

I cleared my throat uncomfortably. "So, can you help me find out more about the girl in the portrait? Her name is Sara Robinson. The date listed only the year. It was 1884."

Millie shook her head as though coming out of a trance. "I'm sorry!" Her cheeks had gone all rosy. She pushed her glasses up her nose and then returned her hands to her hips. "Sara Robinson you say? 1884?"

I nodded.

"Well, that may take a bit of time." She winked at me. "After all, it isn't as though it was yesterday!" She chuckled at her little joke.

"We haven't had any Robinsons living in The Hollows for quite some time." She frowned. "In fact, I think the last Robinson that lived here was Lucius Robinson, a former Governor of the State." She tapped her lips with her index finger. "I guess that is as good a place to start as any."

Millie stepped out from behind the counter and led me to the back of the library. "Lucius Robinson was the twenty-fifth—*no*, the twenty-sixth Governor of New York from 1877 to 1879. He lived here in The Hollows for a time after he left office. Don't remember *why* he left. But I'm fairly certain that we can uncover the truth of it. Maybe we'll learn all about Sara in the process."

I was buoyed by her enthusiasm. She seemed a wealth of information. It was no wonder why she worked in the library. I couldn't imagine a better-suited person to fill the position of librarian.

It took us longer than I had hoped to uncover information about either Lucius Robinson or Sara. I was beginning to feel a little discouraged when Millie finally exclaimed, *"Eureka!"*

She pushed her glasses further up her nose and grabbed my arm, pulling me close to her side. "It seems that the former Governor actually lived in Wellington House for a short time, well, *before* it *was* Wellington House, I mean. Anyway, his young niece, Sara Robinson, died tragically in the nearby woods. There was some type of family gathering going on at the time. No one noticed that she had wandered off. She probably got lost—easy to do in those woods."

I nodded. I understood how that could *easily* happen probably better than anyone.

Millie continued, "They searched for her for days before they found her. It was quite tragic, really. An animal had apparently mauled her. The family was devastated by her loss. They sold the house, all holdings they had in The Hollows, and simply moved away."

Millie squeezed my arm. "It seems that your ancestors bought the estate for a fraction of its worth. They've owned it ever since. After the Robinsons left The Hollows, the Wellingtons were the wealthiest family remaining in the area." She chuckled. "You're practically Royalty!"

"What happened to Sara is so sad," I said.

Millie sighed heavily. "That poor little girl was wandering around alone in the woods—something I would never do! All sorts of wild animals live in these woods. I imagine that there were a lot more of them back then." She shivered uncontrollably. "It gives me the willies just thinking about it! It must have been horribly frightening for her."

She was right, though. There *were* a lot of wild animals roaming the woods. No telling what she may have encountered. My heart went out to the poor girl. It must have been horrible. She was so small... Bobbybear's age...

My thoughts were wandering and I hadn't realized that Millie was still talking to me. I hadn't heard a word that she'd been saying. She shook my arm. "Hellooo? Anybody home in there?"

I could feel the color warming my cheeks. "I'm sorry. I was lost in thought."

Millie smiled. "That's okay, sweetie. I understand."

"You were saying?"

She shook her head. "It wasn't really all that important. I was just asking how life in Wellington House was. We've all heard stories about that place. I was just kinda curious if they were true or not."

"Stories?" I asked. "What kind of stories?"

She seemed suddenly quite shy. She fidgeted with the silver crucifix that she wore around her neck and stared down at her feet. She mumbled something under her breath that I couldn't quite make out.

I took her arm. "Look, Millie, if we are going to be friends, we have to be honest with one another. So, tell me. Please."

"Friends?" she asked, astounded. "You really want to be my friend?"

I nodded. "Why wouldn't I?"

"Well," Millie seemed flabbergasted. "For starters, you're related to the Wellingtons. I'm just a nobody. I couldn't even reach up to your social class if I stood on my tippy-toes. We've *nothing* in common."

"Don't be silly, Millie." I gave her my brightest smile. "We're gonna be the best of friends!"

"Best friends? Really?" Her eyes seemed to water a bit. "Wow! I went from having literally no friends to being somebody's bestie!"

I laughed. "You're the first friend I've made in The Hollows!" I neglected to mention Silas and the others—the jury was *still* out on them.

She wiped her eyes with the tips of her fingers. "So, is Wellington House haunted?"

My jaw dropped. I had *not* expected that. It was a really good question; one that I didn't readily have an answer to. I stared at Millie in silence, not sure of how to answer her question. Finally, I took a deep breath. I decided to plunge right in. "I think it very well may be."

The repeated ringing of the service bell interrupted our conversation. Millie pushed a loose strand of her hair behind her ear. "Sounds like I'm needed up front. You can take your time back here if there is something else you want to look at. I'll pick up things later."

"No, I think I'm good! I'll walk out with you; I really need to be going anyway."

To my surprise it was Aunt Abigail that was impatiently pounding the service bell. "Can I help you?" Millie asked. When my aunt whirled around Millie gasped sharply. "I'm sorry! I didn't realize it was you."

Aunt Abigail rolled her eyes and gave a little shake of her head as though she couldn't be bothered. She ignored Millie who was busy crossing herself. "Are you ready, Kat? I'm afraid we'll have to do our shopping at another time. I need to be getting back home."

I nodded. "Certainly. I turned back to Millie. "Would you like to come up to Wellington House sometime? We could have a sleep-over or something."

Millie's eyes widened in surprise; she hadn't expected an invitation. "Sure! That would be fantastic!"

"How about tomorrow, then? I can send the car for you. Say four o'clock? We can dine with Grandmother and then have the rest of the night to ourselves."

Millie seemed to be blown away. She nodded, speechless.

"Where shall I have Mr. Beckett pick you up?"

"Uh... who?"

"Mr. Beckett, my grandmother's chauffeur. Where shall I have him pick you up?"

"Oh! How about here? I'll lock up and then I'll be ready."

"Great!" I smiled. "I'll see you then!"

After Aunt Abigail and I slid into the back seat of the Bentley I noticed that she was giving me an odd look. "Is there something wrong?" I asked.

"Not at all. I was just wondering if you've thought this whole thing through."

I couldn't help but frown. "What do you mean?"

She practically snorted in response. "Don't you think that you should check with your grandmother before you start inviting strangers into her house? I'm certain she won't take this very well."

Aunt Abigail was starting to get under my skin. Just *whom* did she think she was talking to? I wasn't some naïve little kid. I was practically an adult. "It's my home too. If I want to have a friend over, I don't see what the big deal is." I shook my head. "I'm not a prisoner there after all."

"Oh really?" She laughed. "That is *exactly* what you are! As long as you dwell in Wellington House you will live by *her* rules." She held up a finger, "Number one on her list is quite simple: *She knows what's best!* The sooner you grasp that concept the better. She is *never* wrong, and she is *never* to be questioned." She leaned toward me. "Rules two and three! You get nothing— you do nothing, without her approval. She'll never let you have friends over unless she has *personally* hand selected them first."

"You're wrong!" I said in defiance. "Grandmother isn't at all like that. She may be strict, but she isn't a tyrant!"

"Oh my God! If you are going to start spouting her praises I'm getting out of this car!"

"It's you that you're really talking about, not me. You're afraid that she will let me have friends over when she never allowed you to!" I laughed. "I can't believe it! You're jealous!"

She pounded the back of Harrison Beckett's seat with her fist. "Stop the car! Stop the car this instant!" She had a wild look in her eyes. For a moment I was deathly afraid of her. I could see what Grandmother had meant by *'Crazy Abby!'*

As the Bentley rolled to a stop, she flung the door open and slid out of the car. I wasn't sure what was going on. "I'm sorry Aunt Abby, really I am. Get back into the car and we'll talk about this. I shouldn't have talked to you in that way. I'm sorry."

She wasn't listening. She shook her head and started for the woods that lined the road. I got out of the car, desperate to stop her. "Aunt Abby! Please come back! I'm sorry!"

She started to run away from me. I decided I had to stop her, to make her forgive me. Harrison Beckett grabbed my arm. "The woods are not safe, Miss Katherine. It would be best if you got back into the car and allowed me to return you safely to Wellington House. Your grandmother would be displeased if something were to happen to you."

"What about my aunt?" I said.

"She'll be fine. She knows these woods." I turned and watched Aunt Abby disappearing into the thick undergrowth of the forest. Soon she was out of sight completely. Was she truly insane? I could only hope that it wasn't true.

CHAPTER 12
CLARITY

To my surprise, Grandmother seemed truly pleased that I had invited Millie Bradford to spend the night tomorrow at Wellington House. "That is a splendid idea!" She said. "As a matter of fact, perhaps she could spend the entire weekend!"

"Seriously?" I couldn't believe it. Especially after the apparent meltdown that Aunt Abigail had had in the car. Maybe I had been wrong to put so much trust in her after all. Maybe my aunt was a little peculiar. She was definitely making Grandmother out to be the sane one.

She looked at me quizzically. "Why wouldn't I be? I'm glad to see that you're making friends your own age. I think it is important. Besides, Wellington House hasn't been infused with youth and vitality since your mother and aunt were both girls. It will be nice to hear girlish laughter in this house." She took a sip of her sherry. Harrison told me of the... the *incident* earlier. I hope that it didn't upset you too much. Though I did try to warn you about your aunt, as you will undoubtedly recall. Poor dear isn't all there, I'm afraid."

"It was a bit frightening." I admitted reluctantly.

"You mustn't blame her. It really isn't her fault. I tried to get her help, years ago, but she was just incredibly angry and threatened violence. I probably should have had her committed to an institution that was more capable of tending to her special needs, but I just couldn't bear it. Living in the cottage seemed to help her in ways that I never could imagine. I really tried keeping an eye on her, but it hasn't been easy. I'm old and the walk is just too much for me, I'm afraid."

I shook my head slowly. "I don't blame her. No one's to blame. These things just happen." In reality, I wasn't so sure anymore. Everything that I had believed in had been turned completely upside down since the death of my parents. I mean, I was a werewolf for gosh sakes! *A freaking werewolf!* All of the stability in my life had gone *completely* out the window. Was it really any wonder that my aunt was nuts? Who wouldn't be? The Hollows could send anyone over the edge.

Grandmother placed her glass down on the coffee table. She sat watching me silently for a moment longer. Finally, she smiled demurely. "What will the two of you do with your time? I'm afraid that there isn't a lot for young women to do at Wellington House." She chuckled softly. "I'm sure that you both are too old for tea parties."

I returned her smile and pinched my fingers together. "Just a little bit, I'm afraid."

"So? How will you spend your time?"

I shrugged. "I imagine girl talk, mostly. I'm sure that there is a lot she can tell me about The Hollows that I don't already know. You know, school stuff."

Grandmother nodded understandingly. "I can imagine. Surely 'girl talk' has changed a great deal since my day." She sighed wistfully. Suddenly she seemed years younger. "Well," she said with a grin, "I'll try and keep Robert occupied and out of your hair. Boys will *always* be boys after all."

I forced a smile. I didn't really think that Bobby would be a problem. Besides, I missed spending time with him. "I think Millie will like hanging out with Bobby. The friends I had in the city really loved him."

"Don't be silly Katherine. I seriously doubt that your new friend wants to be entertained by a six-year-old boy. Furthermore, I would think that Robert would be quite bored with your *girl talk*. I can keep him sufficiently amused while your guest is with us." She smiled. "We wouldn't want to alienate your first friend in The Hollows, now would we?"

Grandmother was probably right. I didn't know Millie Bradford very well at all. She might be a bit put-off by Bobbybear's attention. He could be a handful if he wanted. He might see her as a wedge between the two of us, and if that were the case, Bobby could get *very* annoying. So, with that in mind, I nodded. "Of course, Grandmother. That would probably be for the best."

But I felt a sense of unease. I had promised to spend more time with Bobbybear and here I was handing him off so that I could hang out with a complete stranger. I felt terrible. I was certain that Bobby wouldn't understand. I decided to talk to him. Alone. Without Grandmother knowing—I was positive that she wouldn't approve. I forced a yawn. "Oh! Please excuse me. I guess I'm much more tired than I had thought."

Grandmother smiled. I couldn't tell if she believed me or not; she was such a *difficult* person to read. Her eyes seemed to bore into me with an intensity that left me feeling unnerved. They were steely, cold and calculating, belying the warmth of her curved lips that hinted at a smile. "Of course, Katherine. Perhaps you should retire. Tomorrow promises to be a rather big day for you."

"Goodnight Grandmother." I said pleasantly. I was surprised at the amount of self-control it took just to depart graciously. Especially when all I really wanted to do was run from the room. I desperately wanted to talk to Bobby before he fell asleep. I wanted to explain why I was gonna have to delay our time together. I was determined to make it up to him. Somehow. I only hoped that he would understand...

Bobby wasn't in his room. At least he wasn't answering my knock. I could feel my heartbeat quicken beneath my breast. If he was sleeping, I really didn't want to awaken him. I could disappoint him just as easily in the morning. I started to turn away from his door but something made me stop. I could feel the hairs on the back of my neck begin to prickle. *"He's mine!"* The girl's voice resounded in my mind causing goosebumps to appear on my arms.

I placed my hand on his doorknob and opened the door

slowly. Bobby had left a light on in the bathroom. The door was slightly ajar allowing a sliver of golden light to illuminate his bedroom keeping the darker shadows at bay. The covers were turned down on his bed, but the bed was empty. I could see the indentation on his pillow where he had lain his head, and the sheets were rumpled slightly where his body had been.

"Bobby?" I lightly pushed the bathroom door open all the way hoping to hear his protests for the loss of his privacy, but none were forthcoming. Bobbybear wasn't there either. *Where could he be?* It was well past his bedtime and this wasn't at all like him. I glanced back at his bed, frowning.

"He's mine!" The thought continued to nag at me. I had a feeling in the pit of my knotted stomach and it was most unsettling. I wanted to throw up. "Like Hell he is!" I whispered to the voice in my head. I was willing to fight for him if I had to.

I flung open the bedroom door and stepped out into the hallway. With three quick strides I found myself at the foot of the stairs leading up to the storage room. My heart was pounding inside my chest as my anxiety mounted; I had to place a hand on the narrow banister to steady myself.

I hesitated with one foot on the first step. My throat felt tight. My mouth was as dry as a desert. It was difficult to swallow. Fear was threatening to overcome me. I had to force myself to climb the stairs. Despite the chill in the evening air I was sweating. *"Please, Bobbybear!"* I whispered. *"Don't be up there!"*

"Kat?" I very nearly jumped out of my skin when I heard Bobby's sleepy voice call out to me from the hallway below. I turned quickly and saw him standing there clutching his worn teddy bear to his chest. His sleep-filled eyes were staring at me curiously. He rubbed at them with the back of his free hand as he yawned. "What are you doing out here? Why haven't you come to bed?"

I turned from the steps and knelt in front of him, gripping his arms tighter than I had intended. It was a struggle to control my voice. "I came to say good night to you, but you weren't in your room. I was looking for you."

He cocked his head and squinted at me with heavy eyes. "You were?"

I nodded. I pulled him against me and kissed the side of his head. "I sure was!" I glanced up the narrow stairs that disappeared in the darkness and felt chilled. "Why weren't you in your room? Where were you Bobby?"

He chuckled, breathing softly upon my neck, heightening my goosebumps. "I went to your room to see if I could sleep with you. I got scared and I didn't want to sleep in my room."

"Oh Bobbybear! Of course you can sleep in my bed! I've missed your snuggles so much!" I kissed his cheek, then stood and picked him up. I grunted with the effort. He was getting so big and by spending so much time at the cottage I was missing it. "You're growing way too fast Bobbybear! Slow down kiddo!"

He giggled. "It's not me!" He insisted. "It's Mr. Grizzle!"

"Oh really?" I gave his stuffed bear the evil eye. "You'd better watch it Grizz, I've got my eyes on you!"

I laid Bobby onto my bed and pulled back the covers. It wasn't easy, but I managed despite his bodily resistance. I kissed his forehead and tucked him in. "I'll be just a sec Bobbybear. I need to get my PJs on." He nodded, closing his eyes as he rolled onto his side and drew up his knees. I could see his body relax almost instantly.

By the time I finished in the bathroom, I could hear Bobby breathing soundly. Just before turning off the bathroom light I leaned my head against the doorjamb and watched him sleep; he seemed so sweet and innocent, so peaceful. I really did feel guilty about spending so much time away from him. And I feared that in the coming months it would only get worse. I fingered the talisman around my neck thoughtfully. The wolf would have to wait. Spending time with Bobbybear was far more important. As he grew older I knew that he would want his independence, of that I had no doubt. But until then, I vowed to spend as much time with my brother as I possibly could.

I lifted the covers and slid into bed as carefully as I could. I didn't want to disturb Bobbybear's peaceful slumber; he looked so angelic with his soft curls splayed out across the pillow. A small smile curved the corners of his mouth, suggesting pleasant dreams were coming to life in his slumbering mind. A part of me wished he could retain this innocence. I wrapped my arm around him and his tiny body wiggled up against me while he slept. Outside, I could hear the distant, plaintive howl of a lonesome wolf and I felt a stirring deep within me. I could feel the weight of the talisman between my breasts. I nuzzled closer to Bobbybear and kissed the back of his head, content to remain where I was.

Morning found us still snuggling comfortably together as the first light of dawn brightened the windows. I stretched beside Bobbybear, thankful that the heavy curtains were thick enough to keep most of the light out. The room was still sufficiently lit to drive away the shadows of the night.

Bobby stirred beside me, frantically kicking the covers off himself as he struggled to climb from the bed. He was in an obvious hurry to make it to the bathroom. He had me laughing uncontrollably. The rapid pitter-patter of his little feet slapping against the wood floor coupled with his moans of distress, very nearly sent me over the edge.

I could hear his sigh of relief as he relieved himself. He was taking forever, or so it seemed. My own desperate need was starting to bring discomfort. I sat up in bed, tossed the covers aside and slowly rocked back and forth praying that Bobby would be done before I embarrassed myself. My brow furrowed and my eyes closed tightly in a vain attempt to alleviate the rising pain of having to pee, I whispered harshly for Bobbybear to hurry. *Please!*

I opened my eyes as I heard the toilet flush. Bobby was making a beeline for the foot of the bed. I could tell that he intended on jumping, and I knew that I would never survive the rocking of the bed. I hopped up and flew past him just as he landed in the middle of the bed. I could vaguely hear the creak of the frame as he landed cannonball-style in the midst of jumbled sheets and quilted coverings. I was positive that Grandmother would disapprove.

I flicked off the bathroom light and grinned at Bobby as he sat at the head of the bed readjusting the covers. "Ready or not, here I come!" I said playfully as I sprinted toward the bed. As I leapt in the air I stretched out my arms toward him. His eyes growing ever wider as he realized my intent. Before he could escape, I had landed on the bed and was tickling him without mercy. The binding covers of the bed hampered his kicking legs, but his arms were free and he desperately tried to fend me off, though it was only half-hearted at best. His giggles of delight were mingled with desperate gasps for breath.

Exhausted, I plopped beside him. We both had tears running down our cheeks and were breathing heavily. "I love you Kat!" Bobby said softly.

I turned toward him and smiled. "I love you too Bobbybear. More than anything else!"

He held up his teddy bear to me, touching it's head to my cheek. "Mr. Grizzle loves you too!"

I took his stuffed bear in both hands and gave it a big kiss and a hug. "And I love Grizz second best!" I said.

I rolled over onto my side and pressed the bear back into his arms. Then I reached up and smoothed a wayward curl on Bobby's head. "Bobby..." I sighed, not sure how to even begin. "I have a friend coming over this afternoon. She's probably going to stay here all weekend."

Bobby glanced down at the bear in his arms before meeting my gaze. "Do you think she'll like me?"

I pinched his cheek softly. "How could she not?"

He shrugged. "Maybe she doesn't like little boys. Maybe she's like *Whatshername*. She didn't like me."

I had to laugh at that. He was right. Tiffany Stevenson *only* cared about Tiffany Stevenson. She was the obnoxious daughter of our parents' friends. She had been kinda forced on us both. "I'm sure Millie isn't like that. She seems really sweet. I just met her the other day."

"And you invited her to stay here? For the *whole* weekend?" Bobby asked sounding surprised.

Suddenly I felt uncomfortable. My six-year-old brother was making me feel impulsively stupid. "Uh... well, *technically* I only invited her for the night. Grandmother thinks that it would be a good idea if I were to hang out with someone my own age for a change."

I saw his face drop instantly. "Oh," he said. "Meaning Grandmother doesn't want you hanging out with me anymore." His voice sounded sad. Hurt.

I reached out and rubbed his arm. "Oh, Bobby no! I think she just wants me to stop hanging out with Aunt Abby so much. But she really doesn't have to worry about that anymore; Aunt Abigail and I are kinda on the *outs*. I'm sure that Grandmother didn't mean for me to stop hanging out with you."

He nodded. "Yes she did."

I sat up and turned toward him, pulling him onto my lap. I gave him a reassuring hug and kissed the side of his head. "It doesn't matter what Grandmother wants. You are more than welcome to hang out with Millie and I. You know that! All my really good friends back home just love you to pieces!" I could feel him nod against my shoulder.

"Yup! Both of them!" he giggled.

I gave him a soft punch on the arm. "Hey, at least I *had* friends my own age!"

He giggled. "Not *my* fault."

I cleared my throat. "Speaking of Grandmother," I kissed him on the neck causing him to giggle and squirm. "We need to be getting dressed."

Bobby crawled out of my lap and scooted off the edge of the bed. He reached up and grabbed his stuffed bear. "Alright Kat. I'll meet you downstairs." He walked around my bed and paused at the door on his way out. He gave me a pensive look. "Do you think it'd be okay if I made friends my own age?"

"Of course it would! Why on Earth would you even ask a question like that?"

He shrugged. "I just wanted to be sure that it'd be alright with you. That's all."

"Bobbybear, are you afraid that Grandmother won't allow you to have friends your own age?"

He shook his head. "Nuh uh. Grandmother *wants* me to make friends. But she said I shouldn't tell you about it. That you wouldn't like it."

"That's silly! Why wouldn't I want you to have friends to play with? Especially friends your own age?"

He shrugged again. "I don't know."

"Oh, Bobbybear! I'm sure you misunderstood Grandmother. Why would she say something crazy like that?" I found it difficult to believe that she would make such a bizarre statement. But Bobby wouldn't lie. Not to me. Not about something so crazy sounding. He had to have been mistaken. I made a mental note to ask Grandmother about it. If nothing else, I thought we might both enjoy a good laugh.

I watched Bobby heading down the long corridor for a

moment or two longer before I shut the door. As it was, I was going to have to push myself in order to get downstairs on time. There was absolutely no way I wanted to start the day on the wrong footing with Grandmother. Especially not on the day that Millie Bradford was coming over.

Despite my best efforts to be on time, I was still a few minutes late. I couldn't help but blush under Grandmother's smoldering glare. To my surprise she didn't say anything. She even smiled after a moment. Though admittedly it looked a bit forced, like she had just swallowed a bitter pill. "A big day today, isn't it?" She said after taking a sip of coffee.

I placed the napkin on my lap in silence; needing the time to think. I always felt so guarded with Grandmother. Her conversations seemed baited with statements designed to lead you into a corner where she could trap you. Once she'd steered you there, she had you' there was no escaping.

"I suppose." I took a bite of eggs and patted my lips with the napkin. Swallowing, I said, "But I was thinking about canceling with Millie." Grandmother stiffened noticeably. I continued, "I mean, what do I really know about her? I know she works at the library. I only just met her. What if we have nothing in common? It would just make things..." I shrugged, "...weird."

Grandmother placed her hands on the table on either side of her plate. They were closed tightly in fists. "Nonsense Katherine. The whole point of having Miss Bradford over is to get to know her better. To develop a friendship. You cannot do that if you cancel on the dear girl. Besides, you are a Wellington. We keep our word."

I swallowed. "No. I'm not. I'm a St. Claire." I refused to be bullied into losing my identity.

Grandmother pounded the table with her fists and stood abruptly. "Enough!" She gave me a cold stare that burned right through me. "I'll not have your insolence in my home! Like it or not, you have Wellington blood flowing through your veins. You will welcome this Bradford girl into Wellington House where you will be the perfect hostess to her. When it is all said and done, you will thank her for coming and make the offer for her to return. *That* is what *we* do. Do I make myself clear?"

I had never seen Grandmother quite so angry. It was truly

intimidating. Her eyes were like ice but seemed to burn with a white fire that seared to the bone. Her jaw was tightened with her vehemence. "Do. I. Make. Myself. Clear?" she said pointedly; emphasising each word with a pounding of her cane on the floor.

I nodded. Tears stung at my eyes. I couldn't bring myself to speak for fear of losing all of my self-control. My resolve had been completely shattered. I *hated* Wellington House.

We had finished our breakfast with Grandmother and Bobby discussing their plans for the weekend while I silently brooded. It was all I could do to keep from crying. After I had been excused, I went upstairs and removed my talisman, placing it in the drawer of my nightstand and grabbed my small backpack from the closet. I slipped back downstairs and out of the front door. I needed to clear my head.

I headed straight into the woods. I decided a nice daytime run as the wolf might help me to get my mindset right. I would've loved to talk to Aunt Abby, but I figured that we still needed some time apart. I couldn't handle another confrontation like the one we'd had on our way back from The Hollows. Bobbybear was too young to be offering any truly helpful advice. I was on my own.

Besides, Bobby already had plans to help Grandmother in her garden, so I didn't have to worry about entertaining him. They had a lot of work to do to ready the garden for their spring planting. True to her word, Grandmother had devised sufficient plans to keep Bobby busy over the weekend. So, I had some free time available—which I *desperately* needed at the moment.

I would have to keep a tight rein on the wolf. As the wolf, I had no sense of time. If I let her simply run free, I would miss picking up Millie—and *that* would be disastrous. Especially after Grandmother's little speech. She'd think that I had missed it purposely.

After I had gotten far enough from Wellington House, where I knew I wouldn't be seen, I began to undress. The spot that I had chosen was secluded; I didn't fear that someone would stumble upon my belongings while I was in wolf form. I folded my clothes quickly and stuffed them into the backpack. There was a chill in the air, causing goosebumps to rise on my now naked flesh. I found a tree that had a nice little pocket in the trunk that was perfect for storing my stash. I took a deep breath as I studied my surroundings. I was certain that I'd be able to find this place with little trouble. Satisfied with my hasty preparations, I began to run through the undergrowth, transforming as I went. The wolf *loved* to run. I gave her enough freedom to go as fast as she wanted, without having to relinquish full control. She seemed perfectly willing to accept what I offered. At least *something* was going my way, or so I thought.

The wolf was a sneaky beast. She continued to push against my consciousness, weakening my control over her without me even realizing it. When I attempted to regain what I had lost, she pushed back even harder. Now, *she* had control and I was simply along for the ride. I had been careless. I had allowed her swift navigation of the forest to distract me as she dodged the trees in her path and cut through the undergrowth. Finally, I decided to give up my futile attempts at re-establishing any semblance of control and to just enjoy the experience. I pushed an image of Millie to the forefront of the wolf's mind, and she gave out a quick bark, as though in acknowledgement. I could only hope that she would enable me to join Harrison Beckett before he departed.

The wolf stopped quickly, kicking up a low cloud of dust. The earthy scent of the dirt, pine needles and fauna rose up to the nostrils of the wolf in a familiar cascade of aromas. But I could sense the wolf's sudden unease. Her ears stood erect, twitching forward and then to the side. She had heard *something out of place*. I strained to hear what she had heard, and after a moment, I heard it too...

Laughter!

A low snarl escaped the wolf as she eased forward, muzzle close to the ground, nostrils flaring. I could hear the sound of a waterfall not far off. It was in the same direction from which the laughter of several boys could be heard. I recognized the voices of Brock Jacobins and Silas Monaghan. I had no doubt that Tucker and Cho would be in their company. Their guffaws, and the splashing of water made it clear that they were horsing around.

Before I even realized it, the wolf deserted me. I transitioned back into human form and was suddenly conscious of my nudity. Fortunately, I was still deep enough in the woods that I hadn't yet been detected. Curiosity got the best of me; I found myself moving forward for a better look.

I gasped at the sight of Brock Jacobins standing in knee-deep water, his back to me. His broad shoulders glistened in the sunlight as water droplets clung to his well-muscled body. He had a narrow waist; his butt was round and firm. I swallowed, my heart beating rapidly; my mouth was incredibly dry. I could just make out Cho in the distance. He appeared to be showering in the waterfall. Silas' red hair made him easy to spot. He swam toward Brock with strong, even strokes, his cupped hands cutting into the water like knives through hot butter, as his feet splashed upon the surface propelling him forward. I didn't see Tucker anywhere. *That should have set some alarm bells ringing.*

But it didn't.

I eased forward hoping to get a better look. Part of me kept hoping that Brock would turn so that I could see him more clearly; while another part wondered what the Hell I was even thinking! I was so caught up in what I was doing, that I was completely unaware of what was going on around me.

Before I realized what was happening, I felt strong hands grip my biceps and lift me off my feet. Glancing down, I saw the thick, black fingers of Tucker Morrison clutching my arms tightly. I struggled against him, but he was far stronger than I was. He forced me out of the protective greenery and into the open. "Look what I found!" he hollered victoriously. The gloat was clearly evident in his voice.

Brock turned to face us. My eyes grew wide in shock as I gazed upon his full-frontal nudity. I jerked my eyes up to his; embarrassed that he might've caught me looking. He was unfazed. Clearly, he had nothing to be ashamed of. It was then that I fully realized that Tucker was holding me up, displaying me for the entire world to see, and I was naked. I felt the heat rush up to my cheeks.

I was mortified. I hadn't even shaved my legs.

I stomped my heel on the top of Tucker's foot causing him to howl in pain as he dropped his hold on me. Mortified, I ran through the forest, eager to be away from the wolf pack.

CHAPTER 13
THE INVESTIGATION BEGINS

Millie Bradford seemed like a really sweet girl. The truth of it was just as I had informed Grandmother; I didn't really know anything about her. She had a friendly disposition and she worked at The Hollows Public Library. She was obviously eager to help and quite knowledgeable—both of which suited her very well in her work. Beyond that, nada, zilch; I knew nothing.

I had decided to go with Beckett to pick Millie up because I didn't want her to have to suffer through his arrogance alone on the trip from The Hollows to Wellington House. He was more likely to behave if someone else went along. I already knew that he didn't like outsiders impinging on what he perceived as *his* domain. I'm not really certain that Harrison Beckett liked *anyone* other than Grandmother. He could be quite gruff if he wanted to be. He would see Millie as someone that he could intimidate; she would need someone to keep him in check. I could only hope that I was up to the task.

I could tell by the look that he gave me when he opened the door of the Bentley that he was in a particularly bad mood. I knew that the *only* reason he was performing this small task instead of forcing me to open the door myself, was that Grandmother was standing on the front steps of Wellington House, watching him like a hawk. Obviously the two of them had already had words about picking Millie up. It was quite clear where Harrison Beckett stood on *that* subject.

Having inherited my dad's mischievous streak, I couldn't let him off the hook easily. I watched his face reflected in the rear-view mirror. Finally, I said, "Isn't it nice that Grandmother consented to allow me to have a friend over? I mean, I really was expecting her to refuse my request, especially after my conversation with Aunt Abigail. She seemed fairly certain that Grandmother would be displeased."

He shot me a quick glance in the mirror; taking the bait like a hungry fish. I could already see the reddening appear at the back of his neck. His ears were almost beacons. "Mrs. Wellington only agreed out of pity. On account of the fact that you and your brother are newly orphaned."

I was taken back by the cruel way that he spoke the words. Harrison Beckett was just mean! Seeing that his words had stung, he continued to press his advantage. "Fact of the matter is, she doesn't much like kids. Guess your aunt and your momma kind of ruined things for her." He shrugged, "Who can blame her, right? They were both highly disrespectful and ungrateful when they were growing up. Mrs. Wellington certainly deserved better." He sighed heavily. "Now she is saddled with the two of you; an ill-mannered teen and a snot-nosed brat."

I crossed my arms over my chest and turned tear filled eyes to the window. "I'd appreciate it if you'd just stop talking and drive."

He chuckled. "Whatever you say, Mistress Katherine. Whatever you say."

It was readily apparent that the relationship between Aunt Abigail, Grandmother and my mom was strained to say the least. Since coming to The Hollows I had learned enough to know that my parents had left their home to start their lives anew. Had they not been killed in a senseless car accident I seriously doubted that Bobby and I would ever have even seen this place. Mom and Dad had never mentioned the lives that they had left behind. I wouldn't have even known that The Hollows existed if it hadn't been for Aunt Abby sending me the talisman for my thirteenth birthday to keep my inner wolf hidden from the world. Aunt Abby would have sent Bobby a talisman similar to my own when he reached the age of thirteen. But I'm fairly confident that would've been our only contact with The Hollows.

I wonder when my parents would have told me about the wolf? They would have had to tell me rather soon, I think. I knew now that was the reason that Bobbybear and I were home schooled. They had been afraid that I would have removed the talisman during Gym class and simply forget to put it back on. *Why hadn't they told me?* I shook my head in silence as I watched the trees along the side of the road speed by. How would they have told me? I couldn't help but wonder. I chuckled to myself; they would've had to be pretty convincing! Telling your daughter that she was a Lycanthrope and expecting her to buy into the whole concept would be a tough sell. At least to me it would have been.

I have to give Aunt Abby credit for the way she broke it to me. There was no way that I could refute the evidence she provided. It *wasn't* trick photography—I had experienced the transformation! I can remember how the reshaping of my bones felt! I had never been in so much pain in my entire life! If I could spare Bobbybear that agony, there is *nothing* I wouldn't do. That being said, I know I needed to patch things up between Aunt Abby and I. We hadn't parted on the best of terms.

I glanced at a fawn standing at the edge of the woods. I wondered where its parents were. It was dangerous for the young deer to be alone. I couldn't help but remember the deer I had seen when we first got to The Hollows. The wolves had been merciless. My thoughts turned to the wolf pack. I couldn't help but smile as I remembered the boys at the lake earlier. Obviously, they had spent time that morning in wolf form. They had probably even killed another deer and had gone to the secluded pond to cleanse the blood from their own bodies—I remember how I had been covered in blood after my first kill. I thought I had seen Cho washing blood away in the waterfall, but he had been too far away for me to be certain. And then there was Brock... Seeing him naked had made it difficult to concentrate on much of anything.

I could feel myself beginning to blush. I was starting to get aroused. I could feel the heat rising through me. I shook my head. I couldn't think about any of that now. We were pulling up to the library. I could see Millie locking the front door. Hearing the car pull up to the curb, she turned and smiled. She had a relieved look on her face. She waved excitedly.

Harrison Beckett had stopped the Bentley and hopped out rather quickly. He seemed intent on making a good impression. Admittedly, he was putting on a good show. He almost smiled as he took Millie's suitcase. "Allow me to place your luggage in the boot, Miss Bradford."

"What? Oh. Thank you." She looked at him with rather a confused expression and then blushed.

He held her suitcase in his left hand as he opened the passenger door with his right. Millie bent and peered shyly into the car. Seeing me she smiled again and offered another wave. "Hiya." she said as she slid into the backseat. As Harrison closed the door behind her she pushed her round glasses up the bridge of her nose. "To be perfectly honest, I wasn't all that certain you'd show."

I reached out and touched her arm. "Why wouldn't I? After all, I invited you."

She giggled. "I know." She nodded and looked away. "I'm kind of used to disappointment." Millie turned back to face me. "In fact, I've come to expect it from almost everybody—you know how cliques are. There are a few of us that are outcasts at school."

Truth of the matter was, I *didn't* know how cliques were. I'd never had to deal with them being home schooled. I'd seen them in a few movies, but I had thought that was just Hollywood drama. Like monster movies.

As Harrison Beckett moved behind the wheel I smiled at her. "Well you won't be disappointed by me, Millie. I told you, we're gonna be the best of friends."

She nodded and smiled meekly. "Yes. Yes you did say that."

Harrison Beckett turned and looked over his shoulder. "Anyplace else that you'd like to go?"

"Oh, no." Millie said quickly. "Home James!" She gasped sharply placing one hand over her mouth; she reached out the other and touched his shoulder. "I'm so sorry! I don't know what came over me!" She stared at me with wide eyes, "I've always dreamed of being in a chauffeur driven car and saying those *exact* words! I just couldn't help myself!"

I couldn't help but chuckle at her exuberance. I looked into the rear view mirror and watched Beckett's face. He seemed absolutely livid. "You heard the lady, *home James!*"

Millie stomped her feet repeatedly upon the floorboard as she pounded the seat with tightened fists. "Oh, I am *so* gonna remember this experience forever!"

"Oh!" I said as a thought struck me. "Actually, I do need to pick up a few items from the grocery store. If you'd be so kind to stop there on our way, I promise I won't be but a minute or two."

Harrison nodded graciously. He obviously didn't want to appear rude in front of Millie. "As you wish, Mistress Katherine. Just tell the clerk to put your items on the tab of Wellington House. They will happily accommodate you."

I looked over at Millie with a wink and a smile. "That's good to know!"

Millie pointed. "The grocery store is just across the street. It's not what you're probably used to, being from the city, but it is the best that The Hollows has to offer."

I grabbed Millie's hand and we slid out of the Bentley. "We can just walk over."

Harrison started to object but we forged ahead. I needed to speak to Millie without anyone around. This afforded me that opportunity. Just inside the store I squeezed Millie's arm tightly. "We must be careful what we say in front of him. He's Grandmother's little spy. Whatever he hears, he reports straight back to her."

Her smile widened. "Wow! Talk about intrigue! I already feel like I'm living a dream! Now I'm involved in espionage!" she giggled.

I raised my brows as I bit my bottom lip. "You don't know the half of it!" I said with a slight smirk. Since moving to The Hollows I'd felt as if I were in a horror movie. Discovering that I was a werewolf just like my parents had been a startling revelation. I glanced around the grocery store and saw placards with numbers running from 1 to 8, listing the major merchandise located on that particular aisle. "Where would I find the Calgon Bubble Bath?"

She seemed surprised. Glancing up, she pointed, "Aisle six."

I started moving in that direction. "I used up all that I had and I really didn't want to steal my brother's Mr. Bubble."

Millie pushed her glasses up her nose. "Hey! I like Mr. Bubble!" She sounded mildly aggrieved.

I smiled. "Bobbybear does too!"

I didn't see my favorite bubble bath on the shelf so I grabbed the one they had. I walked a little further down the aisle and grabbed a Mr Bubble for Bobbybear - I didn't want him running out—he wouldn't hesitate reaching for mine and I knew he loved lots of bubbles! At the checkout counter I grabbed a peanut butter cup for Bobbybear. "I promised my brother I'd bring him back a treat. This is his favorite!"

Harrison Beckett had the Bentley pulled up in front of the grocery store. To my surprise, he jumped out from behind the wheel and opened the back door for us. As Millie slid in, he took the paper bag out of my hand and *actually* smiled. "I'll place this in the boot for you, Mistress Katherine."

I *know* my jaw must have hit the ground! I think I even heard it.

I slid in beside Millie and Harrison softly closed the door. He walked around to the rear of the car, popped the trunk, stowed the bag and then clicked the compartment closed. As he slid in behind the steering wheel, he turned to the rear view mirror and smiled. "Will there be anyplace else, ladies?"

I shook my head slowly, still astounded. Millie smiled brightly, "Home Ja--!" and quickly placed a hand over her mouth. She turned a bright red.

I tried to hold it in but couldn't. I burst into laughter, and Millie soon followed. Both of us were in tears before we were able to control ourselves.

"Very well," Harrison said stoically. He pulled the Bentley away from the curb and headed down the empty street, back in the direction of Wellington House.

After a minute of silence, just enough time for us to catch our breath, Millie smiled at me. "So, when will you be starting school? It'll be nice to have a friend to hang out with—if you want, I mean. I could like show you around."

I smiled back, giving her arm a gentle squeeze. "Unfortunately Bobbybear and I won't be starting until next year. We already completed the requirements for this year. Mom was pretty adamant about staying ahead of the public schools. She figured it would give us more time together as a family. Vacationing, and all."

"Ah, that's cool!" Millie said sounding slightly dejected.

"But hey!" I said, brightening, "Next year isn't that far off is it? We can hang out at school then! Maybe we'll have classes together."

She smiled. "The Hollows isn't very big. We'll have *all* our classes together."

I blinked at that bit of information. I shouldn't have been so surprised, I guess. The Hollows wasn't the city I was used to after all. "See? Things are looking up already!"

Millie chuckled. "Yeah, now all I have to do is make it through the next two and a half months, and then another three! Yay me!" she held her hands in the air, fingers spread, giving them a royal wave.

I quickly hugged her to me. "Don't fret, Millie. We're best friends now. You aren't going to lose me!"

She chuckled with a sniffle. "I'm gonna hold you to that!"

As we pulled up in front of Wellington House Millie sighed in awe. "It's so beautiful! I can't believe you actually live here!"

I couldn't help but shake my head and smile. To me, Wellington House was anything but beautiful. It looked dark and foreboding, and I was fairly certain that it was haunted by at least one ghost. And I desperately needed to know if Bobbybear was in any danger. Sara Robinson's voice echoed from the back of my mind; staking her claim...

"He's mine!"

An unexpected chill raced down my spine. I could see the upstairs window of the storage room that held the portrait of young Sara Robinson. It looked as though she were standing at the window, watching our arrival.

I reached out and touched Millie's arm as she climbed from the Bentley. I pointed to the figure standing at the window. "There!" I whispered sharply. "Do you see her?" I saw the look in Harrison Beckett's eyes as he looked from the window and met my gaze. *He had seen her too!* Though I seriously doubted that he'd ever admit it.

"Was that someone standing at the window, or just a shadow?"

Millie asked. "I couldn't really tell. I didn't get a very good look." She turned toward me, "Was that maybe your brother?"

Harrison Beckett slammed the door of the Bentley forcefully. "It was just a reflection on the glass, probably that of a tree."

I couldn't believe it. My jaw dropped open and I stared at him feeling flabbergasted. He refused to meet my glaring gaze and I was left standing speechless. I followed Harrison to the trunk of the Bentley as he prepared to retrieve Millie's suitcase and my grocery bag. "I *know* what I saw!" I grabbed his arm briefly before he tore it away. "I know you saw it too! That wasn't Bobby and it *wasn't* a reflection of a stupid tree!"

He shoved the grocery bag into my arms and Millie's suitcase—I very nearly dropped them both. He slammed the trunk closed. "I didn't see anything Miss Katherine. You're letting your mind run wild, I'm afraid." He stepped around me, bumping into Millie, almost knocking her over as he climbed hastily into the Bentley. He sped off leaving us in a cloud of dust.

Millie gave me an embarrassed look. "Is he always like that?" she asked as she took her suitcase from me.

I nodded. "Only when he isn't in the presence of my grandmother." I hugged the grocery bag against my chest with my left arm. I looped my free arm through hers. "Let's get you inside."

Margaret pulled open the front door and smiled shyly. "I'm afraid that Mrs. Wellington isn't free to greet you and your friend properly, Mistress Katherine. Both My Lady and Master Robert are out at the moment."

"Are they in the garden still?" I asked surprised.

"Uh, no Mistress." Margaret seemed anxious.

"Where could they have gone?" I pressed. They certainly hadn't driven anywhere; we had the only car.

Margaret blushed a deep red. She took Millie's suitcase, keeping her eyes averted. "She didn't say. She left instructions for me to have your friend's room prepared. Come, I'll take you up." She started for the stairs.

Millie grasped my arm and gave it an excited squeeze. She looked about with her eyes wide and child-like. "This place is *so* amazing! Better than I'd imagined!"

Surprisingly Grandmother had placed Millie in the spare room next to mine. I had half expected to discover that she'd be given a room far removed from my own; possibly on another floor entirely. After all, Bobby and I couldn't be further apart. Perhaps Grandmother had thought it best to keep Millie and I close, not affording Millie the opportunity to wander about Wellington House on her own. Whatever her reasoning might be, I was glad to have Millie staying so close.

Margaret opened the door and placed Millie's suitcase at the foot of the bed. "If you should require anything," she said as she turned to go, "you know how to get hold of me."

Millie plopped down upon the thick mattress and grinned from ear to ear. "Man I could so get used to this!" She pushed her glasses up her nose. "You are so lucky to live in this place!"

Her eyes grew wide in sudden embarrassment. She placed a hand to her lips and lightly shook her head. "Oh, I'm so sorry Kat! I didn't mean to infer that you're lucky that your parents have died and all..." she shrugged, "...but you have to admit, this beats the Hell out of an orphanage!"

I narrowed my eyes at her. "Millie, I never told you that my parents were dead."

Her eyes widened. "Oh." She squinted. "Are you sure?"

"Positive."

She batted a hand in the air. "Oh well, The Hollows isn't that big a place. Word spreads around here like wildfire! I must've heard it at school." She thought for a second and then snapped her fingers. "That's it! I remember some guys talking about you. At least I'm pretty sure it was you they were talking about— you had gotten lost in the woods—they had to walk you home." She pushed her glasses back up her nose. "Did you get lost wandering around in the woods?"

I blushed. "No!"

Millie crossed her arms over her chest. "Uh huh. That's what I thought."

She hoped off the bed. "Look at me, I live with my Grammy and even that's better than a stuffy old orphan house!" She grinned at me. "But you may seriously have hit the jackpot with this one! And you live in a haunted house! How cool is that?"

"You may have a point—but if this place is haunted, then the ghost may be threatening to steal my little brother away from me—and that isn't cool!" I swallowed. "Can you help me?"

Millie pushed her glasses up. "Lucky for you, you met the

right person at the library the other day. I think that I just might be able to help you with your little problem."

"How?" I asked.

"Well, first off," she said, counting off with a raised finger, "we need to do a little investigating. I need to have a better idea what we're dealing with. And second," she raised another finger, "I'll need to do some further research. Next weekend—if you were to invite me over—I'll come prepared to resolve this whole matter." She smiled at me, giving me a slightly nervous look. "So... are you gonna invite me back?"

I nodded vigorously. "Yes. Yes of course! Anytime. We're best friends now. *Mi casa es tu casa.*"

"Great!" Millie said pushing her glasses back into place. "We should get started then." She seemed to be bubbling with excitement.

We walked down the long hallway in relative silence. Each of us was lost in our own thoughts. While I was thinking about the ghost of Sara Robinson, Millie was marveling at the architecture of Wellington House, or perhaps the antique tables and lamps—that never seemed to be lit—that lined the hall. Old paintings and portraits of those long gone hung broodingly upon the walls; their eyes seemed to follow us. Whichever it was that had captured Millie's attentions it had put a child-like joy on her face and brightened her green eyes. An occasional *"Wow!"* escaped her lips. She'd reach out a hand but her fingers never quite touching, it was almost like she was afraid to disturb anything.

"Your Grandmother should really have these paintings lit with accent lighting! This place is like a museum."

We had stopped in front of an eighteenth-century portrait of a handsome young man with jet black hair, deep blue eyes, long sideburns with a cleft in his chin. Even in the dim light I could see color rise to Millie's cheeks. "Wow! He's absolutely gorgeous! Is he a relation of yours?"

I could only shrug. I truly didn't have a clue. He, like all the others, was a stranger to me. Before my parent's death I had never seen any of my family members. Mom and Dad had carried no photos with them when they left The Hollows. I didn't even know if I had any living relatives on my father's side of the family. Millie had mentioned a hermit by the name of St. Claire when I met her at the Library. *Could Samuel St. Claire be related to Bobby and I?* It was definitely something that I wanted to look into.

After learning all I could about Sara...

We stood at the base of the stairwell leading up to the storage room. I could feel the tiny hairs on my arms starting to rise. I didn't know whether it was from my anticipation or from fear. My mouth was suddenly very dry and I found swallowing difficult. My breathing was sounding a bit ragged, even to me. I felt chilled to the bone. My feet seemed frozen in place, unwilling—or *unable*—to take the next step.

Millie glanced up the stairs and then at me. "Is this the place?"

My lips parted but I couldn't speak. I reached out and grasped the banister to steady myself, feeling suddenly lightheaded and queasy. This was ridiculous! There was really no rationale for the way I was feeling. I hadn't been affected like this before when I was alone, *why now?*

Millie took my arm. "Are you alright Kat?" She had a panicked look of concern etched on her face.

I nodded. Millie's hand on my arm felt warm and comforting. Finally, I was able to swallow back the fear that had taken hold of me a few moments ago. "Yeah. I'm fine." Her subtle reassurances made me feel braver. It helped knowing that I wasn't in this bizarre nightmare alone. Grateful, I smiled at her.

We started climbing the narrow stairs, our bodies close together. Neither of us seemed to mind the contact. I found that the warmth of her body helped to encourage me to continue. Even though Millie had no idea what we might find, I could tell that she was nervous as well. She reached out and took my hand and squeezed it.

Finally, we stood outside the door.

My heart was rapidly hammering inside my chest; I was certain that Millie could hear it. If she glanced over at me, I was positive she would see it pounding against my breast. Looking down at the floor I could see no light coming from under the door. *Was that a good sign or a bad one?* I could no longer be sure of anything.

Millie took a slow, measured breath and then nodded toward the door. Obviously she was waiting for me to open it. I guess it was only fair, had this been her home, I would insist that she made the next move.

I let go of her hand and clenched two fists at my sides. Taking a deep breath, I bounced on the balls of my feet and exhaling a quick breath, I reached for the doorknob. I decided that the best course of action was aggression. I closed my eyes, turned the knob, and pushed.

The door was locked.

I slammed into the door striking it face first. It's a wonder I didn't break my nose. I could hear Millie's nervous chuckle behind me. I turned and glared at her in exasperation. "It's locked!" I said, touching my nose gingerly. It seemed to be okay. Nothing was broken. Maybe aggression hadn't been such a good idea after all.

Millie gave me a *what now* look with a little shrug and I almost growled, stirring the beast within. Millie took an involuntary step backward, almost losing her balance and toppling down the steps. With lightning fast reflexes, I reached out and grabbed her arm, holding her steady. I could see the tiny beads of perspiration breaking out on her forehead. She had sucked in a huge gasp of air and now exhaled it all at once. She blinked, pushing her glasses up her nose. "That was a close one!"

"You're telling me!" I said breathlessly.

"Do you have the key?" Millie said with a frown.

I shook my head. "My grandmother has *all* the keys."

Millie sighed. "I was really hoping to get a good look at the portrait. I did a bit of research after you and your aunt left the library yesterday, but I couldn't find any better pictures of Sara Robinson other than the one in the article we found."

"Maybe I can give you an accurate enough description." I offered.

Turning from the door, she sighed. "I guess that will have to do, for now. But next weekend I'm definitely going to need to get a look at the painting."

We hadn't taken two steps when the door opened with a hauntingly loud screech. Millie's eyes grew wide as she turned her gaze from the door to me. We both simultaneously swallowed the lumps of fear that had lodged in our throats threatening to cut off our breathing completely. Millie reached out and squeezed my arm, her fingernails digging into my flesh rather painfully. I could see goosebumps on her arms. "Are you *sure* it was locked?"

I nodded.

A rush of cold air greeted us; our breath hung in the air before us. "This isn't normal," Millie said.

"Really?" I couldn't keep the sarcasm from my voice. *"You think?"*

Millie tugged at the hem of her blouse with a shaky hand and stepped forward with more bravado than I think she truly felt. "Let's do this!"

We stood in front of the portrait of Sara Robinson without saying a word. The pose was the same as I had remembered, but the smile that the young girl wore on her face seemed *different* somehow. Her expression seemed smugger. It was almost as though she knew a secret that she was unwilling to share. *Was it possible for the painting to actually change?* The portrait I remembered was of a sweet little girl holding a favored toy. Presently there was *no* Victorian era soldier in the girl's hand.

I could feel the icy tingles racing through my body. "That's her. But this painting is somehow different than when I first saw it. It almost looks like a completely different portrait."

"Creepy," Millie said.

I nodded. "You're telling me."

"Could this be a different painting? Is it possible that there are more than one, and somebody switched them just to prank you?" Millie asked.

I shrugged. "I suppose so. But why would they do that? Are they trying to drive me nuts? For what reason?"

Millie stared at me intently as she pushed her glasses back up her nose. "I don't know. It's all part of the mystery that we have to solve, I guess."

"Great." I frowned.

Millie studied the portrait a little longer. She seemed to be inspecting it carefully. She even reached out and tilted the frame forward. Finally, she stepped back and sighed. After a few minutes Millie nodded. "Okay. All right. I think that I've seen enough. I think we can go with what we have, for now."

I couldn't help but shiver uncontrollably. "Good! Let's get out of here. This room gives me the willies!"

Millie hesitated. Pushing her glasses up her nose she glanced slowly around the room. Her gaze seemed to linger upon the thick shadows at the far end of the storage space.

I touched her arm. "Millie?"

She practically jumped out of her skin.

"What is it?" I asked.

Millie shook her head, "I'm not sure."

CHAPTER 14
QUESTIONS UNANSWERED

Grandmother looked from Millie to me. "So, what have you girls been up to this afternoon?" Her brows were raised inquisitively.

I tapped Millie's leg with my foot under the table. I didn't want my grandmother to suspect what we'd been up to. She most certainly, would not approve. I shrugged. "Girl talk, mostly."

Millie shot me a look that clearly said that I had kicked her too hard. She smiled sweetly at Grandmother as she pushed her round glasses up her nose. "You know how girls are."

I quickly looked at Bobby who was sitting at the other end of the table across from Grandmother. "How about you Bobbybear? Surely you didn't toil away in the garden all day. What else did you do?"

He toyed with his peas, disinterested. "I played in the woods with a friend."

"Oh? Who?" I asked.

Grandmother laughed with a roll of her eyes. "What? Robert isn't allowed to have friends his own age? That *hardly* seems fair."

"No!" I quickly shook my head. "No, of course he is! I was just wondering who it was, that's all."

Bobby shrugged. "Just a friend. Grandmother introduced us."

"And did you have a good time Robert?" Grandmother asked as though she already knew the answer.

He nodded as he pushed a pea with his fork. "Uh huh." He drank the last of his milk. "May I be excused? I'm awfully tired."

Grandmother wiped her lips with her napkin. "Of course you may Robert. Say 'goodnight' to our guest and your sister."

Bobbybear slid out of his chair. He beamed at Millie. "It was a pleasure to meet you." He bowed slightly. He turned from her, walked behind Grandmother and stood beside me. "Goodnight, Kat." He stood on the tips of his toes and kissed my cheek.

"Pleasant dreams Bobbybear."

He took a step toward the end of the table. "Goodnight Grandmother. I really did have fun today with Sara."

I felt a shock jolt me. I quickly glanced at Millie, tapping her again with my toe. She jerked slightly at the unexpected contact and stared at me with a perplexed look on her face.

Grandmother placed both her hands on Bobby's temples and kissed him on the top of his head. "Goodnight Robert. Perhaps you can play with your new friend again tomorrow."

He nodded with a yawn. "I think I'd like that."

She patted his bottom. "Run along Robert."

I placed my fork down slowly. I took my time dabbing at the corner of my mouth before I smiled up at my grandmother. "So, who is this *Sara* that Bobby was playing with?"

Grandmother's eyes narrowed as she looked at me. She took a slow sip of her wine and shrugged. "She's the granddaughter of a friend of mine." She glanced at Millie, "Surely you know Henry Tompkins?" She glanced back at me, not waiting for a response. "Anyway, he lives nearby. I believe she's visiting with her parents. Poor girl hasn't anyone around her own age, except for Robert. I thought it would be nice if they met."

She took another sip of her wine. "Why do you ask?"

I took a sip of water and shook my head. "Just curious, that's all."

Grandmother laughed. "For a moment, dear, I was under the impression that you objected to Bobby's new playmate." She eyed me over the rim of her wine glass.

"Not at all. Why would I?"

Grandmother shrugged with one shoulder, a sly smile turning the corner of her mouth. "Yes. Why would you?" She stared at me with one eyebrow raised. "The little girl and Robert seemed to get along well together. It was pleasant seeing him have so much fun, especially after the events of the last several weeks. He is so young to have been subjected to so much trauma. You both are. If I can do anything to make your lives easier, well then, that is my goal. To that end, I shall leave you girls to entertain yourselves."

Finally, I couldn't take any more. I scooped the last of the peas off my plate and practically swallowed them whole. I glanced across at Millie. "Let's head upstairs. I'd like to hear all about school in The Hollows."

Millie nodded as she placed her napkin beside her plate. "Sure." She gave Grandmother a dazzling smile. "That was a delicious meal. I can't believe I ate so much! And it truly was a pleasure meeting you Mrs. Wellington."

Grandmother smiled warmly, her eyes seemed to sparkle. "It's been my pleasure Mildred... uh, Millie. Will you be staying for the whole weekend?"

"Unfortunately that won't be possible this weekend. Grammy needs my help on Sunday. Perhaps another time, though."

I saw Grandmother flinch when Millie mentioned her Grammy. I had to smile.

"Well," Grandmother said pleasantly, "I hope that you enjoy your visit with us."

"I'm certain that I will. Thank you."

I leaned in and kissed my grandmother on the cheek. "Goodnight Grandmother."

She hadn't expected the kiss and seemed a bit taken aback. I was pleased that I had managed to at least startle her somewhat. I gave her a sweet smile, knowing that my eyes were twinkling brightly—I could almost *feel* them sparkle!

She blinked, not quite knowing how she should respond. She glanced at Millie and then turned back towards me, puckered her lips, and kissed my cheek. "Goodnight Katherine. I hope you girls enjoy your evening. Try not to stay up too late."

Still smiling, I kinda hopped toward the door and grasped Millie by the elbow. "We won't." I steered Millie out of the dining room as quickly as I could. She turned to me as though she was going to say something, but I hurriedly placed a finger to my lips. Grandmother had ears like a hawk; I didn't want her to hear anything that might arouse her suspicions.

As we climbed the stairs Millie smiled. "Your grandmother seems like a really nice lady."

I chuckled softly. "Don't be fooled by her pleasant demeanor. Elizabeth Wellington is as shrewd as they come. She's a viper waiting to strike!" I shook my head. "I've never known a more cagey person!"

At the top of the second floor landing we turned toward our rooms. Pausing outside Millie's door, I said, "Did you happen to catch the name of Bobby's new friend? He mentioned her name before he went upstairs."

Millie squinted as she nodded. "Wasn't it Sara?" Her eyes grew wide as it hit her. She pushed her glasses up her nose. "You don't think that his Sara is our Sara, do you?" She shivered. "That would be really freaky."

"But what if she is?" I said.

She opened her door and stepped inside. I could see her lightly shake her head as I followed her into the room. "That doesn't make any sense." She turned to face me. "That would mean that your grandmother also knows about the ghost. What possible reason would that sweet lady have for allowing her grandson to play with a ghost?" She shrugged. "I can't think of anything. Can you?"

It did sound kinda absurd even to me. But it had crossed my mind. "Not really." I couldn't help but sound defeated. "So now what?"

She ran a hand through her hair and blew out the air in her lungs. "We need to try and talk to Sara ourselves. That may be the only way that we can find out what's really going on here."

I sat down on the edge of her bed. "How do you propose we do that?"

Millie plopped on the foot of the bed, and then fell backwards. I laid down too, our heads almost touching. "Well," she said, "there are a couple of ways we can do that."

I kept silent, hoping she would elaborate further. When she remained quiet, I forced her hand. "I'm listening..."

She sighed, rolling over onto her side so that she could face me. "The two options that I know of, are a *séance* or we could use a *Spirit Board*." She paused, allowing that bit of information to sink in. "For a séance we would really need a couple more people. Grammy says that they are best with four or five."

"Wow," I said. "Your Grams is into all this supernatural mysticism?"

Millie smiled, pushing her glasses up her nose. "Are you kidding me? Grammy taught me *everything* I know about this kind of stuff! She's got Gypsy blood running through her veins. I think her mom was a Fortune-teller in a carnival or something." She sighed. "To think I could be like that, travel the country— maybe even the world. How cool would that be?" She had the faraway look in her eyes, the look of a dreamer.

She shook her head and exhaled as though coming out of a trance. "So, where were we? Oh, yeah, the ghost. Sara Robinson. I think our best bet is to use a *Spirit Board* to contact Sara. We wouldn't need anyone else but the two of us. Perhaps we can get her to tell us what is going on here. I just don't buy the possibility that your grandmother would ever allow Bobby to knowingly play with a ghost. Not her. She's too nice." She squinted, "I mean who does that?"

I shrugged. To be perfectly honest I didn't know too many people that had any actual contact with ghosts. This was all really new ground for me. "You got me."

I couldn't stop the tears from welling up in my eyes. I suddenly felt cold. I was starting to feel a bit overwhelmed. Was this really something my grandmother would do - allow Bobby to play with a ghost? Was that even possible? What could she hope to gain from it if she did? I couldn't be sure of anything anymore. All of this was just crazy! My entire life—my whole world—had been knocked off kilter with the death of my parents.

Two months ago I hadn't really believed in the supernatural. To be honest, I had never given it much thought. I had read horror stories, watched movies and the like, but I hadn't truly believed in any of it. It was all just for entertainment; a means of scaring someone, provoke some response. But something changed when Bobbybear and I had seen the two wolves outside the hospital when Mom died. They had seemed to be shrouded in a ghostly aura. Even then I had the bizarre feeling that they were trying to communicate with me. *Had they been?* I had seen them again when I had first run through the woods in wolf form. *Was it possible that those ghostly wolves were actually my parents? Were they trying to watch over Bobbybear and I? Was this truly happening, or had I lost all touch with reality due to my own grief? Was I just crazy? Crazy Katherine? Crazy Abigail and her crazy niece Katherine.*

I honestly no longer knew.

I had been so completely lost in my own thoughts that I hadn't heard anything that Millie had been saying. When she touched my arm I blinked twice, startled out of my daydream. I had been clutching my talisman with my thumb and two fingers, absently rubbing the stainless-steel metal.

"Hullo...?" Millie said with a wry smile. "Where *were* you? You completely zoned out. I thought I'd lost you for a minute there." She chuckled. I could detect a hint of nervousness in her laughter.

I smiled meekly. "Sorry 'bout that."

She pushed her glasses up her nose. "It's okay. You just had me a little concerned, is all." Millie touched my arm. "You don't have a medical condition that I should know about, like diabetes, or anything?"

I took a deep breath and blew it out slowly. I ran a hand through my hair and walked over to the window. I parted the curtains and peered out at the ground below. It was already quite dark outside. I could just see the path leading to Aunt Abigail's cottage. "Okay." I said, more to myself. I turned and studied Millie for a second. "I hope I don't regret this, but there's something that I have to show you."

CHAPTER 15
REVELATIONS

I squeezed Millie's hand as we tiptoed downstairs. We had waited almost an hour and a half, hoping that we could slip out of the house without anyone catching us. I was fairly certain of our chances for success. Grandmother was a creature of habit. After dinner she would retire to the drawing room and enjoy a glass or two of sherry. Then she was usually off to bed, with Margaret in attendance to assist her. After seeing the Lady of the House tucked securely in bed, Margaret would return to the kitchen and finish her chores. Afterwards she too, would retire for the evening. I didn't have any clue what Harrison Beckett did with his time. We had heard the faint, distant tapping of Grandmother's cane upon the flagstones of the hallway leading to her room; signaling it was safe for us to make our move. We just had to hope that we didn't encounter anyone.

As I opened the front door of Wellington House a rush of cool night air assailed us. I was thankful that Millie had insisted on grabbing jackets. She leaned close to my ear. "Where are we going? You still haven't said what it is you're wanting to show me."

I answered by placing a finger to my lips. I again squeezed her hand as we slipped outside. I turned and closed the door as quietly as I could. Then taking her hand once again, I led her quickly around the corner of the house to the cottage path. I glanced over at Millie and wondered briefly if I was doing the right thing. What choice did I have? If Millie was truly going to be my friend then I felt she deserved the truth. I wanted there to be no secrets between us. None at all.

As we walked through the woods I could see our breath shining silver like billowing clouds in the moonlight. I glanced to the sky and could see the full moon through the tall trees. I felt it's magnetic pull with every fiber of my being. And the wolf felt it too. The wolf was demanding to be set free, to run, and to feed... How easy it would be to yank the talisman from around my neck and give into the beast. So *very* easy!

But at what cost? Would I harm my friend? I didn't want to, but could I control the wolf and keep Millie safe? I wasn't certain that I could. I was still only learning what it meant to be the wolf. I didn't think that while I was the beast the human part of me could restrain the animal instincts of my alter ego. Lately the wolf had been getting stronger when it came to establishing control; I wasn't certain that I could rein her in if I needed to.

I thought that by sharing who or what I was with Millie, she might possibly be able to help me deal with the inner turmoil that I constantly felt. It seemed to always threaten to tear me apart. I was never sure that I was strong enough on my own to deal with the raging power of the wolf that longed to be free. Perhaps she could somehow manage to help me hang onto my humanity before I completely lost it to the wolf.

But was I doing the right thing? I *still* didn't know...

Somewhere off in the distance the mournful lament of a lone wolf beckoned to the silver sphere that hung in the night sky. When the wolf's cry faded another began. I could tell that neither wolf was far off. I groaned as the beast within me struggled against my will to keep her suppressed. A part of me wanted to rip the talisman off and cast it into the night; but I couldn't give into my urges and set her free - Millie might never survive. Experience had taught me that the harder I fought to keep the wolf subdued, the wilder she seemed to be when finally released.

"What was that?" Millie sounded panicked.

I stopped and faced her. *God, the pull of the wolf was strong!* "It isn't safe out here. We have to get inside!"

Millie nodded, her mouth dropping open - the fear clearly evident in her wide eyes. "Okay," she managed somehow. She swallowed. "Kat, you're scaring me."

I chuckled. "You have no idea the amount of danger you're in!" I said.

"Me? What about you?"

I chuckled again as I grabbed her hand and pulled her along. Perhaps it was the moonlight shining on my skin that made it so difficult to ignore the pleas of the wolf, I really don't know. I felt that I *had* to get indoors as quickly as possible for the sake of my friend. The weighty pull of the silver moon was almost too heavy to bear...

We rounded the final bend in the path and the cottage was less than a hundred feet away. I was immediately filled with panic. My aunt's bungalow was completely dark! I wasn't even certain that she was home. If we couldn't get in, we were doomed. Millie would *never* survive the night and I'd be *totally* responsible.

I started running faster, practically dragging Millie along. I could feel her stumble and almost fall. I had to stop and help her regain her balance. *"You need to run!"* I heard myself yelling at her in a gravelly voice. I could feel the familiar burning itch of the blood in my veins. *This can't be happening!* I was wearing the talisman but it didn't seem to matter. I could feel the ache in my bones starting to grow stronger; the beginnings of metamorphosis.

As we stepped onto the porch, I threw myself at the door. I pounded my fists against the glass frantically. "Aunt Abby! Please answer the door!" Tears stung at my eyes. "Please!" I begged, adding the toe of a booted foot to my incessant knocking. "Aunt Abby *please* hurry!"

I could feel Millie bouncing nervously beside me. Her fear had brought out her own tears. I could hear them in her wavering voice as she grabbed my arm frantically. "I see a light!"

She was right. I saw the light shine through the window and onto the porch and the lawn beyond. I resumed my pounding upon the door. What could possibly be taking so long? "Aunt Abby please hurry!" I called out one last time. I noticed the hairs on the back of my hand seemed thicker... I could feel the transformation beginning to manifest. We were running out of time!

The door finally opened. Aunt Abby's eyes grew wide as she saw the wolf in my eyes. "Where's your amulet?"

"I have it on!" I practically growled.

She ushered us into the cottage and quickly shut the door. "Pull the curtains!" she snapped.

I couldn't seem to move, as a sharp pain forced me to bend over, but I saw that Millie had sprung into action. In a matter of seconds, the thick drapes were drawn and the moonlight was shut out. Aunt Abigail took my shoulders and stared at me. "Look at me, Kat. *Look at me!*"

I turned my eyes to meet her piercing gaze and saw her smile. She was evidently pleased by what she saw. I no longer felt the wolf asserting her dominance over my will. We had made it! I collapsed against her and sobbed uncontrollably. "I was *so* scared we weren't going to make it!"

"What in the world were you girls doing out there? Don't you know these woods aren't safe—especially at night? What were you thinking?" Aunt Abby's voice was trembling with anger. With fear.

I took a deep breath. "Aunt Abigail, this is Millie Bradford. She's my best friend. Millie, this is Abby."

Aunt Abigail glanced at Millie and then back at me. "I know who she is, but that doesn't answer any of my questions."

"Wow," Millie chuckled with a wide grin. "I can't believe that you actually know who I am."

Aunt Abby scowled at her. "Honestly? The Hollows really isn't that big."

Millie raised a finger in the air and nodded. "Good point."

Aunt Abigail turned back to me. "What's going on? What made you two come out on a night like this?" She glanced over at Millie and then at me. "Do you realize how much danger you put her in? Honey, what were you thinking?"

I was starting to get just a little ticked off. I didn't like the way she was talking down to me. Like this was all my fault. I didn't need her lecturing me. I wanted answers. I stuck out my chin. "First of all, I had no clue that anything like that was going to happen! I felt like I was losing it. I couldn't control it. The wolf was winning. I want to know why!"

Aunt Abby nodded. "Fair enough. I'll do my best to explain it to you." She glanced briefly at Millie. "But not now."

I shook my head defiantly. "No! I want to know now!"

She crossed her arms over her chest. "You seriously think that's a good idea?"

I reached out and took Millie's hand and pulled her against me. I smiled at her. "Aunt Abby," I paused. "She's my best friend. I brought her here to see *the tape*."

Aunt Abigail snorted in disbelief. "You've got to be kidding me! You want her to see the tape?"

I swallowed, nodding slowly. "If she's going to be my friend, I want her to know what that means."

"You trust her with this?"

I looked into Millie's eyes and smiled. I gave her hand a reassuring squeeze. "I do."

"You hardly know her." She snorted with a raised brow.

Millie looked from me to my aunt, and then back again. "Wait. What? What's this tape? What are you two talking about? What's going on?"

I crossed my arms over my chest. "Show her the tape, Aunt Abby."

Aunt Abigail shrugged as she stared at me. "Fine. I'll set up the VCR."

I didn't watch the tape as it played. I didn't need to—I had lived it. But I couldn't bring myself to look at Millie either. Maybe Aunt Abby had been right. But it was too late now. I could feel Millie flinch beside me as she sat glued to the T.V. unable to look away. She gasped sharply and covered her mouth in horror as she watched my transformation into a wolf. A monster.

Aunt Abigail switched off the tape and tossed the remote onto the coffee table after shutting down the television. She sat back against the couch, crossing her arms over her chest. The room grew eerily silent as we waited.

As the silence grew more agonizing, I had the feeling that I'd made a terrible mistake. I had misjudged Millie so completely.

But whom was I kidding? How would I react if our roles had been reversed?

"Wow!" Millie said simply. There was no emotion in her voice.

I felt my heart breaking.

"I can't believe," Millie said, "that my *bestie* is a *beastie*! How absolutely cool is that?"

I hadn't been looking at her. I was wallowing in my grief, letting tears run down my cheeks unheeded. I blinked and wiped my eyes with the backs of my hands. I looked at her in total disbelief. She was grinning from ear to ear.

I looked at Aunt Abby and frowned. "Why was the pull of the moon so hard on me tonight? It took *every ounce* of control I could muster to keep from transforming - heck, I was transforming! It was almost like the talisman *wasn't* even working."

She arched her brows. "Maybe the more you become the wolf, the stronger she becomes. Maybe one day the talisman won't even work at all."

That thought frightened me. I ran a hand through my hair in frustration. I sighed heavily. "So, what do we do now?"

Aunt Abby shrugged. "I'm not certain. I guess I can re-enchant your amulet. The original enchantment is several years old, maybe the magic is starting to wear off." She looked at me helplessly. "Beyond that, I honestly don't know. We're in uncharted territory."

Great! Just what I wanted to hear!

CHAPTER 16

A GHOSTLY VISIT

Millie and I were nearly dead on our feet as we headed back to Wellington House. The sun was beginning to rise through the trees. Neither of us had slept during what had remained of the night. We had been up talking and giggling uncontrollably. How Aunt Abigail had managed to sleep was beyond me.

Aunt Abby had kept my talisman so that she could work on strengthening the enchantment that had kept me safe for the last couple of years. It felt strange not having the weighty medallion around my neck. I had only ever been without it when I had wanted to transform into the wolf. Now I felt *naked* - it was a little unnerving to say the least. I would be extremely happy once it was back where it belonged. Hopefully it wouldn't take long to restore the magical properties. It was imperative I have it before I felt the pull of the moon. The will of the wolf was getting stronger.

Until then, Millie and I had *lots* of work still left to do. Time was wasting away and we hadn't made any progress toward finding out the intentions of Sara Robinson's ghost. Until we knew what they were for a certainty, we absolutely had to go with my belief that Bobbybear's safety was in jeopardy. Once we discovered what her plans were, we still had to find a way to stop her - if we even could. I was determined not to lose Bobby to a supernatural entity - not as long as there was still air in my lungs, at any rate.

As we were sneaking up the stairs in the predawn light I noticed Millie's yawn. It had been a long, tension-filled night to be sure. We had talked about going into town and doing some further research at the library and just spending the day away from Wellington House. I was afraid that now she'd want to back out altogether. I sighed. I knew that I had pushed her hard last night. Was it really fair to ask more of her? I didn't think so; I decided to give her an out. "We don't have to go into town if you don't want to. We can just hang out here and relax if you'd rather. I know we're both tired."

It was true. I was completely exhausted! Having to fight off the wolf for control of my body had left me totally spent. I was running completely on fumes. It was taking all of my reserve energy just to continue climbing up the stairs. A few hours of sleep would do us both a world of good. Surely it couldn't hurt?

Millie bit at her bottom lip. "I've got an idea. Why don't we rest for a few hours before going into town? Once we get to the library, I can call my Grammy and have her bring my *Spirit Board* by. It won't be any trouble really; she meets some of her lady friends for gossip and tea near there anyway. Then we can come back here and try and contact Sara."

I smiled. "If you're certain you're up for it, I'm game. The sooner we find out what Sara's intentions are, the better I'll feel."

Millie grinned. "I agree. But we *really* do need to try and get some rest before we use the board. We need to have our wits about us when we do it. We don't want to leave ourselves open for a possible possession. Trust me, that would be *so* un-cool."

I quickly grabbed her arm. "Is that even *remotely* possible?"

She nodded, pushing her glasses up her nose. "Anything's possible; even likely. Not all spirits are friendly." She shivered. "Danny certainly wasn't." She wrapped her arms tightly around herself, closing her eyes at some unpleasant memory. She shivered again.

"Wow," I said, giving my head a shake. I hadn't even considered the fact that far more could be at stake. I simply figured that we'd sit down, do whatever we had to do to contact Sara; have our little chat, save Bobbybear, and then simply disconnect. I never once figured that we might be at risk of some supernatural malady. I wanted to learn more about this Danny but now probably wasn't the best time, I would ask Millie about him later.

As we stopped outside Millie's door, she reached out a hand and gave my arm a comforting squeeze. "A few hours rest should be enough. If Sara's presence is as strong as you've indicated, it should be easy enough to reach out to her." She nodded once. "I'm confident that we'll be successful."

I offered her a weak smile. I only wished that I shared her optimism. Millie must have detected my doubt. She quickly hugged me and then stepped back, seemingly embarrassed. She shoved her glasses up her nose and sighed as she blushed. "Sorry. You looked like you could use a hug."

I smiled at her and quickly hugged her back. "I did! Thanks."

I crawled onto my bed from the foot and literally plopped upon the quilted covering willing the sleep to wash over me. As soon as my head hit the pillow I sighed longingly; every fiber of my being eager for a refreshing nap. My eyelids felt heavy; I could feel the muscles in my neck and back beginning to relax. Though every inch of me wanted to sleep, my mind refused to let go; my brain was a jumbled mess. It was running the entire gamut between thoughts of Sara Robinson's ghost and Bobbybear's safety, to my own struggles with the wolf. I couldn't help but worry that *somehow* Aunt Abigail wouldn't get the talisman back to me before moonrise. If she didn't, then not only was Millie in danger, but so was everyone else in Wellington House.

Sleep was no longer an option. With so many thoughts to puzzle over there was no way that I could nap - no matter how badly I needed the rest. I ran my fingers through my hair and sighed in frustration. While Millie was no doubt enjoying a bit of a respite, I figured that I might as well take a quick shower. Maybe the hot water would help to soothe my body and my mind. My anxieties were causing my muscles to knot-up and tighten. I could feel the dull ache of an impending headache starting to throb in my temples.

I sighed as an aching pang stabbed at my heart at the sudden memory of my dad. I remembered how good his therapeutic massages always were, and I could definitely use one of them now. Followed by a piping hot, steaming cup of Mom's hot chocolate - no marshmallows! Bobbybear always chided me claiming the melting goo was the absolute best part! Mom loved them too, but Dad and I were cut from the same stone.

Bobbybear and I were a perfect pair. When our parents took us camping in the mountains - *now I knew why* - we'd roast marshmallows that we'd stabbed with sticks, over a crackling fire. I would eat the toasty part and Bobby would eat the heated goo.

I shuffled my feet across the floor into the bathroom lacking the energy to walk properly. I closed the door behind me, crossed to the tub and started the shower as hot as I could stand it. I undressed slowly, even more aware of my bodily aches and pains. The mirror above the sink was quickly fogging up from the rising steam. My reflection was blurred and nearly unrecognizable. I drew a smiley face on the glass with the tip of my finger, hoping it would help to brighten my mood.

It didn't.

What I really wanted was a nice hot bath where I could lay back and relax, letting Calgon *'take me away'* but there wasn't time.

My thoughts turned to Millie. Now I at least had an ally. Millie and I had bonded in a way like I had with no other. Already she was like a sister to me. She had the same desire as I did to keep Bobbybear safe. With her knowledge of the occult I was more confident about our chances of success. Besides, she now knew my darkest secret. And I knew that our bond was unbreakable.

The water pounding upon my skin in tiny forced droplets was almost too hot to bear. I turned away from the shower head and took a half step forward, allowing the pulsating stream to strike my neck and shoulders. Already I could feel the tension in my muscles beginning to relax. I was almost able to completely forget all of my troubles when I heard what sounded like the squeak of a finger upon mirrored glass. I opened my eyes, frozen in place, straining to hear.

"Who's there?" The sound of my voice was tense; even I could detect the rising panic surging through me. I turned to the knobs jutting out of the tiled wall and shut the shower off completely. Grabbing a towel and wrapping it around me I quickly stepped out of the shower. Though the room was shrouded in a thick fog of billowy steam, I could see that no one else was there with me. But I *did* feel a presence. I knew I was not completely alone. Stepping to the sink I could see writing in the mirror above the smiley face I had drawn earlier: *'He's mine!'* Simple. Succinct. To the point. Written by the hand of a child.

Over my shoulder I saw Sara Robinson's image in the mirror staring at me! I jumped back from the sink, nearly slipping upon the wet floor. I whirled around quickly, almost losing my towel. I could see her faintly through the mist. *"You can't save him! He belongs to me!"* She hissed; her words full of venom.

I took a step toward her. "No!" I yelled at her. "You can't have him!"

The bathroom door swung open and the foggy mist was drawn out. Millie stood in the doorway, her eyes wide with fright. Sara was gone. She had vanished. I felt dizzy. I reached out and grabbed the edge of the sink for support.

Millie raced to my side. "Are you alright? I didn't mean to just barge in on you, but I sensed you were in some kind of danger."

I nodded, giving her a wavering smile. "I... I'm okay. Sara, she was here. She said that I couldn't save him. That he belonged to her." I broke down, unable to hold back my tears. I was thankful that Millie held me close, supporting me.

I had just finished getting dressed when Millie returned to my bedroom. "I think we ought to go pick up my *Spirit Board* sooner rather than later. We need to get to the bottom of this. Sara seems to be getting more vocal and I think we need to figure out just exactly what is going on before someone gets hurt."

I tossed the dampened towel over the shower curtain rod. She was right. Sara seemed to be getting a little more direct with her threats. It left me feeling uneasy. The sooner we could put a stop to this nonsense, the better. We had no real idea what Sara was capable of; nor to what extremes she was willing to go.

Harrison Beckett pulled the Bentley to a stop in front of The Hollows Public Library. He twisted his body and flung an arm over the top of the front seat. "I shall be back to pick you up in about two hours. I have some errands to run for Mrs. Wellington, and that should allow you ample time to complete whatever it is that you are up to."

I glared at him with a raised brow. "We're *not* up to anything. I'm helping Millie with some of the research for her schoolwork. Two hours should be more than adequate."

He offered a smile that clearly said he hadn't believed a word that I'd said. "As you say, Mistress Katherine."

I nodded at Millie and she opened the door and slid out of the Bentley. I followed behind her, slamming the door closed as I stepped onto the sidewalk. Harrison Beckett gunned the engine and pulled the car from the curb and headed down the street.

As Millie stuck her key into the door of the library, she pushed her glasses back into place. "Do you think he knows?"

I shook my head and frowned. "How could he? I think he was just fishing for information. He was most likely trying to get a reaction from us so that he could report back to my grandmother."

She turned the key and pushed the door open. "I hope you're right." She flicked on the lights and held the door so that I could enter. The fluorescent bulbs flickered overhead and buzzed as they shed light throughout the library. There were two along the far wall that were barely glowing at all. Millie closed the door and headed toward the checkout counter where the phone was located. "I'll call Grams and have her bring the *Spirit Board.*"

I nodded as I walked down the aisle lined with hardcover books filling the shelves. My fingertips lightly skimmed across the bindings, almost like a romantic caress. I loved the feel of books, but even more than that, I loved the way they smelled! They had a thick, musty smell but it was far more than that, there was the ink, and the glue that bound them together. The books carried more than the author's imagination, there was a history there. Maybe the scent of perfume, or of a flower pressed between the pages. Some carried the hint of exposure to smoke, while others had suffered water damage. Books were keepers of history; their owners, and that of the books themselves. You didn't get that with electronic books. You did, however avoid paper cuts but I believed *that* was a small price to pay to be able to hold an actual book in my hands.

Millie cursed softly as she hung up the phone. "Gram must've already left for her afternoon tea; she's not answering the phone."

Before I could answer, the door to the library opened and two people stepped inside. I could immediately feel the color rising to my face. I hadn't expected to see Silas Monaghan and Brock Jacobins this afternoon. After yesterday's encounter in the woods I had hoped that I wouldn't see them for quite some time. Yet here they were - at least this time we all had our clothes on. For *that* I truly was thankful; I was pretty self-conscious about my body - not that I had a *bad* body, or anything; I just didn't possess the attributes that guys seemed to go for. My breasts were small; but guys seemed to like them larger. My body had a nice little hourglass shape without being overly curvaceous - I certainly wasn't voluptuous by any means. *I liked how I looked* - I just didn't think that most boys would give me a second glance.

Maybe that's why I felt so ill at ease around the guys; *I wanted Brock Jacobins to notice me!* He was *most definitely* worth a second look! Maybe even a third or a fourth, for that matter. Who was I kidding? When I had seen them all naked at the pond the other day, I couldn't take my eyes off him. He was absolutely gorgeous! Well-muscled, deeply tanned and certainly *not* shy.

I heard Brock chuckle. It jolted me out of my daydream. He was standing directly in front of me, an amused smile on his face. "Uhm... did you say something?" I said, feeling the color warm my cheeks.

He reached out toward a strand of hair that had fallen across my face. I took a step back. "Don't" I said, tucking the errant hair behind my ear. I hadn't meant to sound so abrasive.

He dropped his hand to his side and chuckled. "Take it easy, I wasn't meaning anything by it. I was only trying to get the hair out of your eyes."

I suddenly felt stupid. I was *such* a contradiction. A second ago I was thinking how I'd *like* for him to touch me, and now here I was recoiling when he actually tried. I just wanted to run away from him and hide. "The library's closed." I said lamely. I glanced over at Millie; she was smiling and chatting away with Silas. She appeared to be having a grand old time.

Brock smiled. "It's supposed to be. So, what are you doing here?"

I opened my mouth to make some lame excuse but I couldn't

come up with anything intelligent to say. I closed my mouth tightly. I had already made a complete fool of myself; I didn't need to compound that any further by adding something stupid to the conversation.

His eyes sparkled in the fluorescent lighting. "We saw you two come into the library and we figured we'd pop in to say hello." He glanced toward the counter and then back at me. He leaned forward slightly. "Silas has a crush on Millie."

"Oh?" I glanced toward the counter and smiled. It was obvious that she was smitten with Silas as well. "It appears to be a mutual admiration." I smiled.

Brock nodded. "So it would seem." He smiled at me. "Perhaps we should give them a bit of alone time."

"Uhm... Sure. I guess." That meant I was stuck here with him. My palms were clammy. "So," I said, absently touching the spine of a book, "how have you been?"

He grinned. "I've been doing good. The guys and I have been getting some good runs in lately."

I felt uneasy. I didn't know how to respond, or what to say. *I had seen these guys without a stitch of clothing on - and they had seen me!* They might be able to pretend that nothing had happened, but I wasn't so certain that I could.

Millie came to my rescue. "Sorry to interrupt, but Silas says that he and Brock can drive us over to my Gram's house so we can pick up *that item* we need for tonight. It would save us a ton of time!" She had a hopeful smile on her face as she pushed her glasses up her nose.

Brock smile widened. "Sure. No problem."

"Are you even old enough to drive?" I asked. I had him figured to be about my age; I was usually pretty good at that sort of thing.

He chuckled. "This is The Hollows we're talking about, not the big city. I started driving when I was about nine."

"The cops allow that?" I asked, sounding skeptical.

Silas chuckled. "Of course they do! As long as we obey the laws and don't cause any wrecks, they're pretty lenient." He slapped Brock's shoulder. "Brock here is a pretty safe driver, so there's no need to worry."

I glanced over at Millie and after a moment I had to smile. She was giving me a pleadingly hopeful look as she kept inclining her head toward Silas. It was plainly evident that she wanted to spend a little more time with him. How could I, as her friend, deny her this opportunity? "Well, we are a little pressed for time."

Brock beamed. "Great! The truck is right outside."

As we stepped outside, dark clouds were starting to roll in. The air was fresh with the promise of impending rain. Silas took the keys from Millie and locked the library door. He handed them back to her and then placed his hand in hers. He smiled at her warmly and she gushed like the schoolgirl that she was, a nice rosy glow appearing on her cheeks. I couldn't help but be happy for her.

I glanced over at Brock and was startled to see that he was staring at me. His deep blue eyes seemed bluer than they had been inside the library. Now they seemed to harbor an amused expression as he watched me and waited. I blinked, unable to keep his gaze. He made me uncomfortable but in a *good* way.

I glanced around; my eyes settling on a beat-up old Chevy pickup parked in front of the small diner. It was covered with faded green paint, mud and rust. My eyes grew wide as realization sank in. *This* was the truck that we were all to ride in? There was no other vehicle currently parked along the street. I looked at Brock in disbelief. "Are you kidding me? How are we all supposed to fit in that dump?"

Brock grinned. "Well, I guess you could always ride in the bed of the truck if you insist. The rest of us will squeeze into the cab."

Millie gave me a nervous look. "It won't be so bad."

I rolled my eyes upward and sighed. "Fine. But only if you promise me that death-trap is safe..."

Brock smiled. He was absolutely beautiful! The deep blue of his sparkling eyes accented the dimples in his cheeks and the cleft of his chin. How could *anyone* resist him? "I won't let anything happen to you. I promise."

I had to force myself to breathe. What was happening with me? I had *never* before swooned over anybody. I swallowed, shaking my head lightly as I was forced to consider the possibility. Was I starting to fall for Brock Jacobins? When he looked at me that way, I did feel all warm inside. But was I actually *crushing* on him? Was that really what was happening here?

Brock got behind the wheel of the Chevy and turned the key in the ignition. Surprisingly, the truck roared to life. He leaned through the driver's side window and slapped the door twice. "Time's a wasting! Let's go!"

Silas opened the passenger door and Millie motioned for me to get in. She climbed in behind me, forcing me to slide to the middle of the long seat. Silas chuckled. "You gotta keep moving, sister! You have to make room for one more."

"Scoot!" Millie said, pressing her body against me, forcing me to slide up next to Brock.

I couldn't help but notice how rock-hard his body was. He made no effort to move toward the door, where there were a few meager inches to spare. He reached down and grabbed my left knee and pulled it firmly against his right leg. "I need a little more room to operate the stick shift," he said by way of explanation. He slipped the gear stick into reverse and backed the truck out of the parking spot. Had he not moved my leg, he would most certainly have struck my kneecap with the shifter. There was nothing that I could do; I was firmly pinned between Brock and Millie. I couldn't even place my hands in my lap if I wanted to.

Brock kept his hand on the stick-shift and effortlessly worked the clutch and the gas pedal with his feet. As we moved forward, I could hear the engine begin to strain. He shifted gears again and the truck picked up speed. "You live over on Maple right?" he said with a glance over at Millie.

She seemed surprised that he knew where she lived. "Uh, yeah. Twenty-sixteen Maple. You can't miss it." As we turned onto Maple Street she pointed. "The yellow house on the right."

It was an adorable two-story Tudor style home with a wrap-around porch surrounded by perennial plants, mainly Coral Bells. The leafy foliage ranged from white, tinged with green, and two different shades of pink. The leaves of the plant were almost more attractive than the flowers.

Brock nodded as he pulled up to the curb in front of the house and turned off the ignition. "Here we are ladies."

Millie giggled.

The guys opened up the doors and hopped out of the truck. They each held out a hand to assist Millie and I out of the pickup. I misjudged the distance from the seat to the ground and ended up colliding against Brock. He squeezed my hand and quickly wrapped his other arm around me to keep me from falling to the pavement. "Careful!" he said.

I felt the color rush to my cheeks. How could I be so clumsy? "Thanks," I said, totally embarrassed.

He had a smirk on his face as he looked into my eyes. "I told you I wouldn't let anything happen to you."

I jerked my hand from his grasp, suddenly *very* aware of how strong and warm his grip was. I stepped out of the street and onto the sidewalk. I glanced over at Millie; she was obviously enjoying all the attention that Silas was giving her. She didn't seem to be in any hurry to go inside. He said something to her that I couldn't quite hear and she giggled, blushing slightly.

Finally, Millie stepped away from Silas and wrapped her arm through mine and we headed through the white picket fence and up to the front of the house. On the porch were two darkly stained rocking chairs with a small round table in between them. On top of the table was a wicker basket with balls of yarn and long darning needles. Obviously, Grams spent a good deal of her time on the porch.

Millie opened the screen door and then the ornately carved wooden door without using a key. When she saw the strange look on my face, she pushed her glasses up her nose and said, "What?"

I reached out and touched her arm. "You don't lock your doors?"

Millie squinted her eyes and shook her head. "No. Why would we?"

I shrugged and practically snorted. "Oh, I don't know, to keep strangers from coming in uninvited?"

Millie laughed and gave me a quick hug. "I love you, girlfriend! This isn't the big city. Here we are much more casual and trusting. I don't even think Grams knows where the keys to the doors are."

There wasn't even a deadbolt on the door, nor a safety chain. I looked. Back home in the city we had several locks on the entrance, multiple deadbolts. *How did these people sleep at night?*

A long hallway ran toward the back of the small house. Slightly to the right of the front doorway was the staircase heading up to the second floor. A warm and inviting parlor was to the left.

I could see another room off the parlor that had a small round table with four chairs. In the center of the table was a crystal ball and what appeared to be an oversized deck of cards. I glanced at Millie, recalling that she claimed her grandmother had Gypsy blood running through her veins.

Millie smiled at me sheepishly. She must've known what I was thinking. She pushed her glasses up her nose and gave a slight shrug. "I told you that I got all of this mysticism from Grams. She occasionally does readings for her friends; they bring cookies, pies and sometimes even cakes when they come over." She chuckled softly. "They're all so cute!"

I could easily picture several old, blue-and-silver-haired ladies gathered around the table having their fortunes told by Millie's grandmother. Life in The Hollows was far different than life in the city. *But was it really?* I remember seeing numerous shops for Psychic Readings and Tarot throughout the city. There were even several 1-800 numbers you could call to have your fortune read. I had always dismissed it as nonsense - *just as I had the notion of werewolves!* Maybe I needed to rethink things a bit.

Millie left me downstairs as she quickly went up to grab a small suitcase and a few extra clothing items. I wandered back into the hallway and started looking at the family photos that lined the walls. Several of them were pictures of Millie, in various stages of her life. I didn't see any that had her with her parents. There was one with a baby and two people that had similar characteristics that Millie shared; but that was it. Had her parents both died when she was so young? Could that be why she lived with her grandmother? Maybe we had more in common than I had originally thought.

She carried the small suitcase into the room adjacent to the parlor and set it carefully onto the table. She crossed to a shelf in the corner of the room and took down a black velvet cloth that covered a square object. She placed it into the suitcase and pulled back the covering exposing a wooden plank with letters and numbers engraved upon its surface. "Isn't it beautiful?" she asked.

I nodded. "Is that a *Ouija Board*?" I asked, marveling at its beauty.

She smiled. "It's a family heirloom." She held it up for my inspection. She giggled girlishly. "It's *like* an Ouija but not quite. It's what they call a *Talking Board*, or sometimes it is known as a

Spirit Board. Unlike the Ouija this board doesn't use a *planchette* to communicate with the dead."

I couldn't help but frown. Every board that I had ever seen used a planchette, a lens with three glide feet. The participants would place the tips of their fingers on the edge of the device and move it in a circular motion across the board. Supposedly, once you had asked a question, the spirits would respond by moving the lens over various letters. Yes and no answers were indicated by the planchette stopping upon the *Yes* and *No* spaces imprinted near the corner of the board. I knew that the planchette could be manipulated by one of the participants by adding slightly more pressure and 'guiding' the device without the other's knowledge. To say that I had my doubts about the validity of such devices was a complete understatement.

You just *could not* communicate with the dead!

Of course, a few weeks ago I didn't believe that *werewolves* were real either!

I sighed, shoving my hands into the front pockets of my jeans. "Okay, so how does this thing work if it doesn't use a planchette?"

Millie placed the board back into the suitcase and covered it with the velvet cloth. She batted a hand in the air and smiled. "Oh, easy peasy! We can dangle a necklace over the board." She lifted her crucifix. "We can use this since you don't have yours."

My hand went to my neck where my talisman was noticeably absent. I *still* felt naked without it. It didn't seem right not having the weighty medallion where it belonged. Where it had been for almost three years.

Millie zipped up the suitcase. "Okay. I'm all set!"

As we rejoined the guys at the truck, Silas took the suitcase from Millie and placed it in the back. Then we climbed back into the cab, this time I kept my hands in my lap so that I didn't feel so trapped. "Where to?" Brock asked as he fired the engine to life.

"I guess back to the library. Grandmother's driver will be picking us up there in a little while."

"You guys could hang out with us, if you want." Millie said quickly.

Brock smiled. "Unfortunately, we are already running behind. We came to town to pick up some supplies for a friend. Perhaps another time?"

He was looking at me with raised brows. "Uh… sure. Sounds great." I said. "Another time, then."

Millie pulled her glasses off her nose and placed them on the top of her head. She closed the thick book soundly, causing a bit of dust to fly into the air, along with the musty scent of old ink and ancient pages. She rubbed her eyes wearily. "This is getting us nowhere."

My own eyes were burning and I closed them tightly for a second before opening them and trying to focus on her. I closed the book I'd been reading much more quietly than she had. "I feel like it's been a complete waste of our time."

She blinked her eyes rapidly as she reached for her glasses, pulling an errant strand of her brown hair in the process. Her hair had gotten caught in the hinge of the frames. She sighed as she freed her tresses and then slid her glasses into place. "I'm sorry that we didn't find anything useful to help us. Maybe we'll have better luck when we get back to Wellington House."

"Speaking of which," I glanced at my mom's watch, "we'd best be getting a move on, Harrison Beckett is liable to leave us stranded if we're late."

Millie pushed away from the table. "Would he really do that?"

I shrugged as I stood. "Who knows? He'd probably just do it for spite."

"Wouldn't your grandmother be upset with him if he did?"

I smiled. "I certainly hope that she would. Fear of her reprisal might be our only saving grace. I don't think that even Harrison Beckett would want to suffer her wrath."

Millie shivered. "She seems like such a sweet lady, but she has a certain look about her that says she's not one whom you should cross. I certainly wouldn't want to be on her bad side."

"You and me both."

CHAPTER 17

THE SPIRIT BOARD

We found Harrison Beckett waiting impatiently outside. He was leaning against the Bentley puffing on a cigarette, scowling darkly. Clearly, he was not happy with us. He tossed the stub of his smoldering cigarette onto the sidewalk at our feet. I wasn't too sure he hadn't tried to hit us with it, but I decided to ignore his childish provocation. This time he didn't bother taking Millie's bag or opening the trunk. We slid into the back seat of the Bentley and prepared ourselves for the long drive back to Wellington House.

After we had travelled several miles in silence, I glanced over at Millie and smiled. "So, you and Silas seemed to be getting along pretty well."

Millie blushed brightly and the corners of her mouth turned upward. "Do you think he *likes* me?"

I practically snorted. "*Duh!*"

She giggled. "Oh, I hope so! I really like him and all." She glanced out the window dreamily and then turned in the seat to better face me. "It's just that when at school, he's never really talked to me before." She glanced down at her fidgeting hands, her smile disappearing. "No one does."

My heart went out to her. Had people really been that *cruel* and *uncaring* toward her? That just didn't seem right. She was a very sweet girl. You just had to get to know her better. To give her a *chance*! If you did, you couldn't help but love her! I reached out and squeezed her hands. "Well, that is all about to change for you!"

She looked up at me, a hopeful expression on her face as she pushed her glasses up her nose. "You think so?"

I nodded. "Yes I do! Silas Monaghan is truly smitten with you!"

She closed her eyes tightly as a huge grin stretched across her face. She tightened her hands into fists and shook them in the air as she stomped her feet excitedly. "Oh, I *do* hope that you're right!"

Millie exhaled a long, slow breath and waved a hand in the air, fanning herself. "Whew! Is it hot in here or is it just me?"

I couldn't help but laugh.

"So," she gave me a sly look, "you and Brock Jacobins seemed to be doing pretty good. Is there something there that you'd like to share with me? I mean, I *am* your best friend - I should know if there is something going on between the two of you."

I felt a tingling sensation of heat rising up inside me. "Oh, I don't really know how he feels."

"But you like him, though?" she asked.

I couldn't help but smile. "Yeah... I think I might."

On the rest of the drive back to Wellington House we talked about Silas and Brock, giggling until we hurt. I so wanted to tell her about the Wolf Pack but I was afraid of what that little nugget of information might do to her feelings for Silas. I didn't want to put an end to a possible budding romance. Every time we'd laugh, I could see Harrison glance up toward the rear-view mirror in disdain.

Millie saw it too. She stuck out her tongue and made a silly face as she rolled her eyes toward the tiny mirror. I immediately saw the back of Harrison's neck turn a bright red; the color flushed his ears as well. He pressed down upon the accelerator, obviously in a hurry to see us home. We only laughed harder. Before we knew it, we were stopped in front of Wellington

House. Harrison barely allowed us to get out of the car, let alone close the passenger door before he sped off.

We went upstairs to Millie's room and closed the door behind us. She placed the suitcase at the foot of the bed and flipped the top open. She removed the *Spirit Board* and placed it beside the bag, and then set to work unpacking the clothes she had brought along. Yesterday, Millie hadn't planned on spending but the one night, now she wasn't going home until tomorrow afternoon.

My eyes kept wandering to the black velvet cloth that covered the board. I couldn't help but think that we were standing on a precipice. Once we moved forward, there was no turning back. I glanced up at Millie and swallowed. She placed such profound *faith* in this board and what we could accomplish with it. She had used it successfully before. "When do we start with the *Spirit Board*?" I asked.

She shrugged as she gathered up the board and placed it in the top dresser drawer. She pulled out some of the clothes and then placed them down on top of the black velvet cloth. "Not until everyone's gone to bed. We don't want any unnecessary interruptions while we attempt to contact the *other side*. We want to keep the spirits happy. Happy spirits are by rule, nice spirits."

I couldn't help but shiver. What if we contacted an unhappy spirit? Then what? I tried rubbing my arms for warmth, but it did little good. I glanced at my watch; we still had about an hour before it was time for dinner. "So, you've done this kind of thing before? Contacted spirits?" I asked, unable to keep my voice from wavering.

Millie batted the air with a wave of her hand. "Hundreds of times! Well, not hundreds of times - once or twice."

"Once or twice?"

She rolled her eyes and sighed dramatically. "Okay! Once!"

I stopped her by placing a hand on her arm. "*Only once?!*"

She nodded. "Maybe."

"*Maybe?*" I didn't like the sound of this. "What do you mean maybe?"

She looked at me, her eyes beginning to tear. They seemed so large behind her round lenses. "I... I got scared! I was alone, like I usually am, and I started playing around with the Spirit Board. Grammy was at one of her Tea socials. I was bored. I made contact with some dead guy named Danny. I got freaked out!" She started crying. "He... he wanted me to... to let him *do* things..."

I hugged her close. "Oh Millie!"

She sobbed into my shoulder. I could feel her tears against my neck. "If you don't want to do this, we don't have to. We'll find another way."

"No. No, I *need* to do this. I was extremely foolish back then. You aren't supposed to use these things *alone*. They have that whole 'safety in numbers' thing for a reason." She wiped her eyes. "I'll be fine."

"You're sure?" I asked, holding her now at arm's length.

Millie nodded. "Positive."

I glanced back at my watch. We still had forty-five minutes before dinner. Millie must have deduced what I was thinking. "You want to give the *Spirit Board* a try now, don't you?"

I tried unsuccessfully not to smile. She had read me so well. I nodded. "We have a little bit of time before we go down for dinner. I'd kinda like to reach out to Sara's ghost sooner rather than later. I don't know if I can wait until everyone else is asleep. I just worry that it might be too late. I don't want anything to happen to Bobbybear."

Millie pulled open the dresser drawer and removed the *Spirit Board* and a small burlap sack. "The last time you saw Sara was in your bathroom. I think we should at least go over to your room and attempt to contact her there, it may be easier."

"Are you sure you want to?" I stifled a yawn. "Shouldn't we be better rested?"

She opened her bedroom door. "That is a luxury that we can no longer afford. I'm not gonna let this *spooky little bitch* mess with my best friend - or her little brother! It's time we got to the bottom of this!"

I stepped out into the hallway and smiled. I had never heard Millie talk this way. She had taken charge and I certainly wasn't going to stand in her way. "Wow!" I said with a chuckle. "My best friend is *such* a bad ass!"

We walked the short distance to my room and went inside.

Millie went to the foot of my bed and sat down on the floor where there was the most room. She pulled her necklace over her head and held it out for me; it was an old, ornately carved gold cross on a dainty golden chain.

I sat down on the floor across from her with the Spirit Board between us. I took the cross and looked at her expectantly. "What do you want me to do?"

"You hold this over the center of the board, careful not to get too low. We don't want the tip to actually touch the board." She adjusted my hand. "That's *extremely* important. I can't stress that enough."

I nodded my understanding. "Oh... okay."

"Now," Millie continued in a business-like tone, "it is absolutely crucial that you take this seriously. We don't want to seem frivolous or insincere when we ask our questions."

I nodded again.

Millie placed a small burlap sack beside the board and pulled out a small pouch. I could smell a minty aroma emanating from the tiny bag. Millie noticed my raised brow and she smiled. "Patchouli powder. It helps to purify the *Spirit Board*. You can use a sage bundle or any incense like rosemary or frankincense to do the job, but I prefer patchouli. It's easy to find in the woods around here."

I watched as she produced a small white candle and a book of matches. She struck a match and melted a puddle of wax at the edge of the board. She lit the candle and stood it in the puddle she'd created. She held it into place until the melted wax hardened. She closed her eyes and took a deep breath and slowly blew it out. She cleared her throat. Her voice was clear and strong. "We desire that no negative or harmful energies come forth. We banish and dismiss *all* negative forces from our presence!"

I couldn't help but chuckle a little. Millie seemed way too intense. She shot me a sharp disapproving glare. "Sorry!" I said.

Millie closed her eyes and mumbled softly. I could barely discern a few words here and there, like: *'protect us, keep us from harm...'* Oh My God! She was offering up a prayer! I swallowed my fear.

Millie looked up at me as she grasped the golden crucifix between her thumb and two fingers. "Ready?"

I tried to swallow again, but it was difficult. I nodded, tightening my grip on the chain.

She swung the cross so that it spun in a circle over the *Spirit Board*. As the necklace slowed to a stop over the heart of the board, Millie spoke. "We wish to contact the spirit of Sara Robinson."

To my surprise, the cross started swaying back and forth between us. Had I not been the one holding the chain I would have *sworn* that Millie was manipulating it - *but she wasn't even touching it*!

The room felt suddenly *very* cold. The flame on the candle flickered as though caught in a breeze and then went out, filling the air with the rising smell of sulfur. Millie glanced quickly at me and mouthed the words, *'Someone's here...'*

"Sara? Sara Robinson, is that you?" Millie asked.

The gold crucifix pulled sharply to the *NO* at the corner of the board. It held at an impossible angle for several seconds and then returned its sway over the board.

"We wish only to talk to Sara Robinson." Millie said in a firm voice. "Sara? Can you hear me?"

The cross pulled to the *W*, then shifted to the *O*, then the *N*, *T*... Next it spelled out the word *Come*. I could feel the hairs on my arms prickle.

Millie shook her head, frowning. "Why won't she come to us? Who is this?"

I'M SORRY KAT

"Who is this?" I asked before Millie could respond.

BOBBY

I stared at Millie in disbelief. Her lips parted in fear. I could see pain and sadness creeping into her eyes behind her round lenses. I felt cold and empty. Helpless. "Bobbybear?!"

YES...

The Spirit Board literally flew up into the air and we could hear the voice of Sara Robinson proclaim: *"He's mine!"* The two halves of the spirit board clattered upon the floor, now broken and useless.

"What does that mean?" I asked, amazed that I could even get the words out.

Millie wiped the tears from her eyes. "Kat, I'm *so* sorry. We're too late. Bobby is *dead!*"

Her words poured over me like a bucket of ice-cold water. My breath caught in my throat and I couldn't breathe no matter how hard I tried. I attempted to get up off the floor but my knees buckled and I collapsed against the foot of the bed. I felt like I were about to vomit. My mind raced, there had to be something that we could do! I *refused* to believe that he was already lost to me. Tears stung at my eyes, blurring my vision. I staggered toward the door, knowing I *had* to find my brother!

"Kat," Millie continued to sob, "I'm *so, so, so* sorry!"

"*No!*" I shouted back angrily. "I *won't* give up on Bobbybear! *I won't!*" I flung open my bedroom door and raced down the long hallway toward my brother's room. Halfway there I started calling for him. "Bobby! Bobbybear?"

There was no reply.

I ran to Bobby's room and flung the door open. "Bobbybear?"

The room was empty.

I had hoped to find him either playing or even napping, but neither was the case. It was obvious that he hadn't been there since he'd gotten up this morning. Margaret had made his bed while he was at breakfast, and it hadn't been touched since. Mister Grizzle was sitting there, propped against the pillows. I was at a loss. I sagged against his doorway, sobbing uncontrollably.

Millie reached my side and wrapped her arms around me, offering comfort.

I turned to face the narrow set of stairs that led to the attic storage room. I froze. Standing at the top landing was the ghost of Sara Robinson. She smiled down at me, a look of smug satisfaction etched across her face. "I told you he was mine! You can't have him!"

"No!" I shouted back at her. "*You* can't have him!"

CHAPTER 18
GRANDMOTHER'S WARNING

Millie persuaded me to wash up for dinner, but all I wanted to do was confront Grandmother and find out the truth. I didn't see how Bobby's new playmate could be any other than the ghost of Sara Robinson. And, if that were truly the case, how could Grandmother allow that to happen? What did she have to gain from Bobbybear's death? She certainly had a lot of explaining to do. A whole lot!

I stood in front of my bathroom mirror and couldn't believe the disheveled appearance reflected back at me. I was a complete mess. I ran a brush through my hair with three quick strokes and tossed it onto the vanity, uncaring. My hands were shaking. I felt like screaming, and my stomach was twisted in knots.

As we descended the stairs for dinner, I felt the tightness of my shoulders increase with each downward step. I trailed one hand along the banister while I kept the other one tightly fisted at my side. Millie followed along behind me, too afraid to say anything that might set me off. She felt guilty and more than a little responsible for Bobby's death. She had been so certain that we could save him, but in the end we had failed.

I paused outside the dining room door. Every muscle I had

was so tense, I could hardly move. Millie glanced at me as she placed a hand on the doorknob. "Are you ready for this?" she whispered softly.

I tightened my jaw. I couldn't speak. I could only nod. I took a deep breath and exhaled slowly. I was ready to face Grandmother.

Millie opened the door and I saw Bobbybear standing near Grandmother. I couldn't believe my eyes. He was alive! I rushed to Bobbybear and hugged him tightly, the tears flowing freely from my eyes. I kissed the top of his head and whispered, "You're alright!"

He struggled against me, giggling in protest. "Kat!"

I stood beside him, continuing to hold him close as I stared at Grandmother. She was watching my display of affection and relief with a critically raised brow. A thin smile curved her narrow lips. I wished that I could know what she was thinking.

I didn't have to wait long.

"May I ask what this is all about?" Grandmother said.

I didn't want to risk Bobbybear's safety any more than necessary by beating around the bush. I decided to plunge head on. "Millie and I were using her *Spirit Board*. We contacted Bobby's ghost! How is that even possible?" I was angry, and very near tears.

Grandmother's eyes grew narrow and cold. She glanced to Millie and then back at me. "Nonsense."

I glared at her. "Oh really? I know what I saw, Grandmother!"

Grandmother stood abruptly; she was clearly quite angry. Pointing a finger at Bobbybear she said, "Obviously not! I assure you that Robert is quite alive!" She shot a glance at Margaret who was standing quietly in the corner. "Take this all away!" she snapped, waving a hand over the table. "I've lost my appetite!"

I kept Bobbybear close, almost afraid to release him for fear that something terrible would happen. As Margaret began her task of clearing the table of supper, I said, "I know what I saw," I repeated softly.

Grandmother's eyes were furious. She smiled at Bobby. "Perhaps you should run along upstairs, Robert. Margaret can bring a plate to your room. Your sister and I need to have a little talk."

I clenched my jaw tightly. Bobby's eyes were wide and uncertain. He seemed about to cry. My own eyes were tear filled. My heart was breaking. I didn't know what to do, but I knew that I had to do something! I was certain that Bobbybear was in grave danger, but I wasn't even remotely sure how I could convince my grandmother to see that. I had to get a grip on myself; I could see that I was scaring Bobby. I kissed the top of his head. "Do as Grandmother says, Bobbybear."

Bobbybear ran from the room, and my heart went with him. I wanted to go to him, to hug him close and leave Wellington House far behind. There was no safety within these walls, of that I was certain.

Grandmother glared at me icily and said, "A moment, Katherine?" She led me into the drawing room. I signaled for Millie to tag along. I didn't want to be alone with Grandmother.

Grandmother placed both hands on the top of her cane and then tapped it sharply upon the flagstones of the floor. "Would you mind telling me why you have allowed this arcane nonsense into my home?" She crossed to her decanter of sherry, poured herself half a glass; which she quickly tossed back. She slammed the empty sherry glass upon the table and refilled it. She waved the glass toward Millie. "I think that it is time that you went home. I'll have Harrison bring the car around." She turned to me, scowling darkly. "You have a lot of explaining to do young lady."

I raised my chin in defiance. "Funny. I was thinking the same thing!"

I saw the flash of anger spark the fires in Grandmother's eyes. I could practically feel the hot spears shooting from them. Her grip was so tight on her cane that I could see her knuckles turning white. Her jaw was tightly set. It was clear that I had crossed a line with her. I never should've talked to her that way with someone else in the room. It certainly wasn't the way that I'd been raised. Mom would have slapped me without hesitation.

I half expected it now.

But Grandmother showed more restraint than I had given her credit for. She simply arched both brows and nodded. "This conversation has gone on quite long enough. I suggest that you go to your room." She turned to Millie. "It was a pleasure meeting you Miss Bradford. Harrison will have the car out front when you've collected your things."

Grandmother grabbed my arm as I attempted to follow Millie out of the drawing room. I tried to pull from her grasp but couldn't; her long nails dug painfully into the flesh of my arm. She leaned toward me. "If you ever pull a stunt like that again, you will certainly regret it. I have tried to be tolerant with you because of your situation, but you have tested me for the last time. Do I make myself clear?" She squeezed again, forcing a muffled cry of pain to escape my lips.

Tears instantly sprang to my eyes. I could only nod. I tried unsuccessfully to pry her hand from my arm, but she refused to let go. "I can make things extremely difficult for you and that sweet brother of yours. I seriously doubt he has the same stubborn streak that you seem to have. He will break much easier, of that I am certain." Her eyes narrowed, the fire was gone, replaced by ice.

She shoved me to the door. "Now go see that your friend gets packed up. Harrison will be waiting."

I pulled the drawing room doors closed and wiped the tears from my cheeks. I didn't want anyone seeing me like this. Millie would ask too many questions and Bobbybear would be even more frightened. That was the absolute last thing that I needed. I was beginning to understand my mom's desire to leave The Hollows behind and start her life anew, far away from Wellington House, and away from Grandmother.

It was then, as I was about to turn away from the closed door, that it hit me. Despite my parent's best efforts to get away from her, they never truly had. Elizabeth Wellington had known where her daughter had been all along. It was the only answer that made any sense. She had kept constant tabs on them. How else would she have known about the car accident that had ended their lives? After the incident she had sent Abigail to bring her grandchildren to The Hollows.

How could she have known? What other secrets was she keeping?

CHAPTER 19

THE PORTRAIT

Millie gave me a hug as Harrison Beckett placed her bags in the trunk of the Bentley. My eyes were still red and I could tell that she noticed; there was no sense in trying to hide it from her. She squeezed me tightly and kissed my cheek. "We're *not* done here, Kat. I promise you that," she whispered.

I felt empty inside. It was as though with her leaving all hope was going with her. I really was at a loss as to what I should do next. Obviously, something had gone awry with the *Spirit Board*. There was no other explanation. But how was that possible? Was some *malevolent* spirit involved? If so, why had it pretended to be Bobbybear? Was it Sara or were we dealing with someone or *something* else entirely? I didn't really have a clue. My head was still spinning.

Millie squeezed my arm as she climbed into the Bentley. "Don't give up hope Kat!"

I gave her a hesitant smile. I could feel tears of despair starting to well up into my eyes. I felt defeated.

Millie pushed her glasses up her nose. "I'll do a little more research and if I find out anything helpful, I'll let you know straight away. We'll figure something out!"

She sounded so certain; it was hard not to be buoyed. My smile came easier this time. It was hard not to have hope, no matter how fleeting. "I wish you didn't have to go. I wish you could stay longer."

"It is probably better that I don't," she said. "This gives me the opportunity to do some more research."

I moved forward and held the door open so that Harrison couldn't close it on us. "You don't really think that it could've been Bobbybear on the *Spirit Board*, do you? I mean, how could it have been?"

Millie reached out and squeezed my hand reassuringly. "I hope not. We'll see."

I was hoping that she could've sounded more confident. Even the look in her eyes wasn't very comforting. I dropped my shoulders and pouted in an attempt at some levity as I closed the car door. With a crooked little smile I waved to her half-heartedly as Harrison put the Bentley in motion. I shoved my hands into the hip pockets of my jeans as I watched them stir up dust on the way to the main road. Already I missed her.

With luck, Millie would uncover something useful, but admittedly I couldn't even begin to fathom what that might be. We had tried using the *Spirit Board* but that had ended in complete and utter disaster, with the destruction of a family heirloom. What could Millie possibly learn at the library? What could be buried in a bunch of old books and forgotten newspapers that might help us moving forward? We hadn't really found anything useful yet. I didn't have a clue what Millie might uncover, but I knew that if anyone could find something useful, it would be her. I had absolute faith in Millie Bradford. I had to. There was no one else I could turn to.

I turned back toward Wellington House. As I stared at the drab exterior my shoulders dropped and I sighed. Suddenly I was filled with a weighty sense of dread. I could see Grandmother standing, framed in a first-floor window. She had been watching Millie depart with her arms folded regally over her chest. She appeared to have a smug look on her face. '*Good riddance*,' her demeanor seemed to say.

I could see Grandmother shift her gaze away from the departing Bentley to stare at me. Her icy glare sent a cold shiver down my back. She arched a single brow, giving me a slightly condescending look as she raised her chin in arrogant superiority. It was easy to see why so many people feared her. She was a fiercely strong woman who always demanded things be done her way. I was certain that her will extended far beyond Wellington House to every corner of The Hollows. Crossing her wouldn't be easy. I would have to move cautiously so that I didn't incur her wrath.

First, I wanted to talk to Bobbybear about his new friend, Sara. It could be as innocent as Grandmother made it seem; but my gut was telling me different. I don't know *how* it was even possible, but something told me that this new friend of his was actually the ghost of Sara Robinson—who died tragically back in 1884.

Grandmother was standing in the foyer at the base of the stairs as I closed the front door behind me. I took a deep breath before I turned to face her. She had both hands resting on her cane. "I see your friend has left."

I nodded. "As you requested, Grandmother."

She reached out a hand and stopped me as I tried to move past her. I wanted to avoid further confrontation at the moment. I needed to talk to Bobby. She smiled, "It is only for the best, my dear. She should not have brought that arcane nonsense into this house without prior approval from me. It was really quite rude."

Finally, I could take no more. I stared at her defiantly. "I gave her *my* permission. So, it really wasn't so rude of her after all, was it?"

She tried to sink her claws into my arm again but this time I was ready for it. I twisted from her grasp, leaving her to clutch empty air. I could see the hint of surprise in her eyes. I quickly tried to hide my crooked smile of absolute joy.

She turned on me faster than I had thought she was capable of. "Wellington House is *mine!*" Grandmother stabbed the flagstones sharply with the end of her cane for emphasis.

"No Grandmother." I fired back. "Wellington House is *my* home now too! As such, I should be entitled to certain rights!"

I was totally unprepared for what happened next.

Grandmother slapped me hard across the cheek, her eyes ablaze with white-hot anger. "Do not *ever* speak to me in that tone again, young lady! I didn't tolerate that kind of behavior with your mother nor your aunt, and I certainly won't permit it from a spoiled little brat!"

Tears had instantly sprung to my eyes. I could still feel the burning sting of her hand upon my cheek. I glared at her furiously. My hands were shaking as I placed one on the banister. I turned from her, my jaw tightening. "Never strike me again Grandmother." I looked at her through narrowed slits. I spoke in a hissed whisper, "I'll not warn you again." I started up the stairs.

"Are you *threatening* me Katherine?" Grandmother called up at me. I could hear the anger in her voice.

"I'm *talking* to you young lady!"

I continued climbing, ignoring her.

"Fine! Go to your room and stay there until your attitude improves!" She pounded the flagstones with her cane with such fury that I thought it would splinter. It didn't. "I will not suffer such blatant disrespect in my home!"

At the second floor landing I stopped and looked down. Grandmother was no longer standing there. She had most likely headed off to the drawing room for a glass of sherry to calm her rattled nerves.

I glanced down the long hallway toward Bobby's room. I could see a light shining down from the storage room. At first, I only walked, but as the fear continued to grow inside me, I began to run. The silhouette of a child darkened the splash of yellow light that spilled down upon the floor from the stairwell. My heart raced as the door above closed and everything disappeared leaving the corridor once more in murky shadows. I felt an unexpected surge of panic shoot through me. "*Bobby!*" I whispered as I continued down the hallway.

By the time I reached the base of the stairs I was out of breath. "*He's mine!*" I couldn't be certain if I had heard it again, or if the memory of those words had been so vivid that it only appeared that way. My mouth felt incredibly dry. I swallowed, but it wasn't easy. I took a deep breath and climbed the narrow stairs two at a time.

The door was locked.

I pounded on the door with my fist, causing it to rattle. I could feel tears rolling down my cheeks. I was desperate. I was certain that Bobbybear was in danger—more than he'd ever been! I stomped my foot in frustration. I tried turning the knob again but it refused to budge. Turning my body, I slammed my shoulder against the heavy oak door as hard as I could. I felt the sharp stab of sudden pain; but still the door held.

"Bobby?" I called out to my brother.

He didn't respond.

I ran my hands through my hair, feeling helpless and alone. "Sara!" I begged. "Sara, please let me in!"

To my surprise the door opened a crack.

I nudged it the rest of the way with my toe. It opened freely. Cautiously I peeked inside. It appeared empty. There was no one there. Regaining some of my nerve I entered the storage room and looked around. Someone had covered the portrait with that same dingy white cloth.

I was drawn to it for some inexplicable reason. It was as though I hadn't a choice. I stood in front of the canvas-draped portrait, my breath coming in ragged gasps. Almost as though they had a will of their own, my hands reached out for the dust-covered sheet. I drew it off and gasped sharply, not believing what I was seeing. *How was this possible? What did it mean?*

Standing beside Sara Robinson was Bobbybear. *He was inside the portrait!*

I heard the laughter of a little girl. *"He's mine,"* she stated simply. I dropped to my knees feeling utterly defeated. Somehow, I had lost Bobbybear. She had won.

Sara laughed again.

CHAPTER 20

VANISHED

I pushed open the door to Bobbybear's room hoping *desperately* that I would find him alone. He wasn't there. I checked his bathroom only to find it empty as well. Puzzled, I ran my hand through my hair trying to determine a course of action. *Where could Bobbybear have gone?*

Three possibilities presented themselves. He could be in my bedroom—he often did that when he was seeking comfort; I'd find him curled up on my bed snuggling my pillow, waiting for me. He could be somewhere else in the house, or he could have gone outside, maybe to the cottage. Of the three, I hoped to find him waiting for me all safe and sound in my bed, a sleepy smile curving the corners of his mouth.

But the change in the portrait frightened me.

What bothered me about it the most was the fact that his likeness didn't appear to be recently added to the painting. Part of the paint had been cracked, and some flakes had chipped off the canvas due to neglect or carelessness. The portrait of Sara and Bobbybear standing outside Wellington House *looked* old. It had me unnerved. I was terrified by the possibilities it presented.

I had a sick feeling.

I left Bobbybear's room and ran down the long corridor. By the time I reached my door I was out of breath. I took the knob in hand; it felt cold to the touch. I steeled myself before I turned it and pushed the door open. *"Bobby?"* I whispered with breathless hope.

Disappointment greeted me. Bobby wasn't there, my bed had been untouched since this morning. Sighing heavily, I turned from my room and headed back to the staircase. I had no choice. I *had* to ask Grandmother about Bobbybear's whereabouts. Hopefully she knew where he was.

I couldn't afford to waste time searching all of Wellington House on my own. Besides, I was already on Grandmother's bad side from our earlier confrontation. If she caught me snooping around in places where I had no business being, she'd be absolutely livid!

The drawing room door was closed when I got there. I didn't bother knocking. I simply opened the door and went inside. Margaret was pouring a glass of sherry from the decanter. She handed it to my Grandmother who gave me a cold glare as she accepted it. She nodded at the servant. "That will be all for tonight, Margaret. You may retire."

"Yes, M'Lady." Margaret said with a curtsy. She glanced at me and inclined her head. "Mistress Katherine."

Grandmother sipped her sherry and studied me thoughtfully. Finally, she spoke. "Have you come to apologize for your earlier behavior? I must tell you, it is rude to just barge into a room when the door is closed. You should announce your presence with a knock at the very least."

I nodded. "I do apologize for not knocking Grandmother." I smiled nervously as she arched a brow. "And for earlier too." *You get more flies with honey...*

Grandmother took another sip of her sherry. "I will accept your apology with just a bit of advice." She narrowed her eyes menacingly. "Never do it again. I shall not be so forgiving next time."

I fidgeted with my hands. "Yes Grandmother. I won't do it again. You've been more than generous. Thank you."

She eyed me stoically. "Very well, Katherine. What is it that you are wanting?"

I took a step toward her anxiously. "Have you seen Bobby? I can't find him anywhere."

Grandmother placed her glass of sherry on the end table. "What is this about?"

I lightly shook my head. "I wanted to say a proper goodnight to him, but I couldn't find him anywhere. He wasn't in his room. I was hoping you might know where he's gone."

She gave me a sad look. She sighed heavily, her shoulders rising and falling noticeably. She picked up the little bell beside the glass of sherry and rang it. "They said this might happen. I was hoping that you were stronger, but I can see now that I was mistaken." A placating smile appeared on her lips. "Not to worry my dear, we shall get you the help that you need."

"What are you talking about?" To say that I was confused would be a total understatement. I had no idea what she was going on about. "Surely you haven't allowed Bobby to go outside? The woods aren't safe at this time of night."

Grandmother cast a concerned glance at the door. "Where is that girl?" She rang the bell again.

Finally, Margaret reappeared. "Yes, M'Lady?" she said before giving me a nervous glance.

"Margaret, be a dear and help Katherine up to her room. She needs her medication."

Margaret nodded as she grasped my elbow. I yanked my arm from her and stepped away. I shot Grandmother an angry look, unsure what was going on. "What are you talking about? *What* medication? Where's my brother? Where's Bobbybear?"

Grandmother gave me a stoic look. "My dear, your brother Robert was killed in the car accident with your parents. You came to live here because your Aunt Abigail and I are all the family you have left. Don't you remember *any* of this?"

I stumbled backwards in shocked disbelief. *"No!"* I almost shouted at her. "How can you even joke like that? It isn't the least bit funny!"

Grandmother's look was a mixture of concern and anguish. She reached out a trembling hand toward me but pulled it back. "My dear, you're in denial. The sooner you accept matters as they are, the sooner you can begin your recovery. All the doctors are in agreement that—"

I stamped my foot in anger. "I am *not* sick! Bobbybear is alive! He didn't die in the accident; he came here to The Hollows with me!" Her blank stare was infuriating. "How can you stand there and deny any of it? He was at dinner tonight. Millie saw him." I glanced accusingly at Margaret. "So did you! Grandmother told you to take a plate upstairs to him when he got upset…"

She glanced at Grandmother but wouldn't meet my gaze. She shook her head lightly, one hand covering her mouth. "No Mistress Katherine. None of that is true. Only you came to live here."

"Liar!" I said furiously.

Grandmother shook her head slowly. Oh she was good—quite the actress. The tears that filled her eyes *seemed* real. She held a lacy white handkerchief to her lips and attempted to hold back a heart-wrenching sob. "Nothing of what you've said is even remotely possible Katherine. Both your parents and your brother died in the car accident. It is a miracle that you survived."

"No!" I said fighting back my own tears. "I can prove it! His room is upstairs. All of his things are there!"

Grandmother closed her eyes tightly, causing the tears to roll down her cheeks. She shook her head. "Katherine…" Her voice was filled with *such* anguish.

I was more than just angry. I was livid! I didn't know *what* they were trying to do here, but they certainly weren't going to convince me that Bobbybear was dead; that everything that had happened since the accident was all just a figment of my over active imagination. Sure, I knew that people could become so lost in their grief that they could imagine a whole new reality. They could see things that weren't really there. They could convince themselves that what they were experiencing was authentic. But *that* wasn't happening to me. I knew better.

I ran from the drawing room ignoring the plaintive calls of my grandmother. Proof of Bobbybear's existence was right upstairs in his bedroom. I wasn't going to let anyone stop me from getting the proof I needed.

As I was heading up the stairs, Margaret was following along behind me. "Mistress Katherine, please, allow me to help you to your room. I have your medication. It will help you to sleep. Tomorrow when you awaken you will see things more clearly."

She had a syringe in one hand filled with an amber liquid."

I stopped and turned on her, slapping the hand that held the syringe, causing it to fly out of her grasp. It tumbled over the railing and crashed upon the floor a moment later, shattering. "Keep that *crap* away from me!"

Margaret blushed and quickly averted her eyes, refusing to meet my gaze. I should have been instantly suspicious, but my mind was preoccupied. "I... I was only trying to help you, Mistress."

"You want to help me?" I spat at her. "Help me find my brother!"

"Please! You've upset Mrs. Wellington."

I shoved a finger in her face. "Stay out of my way!" I quickly turned from her and raced up the stairs.

The door to Bobby's room was closed. As I reached out to turn the doorknob my hand was trembling. *Why was I suddenly so frightened?* I knew what I was going to find! Bobby's toys and clothes were going to be just as he'd left them.

But they weren't.

No clothes hung in his closet, there were none folded neatly in his dresser. No toys littered the floor. Even his toothbrush was missing from the bathroom. It was as if Bobbybear had never been here at Wellington House. It was as if he'd been *erased* somehow.

He had vanished completely.

CHAPTER 21
LOST IN THE WOODS

I felt cold, isolated and alone. Something was terribly wrong. I should've found some evidence of Bobbybear but I hadn't. *Was I crazy? Had all this been my imagination created out of my grief?* That would definitely explain a lot, for sure. The entire witches and werewolves thing could easily be construed as the wildly vivid imagination of a grief-stricken girl who had just lost her entire family in a horrible accident from which only she survived. The guilt alone could drive you mad. No one would doubt it. It was always much easier to accept a well-conceived lie rather than the simple truth. Trouble was, I was beginning to feel doubt subtly creeping into my own thoughts. One nagging question remained: *Was I crazy?*

I ran through Wellington House calling out my brother's name, searching every room. I had no luck with either. I was now certain of one thing: Bobbybear wasn't *here*. Ignoring Grandmother's pleas to *'stop this craziness'* I went outside. I may be doubting my own sanity, but there were still two people that I felt I could trust: Millie Bradford and Aunt Abby. Neither of them would lie to me. If they told me that Bobby was dead, then I'd *have* to accept it. I wouldn't have a choice. And I'd know for a certainty.

Deep down I knew that none of this could be right. First of all, it didn't *feel* right. But I still had no idea what motive Grandmother could have for such an elaborate scheme. Obviously, she had help. Margaret was in on it, I was certain. And if she were, so too was Harrison Beckett. I believed him to be every bit the weasel that Aunt Abby claimed him to be. But what did they all hope to gain by this deception? I honestly didn't have a clue.

Had there been an insurance policy of some kind?

Money was a powerful motivator in many crimes. *Could that be the reason for all this madness? Were they trying to extort the insurance company out of money? Making me, the sole benefactor, out to be crazy and in need of care?* It would be an easy sell. Especially considering how powerful Grandmother was in The Hollows.

I ran through the woods along the path to the cottage. The sooner I talked to Aunt Abby the better I'd feel. Maybe she could help me sort this all out. At the very least, it would give me another set of eyes searching for my brother. And if she *really* was a witch, maybe she'd have some magical way to locate him quicker than I could on my own. It was a plan, anyway. I *had* to do something! Dad always said that action was often better than reaction.

It was getting late. Already the sun had dipped behind the trees, and with it, darkness was quickly descending. Moonrise would follow not long after. Aunt Abigail still had my talisman; without it I would change—and if I didn't become the wolf, then it really didn't matter. I'd have my answers then.

Bobby would be dead, and I would truly be crazy.

I didn't see any lights on in the cottage at all. It was dark and seemed to be deserted. I felt an empty tug at my gut as fear crept in. Had I somehow missed Aunt Abigail in my mad dash through the woods? Was she searching for me at Wellington House? I hadn't veered from the path; surely I would have seen her. Unless of course she had taken another way to the manor—which was entirely possible; just because I was familiar with this path didn't mean it was the only one.

In desperation I pounded on the door of the cottage calling for my aunt. Maybe she'd gotten busy in the basement and just hadn't turned on any lights yet. I tried the knob, only to discover it locked. I frowned, feeling despair creeping in, extending icy fingers to entrap me. I could just be delusional. I was no longer sure of anything.

I stepped away from the porch and ran my hand through my hair in utter panic. I didn't know what my best course of action should be. I had planned on talking to Aunt Abby and enlisting her help. I needed her to tell me that she *remembered* Bobbybear. I had never expected that she wouldn't be home when I needed her most!

I had gotten so agitated that I wasn't really paying attention to anything. The moon was rising, and I could feel the powerful pull of the wolf staking her claim on my body. I dropped to my knees feeling a sense of *relief* even as excruciating pain coursed through me. Tears fell from my eyes as I clawed at the ground with my hands. I could feel the popping of my bones as they transformed from human to canine. I could hear the far-off sound of my clothes as they were torn to shreds, no longer fitting my misshapen body...

The wolf ran without a care in the world. Fading thoughts of human woes were being left farther behind with each leap and bound she took through the lush forest. Dodging huge rocks and thick clumps of trees, the wolf darted toward newfound freedom. The higher the full moon rose in the evening sky, the more the wolf felt invigorated, invincible, unstoppable. How easy it would be to remain this way; without the trappings of humanity that only served to enslave the wolf like steel shackles upon her skin.

It was only as the wolf that she - or rather we - felt truly happy and carefree. The wolf was not troubled by anything. She wasn't weighed down by worries or insecurities like her human half. When she had a *need*, she satisfied it. When she was thirsty, she drank. When she was hungry, she hunted prey...

The wolf slid to a stop coming out of a dead run. She whimpered, sniffing the ground as though trying to pick up a scent. She paced back and forth, whining to herself in frustration. *What was she searching for?* The wolf snarled in aggravation. *Why couldn't she remember? The human half of her would know!* The wolf stared up at the silvery ball and howled in protest. What was she searching for? An image flickered in the mind of the wolf. A small human boy... *Bobbybear!* The wolf threw back its head and lamented a mournful plea to the forest, to the night, to the stars and to the moon. *Find him!*

A rumbling in the pit of the beast's stomach distracted the

wolf from human thoughts. A cool breeze blew through the tall pines, causing their needles to dance and sing nature's song; a soothing whisper. The strong pungent smells of the forest drew the wolf deeper into the woods. Sniffing the night air, the wolf trotted aimlessly along. The far-off baying of another wolf calling to the moon caused her ears to perk. The answering call of yet another wolf farther off gave her renewed purpose, a sense of direction. The strength of the wolf's mind had pushed my conscious thought to the back, exerting her will over my own. Thoughts of Bobbybear faded into the night.

I awoke just before dawn, curled beneath the boughs of a tall, thick pine, to the sound of a gentle rain. I was naked, cold and dirty. Having no idea where I was, I peered around in the predawn light, hoping to spot something vaguely familiar. It was still quite dark. I saw nothing that I recognized. I exhaled dejectedly; my breath a billowing cloud in the chilly air. There was no telling how far the wolf had traveled.

I was in trouble and I knew it. I hadn't been prepared for my transformation into the wolf, so no precautions had been taken. Somewhere, in familiar territory, I had several stashes of clothing hidden in the nooks and crannies of trees and rocks, so that I wouldn't be forced to wander around in the nude. But since I had no idea where I was, they weren't going to do me much good. I needed a fire. At the very least, some form of shelter from the elements. Now I knew why Aunt Abigail had always insisted that she accompany me into the woods. She could keep a fire going and give me a definitive place to return to when the wolf grew weary. I only wished that were the case now.

But it wasn't.

I was completely lost in the woods, naked and afraid.

But I no longer thought that I was crazy. Grandmother had lied...

CHAPTER 22

THE HERMIT

Maybe it was thoughts of Aunt Abigail, or perhaps a product of my overactive imagination, but I swear that I could smell woodsmoke in the air. It gave me hope. It was a promise of salvation, but one that also frightened me. It meant that another human was nearby. I wasn't exactly dressed for the occasion.

But I had very little real choice in the matter. I desperately needed warmth before I caught my death of cold. If fortune was on my side, though it seemed now that it rarely was, I might be able to sneak up and steal something useful without getting caught. Caution was the key to success. I didn't really have any clue as to what I was going to find. Was it someone's cabin? A campsite? How many people were there? At least one, of that much I could be certain.

Then it dawned on me. I had needlessly been freezing to death when the solution was obvious. I closed my eyes, took a deep breath, and exhaled slowly. I *willed* the wolf into existence. The transformation went smoothly—perhaps because I had so recently been the wolf, but my body easily shifted back into the familiar form. I felt no pain, only an immediate sense of warmth. The thick coat of the wolf comforted me.

The wolf's senses were sharper than my own. She readily detected the location of the woodsmoke's source—the complete opposite direction that I had thought. I could feel the strong tug of the wolf as she fought to gain complete dominance, but I pushed back, resisting her attempt at total control. I couldn't allow the wolf to be in the driver's seat. Not now. There was no telling *what* she might do. It was one thing to kill an animal for food, quite another to kill a person.

After a brief tug-of-war for domination, the wolf relented, giving me full control. Head down, eyes wide with ears pricked up and alert, I moved stealthily through the trees, ready for danger. I stopped at the edge of the clearing where the cabin was centered. I raised my snout and sniffed the early morning air... *What was that smell?* The wolf didn't have a clue—but I certainly did! *Bacon!*

A low rumble sounded from the pit of the wolf's empty stomach. Obviously, she hadn't caught any prey last night; most likely due to the rain. She was hungry now. So was I. Our mutual hunger emboldened us. The wolf whined as she stepped out of the trees and approached the cabin. Still I had seen no physical sign of a human, but their presence was abundantly clear. The wolf detected no man scent.

That seemed peculiar.

The door to the cabin was wide open. I could hear movement inside but couldn't quite make out anything substantial. The cabin itself wasn't very large at all. It was about half the size of Aunt Abigail's cottage; one or two rooms, and probably didn't have a basement. A small porch with an overhang extended the entire length of the cabin's face. The two windows that I could see were presently shuttered. Sitting on the porch on either side of the doorway were two rocking chairs. A thick blanket lay over the back of one. If I could somehow manage to take it without being caught, it might be all I'd need to get back home.

As I drew closer, I heard a man's voice call out and I froze, one paw hovering above the porch. "Breakfast is about ready. I doubt you have any clothes, so that blanket is for you. I've got a fire going and the coffee is strong and hot. Come on inside when you're ready. I don't bite—not unless you give me a reason." I could hear his soft chuckle.

It took a moment for the wolf to determine that the man was talking to *me* and not somebody else. I stood there, not certain whether I should bolt or stay. I didn't sense any danger, so I opted for the latter. The smell of bacon and coffee was too much to resist. I was starving. As soon as I transformed, I felt the biting cold that hung in the early morning air. I quickly grabbed the blanket and wrapped it around my goosebump-covered body, hoping I hadn't left anything exposed for this stranger to see. The blanket was soft, warm and *heavy*. Just what I needed.

He smiled at me, as he stood framed by the doorway. He turned his body so that I could slip by him and inclined his head. "You should get to the fire."

At first, I couldn't move. I was rooted in place. I was sure that my jaw had hit the floor, bounced up, only to drop again. It was like looking at a much older version of my dad! He had the same crooked grin, the same sparkle lighting the same deep blue eyes.

"Come inside girl, before you catch your death of cold!" His voice was more demanding than it had been earlier.

Blinking out of my stupor, I nodded. I had to readjust the blanket that had slipped off my shoulder when I had been so surprised. *"Are you my grandfather?"* Blunt, and to the point. I saw no need in wasting time. Either he was, or he wasn't, but I had to know. Even my fuzzy brain thought it was important to know.

He turned and closed the cabin door, shutting out the cold. Almost immediately the room felt warmer. He moved to the stove and scooped up a generous helping of scrambled eggs. He placed a heap of bacon strips alongside. Then he buttered two slices of toast and placed them on the plate. "How do you take your coffee?"

I was having trouble keeping myself covered as I shoveled eggs off the plate and into my mouth. I was ravenous! The bacon was cooked perfectly; chewy, not too crisp. "Hot. Just a little sugar to..."

"Take the edge off," he finished for me and chuckled. "Just like your daddy."

I smiled.

He sat across from me at the tiny table and placed a cup of steaming coffee in front of me. He raised a cup to his lips and took a sip. "You're about the same size as your mother was the last time I saw her. I've got some of her old clothes in that footlocker yonder, maybe you can find something you like." He had indicated a huge chest sitting at the foot of the cabin's only bed with a nod.

He studied me for several more minutes as I continued to alternate between bites of food and sips of piping hot coffee. Finally, he sighed wearily. "I'm sorry about the loss of your parents."

I had a mouth full of food but I stopped chewing for a second. I could only wonder how he'd found out. This place of his was pretty isolated. I had seen the old beat up Chevy pickup parked just north of the cabin—it looked like the one that Brock drove the other day. I began chewing again as I thought it over. Brock said that he and Silas were picking up supplies for a friend. That must be how he knew. Either the guys had told him, or maybe he had ventured into town for supplies on his own and heard. It didn't really matter, I suppose. The end result was the same. He knew. I still found it rather surprising that something that occurred so far away in the city was a topic of conversation in The Hollows; but then again, maybe not so much. It *did* involve the residents of Wellington House—or at least members of their family.

He still hadn't answered my question. Though he had some resemblance to my father, that didn't automatically make him my grandfather. He could just bear some of the same features as my dad. He could be nothing more than an old friend who knew my parents very well.

I studied him with a critical eye. He had the exact same nose, the same color of blue eyes as my dad and brother and the same crooked grin. His hair was darker, almost black. Dad's was a good deal lighter, just like Bobbybear's. I swallowed. I placed my fork back onto the plate, refusing to eat another bite until I knew for sure. The wolf inside me was not happy with this decision; she was still *very* hungry. "Are you my grandfather, or some relative? A family friend? A distant cousin? What?"

He stared at me, seemingly reluctant to answer. I shoved my plate away in defiance. My stomach growled in protest. I stood. "Well I thank you for your hospitality and the warmth of your fire, but I think I should be going." I took a step toward the door. "I'll leave your blanket outside on the chair where I found it. I'd appreciate it if you'd wait until I'm gone before you come outside."

He quickly stood and blocked my path to the door. "You don't have to go. I don't get a lot of company out here." He scratched his stubbled chin and chuckled softly. "Guess I've kinda missed the company of a young girl." He indicated the chair I had deserted. "Please, finish your breakfast. I'll answer any questions you have."

I crossed my arms over my chest and eyed him with a raised brow. "Are you a perv or are you my grandfather?" I gave him a crooked smile. "It's a simple question. *Yes or no?*"

He sighed with a heavy droop of his shoulders. "Yes. I am your grandfather. Your daddy was my son."

I ran to him and embraced him as best I could without losing the blanket. "I knew it!"

To my surprise, he wrapped his powerful arms around me in a massive bear hug. He kissed the top of my head as he held me close. I could feel his breath as he sighed heavily before releasing me. "Your grandmother's name was Katherine. She liked to be called Katie. She absolutely adored your mother and would've done anything for her. The feeling was mutual. That's why your mom insisted on naming you after her. You would've liked her too, I think." I could hear the emotion in his voice.

"What happened to her?" I asked timidly. Mom and Dad hadn't talked of family, so I knew nothing, really.

He ran a hand over his face as he let out another deep breath. A haunted look remained in his eyes as though he recalled a painful memory that had been repressed for far too long. His eyes watered and he looked away, mumbling something about coffee.

Though I wanted to know more, I decided to let the matter drop. It was obviously still raw and painful for him. Besides, this was all in the past. Nothing could be done about any of it now. But *something* could still be done to help Bobbybear.

"I desperately need your help," I began, watching him with hopeful eyes. He took a sip of his coffee with raised brows, waiting for me to continue. I pressed on. "After my parents were killed, Grandmother Wellington sent Aunt Abby to bring both my brother and I to The Hollows. We've been living at Wellington House for the last several weeks. Now Bobby has just disappeared and Grandmother claims that he was *never* even here—it was *just* my imagination."

He studied me silently over the rim of his cup.

I shook my head. "She's even claiming that I'm in so much grief that I am making up everything about my brother. That no one else sees him, only me. She says that my mind is sick with so much grief that it's distorting reality. All of her servants are agreeing with her, but they're all lying. Bobbybear didn't die in the accident. He came to The Hollows with me. Aunt Abby and my friend Millie Bradford have both seen him."

He raised his coffee cup in the air. "Well there you go."

I shook my head. "Something's going on. I went to Aunt Abby's cottage but she wasn't there. That's strange. She should've been there. She was fixing my talisman. She's gone now too." I could feel the tears well up into my eyes. I was beginning to feel distraught. "Everyone keeps disappearing on me."

I put a hand to my lips, but it was shaking so bad that I thrust it down against my thigh, holding it in a tight fist. "Grandmother wanted to inject me with *something*, I don't know what it was. But I'm afraid if I let them give me anything I'll *never* see Bobby again."

His eyes narrowed thoughtfully. "I'm sure Abby's all right. She can take care of herself. What about your friend? What has she to say?"

"Millie's in town. At least I hope she is. I haven't seen her since Harrison Beckett drove her back." I quickly covered my mouth with trembling fingers as a horrifying thought struck me. "Oh my God! We need to check on her! Harrison Beckett may have tried to make her disappear too!"

He waved his cup toward the footlocker at the end of the bed. "See if you can find anything in there that fits. We'll go into town and check on your friend."

When I opened the footlocker I almost completely lost control of my emotions. Even after all the years that had gone by, the clothes *still* smelled like my mom and dad. Going through these forgotten belongings of theirs was going to be harder than I had initially thought. I wiped tears from my eyes as I sorted through their things. "So, what should I call you?" I asked, my voice sounded husky.

He had his back to me as he cleared the table and started cleaning the dishes form our breakfast. "What would you like to call me?"

I inhaled the fragrance of my mother from an old pullover

sweater I'd uncovered and smiled. I sat it aside and continued to rummage through the trunk. "How about grandpa?"

I could hear the smile in his voice. "I like the sound of grandpa."

An image of a man standing in the pouring rain over the graves of my parents flashed through my mind. I glanced back at him and bit at my bottom lip. "It was you, wasn't it?"

Turning to face me he frowned, his brows furrowing in confusion. "I'm sorry?"

"The day my parents were buried. It was you I saw standing over their graves as we were leaving."

He nodded. "I was there."

"Why didn't you join us at the service? Bobbybear would have loved to have met you, so would I."

He chuckled softly. "That may be so, but I was not welcome. Your Grandmother and I don't exactly get along. It would've caused far much more trouble than any of you needed at that point. I was content to pay my respects after you all had gone."

I studied him a moment longer, wondering if there was any way to repair this rift between the two families.

"I'll let you get dressed," he said as he headed outside, closing the door behind him.

CHAPTER 23
DISTURBING NEWS

Having ridden in the Chevy before, I knew it would start right up. "So, you know some other friends of mine," I said. He seemed surprised by this news. "Brock Jacobins and Silas Monaghan. They were in town the other day getting some supplies for you. They used your truck."

He nodded. "Yep. Those are two really good guys there. Do you know Tucker and Cho as well?"

I smiled. "Yes, I've met them a couple of times."

Grandpa grinned. "They're all a great bunch of guys. I let them use the truck every now and then. They, in turn, pick up my supplies so that I don't have to go into town." He glanced over at me. "I prefer to stay out of The Hollows as much as possible. Your grandmother keeps a tight rein over that small town. I try to keep under her radar."

In no time at all we were leaving his cabin behind and heading through the thick forest. The road we were following was very rough. We hit several ruts in the dirt track that sent me bouncing around the seat. There were no seat belts in the truck, so I took to keeping one hand on the dash in a vain attempt to stay put. It was easy to see that this road got little use and even fewer repairs. Grandpa looked at me and grinned. "This is the road less traveled in case you were wondering."

I chuckled. I had been thinking almost the *exact* same thing. I could feel my eyes grow wide as I fearfully held on as best I could. We were going faster than I had imagined the truck was capable of, and far faster than I thought we should be traveling, especially given the rough terrain. Grandpa obviously knew what he was doing. Years of traversing through these woods had honed his skills. He was pushing the pickup to its limits.

He must have noticed my discomfort, either that or my sharp intake of breath as we made a harrowing turn through some rather large rocks and thick clumps of trees. He chuckled. "Just trying to shave off as much time as I can. I never liked Harrison Beckett. Always thought he was a snake."

I gave him a worried look. "Do you think he'd do any actual harm to Millie? Is she in any danger?"

He kept his eyes on the disappearing path that we were using as a road. His brows rose high on his forehead. "Ain't no tellin' what that scumbag will do." There was something in the way he said it that frightened me.

"Aunt Abby says that he's a weasel," I offered.

Grandpa chuckled; his eyes seemed to sparkle as he glanced quickly at me. "Always did think Abby had a pretty good head on her shoulders. She and your momma were the only Wellingtons I ever cared for. Their mother is a hard woman. I never liked her, but I did always respect her." He shook his head. "I'd *never* turn my back on her, that's for sure. If she'd turn on her own children, then the rest of us should take heed."

"You sound almost as though you admire her." I was flabbergasted.

He glanced over at me with hardened eyes. "I wouldn't say it quite that way." He paused. "Look. Elizabeth Wellington is a powerful woman—especially by The Hollows' standards. She'd be a tough cookie *anywhere*. The life she's had to live has hardened her. All I'm trying to convey is that if we're going to go up against her, we'd best be ready for a fight. She'll play hardball and she won't care that you're her granddaughter. You cross her, she'll be out to crush you."

What choice did I have? I felt certain that she knew what happened to Bobbybear. She may have even been instrumental in his disappearance. But she had tried to make me believe that he had died along with my parents, and that I had come to The Hollows alone. *But why? What possible motive could she have? Would Aunt Abigail stand with me?* I knew she adored Bobby, but could she go against her own mother?

"So, what is the plan?" I asked.

"First we find your friend and make certain she's safe. Then we see if we can locate Abby. Either of them can corroborate your story. The more we have telling our side of things, the better. Like I said, Elizabeth Wellington is a *very* powerful woman. She can pressure most everybody in The Hollows in one way or another. The police are all in her pocket, so we can't go to them. Our best bet is to find Bobby on our own."

"I've searched Wellington House, and there's absolutely no trace left of him. They certainly worked swiftly to make him vanish." I could feel the lump catch in my throat. I was afraid. But at least I wasn't alone anymore. "What if we can't find him?" Tears rolled down my cheeks. I wiped them away with my fingertips.

"We'll find him," he said confidently.

"What makes you so sure?" I asked softly.

He offered me that crooked smile. "Oh, I have my ways."

We continued to drive along the twisting lane that served as our road, lapsing into silence. Each of us lost in our own thoughts. If both my parents were werewolves, but no one else on my mom's side of the family were, then it could only mean one of two things. Either Grandpa was also a werewolf, or Dad and Mom were the first in the line. I *needed* to know... *Would he tell me the truth?* I glanced at him, studying him intently. *Why else would he live in solitude, away from others? Was he protecting them from himself when the moon beckoned? Or was he grieving the loss of his wife still? How had she died?* I had *so* many questions; I figured it was time that I got some answers.

"Grandpa?" I asked softly. I was almost afraid to question him further; but I had to. Not knowing was starting to drive me absolutely crazy! He kept his eyes on the weaving trail that intertwined through clumps of pine and aspen. *Jump in, Kat! The water's fine! Just do it!* I swallowed. "Are you a werewolf too?"

He glanced quickly at me and then returned his attention to navigating the Chevy through the forest. With one last shudder, the pickup left the rugged path behind and turned right onto smooth blacktop. We were heading toward The Hollows on an actual road! He nodded. "I am a wolf. The guys you met in the woods are members of my Wolf Pack." He eyed me for a moment. "We look out for one another like a family." He turned his eyes back to the road. "Guess you're part of that family now too."

I couldn't keep the smile from coming to my lips. It felt absolutely wonderful having a sense of belonging! "Cool!" I said.

We pulled up to the curb in front of the library and I slid out of the truck as swiftly as I could. The old Chevy may have been one of Grandpa's prized possessions but I didn't care for it. The body was dented and badly rusted. On our wild ride through the woods I had felt that it would literally shake apart. In my mind it was a death-trap on four wheels. I didn't relish the thought of having to get back in.

To my surprise the door to the library was locked. It was supposed to be opened up at nine o'clock; it was almost half past now. I looked up at Grandpa with worried eyes. "She's not here."

"We can swing by her house, if you know where it is," he suggested.

"I was just there the other day, I'm pretty sure I can remember where it is."

"*Kat!*" Millie's voice called to me from across the street. Turning, I saw her running towards us with a newspaper clutched tightly against her chest. She had a huge smile of relief etched across her reddened face. "I've been so worried about you! That Harrison Beckett gave me the creeps!"

"Did he do anything?" I asked, touching her arm.

She shoved her glasses up her nose and looked nervously at my grandpa. "Hi," she said with a nervous wave.

"Grandpa, this is my best friend, Millie Bradford." I gave her an encouraging smile. "Millie, my Grandpa St. Claire."

"Did he hurt you at all?" asked my grandpa. He touched her arm giving her a quick once-over.

Millie quickly shook her head, causing her glasses to slip again. As she shoved them back into place she said, "No. But he kept offering to take me home. I told him he could just drop me off here, but he wouldn't have it. I tried to explain that I needed to pick up some groceries first, and he finally relented. When I went into the store, he waited out front. Said he insisted on giving me a lift, it'd only be proper. I slipped out the back, and when he went in to check on me, I ran to the library. I could hear him banging on the door. He even tried the back door." She squeezed my arm. "I've *never* been so scared."

"You're safe now." I tried to sound reassuring and upbeat. It wasn't easy.

"I actually spent all night in the library. I was afraid to go home. I was afraid that he'd follow me. When the diner opened up this morning, I made a dash for it. I was absolutely starving!"

She gave me a serious look. "I found something about Bobby. It's the craziest thing though. I don't know how we missed it the other day."

"What did you find?" I asked. I wasn't sure what she had discovered, but I was greatly relieved that she remembered Bobbybear. I glanced at Grandpa and he offered me a reassuring wink of his eye.

She waved the newspaper in the air. "An article in *The Hollows Gazette* dated April 15, 1884."

"Wait! *What?* And this concerns Bobby *how*, exactly?"

"We shouldn't discuss this out here on the street." Grandpa said, looking around suspiciously.

"We can go in the library." Millie offered fishing out her keys. I looked at Grandpa and he nodded his approval. Anything was better than standing on the curb.

After we had gotten inside, Grandpa locked the door. Millie turned on the lights and then laid the newspaper onto an inclined table where we could all see it easily. When I saw the front-page headline of the *Gazette*, I knew I had seen it before

LOCAL GIRL FOUND DEAD, MAULED.

It was the article that Millie and I had found when we were first researching Sara Robinson.

"I've seen this before." I said.

Millie nodded. "Wait." She turned the page where I knew the black and white picture of Sara was located with the rest of the front-page article. I gasped sharply. The picture had somehow *changed*. Now, standing beside Sara was a boy. I couldn't believe my eyes. The boy in the picture was Bobbybear!

I quickly scanned the news article. It stated the facts with mind-numbing clarity. Sara Robinson, niece of former New York Governor Lucius Robinson, and a young friend identified as Robert St. Claire, disappeared from the grounds of the estate late Sunday afternoon. Both bodies were found late Monday afternoon deep in the surrounding woods, apparently mauled and badly disfigured by wild animals. Wolves suspected.

I took a faltering step backward. I felt cold and lightheaded. I seriously thought I was either going to faint or puke. There was a strong possibility that I'd do both. My legs felt rubbery. I felt Grandpa's hand supporting my back, with the other he guided me to a chair that Millie pulled out. The news of Bobbybear's gruesome death had been very devastating. I was horrified that he had gone back in time and been killed. I could no longer stand and I fell to my knees overcome with my grief.

Millie darted away, returning with a paper cup of cold water. "Here, sip this," she said softly.

I noticed that Grandpa was staring at the article with a haunted look. It was the first time that he'd seen his grandson; it was obviously hard for him too.

CHAPTER 24
REUNION AT THE CABIN
IN THE WOODS

I had wanted to return to Wellington House but Grandpa didn't think it was such a good idea. Unfortunately for me Millie agreed with him. Millie had called her Grammy from the diner and told her she was going to spend some time with her new friend—she was still afraid that Harrison Beckett would discover where she lived. I didn't say anything, because I didn't want to add to her worries; but how *big* did she think The Hollows was? If Beckett truly wanted to find out where her home was, it wouldn't be that difficult of a task even for someone like him—especially if Grandmother controlled all the real power in the town.

The plan was to return to my grandpa's cabin. Once we were safe and secure there, Grandpa would pay a little visit to my Aunt Abigail's cottage. She was the local Healer so it would be easy enough not to arouse too much suspicion if he showed up there. That was the only plan we had come up with. I seriously had my doubts about its chances for success, but once again I was outnumbered. If he found Aunt Abby, he would bring her back here, and then the four of us would decide on a plan of action moving forward.

They seemed to be underestimating Harrison Beckett; or at the very least, my grandmother. She was the one that was telling him what to do and when to do it. He seemed incapable of grand schemes all on his own. Or was I underestimating him too? Could it be that he actually controlled my grandmother, manipulating her to do *his* bidding? I hated thinking that she would simply use Bobby for her own personal gain. He was so sweet, so innocent. He deserved better. I didn't like *anyone* messing with my kid brother! It didn't matter to me who they were.

As Grandpa was preparing to leave the cabin I took him aside. I didn't want Millie to overhear what I had to say. "You really need to be back here before nightfall. I cannot be alone here with Millie when the moon begins to rise. I don't have my talisman and the pull of the wolf has been too strong for me to ignore lately. I don't want to hurt my friend."

He squeezed my arm reassuringly. "I should be back in plenty of time Kat. But if for some reason I'm not, you need to get out and have Millie lock up behind you. Don't wait, get out and get away. If the wolf catches your friend's scent—especially if she is afraid—and you can't control the wolf, it could go badly."

"I know!" I said. "That's *exactly* what I'm trying to tell you."

"You will need to get as far away from the cabin as you possibly can, so give yourself plenty of time." He squeezed my arm again and smiled. "But I will do my best to bring your Aunt Abigail and your talisman as quickly as I am able."

I threw my arms around his shoulders and hugged him tightly. "Please be careful. I don't want anything to happen to you. I just found you and I really want to get to know you better. I have *so* many questions."

Grandpa smiled that crooked smile of his and offered me a quick nod and a wink of his eye. "There'll be plenty of time for that, I promise. First things first, we need to get your brother back."

I stood at the door with Millie beside me, watching my grandpa navigate the old Chevy along the dirt road that twisted through the tall gnarly pines. With the thick shrubs that hugged the narrow road tightly he quickly disappeared from sight, leaving only the squeak of the chassis and the fading rumble of the engine behind, along with the settling dust that the truck had stirred up.

I sighed heavily, deciding it best to confront my fears head-on. I gave Millie a steady look. "You may not be any safer here than you were in town." I could see her eyes slowly wander to my neck; she understood my meaning. Completely.

She swallowed. "We'll cross that bridge when we come to it." She moved to the table and sat on one of the chairs. She held her head in her hands as she plopped her elbows onto the scarred tabletop. I could hear her sigh heavily as I closed the cabin door.

I sat across from her and traced a long scar in the wood with my fingertip. "I don't get it. *How* did Bobbybear wind up in the past? If that was really my brother who was killed along with Sara, *how* did he get there? Time travel just *isn't* possible! According to that article Bobby died almost two hundred years ago!"

Millie shoved her glasses up her nose. She shrugged. "Unless you know someone that's built a Time Machine lately, it would have to be magic of some kind. *Powerful magic!*" I could see her eyes grow narrow as she studied me. "Know any *witches*?"

I knew of only one. Maybe two.

I swallowed the lump in my throat. I found it difficult to believe that Aunt Abigail could do such a thing. She seemed so fond of Bobbybear. I shook my head refusing to believe that she had betrayed us. "There has to be somebody else. Aunt Abby would never put my brother in jeopardy. And she certainly wouldn't allow him to be mauled by wild animals! There simply has to be a better explanation—or another witch that we don't know about."

Millie's cheeks turned a bright ruby-red. "I'm sure you're right. Maybe your grandmother is the witch. Witchcraft tends to run in the family." She looked at me hopefully. She shrugged and looked down at the table, her glasses visibly slid down her nose.

"You really need to get those fixed."

"Sorry." She pushed them back into place and smiled sheepishly. "That costs money and I'm kinda on a tight budget. My job doesn't pay very well. I used to be real fidgety. This gives me something to do with my hands." She studied her fingernails for a moment. They were painted black. "I used to bite my nails. I don't do that anymore." She had a rather pleased look on her face.

It was clearly evident that not biting her nails had been a struggle for Millie. But she had overcome temptation in the end.

I was proud of my friend. I had never chewed my own fingernails but I had known several people that did. It wasn't pretty.

Millie drummed her fingers on the table. "The only witch that I know of in The Hollows for a certainty, is your Aunt Abigail. If she didn't send your brother back in time, then there *has* to be another. Maybe someone your grandmother knows. Maybe even someone that lives in Wellington House."

"It has to be grandmother!" I said. I remember Aunt Abby saying that she was a powerful witch, a *Priestess*, whatever that meant. And it certainly seemed to fit. It *had* to be her. Why else would she fabricate such a story about Bobbybear dying in the car accident that killed my parents? But I *still* didn't understand what she had to gain with Bobby's death.

I slapped my hands upon the tabletop, startling Millie, causing her to jump. "You're the resident expert in all things mystical. What would be needed to transport someone back into the past to 1884?"

Millie shoved her glasses up her nose. "Well... I don't know of any spells that might be able to do it—but then again, I'm not a witch."

I shook my head. "Say it wasn't a magic spell. What would be needed?" I asked. I had a hunch it *wasn't* an enchantment, but something else. But I didn't know what that could be.

"Well," Millie frowned, "you'd have to have something from the past that's present now—something tangible."

I stiffened. "Like a toy?" I was thinking of the wooden soldier that I had first seen in the portrait of Sara Robinson—the toy that Bobby had at the dinner table.

Millie nodded. "I suppose that a toy would work."

I leaned forward, touching her arm with heightening interest. "What else?" My mouth felt incredibly dry. We were onto something I just knew it!

She rolled her eyes up toward the ceiling, as she seemed to mull it over. She started biting her upper lip. She shook her head and frowned. "There would *have* to be some way to pass from one dimension to another."

"What do you mean? Like through a doorway?"

Millie nodded. A small smile curved the corners of her mouth. "Like a doorway." She tapped the table repeatedly. "I'm fairly certain that it would have to be somewhere close to the portrait in the storage room."

"What about the entrance to the storage room? That doorway?" I asked excitedly. "Couldn't that be it?"

She shook her head. "Doubtfully. We would've noticed something *off* about it."

I squeezed her arm. "Sometimes that door seems locked, but then it'll open up without a key. Don't you think that's odd? It certainly seems to fit the bill to me."

Millie chuckled softly. "That's not *quite* what I had in mind."

I crossed my arms over my chest and glared at her. "Well *excuse* me!" I smiled.

She reached out and touched my sleeve. "I'm sorry. I just don't think that's the door we're looking for. It wouldn't be a door so commonly used. That would make potential *crossovers* more frequent. I really think that when we find the right door, we'll know it." She tapped her lips with her finger as a thought came to her. "Of course, the doorway doesn't actually have to *be* a door..."

I looked at her, puzzled. "What do you mean?"

She shrugged. "Well, I guess it could be a window." Her eyes went wide. "I've even heard of full-length mirrors being used. People step through them like stepping through water."

I frowned. "Like a *Stargate*?"

She obviously had never watched the show. "A *what*?" I wasn't even certain she had a TV—I hadn't seen any since I had gotten to The Hollows.

"Never mind. It isn't all that important."

I studied her thoughtfully. "So, are you suggesting that we go back to Wellington House and search for it?"

Millie's eyes grew wide and fear-filled. She swallowed with some difficulty. She gave me a timid smile. "Well..." she began slowly, "...if we're going to get Bobby back, we'll *need* that doorway."

I nodded silently as I absent-mindedly bit at my bottom lip. What Millie was saying made sense. Problem was, we didn't have time to get to Wellington House before nightfall—not without a truck. Without my talisman to keep the wolf in check, Millie would *never* stand a chance in the woods. Though I would never do anything to harm my friend, I couldn't be certain *what* the wolf would do. I wasn't confident in my ability to keep control of the wolf. Her will seemed stronger than mine lately. The day was growing short. If Grandpa didn't return with Aunt Abby's talisman soon, I was going to have to leave the cabin and get as far away as I possibly could. And then I'd have to hope that would be enough to save my friend.

My skin was starting to itch. I could feel the slow burn of the blood in my veins growing stronger; more insistent. It wouldn't be long now. Millie and I had spent the day formulating a plan for tomorrow, but there was nothing we could do about it now. I stood up and massaged my arms in a vain attempt to soothe the prickling sensations that were beginning to drive me crazy. I could see by the look that Millie gave me that she sensed something was going on with me. I walked to the door. "I've got to get out of here!"

She stood abruptly. "Are we going?"

I shook my head. My teeth were beginning to ache. I swear I could already feel them growing sharper. "I'm leaving. You need to stay inside and bolt the door. Don't go outside no matter what you hear."

Millie took a step toward me but stopped. She made a brave attempt at swallowing her fear but I could tell that it wasn't working. Seeing me transform on video was one thing; seeing it first-hand was going to be quite another. It was something that neither of us was ready for.

We were both startled out of our darkening thoughts by the blaring sound of the old Chevy's horn as the battered pickup rumbled closer. We stepped out onto the small porch as the truck braked in front of the cabin sending up a cloud of dust. I was surprised to see Aunt Abby behind the wheel. She had a frenzied expression on her face as she rushed to roll the window down.

"Your grandfather has been shot!" she exclaimed as she abandoned her efforts with the window and opened the door. "He's lost a lot of blood! We need to get him inside and get the bullet out before we lose him."

CHAPTER 25

THE SILVER BULLET

Between the three of us we managed to get my grandpa out of the truck and into the cabin. Aunt Abby insisted that we get him onto the table. "We need to get the bullet out," she said.

"Why didn't you just take him to the hospital?" I asked. Certainly they were far better suited to handle a gunshot wound than we were. And he had lost *a lot* of blood. All the color had gone from his face. He looked ashen.

She gave me a steady look. "Your grandpa is not like most men. He, like you, is a Lycan. It would be far too dangerous for him to go to a regular hospital, even if one were readily available. You forget where you are."

Millie shoved her glasses up her nose. They had come close to slipping off completely. "If he's a Lycanthrope won't he heal quickly?" She looked from my aunt to me, and then back again. "Isn't that like one of their things?"

Aunt Abby shook her head. "I think he was shot with a silver bullet." She glanced at me meaningfully. "Poisonous for Lycans."

I took a step back and blinked. So, the stories told in those old werewolf movies were true. A silver bullet could *kill* a werewolf!

Aunt Abigail looked at Millie. "I need my bag. It's on the floorboard of the pickup, passenger side."

Millie quickly nodded and left. Aunt Abby turned toward me. She reached into the pocket of her blouse and withdrew my talisman. "You won't be much good to me without this. I suggest you put it on quickly, you're already starting to turn."

It was true. My entire body was hurting. And I could see the tiny hairs on my arm begin to darken and grow thicker. Hopefully the restored magic on the amulet would reverse the lycanthropic transformation that was occurring. I put the necklace around my neck. It immediately felt good to have the talisman back where it belonged. The aches in my bones were already beginning to dull.

Millie returned and handed the doctor's bag to my aunt. She smiled at me. "You're looking better!"

I smiled and fondled the talisman. "Thanks to this." I looked at Aunt Abigail and frowned. "Why hasn't he started to transform? He's a Lycan. Is it going to be safe for the two of you to be here?"

Aunt Abby lifted my grandpa's arm. On his right wrist was a thick bracelet with ornate script carved into its smooth surface. "I made this for him years ago. I'm happy to see he still wears it. It works like your talisman."

"Is it silver?"

She shook her head. "Oh no. Stainless steel. Lycans can't wear *anything* silver." She spoke as she withdrew a pair of scissors from the bag and began to cut away his blood-soaked shirt. "Silver would cause an uncomfortable rash to spread on the skin. If left for too long, it would begin to fester. Like I said before, silver is toxic to Lycans. Just touching it isn't deadly, but it can cause discomfort, and make you quite ill with prolonged exposure."

"So," I said with a nod toward my grandpa, "you've done this kind of thing before?"

She nodded as she pulled a long pair of tweezers from the bag and bent over the hole in my grandpa's shoulder. "I told you that I'm a Healer. There are those in The Hollows that do not feel comfortable seeing a medical professional. They ask too many difficult questions."

"I meant extracting bullets."

She half shrugged. "Buckshot mostly. Bear traps are most common. But I treat a wide variety of ailments as well." She glanced up at Millie. "I need more light. See if you can find a flashlight or something."

Millie found a flashlight in a kitchen drawer by the oven. Its batteries were low and the thing barely worked, but it was still better than nothing. The bullet, gleaming bright silver in a sea of dark red, was lodged in the scapula. It was all Millie and I could do to hold Grandpa down and attempt to keep him from moving while Aunt Abby worked the bullet free. The entire ordeal lasted well over half an hour.

When at last Aunt Abby pulled the bullet from the wound my grandpa visibly relaxed. A small smile twisted the corner of his mouth. "About time you got that damned thing out!" he whispered hoarsely. He hadn't been unconscious as I had thought—he'd been awake the entire time!

Aunt Abby chuckled softly as she leaned down and kissed his cheek. I could see the glint of tears in her eyes. "I was afraid that I was gonna lose you."

He chuckled, and then winced in pain. "I'm tougher than I look."

"I've still got some work to do on your shoulder." She ran her hand through the hairs on his chest. "Can I get you anything?"

He nodded despite the pain it caused. "Whiskey."

A smile softened the tension that had been etched on her face as she moved from the table and opened a cupboard. Her familiarity with my grandpa's cabin was the last piece of the puzzle to fall into place. It was now *totally* obvious. The two of them were in love. When she turned from the cupboard her eyes met mine. I smiled and gave a brief nod of acceptance. I was glad that they had one another.

After Aunt Abby had carefully stitched the wound closed, she then wrapped his shoulder with gauze. Through it all, my grandpa kept his silence. *He was watching me as I continued to stare at him.* His good shoulder—if you could call it that—was badly scarred. It looked like some animal had tried to rip it off; but not recently. I met his gaze and he smiled. Flexing the shoulder that had caught my attention. "Battle scars," he said with a crooked grin.

I smiled, my thoughts beginning to wander. Battle scars. I could only wonder what scars I might pick up in the battle to come. For I *knew* that I was going to have to fight in order to save Bobbybear. It was inevitable. Lines had been drawn in the forests that surrounded The Hollows. I was determined to save my brother regardless of what it might cost me personally. *He needed me to save him.* I vowed not to let him down.

Next, the three of us helped to ease Grandpa off the table and take him to the bed where he could be more comfortable. Aunt Abby stretched out beside him, gingerly placing her hand on his chest. She was exhausted. She had every right to be. She had fought hard to save his life. How she had managed to get him into the cab of the pickup truck on her own was beyond me. Yet she had done it. She had brought him here, performed surgery, and saved his life. She was amazing!

I smiled at the two of them. "Millie and I will take care of cleaning up. You two get some rest." Aunt Abigail nodded and nestled against my grandpa careful not to disturb his slumber. Man could he fall asleep fast! Of course, the whiskey and blood loss had definitely helped to that end.

After Millie and I cleaned up the makeshift operating room we stepped outside for some fresh air. It was starting to get dark. The shadows of the forest were growing deeper. Soon the sun would be gone completely and the moon would be on the rise. I no longer felt the urge to transform; the talisman seemed to be working perfectly; better than before.

Millie leaned against the porch post crossing her arms over her chest. She sighed heavily and slowly shook her head. "I have never seen so much blood. *Never!*"

"I know, right?" We were both tired. It had been a long and taxing day. Tomorrow promised to be another. "You did great though!" I said giving her a big hug.

She grinned. "So did you." She shoved her glasses up her nose. "Who do you think shot your grandpa?" Millie asked softly.

I shrugged. "Who knows?"

Millie looked up at the evening sky as she rubbed her upper arms for warmth. As the sun had set, the temperatures had dropped along with it. It was now quite cool. A few stars were beginning to sparkle in the deepening sea of blue and black. "Do you think we'll be in danger when we return to Wellington House?"

I studied the heavens for a minute or two before turning to

face her. Deciding that honesty was the best policy, I said, "It's a definite possibility."

She looked out at the forest now almost completely cloaked in darkness and simply nodded. I was touched by how very near tears Millie seemed to be. She wouldn't face me. To do so would be to give in to her growing unease. She would totally lose it. Knowing this, I said nothing. I just stood beside my friend, quietly waiting.

When she spoke, she had managed to regain her composure. "I just want you to know that I'm willing to do all I can for you." She turned and faced me head on. "Whatever it takes to get Bobby back, I'll do. I've never had a friend like you. The whole *werewolf* thing aside." Millie cocked her head to the side and gave me a quirky smile. "No one has *ever* gotten me like you do! No one has ever accepted me for me!" Tears started streaming down her cheeks. "You are simply the best friend I'll *ever* have!"

I wrapped my arms around her and hugged her close. "We're more than friends, Millie. We're sisters! We're family!"

She chuckled. "What a family! Do you realize, that if your aunt and your grandpa were to get married, your aunt would become your grandma?"

I laughed. "And Grandpa would become my uncle!"

She giggled. "How *crazy* is that?!"

I sighed after a moment. "I haven't told you about the stunt that Grandmother was trying to pull, have I?"

Millie shook her head. She looked at me with patient curiosity.

"She was trying to convince me that Bobbybear had never even come to The Hollows. She wanted me to believe that he had died in the accident that killed my parents. That his being here had all been a manifestation of my grieving, sick mind."

She gave me a quick shove, her jaw dropping. *"Shut up!"*

I could feel the bitter tears starting to form up in my eyes. I shook my head. "Can you believe that?"

"How was she planning to pull that off? You weren't the only one to see Bobbybear! I saw him, and so did your aunt. What was she going to do about that?" She gasped sharply before I could even respond. "You don't think that she would try to get us both out of the picture do you?"

I shrugged. "How else could she hope to convince everyone?

She would have to make both you and Aunt Abby disappear like she had made Bobbybear."

"But you're talking about her own daughter! Is she *really* that cold and heartless?"

She wrapped her arms around me and we sobbed in our mutual embrace for who knows how long. The night was growing colder as crickets began to chirp, calling out to one another. The silvery ball of the moon shown bright through the tall pines; in the far-off distance a wolf howled a mournful plea to the night.

Aunt Abigail opened the cabin door softly. She smiled at us. "I've put some blankets on the floor for you girls. You need to come inside and try to get some rest."

CHAPTER 26
TWO GIRLS AND A CHEVY

I awoke to the smell of coffee brewing and bacon that had been fried in a cast-iron skillet. I thought I was dreaming. The dull ache in my lower back due to sleeping on the hard cabin floor brought me back to reality. To my surprise—and to Millie's as well—Grandpa was up and sitting at the kitchen table. His left arm was in a sling, but he otherwise looked perfectly normal. Color had returned to his face. He *must* be feeling a lot better; he was watching my aunt's backside wiggle as she went about scrambling eggs. Millie and I exchanged knowing glances. Were *all* men the same?

I walked up to Grandpa and kissed his cheek. "How's the shoulder?"

He smiled, his eyes twinkling brightly. "Still a bit sore, but certainly a lot better than it was yesterday."

"I'm amazed at just how fast you seem to have recovered," Millie said with a shake of her head.

He chuckled. "Good genes, I guess."

I noticed that he wasn't wearing the stainless talisman on his wrist. I nodded thoughtfully. "He transformed last night while we slept." It was the only thing that made sense. He couldn't heal so completely, so quickly, in human form. He needed the strength and endurance of the wolf to rejuvenate his body. And he would need to feed to regain his strength and replace all of the blood he'd lost. "I'm surprised we didn't hear you leave the cabin." I said.

Aunt Abby chuckled softly. "You girls were *out*! You didn't even hear—" She stopped and shook her head, blushing slightly.

"Eew!" I said. "Too much information!"

Millie's jaw dropped. *"No way!"*

Aunt Abby dumped the scrambled eggs into a bowl. Grabbing the plate of bacon strips, she placed them on the table. She smiled as she took a strip of bacon and bit it in half. "Breakfast is ready."

I toyed with the eggs on my plate, not really hungry at all. Probably nerves. I knew I should be starving. Aunt Abby didn't miss anything. She tapped my leg with her foot. "What's on your mind kiddo?" She took a bite of toast and studied me expectantly, waiting for me to respond.

I sat my fork down with a soft clink and then placed my hands on either side of my plate. I frowned and then slowly met her gaze. I wasn't entirely certain that I wanted to hear her answer. "Tell me you remember my brother."

She stretched her arms across the table and gave my hands a reassuring squeeze. "I don't know what your grandmother is up to, but we won't let her get away with it. Of course I remember Bobbybear! We'll get him back, I promise!"

Grandpa took a sip of his coffee. "We just need to figure out how."

I glanced from Aunt Abigail to Grandpa and studied his face before I responded. "Millie and I believe we know *how* Bobbybear got sent to the past. We believe that some kind of *portal* was used. Maybe a doorway located somewhere in Wellington House. We just have to go back and find it. Then we can cross over and get Bobbybear and bring him back."

Grandpa shook his head vehemently. "Absolutely not!"

My jaw dropped. I hadn't expected this. "It's the *only* way!"

He stood up from his chair so fast that he knocked it over. "It isn't safe for anyone to go back to Wellington House. Not anymore. Not after yesterday."

"But…" I stammered.

He banged the flat of his hand down upon the table. "I said *no!*" He stormed outside slamming the cabin door behind him in his haste.

Tears forming in my eyes, I shook my head and stared at Aunt Abigail. She sighed. "It just isn't safe to go there," she said.

"We *have* to. *I have* to!" I said.

"Kat, Harrison Beckett shot your grandpa. He almost killed him. Beckett was coming for me, if it hadn't been for Sam I might've been killed. If my own mother sent him after me do you truly believe that she'll think twice about harming either of you? It is just too dangerous for us to risk. Surely you can see that?"

She glanced at Millie. "There *has* to be another way. We'll find it, I'm sure." She stood silently and picked up the chair that had toppled over. "I'm gonna go talk to Sam. He isn't completely healed, he needs rest."

Once she had left the cabin, Millie grabbed another slice of bacon and broke it in half, she took a bite and said, "So, what do you think?"

I wiped the tears from my eyes and shook my head. "I don't know. They act like we have all the time in the world. Do *you* think there's another way to save Bobby? Something that we haven't considered?"

She shoved the last of the bacon strip in her mouth and licked her fingertips. She mulled it over briefly as she chewed absently. "Not without finding the *window* to the past."

"You think it's a window now?"

She laughed. "A door, a window, a set of stairs, a closet, even behind a curtain. It could be *anything*! But I'm *positive* it's up there in that storage space."

"We just have to find it," I said.

Millie groaned as she took a bite of toast. "We're going to Wellington House to search for it, aren't we?"

I nodded. "You don't have to go if you're afraid of getting hurt. Believe me, I completely understand. *Completely!*"

She looked around for something else to eat. "Yes I do! You may not know the *portal* when you see it, but I'm fairly sure that I will. I just hope we don't get killed searching for it. And just so that there's no mistaking it, I *am* afraid of getting hurt!" She gave me a hard stare after shoving her glasses back up her nose. "Any sane person would be."

"Yeah," I laughed. "Know where we can find any of those?"

She couldn't help but smile. "Not here in The Hollows."

We set about clearing away the breakfast from the table. I washed the dishes and Millie dried them and put them away. It took a while for us to find where everything went, but in the end we were pretty satisfied with the job that we'd done.

As luck would have it, Aunt Abigail and Grandpa had wandered away from the cabin. They weren't anywhere nearby—at least if they were, they were being awfully quiet. Chances were, that in the state of anger that Grandpa had been in when he left, he could have gone quite far from the cabin. Given everything that had occurred in the last twenty-four hours it might take a while to calm him down once she managed to catch up to him.

It gave Millie and I time to make our getaway. How much time we had been afforded was uncertain but any at all was better than nothing. Aunt Abigail and Grandpa had made it quite clear that they were against returning to Wellington House. I didn't share their beliefs. To me, it was the *only* viable option that we had in getting Bobby back.

We were too far from Wellington House to walk. We were going to have to take the truck. It was going to make *a lot* of noise. Aunt Abby and Grandpa were sure to hear the roar of the engine. But it couldn't be helped. What choice did we have? Only two problems stood in our way; one, neither of us could drive and two, the old Chevy was a manual transmission, which only made matters worse.

When Aunt Abigail had delivered my badly wounded grandpa to the cabin he had been at Death's door. The *last* thing she was thinking about was removing the keys from the truck's ignition. She had shut the vehicle off—which was a good thing. It had less than a quarter of a tank remaining. Hopefully that would be enough gas to get us where we wanted to go. Another thing that was working to our advantage was the fact that she had did a one-eighty degree turn in the front yard so that it had been easier to get Grandpa out of the pickup and into the cabin. Now, the truck was facing the direction in which we needed to go. If I had to turn the truck around, we might not make it. It was going to be hard enough going straight, the thought of having to go in reverse was inconceivable.

Millie closed the passenger door behind her and looked at me expectantly. "I didn't know you could drive!"

"Neither did I!" I said with a smirk. Frowning, I shook my head as I got behind the wheel. "I've *never* driven anything before." I admitted. Now was not the time for lies to be told.

Her jaw dropped open. "How are you gonna manage a stick shift?"

I gave her a timid smile and turned the key in the ignition. The truck fired to life, jerked with a lurch forward and died. Millie slammed a hand against the dash and stared at me with wide eyes, her glasses perched precariously on the tip of her nose. She looked comical and scared to death. She pointed down at the floorboard. "The clutch thingy!"

"Sorry," I said. I pressed my left foot on the clutch and turned the key again. This time the pickup rumbled back to life but it didn't move. I eased my foot off the pedal and gave it some gas. Again, the truck bucked forward and died. *"What the Hell?"* I yelled in frustration. Brock had made it seem so easy, so effortless. That was obviously *far* from the case!

"Maybe it's in the wrong gear." Millie offered helpfully pointing at the gear stick.

I blushed. *Of course!* It was probably in fourth; I most likely needed to start out in first gear. I depressed the clutch and turned the key. I was relieved that the truck responded with an eager roar. I studied the pattern that still showed faintly on top of the ball. I pulled the shifter toward me, then pushed it up. "First?" I said with a hopeful shrug.

Millie shrugged hopefully.

The old pickup started moving forward as I eased off the clutch.

My confidence building, I gave it a little more gas. The engine started making an unhappy noise like it had too much power. I glanced at the black ball and it had numbers 1-4. I guessed that the truck needed to be in a higher gear. So, I grabbed the ball and pulled it down toward where I hoped second gear should be. It started making a terrible grinding sound as I met resistance.

Millie let out a frightened scream.

The clutch! I quickly depressed the left pedal and the shifter slid easily into gear. I eased off the clutch and pressed on the gas. The truck went faster!

"Tree!" Millie screamed frantically as she bounced in the seat next to me.

I glanced up and saw that we were starting to leave the road! I quickly turned the steering wheel to the right, and we somehow managed to cling to the lane. But I overcompensated and had to quickly steer to the left. Millie's eyes were tightly closed and she was ranting about not wanting to die. "Okay." I whispered to myself. "Focus. Keep your eyes on the road."

"We're going to die!" Millie wailed. Tears were showing wet, on her cheeks.

"You want to drive, Millie?" I shouted back. She quickly shook her head and went silent. "I don't need you acting all crazy over there! It *isn't* helping!" I hadn't meant to yell at her, but I was stressing out. I downshifted gears, and had some difficulty finding the sweet spot. I could hear the transmission grinding in protest, fighting against me. I finally got it into the proper gear but took my foot off the clutch too soon. The truck began to jerk, threatening to stall.

She took a deep breath and blew it out slowly. "Okay. I'm all right. Sorry." She looked at me apologetically. "You're doing great. Really. But *please* don't get us killed!"

I couldn't help but laugh. "I'll try my best." I said. I shifted into third gear a little later than I should have, but overall it went pretty smoothly. I could tell by the whine of the engine that it was ready for another gear change, so I went to fourth.

Perfect!

Millie began to relax beside me. "Alright!" She beamed proudly, as the pickup sailed smoothly along the dirt track. I had to slow to make a bend and the engine started lugging down. I shifted to third and the truck responded with seeming delight. I kept it in this lower gear as I navigated the vehicle along several bends in succession. When the road straightened out, I gave it more speed and shifted back into fourth. Nothing to it!

I had this driving thing down pat!

And then the unexpected happened.

The dirt road ended!

We were going way too fast. I froze, my eyes growing wide. Millie braced against the seat and the dashboard, I was certain this was the end of it all. Millie let out a blood-curdling scream. Gripping the steering wheel tightly, I slammed on the brake and the clutch simultaneously. I jerked the wheel as hard as I could to the left as we reached the blacktop highway.

Thankfully there was no traffic to contend with. The road was deserted. Otherwise we might have been in a horrible collision that could easily have cost us our lives. Thoughts of my parents flashed through my mind. We were lucky and we both knew it. As it was, we were slammed about the cab of the truck unmercifully. But neither of us seemed to have suffered any lasting damage – a few bruises maybe. The truck came to a shuddering stop half on the pavement and half on the right shoulder of the road.

After fumbling with the door Millie finally managed to get it open. She practically fell out of the truck. I could see her crawling away on all fours. Finally, she stopped and began retching violently. My heart went out to her.

I climbed from the Chevy and ran to her. By the time I got to her she had finished puking up her breakfast and was sitting on her butt with her knees pulled up to her chest sobbing uncontrollably. I was positive that she hated me. I plopped down beside her and attempted to give her a hug, but she wasn't having it.

"Don't!" she insisted with both hands in the air to ward me off.

I sat back on my heels with my hands on my thighs. I tightened them into fists to keep them from shaking. I pounded my legs. "What was I thinking?" I said feeling completely unnerved. "I can't drive! I almost got us killed!"

"But you didn't," Millie said meekly. "We survived. Thanks to you. I would've killed us both!"

I couldn't help but chuckle. "Hey, I may get us both killed before the day is over. Just stick around."

Millie took off her glasses and wiped the tears away. She nodded silently and smiled at my attempt at levity.

The light caught her eyes just right. I don't know if it was because of the tears or something else, but I felt drawn to them. "You've got really pretty eyes," I said softly.

She threw a handful of pine needles at me as she blushed. It was good to see the color return to her face. She had been deathly pale a short time ago. "You're just saying that."

I shook my head. "No, I'm not. They're a really pretty shade of blue. I can't believe I hadn't noticed sooner."

She put her glasses back on. "So, are we gonna kiss now?" She was still blushing, but there was a hint of a smile teasing at the corner of her mouth. I couldn't tell if she was kidding or not.

"How about a hug?" I said spreading my arms and rising up on my knees. That, she accepted without hesitation. We were gonna be alright. She *didn't* hate me after all.

"You know," I said as we were driving along the highway, "I can always take you back into town and drop you off at your grandma's. There's really no sense in both of us risking our lives any further. I'll be fine on my own."

Millie slapped my arm as she looked at me in astonishment. "What? No way! Are you kidding me? We've already been over this. I don't think you can find the *portal* without my help. We're in this together, thick or thin. I would seriously rather die than to let you go it alone. You need me, Kat St. Claire."

I nodded with a smile as I looked through the windshield. "Yes. Yes I do!"

"Two peas in a pod," she said.

I couldn't help but laugh. "Yep. Two crazy girls in an old beat up Chevy pickup off in search of a magical doorway."

Millie sighed with a smile. "You make it sound like a fairytale."

I gave her a crooked little smile with my eyebrows raised. "Hopefully we can find our little prince and save him before the big, bad wolf eats him."

Millie grinned. "So, off to Grandmother's house we go!"

"Boo!" I rolled my eyes.

She giggled. "Hey, you started it!"

CHAPTER 27
INTO THE WOODS

I shifted the truck into neutral and let it coast. I guided it onto the shoulder as the engine sputtered and died. We were out of gas. Fortunately, the turn off to Wellington House wasn't that far ahead. It was better that we walk from here anyway. We didn't need the rumble of the old Chevy's engine to alert anyone that we were coming, so it was probably a *good* thing that we were out of fuel.

"So," Millie said, "what's the plan?"

I shrugged. "I guess we wait until dark before we make our approach. It's less likely that we'll be seen that way. We don't want to get shot."

"That would not be my first choice," Millie said with a rueful grin. "But you do realize that it's still pretty early, right? Darkness is a *long* way off."

I nodded. "I know. But we had to take off when we did. Aunt Abby and Grandpa weren't likely to give us another chance. If we're going to save Bobbybear we can't afford to wait around."

"Oh, I totally agree with you."

I opened my door and slid out of the truck. "We ought to get into the woods before somebody sees us just sitting here. They might think that we're in need of help or something. And it certainly wouldn't be good for us if Harrison Beckett happened to come by."

Millie slid out of the pickup. "I can't *stand* that man!" She shot me a look as she rounded the front of the Chevy. "He gives me the creeps!" She shivered, stamping her feet upon the ground.

I shoved my hands in the hip pockets of my jeans. It was the *only* way that I could keep from shivering along with her. "You and me both."

We crossed the highway and carefully stepped down the embankment and into the forest. "I'd like to go around Wellington House and steer towards the cottage. Maybe we can hang out there until it gets quite a bit darker. Grandmother is a creature of habit. She'll retire to the drawing room after her dinner. Margaret and Beckett will most likely be there with her, at least for a time."

Millie glanced at her wristwatch. "She should be sitting down to lunch about now. It's almost noon." There was something in her voice that clearly said that she wished she were sitting down for lunch right now.

I wasn't hungry at all. I had a feeling in the pit of my stomach that was unsettling. I was pretty certain that if I were to eat *anything* it would make a reappearance fairly quickly. But I *was* thirsty. I wasn't sure that I could even keep water down. "I nodded. "Grandmother will have dinner at six sharp. By seven o'clock she'll have sherry in the drawing room. After a glass or two, she'll retire for the night."

Millie sighed, rolling her eyes. "That gives us about seven whole hours to kill." She wasn't a happy camper; that was clearly evident. "We should've stayed at the cabin longer. At least there was food and a bathroom."

"Pick a tree," I said gesturing around. I was *slightly* irritated. "Sorry to inconvenience you. We've been over this already. Had we waited until later we might not have been able to slip away." I shook my head, wishing she'd get over it already.

She stopped and shook a finger at me scolding. "Don't get snippy with me, missy! I *don't* need your attitude on top of *everything* else!"

"*My* attitude!" I placed a hand on my chest in disbelief. "If that isn't the pot calling the kettle black, I certainly don't know what is!" I folded my arms in front of me. "I knew that I should've come alone."

"Oh really?" Millie snapped back. "And just *how* are you gonna know when you even find the portal to 1884?" She placed her hands on her hips. "For that matter, what are you gonna do if you *do* stumble upon it?"

I could feel my jaw tighten in anger. I threw my arms up into the air. "I don't have *any* idea!" I glared at her, furious; thankful that I wasn't the wolf right now. "What are *you* going to do if we find it?" I made quotation marks in the air with my fingers, "What's *your* big plan?"

Millie crossed her arms over her chest and took a stance that clearly said she wasn't budging. She even gave that little shift with her head. "Are we *seriously* going to do this right now?"

Sighing, I raised my hands in the air. "I don't want to fight with you, Millie. We're *so* close to our goal! I just want to save Bobbybear's life." Tears sprang from my eyes as though they were Olympic Gymnasts competing for the Gold. "But I can't do that without your help. We have to be on the same page or it's pointless."

She walked up to me and rubbed my arm with her hand. "I'm sorry, Kat. I don't want to fight with you either." She sighed. "We're both under a lot of stress right now. I get it. I'm sorry."

I nodded. "I'm sorry too." I wiped the tears from my cheeks and smiled at her. "So, what *do* we do when we locate this stupid portal?"

Millie blushed and pushed her glasses up her nose. She said, "Honestly? I don't really know. I'm hoping that something will present itself."

I squeezed her arm. "Well, at least we're on the same page."

Millie smiled in relief. She began hopping from one foot to the other. "Now can we please go to your aunt's cottage? I really have to go to the bathroom and I'm afraid to go behind a tree! I'm deathly afraid of bugs and spiders!"

My stomach growled hungrily in protest. I had eaten very little of my breakfast—picked at it mostly, and now my body was reminding me that it wanted food. *Now!* It was almost as if my stomach knew that nourishment would also be available at the cottage. I couldn't help but laugh. "Fine!" I gave in. "We'll go to the stupid cottage!" At least my stomach was no longer gurgling.

We slipped deeper into the woods wanting added distance between us and anyone who might be watching from Wellington House. Besides, the more trees and undergrowth that we could hide behind, the better. Neither of us were wearing bright colors, so that was a plus. Unfortunately, we had other concerns.

Millie stepped on a long, twisted, dried twig and it snapped loudly underfoot causing us both to stop in our tracks. She stared at me with wide eyes. I put a finger to my lips and strained to listen. "Sorry," Millie whispered. "I didn't mean to make noise."

I shook my head with a crooked grin. She evidently didn't comprehend what a call for silence meant. With the exception of my friend I couldn't hear anything other than normal forest sounds. In response I whispered softly, "It's okay. Just try to be more careful."

Millie nodded her understanding. She bent and picked up the broken branch and tossed it into the shrubbery. It rustled through the leaves and plopped to the ground. Realizing her mistake, Millie covered her mouth with her hand and squinted as though she were in pain. "Sorry!"

Moving more cautiously, it took another twenty minutes to get to within sight of the cottage. Millie was ready to make a mad dash toward the door but I held her back by placing a hand on her arm. I thought I'd seen movement—*two figures*—inside the cottage. That could be a *huge* problem for us.

Millie groaned unable to wait any longer, she stepped quickly behind a shrub to relieve her growing discomfort. I could plainly hear her grumbling to herself in hushed tones. I decided to move to a better vantage point closer to the cottage to give her more privacy. She returned a short time later with a sour look on her face. She whispered, "These woods are full of poison ivy, poison oak and stinging nettle!" She shook her head. "I hope I don't regret this!"

I had to bite my lip to keep from laughing out loud. She gave me a dark scowl. "It isn't funny."

I shook my head and pouted at her. "No, it certainly isn't funny in the least." I couldn't help myself. I broke out into a huge grin. "But yeah, it kinda is!"

Millie slapped me on the shoulder. "The next time you transform into the wolf, I hope you get fleas!"

My eyes went wide. "Ah! I can't believe you'd say such a thing!"

"It would serve you right." She gave me a wink and a lopsided grin.

"Kismet, huh?"

"Exactly!" She sighed as she leaned close to me and peered through the trees toward the cottage. "So, what's our next move?"

"I swear that I saw movement inside. We need to wait a bit longer. Maybe they'll leave."

"They?" Her eyes widened.

I nodded. "I think there's at least two people inside the cottage."

Millie's stomach growled loudly. She rubbed her tummy and gave me an embarrassed glance. "I'm starving. I can't help it. I get hungry when I'm scared or nervous." My own stomach answered the call with similar rumblings. Millie quickly squeezed my arm. "Did you *hear* that? What was that racket?"

"Smart ass." I gave her a little shove.

She giggled.

We watched the cottage with more patience than I had thought either of us was capable of. I was proud of us. Despite our hunger pangs and our physical discomfort, we were doing quite well. It had been over an hour since I had seen any movement through the window.

"What do you think?" Millie's voice sounded hopeful.

I shrugged. "I don't know. I guess maybe we can give it a try. We'll go slowly, stay within the cover of the forest as much as we can. Let's try to get to the back of the cottage."

Millie nodded. "Okay. Whatever you think is best. I'll follow your lead."

We eased further back into the trees and began to circumvent the outer perimeter of the cottage, still taking it slow. Time was on our side—at least I thought it to be. If Bobbybear was trapped in 1884 he was already dead. But could he *still* be saved? That was the question. Could we *somehow* get back in time to the year 1884 and prevent his death? If we could, could we *also* save Sara? *Should we even try to save her?* That would be altering history. What repercussions would that cause?

If Sara Robinson weren't mauled to death by a pack of wolves would Lucius Robinson have remained in his home? If he did, there would be *no* Wellington House, as I knew it. And if *that* were the case, would my mother ever be born? *This was crazy!*

The stress was starting to get to me. I was suddenly feeling dizzy. I dropped to my knees feeling suddenly weak. I felt clammy. A cold sweat had broke out over my entire body. I felt as though I were about to be ill. Millie knelt beside me and put a hand to the small of my back. She pulled the hair away from my face as I attempted to wretch. I couldn't do more than dry-heave. "Are you going to be okay?" she asked after a moment.

Tears stung at my eyes. I felt powerless and shaky. I nodded, not trusting that I could speak. I still felt like I might puke. My stomach rolled and knotted. I couldn't take it anymore. With my left hand I pulled the remainder of my hair away from my face. I stuck my finger in my mouth to get it over with. Fortunately, there was very little in my stomach to purge; I immediately felt better once I was through.

It took me a minute or two longer before I thought that I could stand—and then only with Millie's assistance. I leaned against the thick trunk of an eastern white pine and wiped my lips with the back of my hand. My knees were still a bit unsteady. "Whew," I said exhaling a long breath.

Millie gave me a concerned look. She reached out a hand but stopped short of touching my shoulder. "Are you going to be alright? Maybe we should do this another time."

"No!" I said forcefully. Then, not so sharply, "No, I'm alright. I just let my thoughts run away with me and I got all stressed. When I get all worked up like that it hits my stomach *really* hard. Mom always said if I wasn't careful I'd have ulcers." I rubbed my tummy and squinted. "She may have been right."

Millie pushed her slipping glasses back up her nose. "You're way too young to be having ulcers."

I nodded with a crooked grin. "Yeah, well I have a lot on my plate."

She giggled. "What? So your parents died." She began ticking it off on her fingers. "You found out you can change into a werewolf. You've confronted a ghost. And now your baby brother is sent back one hundred and thirty some years into the past—and killed in these very woods by wolves nonetheless! Seriously girl,

I think you may be blowing everything way out of proportion! I mean, *come on!*"

I couldn't help but laugh. "I know, right?"

CHAPTER 28

THE ANCHOR

We continued along the edge of the forest making our way to the back of the cottage. Both of us were keeping a wary eye on the windows that were still visible through the trees and foliage that we were using for cover as we progressed. Hopefully we'd be able to spot trouble before we were discovered. If not, we could be in *serious* danger.

There was no back door to the cottage and only a couple of windows. I motioned for Millie to approach one of them while I moved toward the other. The idea was that we were going to peer quickly through the glass to see if anyone was inside. If we didn't see anyone, then we would go around to the front and attempt to enter.

That was the plan. But my plans rarely turn out the way that they're supposed to. And this was certainly no exception. As Millie peered through the window, she almost immediately screamed. She backed away from the cottage faster than she could manage and fell to the ground. Her glasses slipped completely off her nose and landed in her lap.

I ducked down in front of the window that I had chosen and glanced at Millie. "What did you see?" I whispered harshly.

Millie was fumbling with her glasses and sliding backwards

on her butt to get further from the window. "S... someone's in there!"

"Did they see you?" I asked feeling my own panic starting to rise to the surface.

She nodded. "They were looking right at me!" She was frantically trying to put her glasses on her nose and stand at the same time. She wasn't having much luck with either task.

"Could you tell who it was?" I pressed.

Millie shook her head. "Some woman—or maybe a man! Jesus! I don't know!"

We were about to find out. The window was sliding open. I froze in place. There was nowhere to hide. It was already far too late to run. We were caught! Completely at the mercy of whomever was inside the cottage. If it was Harrison Beckett, why didn't he shoot us both and get it over with? Could it possibly be Grandmother? The thought of her skulking around my aunt's cottage made it seem unlikely; perhaps it was Margaret, her housekeeper?

We were about to find out.

Aunt Abigail crossed her arms over her chest. The fingers of one hand impatiently tapped her bicep. She arched a brow as she leaned against the kitchen counter. Her unrelenting stare seemed to bore right through me. She was obviously *still* fuming but she was controlling her anger remarkably well. "What were the two of you thinking? Harrison Beckett shot your grandpa, what's to stop him from shooting either of you?"

I shrugged feeling inadequate as tears sprang to my eyes. "I hadn't really even considered that. All I can think about is the simple fact that Bobbybear needs my help." I ran a hand through my hair. I seriously couldn't see any other options. "This seems to be the only way that I can save him. I have to try!"

"How?" She sounded skeptical.

I glanced over at Millie for help. She wiped a cookie crumb off her bottom lip with a flick of her tongue. "Me?" She swallowed. "Okay. We believe that there is some sort of *portal*—a doorway— into the past, somewhere inside Wellington House. If we can find it then maybe we can go back in time and save Bobby."

Aunt Abby practically snorted. *"Time travel? Seriously?"* She shook her head and slapped her thigh. "Now I've really heard everything! That's crazy! It isn't even a real thing!"

I was suddenly furious. "Before I came to The Hollows I didn't believe that werewolves were real either! Same with witches. But somehow Bobbybear was sent into the past. If he can go back in time, then why can't we?"

She smiled. "Fair enough." She crossed to the window and parted the blind, peering outside. Searching for what, I didn't know. Seemingly satisfied she faced us again. "So, what is this plan of yours? How do we ensure that we go back to the right time?"

"We use an anchor." I said.

She squinted. "How is a boat anchor going to help us?"

Millie laughed as she batted a hand in the air. "Not a boat anchor—that would be just *silly*!" At Aunt Abby's harsh glare she quickly sobered. "Not *that* kind of an anchor. Just something of Bobby's to kinda draw us to him—that type of anchor." She shrugged, feeling uncomfortable.

Aunt Abby nodded as she bit at her bottom lip thoughtfully. "How can you be certain that you'll arrive in time to save him? If you're off by just a little bit you could be getting there too late to actually do any good. And once you're there, you still have to find him." She shook her head. "I don't like it. Too many unknown variables." She narrowed her eyes at me. "Besides, even if you do manage to get back in time to save him, how do you get back?"

To that, I didn't have a readily available answer. My main focus had been going back in time, finding and saving Bobbybear. I never even considered a return trip through time. I had completely taken that for granted; but now the question seemed to just hang in the air—like an elephant in the room, it demanded attention. I could only shrug. I glanced helplessly at Millie.

"Easy peasy!" Millie said.

We both turned our attention to Millie, causing her to suddenly blush. She pushed her glasses up her nose, a slight tremble in her fingers. "We provide an anchor here. Simple." She took another chocolate chip cookie from the plate on the counter and bit into it. She shrugged. "No big deal."

Aunt Abigail shook her head, her brows raised. "Forgive me for being skeptical of our chances." She looked at me. "You said that all traces of Bobby had been removed from his room. With nothing there to tie him to Wellington House, what are you going to use as an anchor? How will you get back in time to save him?"

"Remember Mr. Grizzle?"

"Bobby's stuffed bear?" Aunt Abby looked confused.

I nodded. "I found one of his eyes. It must have fallen off in my bedroom the last time he was there."

Aunt Abby glanced doubtfully from me to Millie. "Is that going to be enough?"

Millie shrugged. "It's all we've got."

I felt a sudden surge of panic go through the pit of my stomach. *Was* Mr. Grizzles' button-eye going to be enough? I didn't have anything else—all of Bobbybear's other belongings had vanished from his room or been left behind in the city. Grandmother—*or someone*—had had them removed. They had probably already been destroyed. At any rate, they were inaccessible. The stuffed bear's eye was our *only* remaining option. It would have to be enough.

Aunt Abby sighed as she slowly shook her head. It was obvious that she wasn't thrilled. "Where is this eye?"

I could feel a huge lump stick in my throat. I tried with little success to swallow it. "I... I... don't actually have it."

Millie's jaw dropped as she looked from my aunt to me.

Aunt Abby's eyes narrowed. "What do you mean, you don't have it?"

I blushed. "I couldn't very well carry it when I was expecting to transform into the wolf—it might've gotten lost somewhere in the woods. It's back in my room at Wellington House, where it's safe."

"You mean it's safe only if your grandmother hasn't found it." Aunt Abby said pointedly.

"She wouldn't go through my things. She'd have to go snooping around to find it. She wouldn't do that."

Aunt Abby practically snorted. "Oh please! Of course she would! If she didn't do it herself she'd have one of her lackeys do it for her. But rest assured, if she hasn't gone through your belongings, she most certainly will."

"All the more reason why we can't afford to *screw* around

waiting. Millie and I need to get into Wellington House and find the *portal*." I could see Aunt Abby tense up when I said *'screw'*. To her credit, she didn't chastise me on the spot.

Aunt Abby drummed her fingertips on the counter. "If Millie and I go to Wellington House it might be suspicious. You returning home can easily be explained. I can sneak Millie in once you have your grandmother occupied."

"So you want me to go back now?" I asked.

"Why not? Besides, we need to give your grandfather more time."

I could feel my body *jolt* unexpectedly. "Give him time for what, exactly?" A weighty sense of dread bore down upon me.

Aunt Abby had a slight raise to her chin. "He's gathering the pack. After Harrison Beckett shot him, it is clearly evident that *war* is coming to The Hollows."

"Whoa." Millie blinked.

"War?" I said. *"Are you freaking kidding me?"* I couldn't believe what I was hearing. How had things gotten so out of hand? "I don't want to start a war, I just want my kid brother back where he belongs." I didn't know if I was ready for this. There was *always* collateral damage in war. I had lost too much already; I wasn't sure if I could take any more.

Aunt Abby sighed. "There has always been tension between the Lycans and the Coven."

I shook my head. "The Coven?"

"Witches," Millie supplied.

I stared at Aunt Abby. She shrugged nonchalantly. "I've always been kinda caught in the middle."

"But *you're* a witch." Confusion had to be written all over my face.

Aunt Abby nodded. "Yes, I am. But I am in love with Samuel St. Claire, who just happens to be the *Alpha* of a very strong wolf pack."

"So, when did Grandpa leave?" I could see his clothes piled up on the floor through the open door to Aunt Abby's bedroom. Either he had transformed and left or he was hiding naked somewhere in the cottage. She had said that he had gone to gather the others, but I hadn't even considered that he might go in wolf form.

"He was on his way out when I spotted you two."

Millie's eyes grew wide. "I hope he doesn't encounter Harrison Beckett. That man isn't kidding around. He's likely to shoot the first wolf he sees."

Aunt Abby frowned. I could see the worry and tears fill her eyes. "I know. I tried to talk Sam out of it, but he wouldn't listen. He was saying that it was time to end this." She shook her head. "I've never seen him quite so angry."

I sighed and shook my head slowly. I didn't want to see anyone get hurt. The sooner we could save Bobbybear the better things would be—at least that was my thinking. I didn't want Grandpa getting shot by another silver bullet—or any of the guys for that matter. "We need to end this before anyone gets killed."

Aunt Abby gave me a sad look. Tears fell from her eyes and left a wet trail down her cheeks. She bit her bottom lip and then shook her head slowly. "I'm not certain that we can."

I reached out and squeezed her arm. "We have to at least try."

She nodded, exhaling slowly. "You're right. We can't afford to drag our feet on this. We have to try and make a difference in the outcome somehow; we can't just leave it to chance." She looked from me to Millie. "I hope you know what you're doing."

Millie couldn't meet her gaze. She shoved her glasses up her nose and nodded. "Me too."

I studied Aunt Abigail for a moment. "You mentioned that a Coven might be involved in this mess. What can you tell me about them? Why would they want to sacrifice Bobbybear by sending him into the past to be mauled by wolves? What do they hope to gain?"

She chuckled softly. "I guarantee that if my mother is responsible for sending Bobby back in time, then she has involved the Coven as well. I really can't say what their agenda is, but I may be able to find out. There are still a few of them that are friendly towards me; some that have long desired to break with the old ways but haven't had the strength to walk away as I had. I can reach out to them, see what I can find out. They may be willing to talk."

I nodded. "That might prove helpful."

CHAPTER 29
THE RETURN TO WELLINGTON HOUSE

I walked to the front of Wellington House feeling a lot less certain than I had when the day began. There seemed to be so much more at stake. Now, many more lives were hanging in the balance. It wasn't just Bobbybear's. When Harrison Beckett shot Grandpa with the silver bullet, it showed just how far Grandmother was willing to go but it *still* didn't explain what her motive was for sending Bobby back in time to 1884. And was it just Grandmother and her *lackeys*, as Aunt Abigail liked to call Beckett and Margaret, or was this mysterious *Coven* also somehow involved? And if so, what was their driving force? Why would they want to send a six-year-old into the past? What could he accomplish that they could not?

A part of me wanted to confront Grandmother right now, tell her *everything* that I knew, and demand answers. Aunt Abby had cautioned me *against* doing just that however. She claimed that Grandmother wouldn't listen and she would block all attempts at getting to the truth. But I just wanted to know *'why?'*

Steeling myself, I took a deep breath as I climbed the steps and stood at the front door of Wellington House. I grasped the door handle as I exhaled slowly. I glanced around, hoping to see some sign of Aunt Abby and Millie. They hadn't followed me right away like I had anticipated. *What were they waiting for?*

I couldn't wait for them; if I did I knew that I'd lose my nerve. So I forged ahead, I opened the door and stepped inside. The place was eerily quiet. Of course, I hadn't expected to hear a great deal of noise, but I had expected to hear the normal everyday household sounds. There were only the two servants, Grandmother, Bobbybear and I after all. I felt an immediate tug at my heart at the thought of my missing little brother.

I'm coming for you Bobbybear. Just hang on!

I closed the front door as softly as I could. My throat felt tightly constricted and incredibly dry. I rested my head against the door and closed my eyes as an unsettling wave of nausea passed over me. I felt as though I were either going to blackout or vomit. My skin felt cold and clammy. *I don't have time for this!* I could feel the tremor in my knees threatening to buckle them beneath me. I had to get moving; there was no time to waste. Each minute I delayed, Bobby came closer to being lost to me forever.

I crossed the grand entrance and had just placed my foot on the first step of the staircase when I was stopped in my tracks by Grandmother's voice. "Katherine! Where have you been?"

I took my hand from the banister and turned to face her. "You wouldn't believe me if I told you Grandmother." My voice sounded shaky *even* to me.

"Try me." I saw the slight raise to her chin even as her eyes narrowed.

I swallowed, unable to meet her gaze. "I needed to think, so I went for a walk in the woods and I got lost." Finally, I was able to look her in the eyes. "I've never been good at directions. Guess I inherited that from Mom." It was true. Sometimes Mom couldn't find the nose in front of her face without a detailed map. It was funny though, but you'd figure that her *wolf-sense* would've helped her more while she was in human form—but then again, I hadn't done so well in that department either.

Grandmother smiled, she obviously remembered how bad Mom could get. She took a step toward me, a look of concern lighting her face. "Are you feeling unwell?"

I shook my head. "No, I'm fine. Really."

"You must be hungry. I'll have Margaret prepare you something."

I nodded. "That would be nice. I'd like to clean up first." I could think of no other way to stall for time.

"Of course. Dinner will be ready in ten minutes. Afterwards I will expect you in the drawing room."

I nodded in response, and turning I took the stairs two at a time. I needed to get up to my room and make certain that I still was in possession of Mr. Grizzle's eye. Without it, I might never see Bobbybear again.

I closed my bedroom door behind me and leaned against it as I carefully scanned the room. It appeared to be just the way I had left it, but I seriously doubted that it had gone untouched. I was fairly certain that either Grandmother or Margaret had gone through it while I had been gone. If they had, they took great care in not making it obvious.

I went into the bathroom and splashed some water on my face. I gripped both sides of the porcelain sink and closed my eyes tightly as I slowly exhaled. I just needed a moment to collect my thoughts and clear the jumbled mess in my brain. I looked at my reflection in the mirror and was startled by what I saw. It looked like I hadn't gotten a decent night's sleep in days. My hair was a mess and I could use a little makeup and a change into fresh clothes. I sighed, reaching for my toothbrush. First things first.

I had found Mr. Grizzle's loose eye right where I had left it; in the front left-hand corner of my underwear drawer buried beneath my panties. I stuck it in the pocket of my jeans and left the bedroom, closing the huge double doors behind me. I stared down the long hallway toward Bobbybear's room and sighed, hoping that we'd be successful in bringing him back where he belonged. Our chances of success seemed dismal at best. But I had to remain optimistic nonetheless—especially if I wanted to see my brother again. I headed slowly toward the staircase. As I started to descend, movement off to my right brought me up short. Millie was coming toward me, motioning for me to join her. "How did you get up here?" I asked.

She squeezed my arm. "Did you know that your aunt has a secret tunnel that runs from her basement all the way to Wellington House? It has rock walls and a string of lights to guide the way." She smiled shaking her head slowly, clearly awed. "I've never seen anything like it."

"I wonder if it has always been there?" I knew that Wellington House was a lot older than my aunt's cottage. So if the tunnel had always been there it must've been secretly hidden—perhaps a method of escape used by the residents in case there were ever a need. At any rate, I had been in Aunt Abby's basement and I hadn't known about the tunnel. It must've been cleverly hidden.

"Where is my aunt, anyway?" I asked.

"She said she was going to keep your grandmother occupied while you and I searched for the *portal*. I'm not certain how much time she can buy us—she wasn't even sure."

Time! "Grandmother is expecting me downstairs for dinner in under a minute. We'd better make this quick!" The amount of time that Aunt Abby could buy us would be directly related to how long she and Grandmother could stand to endure one another's company. Recent experience had shown that Millie and I didn't have *any* time to waste.

Millie nodded. "Do you have Mister Grizzly's eye?"

I couldn't help but chuckle. "You mean Mr. Grizzle's eye? Yes, I've got it."

"Oh!" She looked around in obvious embarrassment as if she was afraid that Bobby might catch her error. But sadly, there was no fear of that. "Sorry," she said, pushing her glasses up her nose.

Millie inclined her head down the hall. "Shall we?"

Taking a deep breath to once again steel my nerves, I nodded. I could only hope that Millie knew what she was doing. We didn't really have much of a choice. We *had* to find the *portal*. We *had* to use it to save Bobbybear before he was truly lost to us. I couldn't help but feel that time was slipping away from us. *Hang on Bobbybear. I'm coming!*

CHAPTER 30
THE HOLLOWS, 1884

I took Millie's hand in my own as we stood at the base of the stairwell that led up to the storage room. I swallowed the lump of fear that was lodged in my throat but it wasn't easy. As I glanced at Millie I could tell that she was just as afraid as I was. Her hand was clammy to the touch. I gave it a reassuring squeeze and tried my best to sound optimistic. "Are you ready for this?"

She shook her head from side to side, blinked and then nodded as she shoved her glasses back into place. She swallowed with some difficulty. "Uhm... yeah... Yes. Ready!"

I almost laughed. Smiling at her, I said, "Are you sure?"

Millie slipped her hand out of mine and turning, she faced me. "Okay, to be honest I'm a little freaked out. Scratch that. I'm a *lot* freaked out!" She closed her eyes and took a deep breath. She handed me a flashlight, keeping one for herself. "We may need these."

I tried out the small Maglite. The LED bulb burned brightly. The entire flashlight looked like it was only slightly larger than a single AAA battery but it's power of illumination belied its size.

Facing the stairs, Millie exhaled slowly. Squaring her shoulders, she nodded twice, and then started up the steps. "Let's go get Bobbybear!"

I blinked in surprise. "Okay then!" I climbed after her.

About mid-way the air started to chill and we could see our breath waft before us like small wisps of rapidly receding clouds. I could feel a presence in the surrounding atmosphere that hadn't been there at the foot of the staircase. The goosebumps on Millie's arms told me that she sensed it as well. At first I thought it was Sara trying to manifest some way to stop us, but I didn't feel *any* hostility. I was comforted. I smiled knowingly. *Hang on Bobbybear. I'm coming!*

Millie paused at the top of the stairs waiting for me to join her. "Did you feel *him*?" In the darkness her eyes seemed moist, ready to tear.

I nodded. "Bobbybear is close."

She smiled timidly. "That's a good sign, I think."

I smiled back, trying to bolster her confidence. "I think so."

I reached out and turned the doorknob and gave the door a little push. I had honestly expected there to be some resistance. I knew Sara would try *something* to keep Bobby and I apart—she had locked the door on me before; why not now? But there was nothing. It swung open easily. Millie had expected some high jinks from Sara as well; she gave me a shocked look.

Stepping into the room, I was surprised by how dark and gloomy everything looked. But the sun was setting, and only a little sunshine was making its way through the shuttered windows.

Sara was there, standing in front of the portrait. She glared at us angrily as we approached, her face twisted in a bratty, pouty expression. *"He's mine! I won't let you take him!"* She was pointing directly at the painting; at Bobby's image.

I took an emboldened step forward. "No! He belongs with me!" I couldn't help but shout, feeling my own anger rising within me. She could still so easily goad me.

Sara stomped her feet angrily as though throwing a tantrum, her hands balled tightly into fists at her side. She screamed. *"NO!"* She ran at us her fists turning to claws that threatened to rake over us in her fury.

We stopped, gasping in shock at her sudden vicious attack. But as Sara's ghostly image got within a foot of us, she completely dissipated into a swirl of mist and nothingness.

Millie blinked with eyes wide and shoved her glasses up her nose. "Whoa! *That* was unexpected!"

I swallowed, taking a couple of quick steps forward I stared at the painting. There, at least, Sara looked sweet and innocent, holding her toy soldier. Bobbybear stood beside her, clutching a one-eyed stuffed bear under one arm. I felt a single tear roll down my cheek.

Millie turned on her flashlight and started panning it around the room. I did the same with the one she had handed me at the base of the stairs. I wasn't at all certain what I was looking for; I was glad that she was here with me. She had been fairly confident that she would be able to somehow *sense the portal.* I was completely clueless. But at least I was here offering her moral support.

I detected a faint trail of footprints on the floor leading deeper into the room. I was surprised that I hadn't seen them before. One set belonged to my brother, the other was larger—adult sized, a woman's. They belonged to Grandmother. I could see the faint dot left upon the dusty floor where her cane had touched in passing. "This way," I said softly.

Millie continued to scan the walls ahead of us. She stopped the beam of light on a closed door. She swallowed. "I think that may be it!" she said excitedly. There was nothing particularly special about the door. It seemed absolutely ordinary.

I scanned my light onto the floor in front of the door. The two sets of prints led from somewhere off to the left and stopped at the doorway. Only one set of footprints led away from the door... the adult's. *This had to be it!*

"Do you *sense* it?" Millie asked softly, almost in awe. She gripped my arm tightly with her free hand and squeezed.

In all honesty, I felt nothing. I guess I had expected to feel a surge of power or energy, but I didn't. All I felt was rising anger. Two sets of footprints led up to the door, only one walked away. Bobbybear had gone through the doorway, but he hadn't returned. I stepped forward and opened the door. In anger, I stomped into the room beyond.

Whatever I had been expecting to happen didn't—at least I didn't *think* that it had. I felt perfectly normal. My tensions eased as I looked back at Millie. "Did it work? Am I back in 1884?"

I could see the hopeful expression melt away from her face. She shook her head. "I think if it had worked, we wouldn't be able to see one another."

"If *this is* the *portal* why didn't it work?" I was beginning to feel frustrated. I needed to get a grip on my annoyance *before* I lashed out at Millie. She certainly didn't deserve to receive the brunt of my hostile feelings. It wouldn't be fair to her, and she had done so much already.

An idea seemed to go off in Millie's head—I could practically *see* the light bulb illuminate above her. "Maybe if I close the door!"

I shrugged. "Give it a try."

She closed the door.

I looked around the room. The furniture was fancy. Old. Covered with layers of dust. *This can't be...*

Millie opened the door and was immediately disappointed at seeing me standing in the middle of the room. She crossed her arms and tapped her lips with the forefinger of her free hand. "What am I missing?" She snapped her fingers. "A key!"

I looked at her curiously. "A key? But the door wasn't locked. Do you really think that by locking the door it'll make a difference?" It sounded crazy. I thought Millie was so out of her element that she was grasping at straws. But I was willing to go along with her simply because if I didn't, Bobbybear was gone. Lost to me forever.

She started scanning the floor with her flashlight, shaking her head. "No," she mumbled softly, "not anything like that." As I joined her, she backtracked the double set of footprints leading to the doorway. A tall, ornate armoire stood against the far wall. Millie's face brightened. *"Of course!"*

"What?"

She panned her beam of light across the floor. Bobby's clothes were in a pile next to the armoire. "*Aha!* They entered the storage room, went to the armoire, changed Bobbybear's clothes, and then went to the door and entered the room!" Millie smiled with satisfaction.

I could see the trail of prints playing out across the floor just as she said. Was it possible? Could it really be *that* simple? I could feel the small hairs on my arms and the back of my neck begin to tingle.

Millie grabbed my arm. "Let's see if we can find something that'll fit!"

"Are you serious?"

"Yes! Absolutely! Those clothes that you are wearing don't *belong* in 1884! You need something that *does*!"

I guess that made sense. It sounded right, somehow. At least Millie seemed to believe it—and she was my expert in all things supernatural. Aunt Abby may be a witch and have the corner market on mysticism and healing, but Millie Bradford was the reigning champion when it came to the occult.

Rummaging through the armoire we found a silk dress that looked to be about my size. It had ruffles below the waist and extended to about midway down my shins. It had a high collar that absolutely choked. It was hideous! To go with it we found a pair of black-laced boots that went to just below the knee. I felt ridiculously uncomfortable.

Millie beamed at me gleefully. "You look marvelous!"

I rolled my eyes and tried to loosen the collar with a finger. "I feel like I'm suffocating! Did people *really* wear this torturous clothing?" My feet were beginning to hurt. The boots were probably a half-size too small.

She bit at her bottom lip as she eyed me critically. I could tell that there was something bothering her. "I think we need to lose the makeup."

"Are you serious?"

She nodded. "Yep. You don't want to be taken for a harlot, do you?"

I put a hand on my hip. "Seriously? In *this* gaudy outfit?"

She shrugged. "Well, I just don't think it is wise to draw unneeded attention to yourself. It might make things harder for you in the long run."

I stomped my foot, and immediately regretted it. "Fine! Let's do this!"

It no longer mattered to me if I were comfortable or not— getting back in time to 1884 was all that concerned me. I had to journey through the years of bygone days and reach Bobbybear *before* he was mauled in the woods alongside Sara Robinson. I decided that I'd save her too, if I could—but Bobbybear was my *top priority*.

We stood in front of the open doorway waiting for I don't know what, exactly. Courage, maybe. I held Mr. Grizzle's eye tightly in the palm of my right hand; trusting that it was the anchor that would guide me to my brother. Millie reached up to the back of my neck and unclasped the chain that held my talisman. I could scarcely feel the weight of it lift off of me through the fabric of the dress. I swallowed, knowing that *only* my self-control and will power would stop my transformation when the moon beckoned to the wolf.

A small antique pedestal stood beside the door with a dust-covered, potted plastic plant atop it. Millie placed the talisman in the pot for safekeeping. "This will be your anchor. Concentrate on it when you wish to return and it should guide you and Bobby back." She placed a hand on my arm. "Understand?"

I nodded. I stepped into the room and swallowed my fear as I turned and faced my friend. "I don't know how to thank you, Millie. I... I..."

She waved a hand in the air. "Oh puhlease! What are friends for?"

"Katherine! What is the meaning of this?" Grandmother was stalking toward us, cane pounding upon the floor with each step. She was angry. *Furious!* I could hear her sharp gasp as she drew closer and realization struck her. *"Katherine!* You come here *this* instant!"

Millie cowered as she mouthed the words *'Good luck!'* She swung the door.

"KATHERINE!!!" Grandmother roared in a demanding voice.

The door slammed closed.

Silence engulfed me. I felt a wave of dizziness wash over me, but it was gone in a matter of seconds. The dust faded from the furniture, replaced by a polished sheen that glistened in the sunlight flooding through an open window.

I walked to the window and peered out. Down below, in the courtyard of Wellington House, several men were standing around a bizarre looking early automobile. Women were there too, all dressed in the attire of the late eighteen-hundreds, parasols included. Everyone was marveling over the automobile like it was some rare gem.

And it was. It was even earlier than the pictures I had seen of the Model-T. But of course the Tin Lizzie wouldn't exist for almost another quarter of a century.

Had I made it? Was I back in 1884? Only *time* would tell...

Glancing around the room I saw another door on the opposite wall from the door I had entered. Moving as quietly as I could, careful not to make a sound or disturb anything, I crossed the room and put my ear to the door. I listened intently for any signs of life. Though had there been, I'm not entirely certain that I would've heard it over the pounding of my own heart.

Grasping the doorknob in one hand I placed my other on the crack of the door as I slowly pulled it open. A narrow staircase was on the other side of the door. It too led downward. When Bobbybear and I first arrived at Wellington House we had scoured over the place and I don't recall another set of stairs. Intrigued, I stepped out onto the landing closing the parlor door behind me. To my surprise there were electric lights along the walls, though far different than those to which I was accustomed. With a last glance behind me, I cautiously descended the stairs.

I was in what seemed to be a small shaft. The stairs hugged the wall and continued to spiral downward, well beyond the second floor where my room was located. Obviously—or at least I hoped, the stairs would take me to the ground floor. They did.

A closed door stood before me. I was trying to cipher *where* this door was in *my time*, but I was hopelessly lost and quite honestly, confused. Puzzles like *this* were beyond me. They were more in Bobbybear's wheelhouse. He was the smart one - the truly clever one. He had such a beautiful mind. His sense of direction was *absolute*. I wasn't even certain if I was presently facing toward the front or the back of Wellington House; the stairwell had made so many turns in my descent. I had two options. I could go through this door or go back upstairs and go through what I knew as the storage space. Not knowing *what* or *who* was on the other side of either door was completely nerve racking.

Rather than retracing my steps I decided to press forward. In order to save Bobbybear I first had to find him, I couldn't do that unless I continued on. *The Hollows Gazette* proclaiming that Sara Robinson and Bobby were found mauled in the woods was dated April 15—that meant that they had been killed on the 14th. I didn't even know what day *today* was. I had no idea how much time was afforded me, but I was fairly certain it wasn't a lot.

Slowly and as quietly as possible, I opened the door and stepped into the room beyond. I knew where I was! I was in the library that was on the ground floor almost directly below my bedroom—or at least the bedroom door that *would* become mine in more than a century later.

Fortunately, no one was occupying the library at the moment, so it gave me the opportunity to close the door behind me and cross the great room to where a massive cherry desk was located. I could see a newspaper folded on top of the desk and I was drawn to it like a moth to a flame.

I scooped up the copy of the *Gazette* and scanned it quickly. It was dated Monday April 14, 1884... Today Sara and Bobby would die horribly in the woods. I felt my gut wrench. My knees buckled beneath me and I collapsed on the floor, still clutching the newspaper in a tight fist.

"My dear girl!" I heard the man's voice behind me, sounding alarmed. "Are you all right?" He was kneeling next to me.

I turned and faced him, feeling as though I were about to pass out. He was a large man with a big bushy beard that was snowy white. His upper lip was bare. He had a full head of silver hair. I recognized him from the paper that Millie had shown me just the other day... he was the former Governor of New York State, Lucius Robinson. Sara's uncle!

CHAPTER 31
CONFRONTATION IN THE WOODS

It took a moment for me to gather my wits. When I finally came to my senses I could only nod. I hadn't expected to encounter *him*, the former Governor, let alone have him tend to me when I had very nearly fainted. He helped me to my feet and guided me to a nearby chair. He had kind eyes that seemed to sparkle with concern. "Perhaps I should summon someone..." His voice was soft and gentle. Kind.

I couldn't afford for him to make a big fuss. I had already brought more attention to myself than I had intended. "That won't be necessary. I'm quite all right."

He eyed me critically. "All the same, it would be best to make certain." He gave my arm a firm pat.

I placed my hand on top of his and gave it a squeeze. "Please, Sir, don't trouble yourself on my account. I... I just need to find my brother. He was playing with your niece, Sara. I thought that they had come inside..."

He shook his head. "I believe that I saw them heading into the woods. I think they were playing Tag or some such. I'm sure they will return forthwith. Sara knows not to stray too far."

My face must've betrayed my alarm. His brows furrowed with

concern. "Let me get you some water." Perhaps he again feared I was about to faint.

When he turned away, I seized my opportunity. I stood and raced to the French doors that led out to Grandmother's garden—or it would be in just under two hundred years or so. I felt bad leaving the old man so abruptly, especially when he had been so kind and helpful. But what choice did I have? Bobby and Sara were *already* in the woods—who knew how long I had before they were attacked?

There were several people milling about the lawn with mallets, some slung over their shoulders. They were too caught up in their Croquet match to even notice me dashing madly across the lawn. To them, I was just a normal teenage girl to be ignored. As I reached the edge of the woods, I paused to catch my bearings. *Which direction should I go?* I wished I knew where the attack had taken place—*or would take place*—but that would make things way too easy. I was going to have to do things the *hard* way.

It would take more time than I had for *me* to track Bobbybear and Sara down; but there was a much easier way... *the wolf!* She could track Bobby's scent and find them much quicker, hopefully in time to save them from certain death. I froze, my mind racing to a scenario that I hadn't considered. *What if I was the wolf that mauled them?* I knew I'd never reach them in time if I remained in human form; but what if by transforming into the wolf I found them, and I wasn't able to *control* the wolf? *Would I actually be the one to maul poor Sara and Bobbybear?* I would *hope* that I could control her. I didn't believe that I'd harm Bobby even as the wolf—our bond was too strong. But Sara was another story altogether; her and I were not on the best of terms. To what lengths would Bobbybear go to try and save his friend? Would he somehow manage to enrage the beast within me enough to provoke an attack against him?

I was beginning to feel ill. The stress was causing my shoulders to tense and ache immensely. I wish I hadn't come alone. I needed someone here that could help me through this. I didn't know which of the two paths before me was the correct one. The choice that I was about to make could have lethal consequences. It truly was a life or death decision for Bobbybear. Do I transition into the wolf and track him, or do I remain in human form and hope by *chance* that I encounter him before he is killed?

The decision seemed obvious. I had to *trust* that the wolf would exercise restraint when she found them. I *had* to believe that she wouldn't harm Bobbybear. *I had to believe in myself! I had to keep the wolf under control.*

I needed to go deeper into the woods—far enough away from Wellington House so that I wouldn't accidentally be seen by anyone on the grounds when I made the transformation. Plus, I was extremely aware of the fact that I needed to stash my clothes so that I wouldn't have to wander around naked afterwards. I didn't want to traumatize anyone—not Bobbybear, and *certainly* not myself.

The sounds of gaiety that surrounded the grounds of the great estate were beginning to wane the further I ventured into the woods. I began looking for a good spot to disrobe and a good place to hide my clothes. I stopped in my tracks and had to smile to myself. Looking around, I couldn't believe it. I recognized *where* I was! This section of the forest was *very* familiar. This was where Aunt Abby's cottage would eventually stand. I couldn't think of a more perfect spot to summon the wolf.

I stripped down quickly and pulled the loose eye of Mr. Grizzle from the pocket where I had stashed it. It still had a patch of cloth sewn onto the back. I took a long sniff of the remnant—even this tiny piece smelled of Bobbybear! I closed my eyes and *willed* the wolf to come...

In a matter of seconds, the transformation from human to canine was complete—thanks largely to all the repetition that Aunt Abby had insisted upon during her training. As I transformed, I dropped Mr. Grizzle's eye—as the wolf wasn't able to hold on to it. It was on the ground inches away from the wolf's front paw. The wolf took two sniffs and then started forward through the pines searching the woody terrain for Bobby's scent.

Surprisingly, the wolf wasn't insisting on taking full control over mind and body. She seemed content to share headspace. It was almost as though she *understood* the importance of the situation. For that, I was thankful. I vowed to make it up to her. Now, I was in desperate need of her speed and her great sense of smell. Time was of the essence!

A frightened girl's scream sounded from deeper in the woods. I urged the wolf in that direction. Bobby's musky scent was growing stronger as well. The wolf's ears twitched, detecting a familiar sound. Bobbybear was crying for *something* to stay back! I felt the thick hair on the wolf's back begin to prickle; even I could detect the pungent smell of fresh blood spilling into the forest.

The wolf slowed, sensing the clear and present danger she wanted to move with increased caution, but I couldn't afford to waste any time. Bobbybear may already be hurt—I needed to get to him as quickly as possible!

As the wolf neared the edge of a small clearing I quickly took in the milieu. I was already too late to do poor Sara any good— her mauled body lay beneath the broken boughs of a twisted pine tree—but I could still save Bobby if I acted quickly. A large black wolf, its jowls matted and dripping blood, was snarling viciously as it approached its cornered prey.

Bobbybear was wielding a gnarled pine branch half his size in a vain attempt to ward off the beast with repeated jabs. His strength was waning and the forked pine limb was too heavy. He didn't have a chance. Exhausted, he lunged at the great beast in an awkward attack hoping to stab the wolf in the face. The wolf struck out with a fierce swipe of his paw and knocked the weapon from Bobby's hands. Bobbybear fell to his knees as he faced certain death.

The wolf lunged.

I sprang into action, striking the black wolf in mid-air less than a foot away from Bobby's outstretched hands; a second later and I would've been too late. Surprise was on my side. The black had been concentrating so hard on Bobbybear that he hadn't even noticed my approach. I sunk my canines deep into the black's shoulder and did my best to rip his foreleg from his body—I didn't succeed, but I tried. His ferocious snarls turned to whelps of pain in an instant.

But he wasn't about to give in. He turned his attention on me. We hit the ground all tangled together, still biting and clawing for dominance in a whirlwind of nonstop barrages. Pine needles, clods of dirt and bits of rock were thrown in every direction as we continued to fight. We separated and I did my best to keep myself between Bobby and this monstrous black wolf.

He was larger than I was and far stronger. I knew I didn't stand much of a chance against him, but I wouldn't back down—I *couldn't*—for Bobby's sake. I just had to hope that Bobbybear would take the opportunity I was affording him and get as far away as he possibly could. I wasn't sure how much time

I could buy him, but I was willing to sacrifice myself to give him a fighting chance. But that could *only* be accomplished if I managed to hurt the black wolf enough to make him give up the fight and search for easier prey. The only problem was, I was *willing* to do my part, but Bobby wasn't doing *his*. He was still on his knees staring at the two wolves in front of him—*I needed him to be running!*

I turned from the black and faced Bobby, baring my teeth I snarled at him. When that had no affect, I barked menacingly. My focus on Bobby was all the opportunity that the black needed. He pounced on me, sinking his fangs into the thick fur at my throat. I tried shaking him off but he was just too strong. There was literally *nothing* that I could do to get him off of me. He had me right where I wanted him—he was far more experienced at this than I was. His powerful jaws were beginning to crush my neck. I was in some *serious* trouble...

Darkness was seeping in and beginning to cloud both my vision and my judgment. I could no longer be certain what was reality or mere imagination. I *knew* I was dying—or maybe I was dead already. I didn't know, nor did I care. All I was aware of was the fact that the black demon had released his death-hold on me and was now facing two ghostly wolves—*a gray and a white*—and that apparently, they were more than he'd bargained for. He turned and disappeared into the deepening shadows of the forest, limping as he went.

Somehow, the two wolves shrouded in the ghostly bluish-white aura had managed to get Bobbybear and I back to the place where I had stashed my clothes. I had this bizarre sensation of being dragged along by the scruff of my neck like a little lost puppy, and what made it stranger still, was that I seemed to recall Bobbybear *riding* on the back of the gray wolf... At some point I must have blacked out— I must have been completely delusional!

When I came to, I was lying with my head in Bobbybear's lap. He was gently stroking my hair with one hand while holding a cloth to the wound on my neck. I jumped with a startled jolt as it *all* came back to me in an instant. He smiled through his tears, "I thought I was gonna lose you!"

I tried to swallow, but it caused an unbelievable amount of pain in my neck and I cried out. Bobbybear's eyes grew wide with concern. I attempted to smile, hoping to dissuade his growing fear. It seemed to help a little.

To be perfectly honest, I was relieved to find that I was back in *human* form—and dressed. I didn't even concern myself with *how* I got dressed. I didn't really care. I sat up and hugged Bobbybear tightly not sure I'd *ever* let him go. I kissed the side of his head; happy he was alive. I could feel the intense burn in my neck caused by the wound that I'd received at the hands of the black—or rather by his sharp canines; but though it hurt like *Hell*, I didn't think it was going to be fatal. "How bad am I hurt, Bobbybear?"

He pulled away from me and wiped the tears from his face. It was all I could do to keep from laughing. My brother's face was a smudged, dirty mess. There was a mixture of tears, dirt and blood almost everywhere. He swallowed and shook his head. "Not too badly, I think. Most of the bleeding seems to have stopped, except for that one spot." He pointed to a place on the side of my neck—where I could still feel the throbbing pain.

I nodded. He was being *so* brave! I couldn't be prouder of him. I glanced him over, turning his body this way and that, as best I could. "How about you? Are you injured at all? Did the black wolf hurt you?"

He shook his head. "Nuh-uh." He swallowed again as tears sprang from his blue eyes. "Sara pushed me out of the way or he would've got me first. I... I was trying to do what Grandmother wanted, but Sara shoved me to the ground," he sniffled. "And then... then the bad wolf got her."

I reached out and squeezed his arm. "She saved you?" I couldn't keep the surprise from my voice.

He nodded. "Uh huh."

I hugged him close as he sobbed; his tiny body quaked against my breast. "Why did he have to kill her? We didn't *do* anything wrong." He sniffled again and wiped the back of his hand over his nose. "We were just playing..."

"I know Bobbybear, I know." I didn't have any answers for him. There was no rhyme, nor reason to what had happened. I don't know that there was *anything* that could've been done to prevent Sara's death. In *our* time she had *already* died just as she had, though the circumstances may have differed slightly, she was still just as dead. But Bobby was alive. Sara Robinson had saved him by sacrificing herself. Now, I just needed to get him back home where he belonged.

"Bobbybear," I turned him so that he faced me head-on. There was something that had been bothering me. I had to know. "You said that you tried to do what Grandmother wanted."

He nodded.

"Bobby, *why* did Grandmother send you here?" My mouth felt incredibly dry, my nerves on edge.

He shrugged. "Sara was my only friend. If I wanted to continue to play with her, I had to come here, when she was still alive." He started sobbing, his shoulders heaving in his grief. "Grandmother said that she needed my help. She... she gave me something for... for when the beast came." He wiped the snot from his nose with the back of his hand. He shook his head. "But I... I... couldn't... I was too... too scared!"

I hugged him tightly. "Oh Bobbybear, it's not your fault. It's not. Grandmother shouldn't have sent you to do this—whatever it is! She was wrong, and that wasn't very nice of her." I stood up and squeezed his hand. "Come on, it's time we went home."

To my surprise Bobbybear slipped his hand out of mine and shook his head. A determined pout was carved, like stone, upon his face. "I can't go yet. I have to save Mom and Dad first." He placed his hand, instinctively, on his pocket.

I knelt down in front of him, placing a hand softly on his arm. "What do you mean you have to save them?" I had no *earthly* idea what he was talking about. I was angry, furious even, that Grandmother would put such a notion into his head. When we got back, she had a lot to answer for, and I was determined to get those answers—no matter what.

"That's what Grandmother said. She said that if I saved them, we could all be together again." A little light of hope shone in Bobby's tired eyes. It was heartbreaking. She had put so much on his tiny shoulders and he had bought into *everything* she said. He wanted *so desperately* to believe that we could all be together again, that he was willing to try *anything*.

I held Bobby's arm and gave it a light squeeze. "Oh Bobbybear!" My heart was breaking for him. How could I make him understand when I wasn't even certain that I understood it all? *How could he hope to save them now?* "You *do* know we are back in 1884, don't you?"

He nodded, giving me a little look that clearly said, *'duh!'*

"Then *how* were you supposed to save Mom and Dad? They aren't even born yet."

He frowned at me like the answer was obvious and I was a *complete* idiot for not seeing it. "By stopping the curse," he stated simply.

I felt like I had been struck in the chest with a ton of bricks. I almost fell over. "What *curse* are you talking about?"

He sighed heavily. "*You* know. The one that turns you all into werewolves."

BOOM! There it was. You could literally knock me over with a feather—not a *big* feather, mind you, a little one, like from a soft downy chick. I could only blink. I tried to say something—*anything*—but I couldn't. I could only blink. Problem was, I didn't have any idea what to say. I hadn't even been sure that Bobbybear knew about the whole wolf thing. But evidently, he had known. Grandmother probably told him.

Bobby took a small bottle out of his pocket and showed it to me. "Grandmother and her friend Sebastian said that all I had to do was splash this on the monster when he attacked and it would do the trick. But when he attacked us, I got too scared. I... I... I lost my nerve." He began to cry again. It was more a whimper than an actual sobbing.

Taking the bottle from him I hugged him close and kissed the top of his head. "Ssh Bobbybear. It's gonna be okay. It's all right to be scared. I would've been too."

He pulled back and wiped at his face. "But *why* did Grandmother say I had to wait until *after* Sara was hurt? Why couldn't I do it before? After—there was *so* much blood I got too scared." He frowned sadly. "I shouldn't have waited. I should've done it before."

I shook my head. "None of this is your fault Bobbybear. You have to believe me when I tell you that."

I had my suspicions as to why Grandmother had instructed Bobbybear to wait until after Sara was hurt, but he didn't need to know that. To me, it was obvious. Sara *had* to be sacrificed in order to preserve history. *How cruel was that?* If Sara didn't die, then Wellington House would remain in possession of the Robinsons. There would be *no* Wellington House. Ever. I glanced at the small white label on the bottle. Written in Grandmother's hand were two simple words: *Liquid Silver.* I had expected *Holy water.* But this made much more sense considering what I already knew about werewolves and silver.

"It's too late to save Mom and Dad." I really believed it was, but I wished that there *was* a way that we could save them. But neither of us was in *any* shape to go up against the black wolf again. He had very nearly killed us the first time. "We need to go back and help Aunt Abby, Millie *and* Grandpa."

"*Grandpa?*" Bobbybear's face lit up.

I tousled Bobby's hair. "That's what I said kiddo! He's looking forward to meeting you."

It was surprisingly easy to get back into the manor. All of the men were heading into the woods to search for Sara, while the women rounded up the children. Bobbybear and I were able to blend in almost effortlessly. I had hoped that we could find the tunnel that Millie had mentioned, but evidently its construction was later than 1884; probably after the cottage was built.

We made our way into the study and crossed to the door with the stairs leading up to the *portal room.* I ushered Bobby inside and we climbed the stairs quickly. Fortunately, the upstairs parlor was unoccupied. I grasped Bobby's hand tightly, my own feeling suddenly clammy. "Don't let go of my hand," I urged, giving his hand a little squeeze for emphasis. He nodded.

I closed my eyes, concentrating on my talisman, and slammed the door to the stairwell closed.

CHAPTER 32
THE SCENT OF TRUTH

Whether it worked or not, I didn't know right away. As I opened my eyes, I unexpectedly felt dizzy. I took a faltering step forward and felt my knees buckle. I tightened my grip on Bobby's hand, pulling him down on top of me. The dusty cobwebs that filled the room fluttered and I sneezed.

This was a *good* sign. Bobbybear was squinting and shaking his head as though trying to clear it after waking up from a bad dream; *another* good sign. I pushed myself up and walked to the other door in the parlor—the one leading to the storage space. I pressed my ear to the door and listened intently.

Nothing. All was quiet. I didn't know what to expect. When Millie had closed the door, sending me to the past, Grandmother had tried to stop us. I could only hope that Millie was okay. I reached back and took Bobby's hand. "Stay close to me." He simply nodded.

I slowly eased the door open and found my talisman where Millie had left it. I started to put it around my neck but decided against it. I kept it in my free hand. It was dark in the attic storage room, so we took our time walking over to the armoire. Fumbling in the dark I found the Maglite and twisted it on. I stood it on end and its bright beam of light struck the ceiling giving us plenty of illumination by which to change back into our clothes. I saw no sense in wandering around in the uncomfortable attire of a bygone century. Besides, I missed the comfort of my jeans and shoes that actually fitted properly.

"Okay Bobbybear, we need to be as quiet as we possibly can be. I don't want anyone hearing us," I whispered.

Bobby nodded his understanding as he whispered back, "Where are we gonna go?"

"We'll start by going to the cottage. Hopefully Aunt Abby and Millie will be there waiting for us. We'll decide upon a plan once we regroup."

A small smile curved the corner of Bobbybear's mouth. I could tell so *easily* that he had something burning on his mind. He looked up at me, his blue eyes bright and hopeful. "Will Grandpa be there too? I can't wait to meet him." He frowned suddenly. "You never said *which* grandpa he was."

I couldn't help but grin as I took up the flashlight. "Let's just say it's easy to see where you and Daddy get your ruggedly handsome good looks."

Bobby's smile grew. "Cool."

With the aid of the flashlight we were able to move much faster through the storage room. *Something* compelled me to stop in front of Sara Robinson's portrait. It hadn't changed since the last I'd seen it. She was standing there next to Bobby, smiling sweetly, holding her toy soldier in one hand. Bobby was smiling as well, holding Mr. Grizzle in one arm. I hadn't really noticed it before, but Bobby and Sara were holding each other's hand.

"When did you two pose for this portrait?" I asked softly.

Bobby shrugged. "There was some guy who wanted to paint Sara's portrait. She said she'd only do it if he painted me too. We had to stand there for the longest time." He squinted. "I think it was this morning, sometime."

I smiled. "It isn't that important. I was just curious."

He looked up at me. "Do you think I can hang it in my room to remember Sara by?"

I nodded. "I don't see why not."

I scanned the painting one last time. I could only wonder if the newspaper article had changed. It had stated that both Sara and Bobby were mauled in the woods by a wolf. Now that Bobbybear had been saved, I wondered what it would say?

I smiled at my brother as we walked to the door. "You know this old house better than I do," I could see a slow grin play across his face. He kept silent, but he had a knowing look in his eyes. "Millie says that there is a tunnel that goes from Wellington House to the basement of Aunt Abby's cottage. Do you, by any chance know where it is located?"

His brow crinkled in thought. After a moment he shook his head. "Probably somewhere in the basement."

I frowned. In all likelihood he was right. Getting down there wouldn't be easy, the stairs were just off the kitchen. Margaret was probably preparing the evening meal, or cleaning up after it, depending on what time it was. I had stopped wearing Mom's wristwatch some time ago so I had no idea. And if we even managed to get down to the basement without being detected, we'd still have to locate the passage. It would most likely be easier just to sneak out the front door—I had already done that a time or two.

So that was the plan. We'd go down the stairs, straight out of the front door and around the house, along the path through the woods to the cottage. Simple. We just had to hope that no one caught us trying to slip out of Wellington House.

I eased the front door closed as quietly as I could. Bobby had already stepped out into the drive and was slowly walking towards the corner of the manor, the gravel crunching under his feet; he was eager to see Aunt Abby again and to meet Grandpa. In the distance I could see headlights bouncing through the trees, as a car was navigating the long drive, approaching Wellington House. I quickly grabbed Bobbybear's hand and led him into the woods. We scrunched down behind thick foliage just in the nick of time. It was Harrison Beckett behind the wheel of the Bentley. I could just make out Grandmother and another passenger in the back seat. He seemed to be a very distinguished looking man.

We continued to watch from our hidden vantage point as Beckett climbed from the car and opened the rear door. The male passenger was the first to exit. His hair was jet black with a touch of silver at the temples. He had a thin mustache and goatee. He was impeccably dressed in a black pinstriped suit, under a charcoal gray overcoat. He carried a walking stick in his left hand. As he climbed from the car he seemed to stare *directly* at me. A small, *cruel* smile curved the corner of his mouth. I wanted to turn from his gaze but found that I couldn't. Finally, he broke contact by turning and offering Grandmother his hand to assist her from the Bentley. Bobby and I watched as he and Grandmother went inside.

"I wonder who that was," I whispered softly. Something about the man made me shiver.

Bobby gave me a frightened little look. "He... he's a friend of Grandmother's. But I don't think he's very nice. I don't think that he likes me very much."

"You've met him?" I asked, touching his shoulder.

Bobby nodded, swallowing as though it were difficult. "His name is *something* Barristrade." He quickly shook his head. "No! Barrister. Something Barrister."

Neither was a name I had heard. I watched as Bobbybear bit at his bottom lip and frowned darkly. I rubbed his arm. "What's the matter kiddo?"

"H... his name is," he swallowed. "Sebastian Barrister!" He nodded resolutely. "He's the one who told Grandmother to send me back to help Sara." Tears were forming in his eyes. "I don't think he's a very nice man. I told Grandmother that I didn't want to go back to see Sara. But he said that if I... if I didn't, something terrible would happen to you!" He wiped his runny nose with the back of his hand. "He scares me Kat."

Something about him had frightened me too. *Why would he threaten to harm me if Bobby didn't do what he wanted?* I couldn't stand bullies. But what was worse was when an adult bullied a child.

The front door to Wellington House opened and Sebastian Barrister stepped back outside. He took slow, confident strides toward the shrubbery where Bobbybear and I were still hiding. Not ten feet from us, he stopped. He puffed on a thin cigarette, blowing the smoke from his nose. The red stone on the ring he wore on his index finger seemed to glow in the darkness. It seemed he was looking straight at us when he spoke. "You managed to survive, I see." He dropped the cigarette and crushed it with an impeccably polished shoe. "No matter. I am ready for what is to come. I suggest you prepare as well."

I could feel the hairs rising on the back of my neck as a low snarl sounded from behind Bobby and I. Fear gripped me as a gentle breeze carried with it a *familiar* scent. I gripped Bobbybear's hand tightly as I turned to face the black wolf that I had battled back in 1884! *Somehow it had followed us!*

"Kat!" Bobbybear's harsh whisper was full of panic. I could feel him trying to scramble away from the approaching wolf.

I did my best to get between Bobby and the danger. The problem was, we seemed to be facing it from two sides. I looked back toward Wellington House and was relieved to see that Barrister was no longer standing there. *Good!* That meant I could focus on just the black wolf. I ripped the talisman from my neck.

I tried to direct Bobbybear toward the cottage. "Run to Aunt Abby! Don't stop until you get there! Already I could feel my body starting to change as I summoned the wolf to defend my brother.

In an instant Aunt Abigail was by my side. She placed a firm hand on my arm. "Kat! No!"

Something in her voice made me stop and listen, I pushed the wolf away, and I could sense her displeasure, but she obeyed. I could feel my heart pounding inside my chest at the rush of adrenaline coursing through me.

Aunt Abby took a step forward, placing herself between the black wolf and us. Her hands were raised in the air, one directing Bobbybear and I to stay put, the other doing the same thing for the black. "Sam! Stand down!" she said sharply.

To say that I was blown away was the understatement of the century. A moment later the black wolf stood up on its hind legs and morphed into Grandpa behind some shrubbery. I coudln't believe it - my grandpa had been the wolf that killed young Sara Robinson back in 1884! *How was this even possible?*

I felt lightheaded.

CHAPTER 33
THE BLACK WOLF

As we walked up to Aunt Abby's cottage, I could see Millie bouncing on the balls of her feet, her arms outstretched above her head. To say that she was obviously excited to see us was another *understatement*. I couldn't help but smile at her unbridled enthusiasm. Finally, she couldn't take it anymore. She ran up to me and hugged me tightly. *"You did it!"* She released me and pulled Bobbybear into a warm embrace. *"Heya kiddo!"*

Aunt Abby tousled Bobby's hair. "He's probably hungry. Why don't you take him inside and give him some cookies?"

Millie nodded. "Fresh baked chocolate chip!"

Bobby jumped up and down in eager anticipation. "I love chocolate chip!"

As they went inside, Aunt Abby placed a hand on my arm, holding me back. "A word?" she said simply.

I turned and faced her, one eyebrow raised expectantly. I could see Grandpa coming through the woods behind us, buttoning his shirt. My jaw tightened. "What?" I said a little too harshly.

She blinked. "Okay, *something* on your mind?"

I raised my chin slightly. "He was back in 1884. He *killed* Sara

Robinson. He *tried* to kill Bobbybear." I pulled my collar so she could see my wound. "When I intervened, he *almost* killed me."

She gasped at the sight of the torn skin on my neck. It *still hurt like Hell*, so I know it didn't look good. "I need to get you inside and get that tended to," she said. She glanced angrily at my grandpa and I could see the hard set of her jaw; she was far from happy.

Millie continued to see to Bobbybear while Aunt Abby, Grandpa and I went into the bedroom. After Aunt Abby securely closed the door behind us, she whirled on Grandpa. *"You did this?"*

He paled. *"What? No!"* He looked from my wound to Aunt Abby and then back at me. "I would *never* hurt you."

Aunt Abby was livid. "Kat says that *you* attacked Bobby in the woods and when she tried to stop you, you almost killed her. You murdered that poor girl and would've done the same to them if she hadn't stopped you!"

Grandpa's face flushed a deep crimson. "That's crazy! I didn't attack anyone tonight! You *know* that, Abby."

I shook my head. "It didn't happen tonight. It happened over a hundred and thirty years ago, back in 1884. You mauled Sara Robinson and almost got Bobbybear too. He'd be dead right now if I hadn't attacked you." I pointed to where I knew the scar on his shoulder to be. "I was the wolf that gave you that."

He instinctively placed his hand over his right shoulder, remembering. He plopped down on the edge of the bed with his head in his hands. He had visibly paled; all of his anger vanished. He shook his head. "I'm *so* sorry Kat. I *didn't* know it was you."

I swallowed. "Just how old *are* you?" I asked as realization started to dawn on me.

He chuckled. "Far older than I look."

"Sam, how could you?" Aunt Abby said with her arms crossed over her chest.

He sighed heavily. "When I killed that girl—in 1884—I was newly turned. I had been attacked in the woods about five days before that by a monster of a wolf while I was hunting. I barely survived the encounter. A few nights after that, I transformed for the first time. I... I couldn't control the beast I'd become. Not until much later." His shoulders shook with his grief.

Aunt Abby moved to his side and sat beside him on the

bed. She hugged him against her body and rubbed his back vigorously. "You've never told me that story. Why?"

He chuckled without humor. "It's not a tale that I'm particularly fond of. I found out that I'd killed the girl—Sara Robinson, a few days later. I had hoped that it wasn't me that had killed her. I wanted to believe that I wasn't capable of such a heinous act. I told myself that the wolf that had attacked me was the one that did this to that girl, not me." He glanced at me with tear-filled eyes. "I know now that it *was* me."

Aunt Abby stared at me as though she were waiting for me to speak. Clearly, she wasn't going to weigh in any further. I knelt on the floor in front of him and placed my hands upon his knees. I gave them a little squeeze. "It wasn't your fault, Grandpa. I see that now. It has taken me several weeks to learn to control the beast within—and at times I am *still* having to fight for dominance." I glanced at Aunt Abby, "I had someone helping me to adjust. You had no one. It wasn't your fault. I forgive you. Bobbybear will too."

I reached into my pocket and handed the bottle of *liquid silver* to Aunt Abby. "Grandmother had given this to Bobby with specific instructions on using it. He was to wait until he got attacked in the woods." I glanced back at Grandpa. "She *knew* when and where you'd attack."

He glanced at the bottle and nodded as comprehension dawned. "She wanted me dead."

Aunt Abby stood abruptly. "How could she send her grandson to do such a thing? She's *not* going to get away with this crap!" She took a step toward the door, but Grandpa stopped her.

"Hold on a sec, Abby. You need to treat Kat's shoulder before you go running off to confront your mother. Besides, we've got bigger problems than just your mother to worry about."

"What do you mean?" she asked.

"Ever hear of a man named Sebastian Barrister? He's bad news. I saw him going into Wellington House tonight. He made it clear to me that it's going to be all out war."

"I've heard of him. He has quite a bit of influence in Mother's coven. I've never cared for him. He's one of the reasons that I refused to belong to the coven in the first place." She smiled. "You're the other."

Grandpa grinned. "I'm flattered."

"Bobby said that Barrister was the one that suggested Grandmother send him back in time to kill you with the *liquid silver*. He gave Bobbybear quite a scare."

Grandpa's brows rose as he nodded, spreading his hand in the air. "With good reason. Sebastian Barrister is a *very frightening* man."

"How do you know him?" Aunt Abby asked.

He chuckled without any trace of humor. "Sebastian and I go way back."

She arched a brow, placing her hands on her hips. "How far back?"

He smiled slyly. "All the way."

"Care to enlighten us?" Aunt Abby said as she directed me into the bathroom. She had me sit on the toilet lid and then made me take off my blouse. I cringed when I saw that it was caked with my blood. I hadn't even realized that I had been bleeding again.

I could hear Grandpa's exhausted sigh. "About the time that I became a Lycan, Sebastian Barrister was gaining a considerable following here in The Hollows. There were whispers that he was a powerful warlock, though nothing had ever been proven. No one had ever seen him perform any magic to speak of. He developed a close relationship with the local coven—the very one that your mother leads now. At any rate, he and this coven began to hunt the Lycan with the intent to eradicate them. They were almost successful. *Almost.*"

"Sebastian and I crossed paths several times; neither of us managing to do any significant damage to the other. Then, one night I happened to come upon him unexpectedly. He was in a weakened state, and I very nearly ripped him to shreds. He *somehow* escaped, but I was *certain* that his wounds were fatal. I thought he'd gone off and died. He simply disappeared; vanished without a trace. I hadn't seen him since—until tonight."

Aunt Abby shook her head as she continued to dress my wound. "Obviously he is an *Immortal.*"

I winced as a sharp stab of pain shot through my neck. "An Immortal?"

She glared at me. "Hold still."

"Sorry." I frowned.

Aunt Abby continued. "People aren't just immortal. Something usually *makes* them that way. In order to stop him, we'll need to find out his secret."

Grandpa slapped his hand against the doorjamb. "Well, hopefully we can discover his dirty little secret soon—he already knows mine *and* he knows how to defeat me." He gave me a meaningful glance. "And in turn yours as well. Our weaknesses are the same."

Abby smiled, "You both have something that he doesn't have - you have each other."

And Grandpa nodded, "He has the coven backing him."

Stepping away from me Aunt Abby looked at both of us. She spoke with absolute conviction; her eyes deadly serious. "I'm *not* losing either of you to my mother *nor* this Barrister. I will do *everything* in my power to keep you both safe." Tears were starting to form in her eyes.

Grandpa pulled her into a warm embrace. "We can't ask for anything more." He kissed the side of her head. "I want you all to stay put for the rest of the night. I've got the Wolf Pack waiting for me at my cabin. I need to fill them in on everything that's happened. We'll come up with a plan."

I got up and squeezed past them. "I'm going to check on Bobbybear. He was pretty shaken earlier." I left the two of them alone, closing the bedroom door behind me as I went.

To my surprise, Bobbybear was sound asleep on the sofa, his head resting in Millie's lap. She was gently running her fingers through his soft curls, singing softly to him. She had a very pretty voice. She hadn't noticed me yet. I continued to watch and listen for several minutes longer.

When she finally noticed me, she blushed brightly. Shoving her glasses back up her nose, she said, "I didn't hear you come in. Poor thing was exhausted."

I smiled. "I know the feeling." I sat down next to her and laid my head on her shoulder.

Millie wrapped her arm around me. After a moment she resumed her song, soft and sweet. My eyelids felt heavy. I had trouble keeping them open. Finally, I stopped trying.

CHAPTER 34

PARADOX

I awoke with the startling realization that I was laying on Aunt Abby's bed alongside Bobbybear. The bedroom door was closed and the shades were drawn over the windows. How I had gotten there I hadn't a clue. Nor could I be sure how long I'd been there. My mind was in a fog. I felt lethargic. It would be *so* easy to simply close my eyes and drift back to sleep. But I *knew* sleep would not come. My mind was already churning. There was too much that I needed to do. And so little time...

I eased up off the bed as carefully as I could; I did not want to disturb Bobbybear. Poor kid was exhausted—I'm not even sure I could wake him if I tried. He was making soft, cute little snoring sounds and seemed to be perfectly at peace. I watched him a moment or two longer and couldn't help but smile. The corners of his lips were slightly curved upward. I wondered what he was dreaming. I had to resist the urge to wake him and snuggle him close. In this moment he seemed so sweet, so innocent—I wished that I could keep him that way.

Finally, I forced myself to move. I needed to find out what was going on. Things had been a bit uncertain when I last was among the living. The mysterious Sebastian Barrister had arrived and seemed to be working with Grandmother. Thinking back now to the words he had spoken, about preparing for what was to come, had me wondering *what* he was referring to. *Was he talking to Bobby and me? Or had he been talking to Grandpa—the black wolf?* It really didn't matter. Bobbybear and I were caught in the middle of *something* that seemed far bigger than either of us. I had to try to find a way to keep us both safe.

I found Millie curled up on the living room sofa with a thin blanket tucked under her chin. No one else seemed to be in the cottage. I knelt beside my friend and gently shook her shoulder. She awoke with such a start that it even took my breath away. She pushed herself up, squinting as she hunted for her glasses. "What is it? What's wrong?" she asked.

I took her glasses off of the coffee table and handed them to her. "Nothing's wrong." I shrugged glancing around, "Do you know where everyone's at?"

She slid her glasses up her nose. "They said that they had a few things to take care of and that they'd return as quickly as they could."

I practically growled at her. I couldn't afford to just wait around—I *had* to do something! "Can you watch Bobbybear for me?"

Millie's eyes grew wide. She pushed her glasses back into place. "We're... we're *not* supposed to go anywhere. Both your aunt and your grandpa wanted us to stay put. They said as much. They said, *'You girls stay put and keep Bobby safe.'* That's what they said— their exact words. So we can't *go* anywhere." She was nervous, she was starting to talk faster.

"That's what I intend to do, keep Bobbybear safe. But I can't very well do that sitting on my hands."

Millie had a worried expression on her face. She wasn't liking this at all. Clearly it made her uncomfortable. And whiney. "Please, can you just stay here until they get back? They're gonna be *so* mad if you don't!" She sniffled.

I stood and shook my head. I *almost* felt sorry for my friend. "I need to talk to my grandmother. Will you keep Bobbybear out of mischief until I return?"

She started crying. "I don't think you leaving is a very good idea. Really, I don't."

I squeezed her arms. "I really need to see if I can talk some sense into her before this mess gets *totally* out of control. I have to try and reason with her. Can I count on you to protect my brother, or not?"

She nodded, unable to speak. I couldn't help but feel sorry for her. I was asking a lot of her, but I couldn't afford to back down. I kissed Millie's cheek. "I won't be long. With luck no one will even know that I've gone."

She had a miserable expression clouding her face. "That's just great." She said sounding all mopey.

As I turned to go, Millie reached out and grabbed me by the arm. Her glasses had slipped down her nose again but she didn't bother pushing them up; she glared at me over the rims. "You *do* realize that your grandpa is a werewolf and your aunt is a witch and I am just a *mere* mortal, right? They can do unspeakable things to me and I'd be absolutely at their mercy; totally helpless. *Totally*." She shoved her glasses back in place for emphasis. "So, if you're okay with that, by all means, *go*."

It was a nice try, a truly valiant effort. It wasn't gonna work. I patted her shoulder and smiled brightly. "Great! See you in a bit!"

Millie's jaw dropped. She obviously thought she had delivered an Oscar-worthy performance and had me swayed. But it wasn't happening. Admittedly she'd poured it on rather thick, but I wasn't going to jeopardize Bobbybear's safety. Besides, I was pretty sure that neither Grandpa nor Aunt Abby would do her harm.

Still, as I stepped outside and pulled the cottage door closed behind me, I *felt* horrible. I was being a terrible friend. Millie deserved better from me. But I had to think of what was best for Bobby. He had been orphaned, and now his own grandmother had sent him into the past to either kill his paternal grandfather or be killed *by* him. *How screwed up was that?* He needed me to do all that I could—for the both of us. I knew that Millie was stronger than she gave herself credit for.

I walked along the path at a fairly quickened pace. I was hoping that I could get to Wellington House before I encountered anyone else, or before I completely lost my nerve. I *needed* to speak to my Grandmother alone. She had a lot of explaining to do as far as I was concerned. I needed to hear her reasoning for all that she had done. It would have to be pretty good to get someone to betray their own blood.

She had already tried to eliminate my grandpa by having Harrison Beckett shoot him with a silver bullet. Having failed in that attempt, she had now evidently enlisted the aid of this Sebastian Barrister—an old nemesis of Grandpa's. I needed to learn as much about him as I could. Somehow, he had also managed to keep his youth and vitality over the years. *If he wasn't a Lycan, then what was he - could he be a powerful warlock as the rumors suggested? Had he used dark magic to maintain his prime? What else was he capable of?*

As Wellington House came into view through the pines, I slowed my pace. It gave me the opportunity to study the manor for signs of increased presence. I didn't see anything that would be a cause for alarm. Everything seemed perfectly normal—if anything could ever be considered *normal* in The Hollows. That was still up for debate.

I walked around to the front of the old house and approached the door slowly. I was trying to decide whether or not to knock or just barge in. Finally, I made up my mind and just went inside—it was still my home after all. I may no longer be welcomed with open arms, but I didn't think that Grandmother would throw me out—that wouldn't *look* good. She was all about keeping up appearances.

I closed the door behind me, careful not to slam it shut, but I wasn't trying to be quiet either. As I turned around I saw Margaret hurrying toward me with a frantic look on her face. I smiled.

"Good morning Margaret. Would you happen to know where I can find my grandmother? I need to have a word with her."

She stopped, opened her mouth to speak, but no sound came out. She blushed slightly as she bobbed her head in affirmation and indicated the direction from which she had just come. She coughed into her fist. "She is expecting you in the drawing room."

Of course she was. Margaret had most likely seen me coming through the kitchen window and informed the Lady of the House of my impending arrival. So much for catching Grandmother by surprise—though I hadn't truly thought that possible. She *always* seemed to know what was going on in and around Wellington House.

As I took a step in her direction Margaret turned and led the way. The door of the drawing room was securely closed and as we approached Margaret quickened her pace. She knocked upon the door before opening it. "Madam, your granddaughter is here to see you." Her body blocked my entrance.

"Show her in." Grandmother's voice was cold, emotionless.

Margaret turned to let me pass, she said, "Mistress Katherine, Mrs. Wellington will see you now." As I entered the room Margaret pulled the door softly closed behind me, leaving me alone with Grandmother.

"Good morning Grandmother." I tried to keep my voice pleasant. My throat suddenly felt dry, my hands a bit clammy. Seeing her stoic expression unnerved me in inexplicable ways. I swallowed, steeling my waning nerves.

She studied me longer than I was comfortable with. Finally, she spoke. "You've been quite a busy girl, Katherine." Her hand tightened upon her cane. "I should caution you to mind your own affairs..."

I was angry now. "Stop it Grandmother!"

Her eyes grew wide as her jaw hardened. She tapped the end of her cane upon the flagstones repeatedly. "I'll *not* be spoken to in this manner in my own home. You should proceed with extreme caution. I—"

I didn't let her finish. "When I first got here, I tried to give you the respect that you deserved. Hell, I was even frightened by you. I was living under your roof and I was willing to live by your rules. But when you started *screwing* with my kid brother, you crossed a line."

"Are you threatening me Katherine?" One eyebrow arched.

"You sent Bobbybear back through time to die!" I was furious now. My hands were shaking. I so wanted to throttle her!

"Not to die," she said shaking her head.

"Oh no? What did you expect would happen to him when you sent him up against a werewolf? How could you possibly expect him to survive against such a monster? He's *only* six years old for gosh sakes!"

"You don't understand."

I knelt in front of her and placed my hand over the one she held on the arm of the chair in which she sat. "No, I *don't* understand.

Help me to." It was almost a plea.

"If your brother had managed to strike that *monster* with the *liquid silver*, he would've killed him." Her eyes narrowed as she looked into mine.

"He's my grandpa," I said hoarsely.

She pulled her hand away. "Exactly. If he had died back in 1884 then my daughter *couldn't* have married his son. She would *never* have become one of those *horrid creatures*. She would be alive today." She stood up abruptly, almost knocking me off balance. She crossed over to the fireplace, staring down into the crackling flames.

Horrified, I slowly stood up and stared at her back. Realization hit me like a ton of bricks. If Mom and Dad never married, then Bobbybear and I would never exist either. *Talk about a Paradox!*

Tears filled my eyes making everything a watery blur. They rolled down my cheeks unhindered. I blinked, trying to come to terms with what I'd heard. Finally, I thought I understood everything. I burst into laughter despite myself, causing tears to literally shoot from my eyes. "Is that why you've always been so cold to us?"

Grandmother's nod was almost imperceptible. "I didn't want to get close to either of you if I were just going to lose you." She turned and faced me. "I've lost far too much in my life as it is."

I shook my head slowly. "So, you are okay with simply *erasing* Bobby and I from existence? How can you be so cruel?"

"Had Robert succeeded, I never would've even known of the two of you. History would have been forever altered. You cannot miss something if you never had it in the first place."

"But we're not some trinket that you can just dispose of on a whim. We're living, breathing, human beings."

She frowned. "Oh please. Spare me."

"So, what happens now?" I asked.

"What do you mean?"

"What are your plans for us, for Bobby and I?"

"I am *not* a murderess, despite what you might think. Robert can continue to live here at Wellington House. I have grown quite fond of him after all. There is still the chance that he may never become like you and your parents."

"A Lycanthrope, you mean."

Her chin rose slightly. "Precisely."

I swallowed. "What about me? Where would you have me go?"

"Live with Abigail. I'll have no *dogs* here."

I couldn't help but notice that she failed to mention living with Grandpa as an alternative. "And our grandpa? What of him?"

Her eyes burned cold. "Samuel St. Claire has lived longer than he has a right to. He will be made to pay for his sins. He will be dealt with soon enough. Once he has then you and Abigail must leave Wellington House."

I stared at her in disbelief. "I thought murder was beneath you."

She laughed without any trace of humor. "Oh, Samuel St. Claire will not suffer my wrath. There are others willing to deal with him."

"Who? The Coven? Sebastian Barrister?"

She smiled thinly. "You've certainly done your homework, haven't you?"

CHAPTER 35

ULTIMATUM

I left the Manor in a daze. Before I departed, Grandmother gave me an ultimatum; her terms. I had to convince Aunt Abby to return with me to Wellington House where our safety would be guaranteed. If we chose to stay in the cottage or with Grandpa we would be destroyed right along with him and his Wolf Pack. Simple. Whether or not we accepted her offer we were to send Bobbybear tonight, so that he would survive the impending conflict.

Aunt Abby glared at me. "What the *Hell* were you even thinking?" I couldn't really tell if she were *furious* or *flabbergasted*. I felt as though I was in the sights of her proverbial shotgun and she was letting me have it with *both* barrels.

Millie waved her hands in front of her in a blur of rapid movement. She looked at me. "Sorry!" she exclaimed nervously.

It was *almost* comical. But I knew if I started laughing it would *only* make matters far worse. I offered Millie a wink instead.

Aunt Abby fixed Millie with a hard stare. "We asked you to do *one simple thing!* Keep everyone here while we were out."

I pointed a finger at Aunt Abby. "Don't you *dare* blame her! This isn't her doing by any stretch of the imagination. Your mother is to blame."

Aunt Abby took a deep breath, trying her best to reel her emotions in. To say that she was livid was an understatement. Her eyes were wider than I ever thought possible; her complexion a deep ruby red. She opened her mouth to say something but Grandpa placed a calming hand on her arm. The rest of the Wolf Pack looked uncomfortable, they exchanged silent looks as they tucked their hands into the pockets of their jeans. The tension in the cottage was so thick you could cut it with a knife.

Grandpa sighed. "There's no harm done. We need to think this through."

Aunt Abby's eyes were suddenly clouded with tears. "We can't afford to take any unnecessary chances. We know very little about Sebastian Barrister. Surely you know something more than what you've already told us. You said the two of you went *way* back." She gave him a hardened look as she wiped away the tears from her cheeks. "He is obviously *very* dangerous. *Is* he a warlock? We need to know what we're dealing with. We all do."

Grandpa sighed wearily as all eyes turned toward him. He sat heavily down upon a kitchen chair. "Okay, I'll tell you everything I know." He stretched his legs out in front of him. "Sebastian Barrister and I have always been at odds. He comes from old money whereas my family has always struggled for everything we've gotten. Because of that, he's always believed that he was better than me—better than *most* people for that matter. I've never believed that." He shook his head slowly. "He puts his pants on the same way as I do, one leg at a time."

Aunt Abby handed him a glass of whiskey as she sat across from him. He smiled appreciatively as he threw it back, draining the glass in one swallow. "He was never a very strong man, physically. Hell, I'm *twice* his size." Grandpa smiled that crooked grin that I recognized as a St. Claire trait. "Barrister decided one day that he'd pay a couple of his cronies to take me down a peg or two, teach me a bit of a lesson, I guess. But I've always been an outdoorsman, built from hardy stock. I didn't back down when they came at me. I took care of his goons and then I hit Sebastian in the face, breaking his nose." He chuckled softly. "He bled all over his tailored suit, and *boy* was he mad. People started laughing at him and it only made him angrier. He swore he'd make me pay."

Grandpa took the whiskey bottle and refilled his glass. This time he only took a small sip. "I didn't see much of him after that. When I did, it was a fleeting glance, like he couldn't get away fast enough. I thought the problem was solved; he'd learned his lesson." He shook his head. "But he hadn't."

He took another sip. "It was about that time that he started hanging out with members of the coven, and I had just been bitten. As I said earlier, we tangled a few more times—I think he was testing out his newly discovered powers." His eyebrows arched. "Each time we met, he was a little more powerful. Then we fought, and I thought I had finally finished him for good; but now I see that I haven't."

Aunt Abby reached out her hand and touched his sleeve. "There has to be something else. Being a warlock doesn't make you immortal."

Grandpa nodded. "I agree."

Brock crossed his arms over his chest. "So, what are we going to do? Take down this Sebastian Barrister and then deal with the Coven?"

Grandpa put a hand in the air. "Not so fast. First off," he glanced at Aunt Abby, "I think we should accept your mother's offer. I think Millie needs to take Bobby to Wellington House for safety reasons. And," he grinned, "it wouldn't be a terrible plan to have you and Kat there as well. You can be my eyes on the inside."

Aunt Abby shook her head. "If you think my mother is being honest about them being safe inside Wellington House, then you truly do not know her. She'll find some way to use us against you. We'd be nothing more than ransom. In the end, she'd have Sebastian kill us all, probably."

Grandpa sighed, running a hand through his hair. "At least in there you won't be the primary targets. If you stay out here you could just as easily be collateral damage. I can't risk that. I won't." He crossed his arms over his chest as though daring any of us to defy him.

Aunt Abby was up to the task. She stood up from the table and placed one hand on her hip and cocked her head with a raised brow. "You may need my services out here, especially if Harrison Beckett continues to take potshots with silver bullets. Besides, the others are *just* boys."

Grandpa chuckled as he stood and faced her. "They are *far* from being *just* boys, and you know that—probably better than anyone else." He put his hand to the side of her head and lovingly played with her hair. "Besides, I'm counting on you, Kat and Millie to keep your mother and the house staff out of the fight. You stand a much better chance of doing that from inside Wellington House. That way the Pack and I can deal with Sebastian." He pulled her to him, kissing her lips. "I can't focus on him if I'm worried about you."

She started to object but he planted another kiss on her lips. "Abby, I need you to keep my grandkids safe. Barrister will have no qualms about doing them harm. It *has* to be this way. You know it does. Besides, I truly believe what your mother said. If they are at Wellington House they will be under her protection."

Aunt Abby's nod was barely perceptible. I saw the tears fall from her eyes and roll untouched down her cheeks. She pressed her forehead against Grandpa's. "You know why she made this offer, don't you? It's not about keeping all of us out of harm's way; it's to ensure her own safety. She knows that as long as we are there with her, it limits what you can do. You can't simply burn her out."

Grandpa chuckled softly. "That thought had never even crossed my mind."

Millie shyly cleared her throat. "Uhm... guys?" As all eyes turned to her she blushed and nervously shoved her glasses back onto her nose. "What about the secret passage from here to Wellington House? Could, maybe... ah... it be useful? Or not?"

Grandpa seemed surprised. He stared blankly at Aunt Abby. "There's a secret passageway?"

She nodded. "Yeah, there is. I wasn't even thinking about it. You could get inside the basement of Wellington House. You know, I don't think my mother even knows it exists."

Grandpa scooped Millie up into his arms and gave her a big bear hug. Millie just let out a surprised "Oh!"

Setting her back down he cradled her head in his hands and kissed her on the forehead. "You are *absolutely* brilliant!"

Silas spoke up for the first time. "Hey! That's my girl you're kissing!"

Millie crinkled up her face as she looked at him with a big smile. "*Really?* I'm your girl?"

Blushing slightly, he quickly shrugged. "Uh... if you wanna be."

Millie flashed me a wide grin. "Well, what do ya know? I've got a boyfriend!"

Silas gave her a questioning look and said "so the fact that I can turn into a wolf doesn't bother you - not even a little bit?"

Millie batted a hand in the air. She said, "Please, my best friend is a wolf! Maybe I can be an honorary member of your Wolfpack?"

All eyes turned to my grandpa, he nodded as he took Aunt Abby's hand and said, "Why not."

CHAPTER 36
FACE TO FACE WITH THE ENEMY

Grandmother was obviously displeased at the sight of Millie joining us. "I don't recall inviting you here." Her attitude caused my friend to gasp sharply and turn quickly toward the door. Thankfully Aunt Abby blocked Millie's retreat, closing the door behind her.

"Really, Mother? Where's that Wellington charm and hospitality? You seem to have lost your manners." She glared defiantly at Grandmother as she crossed her arms in front of her. "We couldn't very well leave the poor girl alone in the woods, now could we? Especially since you've gone and stirred up all this ruckus."

I could see Grandmother's grip tighten on her cane, her knuckles almost turning white. Her jaw was clenched tightly and appeared to be chiseled from stone. She turned to me and smiled, but it was far from warm and inviting. "You should all go up to your rooms. I trust you recall where they are located." She glanced at Aunt Abby. "Abigail, a word in the drawing room."

"I don't think so, Mother. I shan't be staying. I only came along to get your promise that they will be safe here."

"What do you mean you won't be staying? If you go out there, I cannot guarantee your safety. Whatever fate befalls those *dogs* will be yours as well."

"I want your promise Mother. Will you keep them safe?" She glanced meaningfully at me and then back at Grandmother. "And you promise to keep Kat safe as well?"

Grandmother's eyes narrowed. "As long as they behave they will be safe in Wellington House. You have my word." She raised her chin. "Katherine as well. But when the dust settles, she must leave Wellington House for good. I'll not tolerate dogs in my house for long."

Aunt Abby nodded. "Thank you."

"Abigail," Grandmother reached out a hand and placed it on her arm, "if you go, there is nothing I can do to save you from him."

"Mother," Aunt Abby said with a smirk, "I'm not the one who needs saving."

Grandmother straightened. "Very well. Then this is goodbye." She turned and walked away; the sound of her cane tapping the floor sharply as she went.

Aunt Abby turned to me. "I'm trusting you to keep them safe. Don't try anything foolish."

Unexpected tears stung at my eyes. "Grandpa wanted you to remain here, with us. He won't be happy if you defy him."

She kissed me on the forehead, chuckling softly. "A little defiance is good for the soul." She squeezed my hands. "They may need my services. I can't tend any of their wounds from in here. I'll be safe at the cottage."

She knelt down and hugged Bobby. "You take care of your sister for me, okay?"

"I will." He threw his arms around her. "Be careful!"

She stood and glanced at Millie. "I'll send Silas through the tunnel as soon as I can."

Millie nodded. "We'll be ready for him."

"Okay, then." Aunt Abby smiled. "Try to keep as low a profile as possible? I think that your grandmother will keep you safe as long as you don't anger her. I'll see you all soon." She opened the door and stepped out into the fading sunlight. She glanced back at us, smiled, and then pulled the door closed.

An eerie silence seemed to descend upon us. As we climbed the stairs to the second floor Bobbybear tugged at my hand.

"Kat, I don't want to be alone."

I gave his hand a squeeze. "Don't worry sweetie. You're *both* coming into my room!" After all that had happened here in Wellington House, I wasn't about to let either of them out of my sight.

"You mean like a sleepover?" Bobby's face lit up.

"Yup! Just like a sleepover!"

Millie grinned. "Yay!" Her eyes went wide as she shook her head. "Your grandmother scares the you-know-what out of me! I think she *hates* me!"

I chuckled. "Well you *did* spoil her plans!"

"Me?" Millie said. "You're the one who went back in time to 1884!"

"But I couldn't have done that if not for you. You were the one who found the *portal*," I reminded. "And you figured out how to activate it. If it hadn't been for you, I would've lost everything!"

Bobby smiled up at her. "You're my hero! You saved me!"

Millie's smile grew as she blushed happily. "Aw, I'd do anything for you kiddo!"

He wrapped his arms around her and hugged her tightly. He looked up at her with bright eyes. "I love you Millie!"

In radiant surprise Millie looked at me with tear filled eyes. She hadn't expected Bobby's sudden display of affection. "Aw, I love you too, Bobbybear!"

At the top of the landing we turned toward my room in silence. Millie had hefted Bobbybear up into her arms and he was now resting his head on her shoulder. He stifled a yawn. "Tired?" I asked. He simply nodded.

"There's time to rest before dinner," I said as I opened the door. Millie stepped past me and plopped Bobby onto the bed causing him to giggle in delight. I glanced around the room not really expecting to see anything out of the ordinary. The room was pretty much as I had left it. I popped my head into the bathroom for a quick look but saw nothing out of place. I knew that Margaret had already been here for her morning cleaning. She always came after serving breakfast, wiping away any particles of dust that may have settled overnight; she'd return again while we ate dinner. She was a creature of habit or was she simply taking the ideal opportunity to snoop? I was never truly certain—especially with all the events that had transpired in this strange house.

Millie and I stretched out on the bed with Bobbybear nestled between us. The events of the last several days had left us all exhausted. In a matter of seconds I could hear the soft snores from the both of them. Listening to their uneven breathing my eyelids grew heavier. My aches slowly melted away as my body seemed to sink further into the thick mattress. It wasn't too long before sleep overcame me.

I don't know how long we'd been asleep but it felt like it had only been a few minutes at best. I reached over and gave Millie's shoulder a quick shake. "Wake up sleepy head." There was no way I was going to tell her that I had just woken up myself. What she didn't know wouldn't hurt her.

Millie glanced at her wristwatch and she frowned. "Seriously? It's only been about twenty minutes."

"I know, but we need to get down to the kitchen so that we can create a distraction for Silas. If Margaret is in there preparing dinner, then she will undoubtedly see him when he comes up from the basement."

"Oh! I almost forgot!" she said scooting off the bed. I noticed a small smile of pleasure appear on her face. At least *something* good was coming out of this mess.

Bobbybear opened his eyes and stretched his arms and legs as far as he could. He sat up and looked from Millie to me. "I'm not hungry. I just wanna sleep."

I smiled. "It isn't time for dinner yet, Bobbybear. But we do need to get up and see if Silas is in the basement, he may need our help getting upstairs without being seen."

Bobby's face brightened. "I can help!"

I chuckled softly. "We're counting on it!"

Millie glanced at her watch. "It's four forty-two. We'd best get moving if we are gonna do this before everyone goes for dinner."

My stomach growled noisily. "Wow, just the thought of food is starting to make me hungry."

"Well it's no wonder," Millie scolded, "you've hardly eaten anything in the last couple of days."

We got to the base of the stairs without any other signs of life stirring in Wellington House. As we walked down the hallway toward the kitchen, we could hear Margaret as she went about preparing the evening meal. I glanced into the dining room and saw that there were six place settings. Evidently Grandmother was having a couple of guests.

Bobbybear made his way into the kitchen and stood on the opposite side of where the basement door was located. He looked up at Margaret and smiled brightly. "Can I have a cookie?" he asked sweetly.

She turned from the stove to face him, a wooden stirring spoon in her hand. "Master Robert, you know I cannot let you have any sweets before dinner; it would spoil your appetite. Mrs. Wellington wouldn't take too kindly to that, I promise you."

Bobby frowned. "I only want two. Two won't spoil my appetite."

Millie and I slipped down into the basement as Margaret continued with another refusal. I closed the door softly behind me. It was pitch black. Fortunately Millie still had her tiny flashlight with her, and in a matter of seconds she had it on so that we had light to see by. The steps were narrow, and without the light I seriously doubted that we could have descended safely.

"Where is the tunnel?" I whispered softly in Millie's ear.

"Over there," she directed the beam of light off to the right.

We had to wind our way through several stacks of cardboard boxes, old furnishings, dusty crates and who knows what else. It took us over a minute, but finally we were standing in front of an old wooden door. "That's it," Millie said.

I turned the doorknob and pulled the door open. The passageway beyond almost immediately turned to the right and then switched back to the left, where I could see a faint glow of light coming. As I rounded the final bend, I came face to face with a wide-eyed Silas Monaghan. He reminded me a little bit of how Bobbybear looked when he was caught doing something he shouldn't.

His look of panic dissipated into one of pure joy. "I thought you might be either Beckett or Barrister!"

"We have to be extremely quiet. Margaret is up in the kitchen. It looks like my grandmother has two other guests here for dinner. One of them is probably Sebastian Barrister, so we need to be very careful. If anyone sees you there'll be trouble for sure."

He slipped his hand into Millie's. "I'll follow your lead."

At the top of the basement stairs I eased the door open a crack. Margaret was near the stove. I could hear Bobbybear moving across the room. "Can I have another cookie?" he asked.

"Certainly *not*!" Margaret said shaking the spoon at him. "You've already talked me out of three as it is!"

"How about a glass of milk then?" Bobby said. "The cookies were kinda dry, I need something to wash them down with."

"Very well, Master Robert. I'll pour you a glass of milk, but then it's off with you. I need to finish getting dinner ready. If I'm late Mrs. Wellington will have *both* our hides; she's got special company tonight."

"Who?" I heard him ask as I ushered Millie and Silas out the door.

"Never you mind who it is. You'll see them at dinner, not before. They are visiting with Mrs. Wellington in the drawing room; best you steer clear!"

I took a step forward. "There you are Bobbybear! I've been looking for you everywhere! You're not pestering Margaret are you? You know she has her hands full preparing dinner."

I smiled at Margaret as she took a gallon jug of milk out of the refrigerator. "Is there anything I can help you with?"

She shook her head. "That won't be necessary Mistress Katherine, I've things well in hand."

I took Bobby's hand. "Come along Bobbybear. Let's go get cleaned up."

"What about my milk?" he asked.

"You can have a glass with dinner."

He grinned up at me as we left the kitchen. "How'd I do?" he whispered.

"You were fantastic!" I said. I hesitated outside the drawing room door. "You go on ahead, I'll be just a second."

I pressed my ear against the closed door and listened intently. I could hear the muffled voices of Grandmother and another woman. And then I heard his voice—the rich baritone—quite unmistakable. He must have said something clever because both of his female companions laughed.

Nothing like being caught red-handed with your hand in the cookie jar. I still had my ear up to the double doors of the drawing room when they opened suddenly. I was practically touching Sebastian Barrister's chest with my ear.

He grasped my arms and pulled me against him. "What have we here?" There was a hint of humor in his deep voice.

I tried to pull out of his grasp but I couldn't. His icy grip tightened, the ends of his fingers digging into me. *"Let go of me!"* I hissed, struggling to get free. I could feel my feet leaving the ground. My eyes were now level with his.

"Such a *feisty* lass," he said, the corner of his mouth twisted.

"Put. Me. Down." The fire in my eyes failed to match the intensity of his. His were like ominous black pools—the kind you can easily drown in. I had no idea where the bottom was in those murky depths but I was certain that I didn't want to find out. I was afraid that I'd be lost forever. Even as his gaze met mine I felt like I was being drawn in—like from the pull of a black hole in the depths of outer space; I was unable to escape. Had Millie not suddenly appeared by my side I might have been lost forever.

Sebastian took one look at her and then firmly set me down. He turned toward Grandmother. "There are matters that require my immediate attention. I'm afraid that I will not be able to stay for dinner after all. My sincere apologies." With that he took Grandmother's hand and pressed his lips to the back of it. "Perhaps another time?"

Grandmother seemed more than a little disconcerted. "If you'd rather we dined alone, that can be easily arranged. The children can eat in the kitchen."

Sebastian Barrister turned and faced me. "I look forward to getting to know you better, my dear." He glanced at Millie, his eyes drifting to the golden necklace that she wore. His gaze seemed to harden and grow cold. He walked from the drawing room without another word.

Grandmother blinked as though coming out of a stupor. The other woman was glaring at Millie and I with disdain. I had never seen her before. She was about the same height as my grandmother, maybe slightly taller. Her hair was dark with streaks of silvery-white throughout. She wore a black, high-collared, flowing gown that went to the floor; clearly she was attempting to impress Sebastian Barrister. She had large, silver rings on each of her index fingers.

I could feel Millie tug at my arm. "We need to get upstairs!" her whisper was barely audible, but urgent.

I carefully backed out of the room and pulled the door closed. We walked away as quickly as we could. "Who was that woman?" I asked.

"Marybeth Collingsworth. I don't know much about her but I think she's a member of your grandmother's coven. I think she's another High Priestess or some other important figure. She can be a *nasty* woman when she wants to be." Millie shivered uncontrollably. "I think we should leave Wellington House!"

"She can't be that bad, can she?"

"Worse." Millie said pointedly.

CHAPTER 37
THE DISCOVERY

When we got back to my room we saw Silas and Bobby sitting on the edge of the bed. They were both grinning from ear to ear, speaking in hushed tones, conspiratorially. As soon as we entered, they stopped talking. I gave them a narrow look. "What were you two talking about?"

Bobby glanced up at Silas. "Nothing."

Silas slapped him lightly on the shoulder. "My man!" he said grinning wider—if that was even possible. He clapped his hands together and stood up abruptly. "So, when do we eat around here?"

"Dinner is usually at six sharp," I said.

Millie glanced at her wristwatch. "Almost an hour from now."

He frowned as his stomach growled noisily. "I don't know if I can make it that long."

"Well," I said, crossing my arms over my chest, "you'll have to wait even longer than that. You can't go down to the dining room. We'll have to see about sneaking you up something."

His face dropped. "Bummer." Defeated, he plopped back down beside Bobby.

Millie pushed her glasses up her nose. "Why do you suppose Sebastian Barrister left so suddenly?"

I shook my head. "I don't know. Besides being very rude, it was very odd. His entire manner seemed to change when you appeared beside me. It's like he saw something that disturbed him."

Millie blushed. "Wow. I never realized that I had that effect on guys. Maybe he doesn't like girls that are a little plump."

"Hey!" Silas frowned darkly. "Don't talk yourself down. I happen to *like* the way you look!"

Millie blushed again, her glasses slipped down her nose.

Bobbybear giggled. "You need to get those fixed."

Millie chuckled as she pushed her glasses back into their proper place. "Your sister tells me that all the time."

"Barrister was staring at your neck. He seemed fixated on your necklace," I said recalling the look he'd given her.

Millie's fingers went instinctively to her crucifix. "Hmm," she said thoughtfully.

Silas pursed his lips. "What do you think it means?"

She shrugged. "Who knows? It's an old family heirloom. Maybe he's seen it before. It's been passed down for generations."

I shook my head slowly as I considered what she'd said. "No, I don't think so. It wasn't recognition that I saw on his face. It was more like anger. *Something* about your necklace made him terribly angry."

"Hmm," she said tapping a finger against her lips.

"What?" I could practically see the cogwheels turning inside her head.

Millie shook her head, but didn't say anything. She had that faraway look clouding her blue eyes as she slowly drummed her fingers against her hip. Finally, she pushed her glasses up her nose and squinted her eyes at me. "I think we need to take a good long look at your grandmother during dinner."

"Why? What are you thinking?"

She shrugged. "It may be nothing, but she seemed to change once Barrister left. It was kinda like she snapped out of a trance, or something."

"You think she was hypnotized?"

Millie shook her head as she toyed with her necklace. "No. Something else, maybe."

I placed a hand on her arm. She was starting to drive me crazy. "C'mon Mille, what's going through your head? Please tell me."

She chuckled. "After dinner, I promise. But it may turn out to be nothing at all."

I gave her my best pout as I crossed my arms over my chest. *She knew something! And she wasn't talking...*

Silas stretched out on the bed as we headed out the door. "Don't forget to bring me back something to eat—I'm starving!"

"Stay put!" I warned.

He chuckled as he raised his hands in the air. "I'm not going to go anywhere. Just gonna take a little nap while you're all gone."

We were heading downstairs a little early but I was anxious to get a good look at Grandmother. Whatever Millie was hoping to discover, I wanted to see it for myself. But, admittedly, I had absolutely no clue as to what I was looking for. I was just hoping that I'd know it when I saw it—whatever *it* happened to be.

We took our seats at the dining table and sat in silence as we waited. Bobbybear was sitting next to Millie, who was directly across from me. She leaned down and whispered something in his ear. His eyes grew wide as I watched the two of them. When Millie straightened Bobbybear swallowed, a dark frown creasing his brow. Before I could ask what was going on, the door to the dining room opened and in walked Grandmother and Marybeth Collingsworth.

My eyes were glued to Grandmother. She looked a little pale but not too poorly. It was probably all of the stress of late. She wore a pale pink evening dress with a high collar. A pink chiffon scarf was loosely tied at her throat. I know she had been complaining about the coolness in the air.

As they took their seat, Grandmother glanced about the room. "Children, I'd like for you to meet a dear friend of mine, Mrs. Collingsworth. Marybeth, these are my grandchildren, Katherine and Robert." She turned her attention upon Millie, "This is Miss Bradford, one of Katherine's friends."

Marybeth Collingsworth smiled pleasantly. "I've heard a great deal about you all, already." She fixed her eyes on Millie. "Aren't you the granddaughter of Esmeralda Donea, the Fortune Teller?" She smiled at Grandmother, "You remember her don't you?"

Grandmother rolled her eyes. "I should have known." She indicated Millie with her wave of the wine glass she held in her left hand. "She brought her supernatural nonsense into my home."

"With your permission, I'm sure," Marybeth said.

Grandmother shook her head. "Hardly."

"Heavens! But should we really expect anything less?"

I slammed my hands down upon the tabletop, nearly spilling my glass of water. Millie visibly jumped in her seat. *"Enough!"* I stared at Grandmother, appalled that she could stoop so low and be so rude. "Millie is a *guest* in Wellington House. She should be treated with respect and courtesy." Tears stung at my eyes. I was getting tired of Grandmother's double standards.

Grandmother placed her glass of wine down carefully. She stared at it for a moment before she turned her gaze upon me. "The only reason that any of you are here is so that you may be spared the fate that awaits the others." She pointed a finger at Millie. "She brought that *nonsense* into my home and I told her she was not welcome back, yet I have been gracious enough to allow her to return to Wellington House so that she too might be spared because she is your friend. Do *not* make me regret that decision!"

I stood up. "May we be excused?"

"Sit down!" Grandmother insisted sharply.

I could see that Millie's eyes were moist. She looked up at Grandmother and spoke softly. "I... I thank you for your hospitality and... and your graciousness Mrs. Wellington. I do." She swallowed as she placed her hands in her lap. "And I just wanted to say how lovely you look this evening. That pink dress with the lace is very beautiful, and that scarf," she nodded as Grandmother placed a hand to her throat, "it's lovely." Millie glanced at my brother. "Don't you think that it is a lovely scarf?"

Bobby nodded.

Grandmother took a deep breath and exhaled it slowly. "I think I'd like to finish this meal with a little quiet, please."

We ate in silence. The only sounds to be heard were the clink of the silverware upon the plates. Bobbybear was the first to finish. He patted his lips with his napkin and then placed it beside his empty plate. "May I be excused now, Grandmother?"

"You may, Robert."

He slid out of his chair and smiled up at Marybeth Collingsworth. "It was a pleasure meeting you Mrs. Collingsworth. I hope to see you again."

"Oh, what a fine young man you are!" she said with a smile. "I do look forward to getting the opportunity to know you better."

Bobbybear continued to put on his display of good manners as he stepped up to Grandmother. "Goodnight Grandmother." As he went to kiss her cheek, the tips of his fingers pulled down the scarf slightly—it was enough to see two small puncture wounds, perfectly rounded, only inches apart upon Grandmother's neck. A thin trail of dried blood streamed down toward her shoulder. She had been bitten...! Bobby's action seemed accidental, and I didn't think anyone had noticed.

I felt Millie's toe lightly kick my shin. She had seen it too. I glanced at Marybeth Collingsworth; she was watching me over the rim of her wineglass with shrewd, *knowing* eyes.

I closed my bedroom door and leaned my back against it. "So, what was that? Did you and Bobby have that little stunt planned all along? Is that what the two of you were discussing before Grandmother and Mrs. Collingsworth arrived? What if you'd been caught?"

Millie smiled sheepishly. "Relax. No one even noticed."

"Are you sure about that?" I said raising my hands in the air. The way that Marybeth Collingsworth looked at me flashed through my mind.

"Did Grandmother get bit by a wolf?" Bobbybear asked.

"That *wasn't* the bite of a wolf," I said with conviction.

Millie shook her head. "I was afraid you'd say that." Her voice sounded full of dread. "That leaves only one other option."

"I'm listening."

Bobbybear spoke with undeniable certainty. It left me with a chill that cut to the bone. "I think that Sebastian Barrister is a vampire," he said.

I blinked in disbelief, my eyes growing wide as I looked from

Bobby to Millie. She nodded. "It's the *only* explanation that makes any sense."

"Whoa!" Silas said as he shoved a dinner roll into his mouth.

I shook my head in denial. "No way. There *has* to be another explanation that fits. Vampires *aren't* real."

Bobbybear looked up at me with large, round eyes. "How can you be so sure? They're in all those scary movies Mom and Dad didn't like us watching."

Millie chuckled nervously. "Why can't vampires really exist? I mean, a week ago I didn't think werewolves were real either. Now my best friend and my boyfriend are part of a real-life wolf pack. We've seen witches and ghosts, why not a blood-sucking vampire too?"

She had me there.

I sighed heavily. "We need to be sure of this."

Silas looked from me to Millie. "Is there some kinda test we can do? Make him stand in front of a mirror, maybe?"

Bobby grinned. "We could squirt him with Holy water!"

Millie giggled at Bobbybear's enthusiasm. She tousled his hair. "Sorry kiddo, I'm fresh out of Holy water!"

I gave her a look. "Would that even work?" I knew it did in most of those old horror movies but there was no telling if it was based on any hard facts or simply *creative licensing*.

She shrugged as she pushed her glasses up her nose. "Who knows?"

"Well," Silas said glumly, "with the absence of any Holy water to squirt on Sebastian Barrister we need to come up with another way. I still think we ought to see if he has a reflection in a mirror."

I shook my head. "And just how do you propose we do that?"

He shrugged. "Beats me."

I looked at Millie with wide, questioning eyes. "We need to be sure about this whole vampire thing before we drive a stake into the man's chest."

"There's some pretty hefty tomes in a back section of the library. Mostly dealing with the occult and what-not. I'm pretty sure that one of them would have details on vampires and such." By the color rushing to her cheeks I knew she was also referring to werewolves and witches but she just couldn't look me in the eye.

I tapped my bottom lip. "So, what you're saying is that you want to go do some research."

Millie shrugged. "Well, you wanna be certain."

I nodded. "I do. We can't afford to be wrong."

She crossed her arms over her chest. "Then get me to the library."

CHAPTER 38
THE CONFRONTATION

Bobbybear's voice was small and filled with fear. "So, if Sebastian Barrister really is a vampire, does that mean that Grandmother is a vampire now too?"

I started to say something reassuring, but my mouth opened and nothing came out. The truth of the matter was, I didn't know *anything* about vampires. I'd heard of Dracula, and I knew about Edward Cullen from *Twilight*, but those were just fictional characters—and they were nothing alike. I knew nothing about *real* vampires. I didn't want to frighten Bobbybear any more than he already was. I looked at Millie for answers, my eyes pleading for help.

She pushed her glasses up her nose as she knelt in front of Bobby and took his arms gently. "Oh, no, Bobbybear. I'm pretty certain that you don't turn into one of those things from just a single bite. There's a whole process to it."

"There is?" Bobby looked hopeful.

"Sure is!" Millie said with conviction. "She'd have to be completely drained of blood first, and then she'd have to drink the blood of the vampire. We just need to watch her and make sure she doesn't get bitten again."

Bobby had fallen asleep on the bed and Millie, Silas and I were watching him from across the room. Silas frowned. "I need to get word to the Pack that we think Barrister might be a vampire. That is something that they *need* to know. Maybe Abigail will have some Holy water or at least know how to combat him."

Millie nodded, "If you can find his lair during the day when the vampire is *most* vulnerable, we might be able to destroy him. It's probably our best chance."

"If he *is* a vampire," I said.

She quickly nodded again. "Of course. That's what I meant."

Silas started to unbutton his shirt. "What are you doing?" I said, placing a hand over his. I didn't know what he was fixing to do, but I was starting to feel just a little bit uncomfortable.

"I'm gonna go tell the others. I'll go out of the window, and then jump to the ground," he said with a slow grin.

Millie stared at him in disbelief. "Are you *crazy*? We're on the second floor! You'll break your neck jumping to the ground."

He chuckled and kissed her quickly on the lips. "I wasn't planning on jumping in human form. I was gonna let the wolf do all the hard stuff." He glanced at me. "This is my favorite shirt and jeans, not to mention all that I have with me. I don't really want to run around naked when I'm not the wolf."

I crossed my arms over my chest and gave him a crooked little grin. "It certainly wouldn't be the first time for you—and your friends for that matter."

He glanced quickly at Millie and blushed, which I found rather surprising. "We weren't running around, actually. We were at a swimming hole, and we had our clothes nearby."

Millie's eyes went wide as she looked at me in astonishment. "You saw them naked?"

I nodded. "Yup. Every single one of them." I couldn't keep the smile from my face.

Silas suddenly got defensive. "Hey, we weren't the *only* ones without clothes!"

Millie gasped.

I could feel the heat rising up my face. "Okay, we're getting off track here. We need to reel it in a bit."

Millie shook her head. "I can't believe it. You've seen my boyfriend naked. *He's* apparently seen *you* naked! I don't know how I should even feel about any of this." She pushed her glasses up her nose. "Should I be jealous? Should I feel like I've been cheated on? I mean, jeepers creepers! My best friend and my boyfriend have been naked. Together. Did you guys like touch?"

"What?" I quickly grabbed her by the arm. "No way! It was nothing like that! Honestly, it wasn't! *Ew!*" I shivered.

Silas climbed through the window after giving Millie another kiss. "Stay safe!" he said. Outside, he stripped down and threw his clothes back through the window. Before we could say anything, he started walking across a section of the roof.

Millie watched as he made his way toward the back of the house, a slow smile crept across her blushing face. "Wow... would you look at that!"

"No thank you," I said turning away. I'd seen enough already.

"What? Afraid that two moons in one night will be too much for your inner wolf to handle?" Millie teased.

"Ew!"

Millie touched my arm. "We're not out of the woods yet, with your grandmother, you know."

"What do you mean?"

"Well, if I'm right, that initial bite was just Barrister's way of exerting control over your grandmother. That's why her mood seemed to shift so drastically when he left earlier today. If I'm right, he'll have to re-establish his link." She gave a little chuckle. "I know what you must be thinking. You're wondering how I know so much about vampires. Well, first you have to consider *where* I work. I'm not popular in school- not even with the geeky nerds - I'm a total outcast. So I read. A lot. I read *everything* I can get my hands on. You may have noticed that I like the supernatural elements." She chuckled again, pushing her glasses back up her nose. "But *hello*! We are in The Hollows! We have witches, ghosts, werewolves and now, vampires! *Somebody* needs to be up to date on all this insanity. Why not the fat girl?"

I wrapped my arms around her and pulled her into a tight hug. I kissed the side of her head. "But I thought you didn't know a lot about vampires. You said you needed to do some research. Now suddenly it seems you're an expert."

She pushed her glasses up. "I'm far from being an expert so don't sing my praises just yet. We still have to find a way to stop Sebastian Barrister from getting to your grandmother. I seriously doubt if she'll be willing to assist us in that department; we're not in her good graces."

I nodded, hooking my thumbs through the belt loops of my jeans. "Okay. How do we do that?"

Millie chuckled. "You're asking me? She's your grandmother."

I gave her a helpless look and she rolled her eyes, giving in without a fight. "Well, for starters, we don't leave her alone; someone needs to be around her at all times. He's less likely to try something when somebody else is present. If he can't get to her, then he'll try to get her to go to him. He's only bitten her this once—I think, so his control shouldn't be that strong. The more times you're bitten by a vampire, the stronger his control over you becomes. And, it would be helpful if we had more crucifixes around—that whole thing with vampires not liking them isn't just in the movies."

It was like a light bulb just went off in my head. *That totally explained Sebastian Barrister's reaction when he first saw Millie—he had seen her crucifix!* It made him uncomfortable enough that he had to leave rather abruptly. Trouble was, I didn't recall seeing very many crosses in Wellington House since I'd gotten here. Come to think of it, Millie's was the *only* one.

Millie toyed with her crucifix. "It would be nice if we could get your grandmother to wear this. If Barrister does manage to get to her, or causes her to go to him, she'll need the protection. He can't bite her neck if he can't get to it."

"But what about you?" I was touched by her generosity.

She practically snorted as she batted a hand in the air. "Are you kidding me? My best friend is a bad ass werewolf!"

I couldn't help but laugh. "I don't know how much good I'll be against a vampire," I said. I wasn't able to keep the skepticism out of my voice no matter how hard I tried—and I did try.

"Of course," Millie said thoughtfully, "if the guys could find the vampire's lair, maybe we could end this in the morning. I'm pretty confident that we can survive the night—as long as we stick together. There is safety in numbers, especially when confronting a vampire."

I saw movement out of the corner of my eye. Bobbybear was tossing restlessly in his sleep. His brows were drawn together in a deep frown, his hands fisted tightly. *"No!"* he yelled.

I moved to the bed, hoping to offer him comfort. His feet were kicking about wildly as though he were running. His eyes shot open, and he sprang up to a sitting position. As though he were looking through me he said, "Grandmother needs our help!" He slid off the bed and headed to the door.

I reached out to stop him but Millie grabbed my arm. "He's not awake, look at him."

Looking at my brother I could see that she was right. His eyes had a glassy stare; it was almost as if he was walking in a dream-like state, not truly conscious of where he was.

"We need to follow him," Millie said urgently, "he may lead us to your Grandmother!"

After he opened the bedroom door, he continued to shuffle toward the stairs. I wanted to run to him, and wake him up before he could fall, but Millie wouldn't release her hold on me. "We don't want to wake him. It might do more harm than good."

"But what if he falls?" I could feel the fear for my brother's safety rising within me. "He could break his neck tumbling down those steps."

Millie pointed at Bobbybear as we followed close behind. "He won't."

Bobby was taking each step slowly, one hand gliding along the polished maple handrail. We were careful not to make any sound, but I doubted if it would've really mattered. Bobbybear still seemed oblivious to his surroundings, walking as though in a trance. At the base of the stairs he turned right and walked down the hallway toward the drawing room. We continued to follow him, keeping as close as we dared.

My nerves were on edge as we continued past the kitchen. We could hear Margaret scrubbing pots and pans as she worked diligently at her tasks, humming softly to herself. We continued along the dimly lit corridor towards Grandmother's chambers, past the servant's quarters. Margaret and Harrison Beckett had larger rooms than one would expect due to their station but Grandmother wanted to keep them close at hand.

As we drew closer, we began to hear muffled voices but I was unable to make anything tangible out. Bobbybear opened the door to my grandmother's room and went inside. The door closed behind him. I quickened my pace and as I reached the door I clearly heard Bobbybear state, *Let me go!* He seemed to be struggling with someone.

I pushed open the door and I could see Marybeth Collingsworth and Bobbybear in the middle of the room. She was holding his arm as he fought to free himself from her grasp. In the adjoining room I could see Grandmother standing with Sebastian Barrister.

Somehow, in his struggles with Marybeth, Bobby managed to see Millie and I enter the room. His eyes grew wide as he frantically pointed to Grandmother. "Don't let him hurt her!" He clawed at his captor, scratching her on the arm, drawing blood.

Marybeth's eyes narrowed and she slapped him hard, upon the cheek. *"You little shit!"* she hissed angrily. He fell at her feet but she retained her tight grip on his forearm, twisting the skin.

Millie gave me a nudge toward them. "See to your brother, I've got your grandmother!"

Nodding I moved forward transforming.

Marybeth Collingsworth screamed as the wolf's front paws struck her chest. She fell backward, releasing her hold on Bobbybear's arm. I landed between the two of them, snarling viciously, ready to attack again if the need arose. Marybeth cowered in the corner of the room, her arms raised to ward off another attack.

The wolf turned and nudged Bobbybear with her muzzle as though checking him for injuries. Satisfied that he was unhurt, the wolf turned again to Marybeth Collingsworth and exposed all of its teeth in silent warning.

"Please, don't hurt me!" Marybeth said in a wavering voice as she drew her knees closer to her chest.

Turning the wolf trotted toward the other room, letting out a soft bark for Bobby to follow. He seemed to understand.

Sebastian Barrister was standing in front of a shiny black coffin that was sitting upon a stained pine bier on the far side of the room. Grandmother was standing just to the side of the vampire; her head cocked at a slight angle to better expose her neck to him. Her eyes were glassy, as though she were drugged or in a trance. A small smile curved the corners of her mouth. She seemed perfectly at ease, offering herself up to him. He seemed to snarl at the sight of the wolf coming into the room to confront him. His fangs were exposed and seemed to glisten in the candle-lit room. He pulled Grandmother against him, almost as though he intended to use her as a shield.

As he sunk his teeth into her pulsing neck, she let out a soft gasp, her eyes squinting in momentary pain. Millie rushed forward and pressed something against the vampire's cheek. Faint wisps of smoke seemed to rise through the small gaps between her fingers and the pungent smell of burnt flesh filled the air. Sebastian Barrister recoiled in agony, ripping Grandmother's tender neck in the process. She crumpled to the floor. With a clawed hand he struck out at his assailant, knocking Millie off balance. She stumbled backwards, awkwardly trying to regain her footing. She bumped into Bobbybear and together they fell to the floor in a tangled heap.

Sebastian maliciously glared down at them, his sharp-nailed fingers flexed at his sides. His eyes were red, the pupils elongated like a cat's. His left cheekbone had the imprint of Millie's crucifix burned into it. His chin was covered with blood. Furious, he snarled as he stepped forward, ready to strike. The wolf growled and sprang toward the vampire, striking him in the chest.

Barrister fought back. I could feel his sharp claws digging into my sides as we stumbled backwards. A rush of cool air surrounded us as we crashed through the window. The wolf bit at the vampire's shoulder as we fell through Grandmother's rose bushes snapping several stems as we went. We impacted the hard-packed ground and I heard Sebastian grunt in my ear.

The vampire was first to his feet. We could hear others fast approaching. He glared at me. "This isn't over!" He transformed into a bat and flew off into the night. I shed the wolf returning to human form. Both of my rib cages bore the deep scratches from the vampire's claws, but I wasn't too concerned. I was fairly certain that I would heal in time.

Grandpa and Aunt Abby were the first to reach me. The rest of the Wolf Pack transformed and attempted to follow the bat through the forest. Grandpa peeled off his jacket and wrapped it around my shoulders. "Are you okay?" he asked.

Aunt Abby had given me a cursory examination. "She'll be fine in time."

"Grandmother's been injured. Marybeth Collingsworth was in the other room."

Grandpa glanced through the shattered window at the mayhem inside the room. "Can you get to the cottage?" I could tell that he was concerned about me still.

"I'll be fine. Go." I inclined my head towards the house.

He helped Millie and Bobbybear out of what was left of the

window. Then he and Aunt Abby went inside to see what they could do about Grandmother and Marybeth Collingsworth. I thought it strange that neither Harrison Beckett and Margaret did not appear during all the commotion.

CHAPTER 39

AN ALLY OR AN ENEMY

Not surprisingly, the vampire had eluded the Wolf Pack. They had managed to follow him a good ways in the woods before losing him completely in the deepening shadows. Cho Ming and Tucker Morrison were still searching the forest. They were following a very small and intermittent trail of blood caused by the wound I had inflicted to Sebastian Barrister's shoulder, while Brock and Silas returned to the cottage.

Aunt Abby returned not long after the guys had arrived. She quickly sent them back to Wellington House. She looked at me with concern. "I need to tend your wounds. We don't want them to become infected."

Millie was sitting on the living room sofa with Bobbybear in her lap. His eyes were wide, and red-rimmed from crying. He was absolutely terrified by all that he had seen happen. She had her arms around Bobby and was rocking him as she sang softly to him. She was doing a great job in soothing him and giving him comfort.

Aunt Abby took me into her bedroom and had me sit on the edge of the bed. "Are you in any pain?" she asked as she helped me remove Grandpa's jacket.

I winced. "Only when I breathe."

She gingerly touched my wounds. "The bleeding has already stopped. You seem to be healing nicely. I see no signs of infection."

"That's good to hear." I said.

She put some antibacterial ointment on some gauze and then had me hold them in place as she taped them to my sides. "You probably won't have to keep this on for more than a few hours if you heal anything like your grandpa. Otherwise I'd wrap you up like a mummy."

"How's Grandma?" I asked.

Before she could respond, Grandpa came in carrying Grandma in his arms. She was unconscious and looked *very* pale. He laid her down on the bed and glanced at my aunt. "I've got Brock and Silas destroying that coffin. That's one less sanctuary that Barrister can take refuge in."

Aunt Abby removed the bandage from Grandmother's neck; her skin was badly torn and almost shredded. I could see the worry in her eyes as she examined the wound. It didn't look good. I was worried, but I wasn't about to say anything. Aunt Abby shook her head. "I doubt that coffin was Barrister's. It was probably there for Mother."

Grandpa glanced down at my grandmother. "Do you think that your mother is going to become a vampire?"

Aunt Abby glared at him and then glanced at me. "I honestly don't know. My knowledge about the undead is limited."

I couldn't keep quiet any longer. "Millie says that a vampire has to almost completely drain you of blood before you turn. Either that, or you have to be bitten and then you have to drink blood *of* the vampire." I indicated Grandmother with a nod of my head. "We saw bite marks on her neck when we were at dinner tonight. So, I think she was at least bit one other time before this one. Millie said that was so that Barrister could gain some control over her. The more she was bitten, the more control he'd have."

Grandpa shrugged. "That sounds reasonable, I guess."

Aunt Abby looked at me. "Where does she get this information?"

I shrugged. "She's really into *this* sort of thing. She says that they have a whole section in the library dedicated to the supernatural. She reads a lot. We need to see if we can find more information though. Like all the ways to destroy a vampire. Anything that may be useful."

She began to stitch up Grandmother's neck as best she could. Due to the severity of the ripped flesh, there was going to be a lot of scarring. She covered it with a thick greenish paste. "This will draw out any toxins from the blood." She shook her head. "I don't know if it'll do any good against a vampire bite though. Time will tell."

She glanced at Grandpa. "Did you find any signs of Marybeth Collingsworth?"

"No," he said shaking his head. "She simply *vanished* without a trace. Probably flew off on her broomstick." He grinned at his own joke.

Aunt Abby shot him a scathing glare. She was in no mood for his humor. He cleared his throat. "Sorry."

I glanced at Aunt Abby, "Did you ever hear from your contact in the *Coven*?"

Aunt Abby sighed. "She couldn't tell me anything that we don't already know. It seems that she split from the Coven when they brought in Sebastian Barrister. She confirmed that he *is* a vampire. She and a couple others wanted no part in his plans, so they quit."

Grandpa sighed. "Not very helpful."

Aunt Abby gave him a meaningful look. "You and that Pack of yours need to find his lair. We need to put an end to his plans whatever they may be. In order to do that, we have to destroy him."

"Killing a vampire isn't going to be an easy task, I'm afraid. Not even for the Wolf Pack. I may have to bring in reinforcements."

She sat beside Grandmother and placed a cool, damp washcloth on her forehead. "She's burning up."

"Is that a bad sign?" I asked.

"Depends," she shrugged. "It could be her body's way of fighting off the bite of the vampire. If it breaks, I'm fairly confident that she'll be fine."

"If it doesn't?" Grandpa asked.

"Then we may have a bigger problem on our hands." She glanced at him. "At any rate, there's nothing more you can do here. Go do what you have to do to deal with Barrister and the Coven."

Grandpa hesitated. It was like he still had something on his mind that was really bothering him. He frowned and then reached out a hand toward my aunt. "I need to find Keegan Rourke. He's probably our best chance of dealing with Barrister."

I saw Aunt Abby flinch at the mention of Keegan Rourke. It made me curious. Obviously, he was someone whom she didn't like very much. *Who was he? How could he help us deal with Sebastian Barrister? Was he a modern-day Van Helsing? I had never heard the name before.*

Aunt Abby shook her head. "There *has* to be a better way." She glanced quickly at me and then back at Grandpa. She lowered her voice to a whisper, hoping I wouldn't hear. "I don't trust him. You shouldn't either."

Grandpa chuckled. "It's not a matter of trust. *Hell, I don't trust him!*"

"Then why bring him into this mess? We're in enough trouble as it is."

"Sebastian Barrister is just too strong for the Wolf Pack and me to face. The powers of a vampire are formidable. I just don't think we should risk it. If we were to fail," he shuddered, "then The Hollows would be lost."

I couldn't keep silent any longer; besides, I was starting to get a crick in my neck straining to hear their conversation. "Who is this Keegan Rourke?"

Grandpa glanced at my aunt. "An acquaintance of mine. We go way back."

I crossed my arms over my chest. "Seriously?" I was getting annoyed.

Aunt Abby sighed. "He's the man—*or the wolf*—responsible for turning your grandpa into a Lycan in the first place."

"So what's the issue with him, then?" I pressed.

Grandpa sighed. "Let's just say that we don't exactly get along very well." He took a deep breath. "I'm gonna see if I can locate him. I've instructed the guys to stay close to keep an eye on things." He reached out and squeezed Aunt Abby's hand. "Everything's gonna be okay. You'll see."

She nodded without looking at him. I could tell that she wasn't happy with his leaving.

After Grandpa had left I looked at Aunt Abby, "What's the real story between this Keegan Rourke and Grandpa?"

She took a deep breath and exhaled slowly before she answered. "Keegan Rourke killed Sam's wife, your grandmother. Sam's never forgiven him for it, and every time he has the opportunity, he tries to kill Rourke."

This new information had me wondering if Keegan Rourke was going to be an ally against the Coven and the vampire, or would he turn out to be just another enemy that we would have to face. Things were looking pretty grim.

CHAPTER 40
WHERE THERE'S SMOKE

Bobby had fallen asleep on the sofa and now Millie was standing beside me. She must have sensed my tension as we watched my aunt administer Grandmother's wounds. I could feel her fingertips caressing my back in tiny circles. Aunt Abby sat on the edge of the bed and pulled back the bandage on Grandmother's neck taking the utmost care. Millie froze. I doubted she was even breathing at this point.

Aunt Abby placed the back of her fingers against her mother's forehead. Even I could see the beads of sweat that had formed on Grandmother's brow. "Oh my," Aunt Abby said softly; it was scarcely more than a whisper. She stood up and disappeared into the adjoining bathroom and we heard her open the medicine cabinet. We could hear the soft clink of glass bottles as she rummaged through them searching for only she knew what.

She returned with a mortar and pestle and a small bottle. She placed them on the dresser and then dumped the contents of the bottle into the bowl. Millie took a step toward her. "Can I help?" she asked.

Aunt Abby smiled at her. "That would be nice. If you will just crush this until it turns into a paste."

"What is that?" I asked, joining them.

"Yarrow," Aunt Abby replied.

Millie looked up. "I've read about this. Doesn't it help to lower fever and prevent infection?"

Aunt Abby looked at her with raised brows. "You are an amazing young woman."

Millie's cheeks had a rosy glow. She shrugged. "I read a lot."

Aunt Abby smiled at me. "So I've heard."

After Millie had ground the yarrow into a thick paste, Aunt Abby spread it over the wound on Grandmother's neck, covering it completely; afterwards she put a fresh bandage in place. "We'll need to change this daily and keep the wound covered with the yarrow paste."

I stared at Grandmother and couldn't keep the tears from forming. "Do you think she'll be okay? I mean, seriously?" She'd had a *huge* chunk of her neck torn away. I was surprised that Aunt Abigail had managed to stop the bleeding as quickly as she had. But Grandmother had lost a lot of blood. She was deathly pale and it frightened me.

Tears fell from Aunt Abby's eyes. She quickly wiped them away. "Only time will tell." She straightened. "How's Bobbybear?"

"He's sound asleep."

"Good. He's been through a lot. He needs to rest." She squeezed my hand. "How are you doing?"

I wiped the tears from my eyes. "I'll be okay."

She gave my hand a pat. "Good. I think you and Millie should go and see what you can learn from the library. Take Brock and Silas with you."

I shook my head in protest. "But..."

"The more we learn about this vampire threat, the better off we'll be."

"But what about you? You might need some help with Grandmother."

"I'll be just fine. The rest of the Wolf Pack will keep an eye on things here." She fave me a gentle shove. "There's nothing you can really do here. Your grandmother needs to rest. It will take some time for the fever to break. Until then, there isn't anything that we can do for her, except try and keep her comfortable. I can handle that much."

Dawn was still several hours away and the threat of the vampire was still very real. I hated the fact that we were spreading our forces so thin, but what choice did we really have? Grandpa had gone off in search of this Keegan Rourke who sounded like a very dangerous man. Would he help us fight Sebastian Barrister? *Who knew? And what of the Coven? What was their role in this mess?*

"I hope we're doing the right thing," I said softly as Brock drove grandpa's truck toward The Hollows. Millie was sitting to my right, with Silas' arm wrapped around her. "I hate splitting up like this, it makes us more vulnerable."

Brock chuckled softly. "Relax. Cho and Tucker can handle things at the cottage. Silas and I can keep you and Millie safe."

I sighed. "Are we *really* safe though? I mean, even Grandpa seemed concerned about facing a vampire. I just think we need to be careful. It may take all of us together to defeat Barrister."

"There's no need to worry," Silas said. "We've been doing this for a long time. The Pack is strong."

"I know you are when you're all together," I said. "But now we're all scattered." I shook my head and shrugged. "I mean, who's even leader of the Pack in my grandpa's absence?"

Silas chuckled. "It sure ain't me! I can tell you that!" He leaned forward. "And I *know* it isn't Tucker or Chow Mein. How about you, Brock?"

Brock laughed as he looked over at Silas. "No way! I'm not stepping into the role of the Alpha." He pressed his shoulder against mine, giving me a gentle push. "Your part of the family line. That makes you the Alpha!"

I glared at him. "You've got to be kidding me, right?"

"Nope," he said smugly.

"That settles it in my book. You're the Alpha!" Silas said.

Millie slapped a congratulatory hand on my knee. "You go girl! Show these boys!"

I rolled my eyes as I leaned into the seat. This was *so* not what I was going for.

As we neared The Hollows city limits, we could see a thick billowing cloud of smoke rising upward into the night sky, highlighted by a fiery orange glow from underneath. Millie gasped sharply.

"That's coming from the direction of the library!"

We could see the flashing lights of the only fire truck and police cruiser that the city had as we rounded the last corner. A throng of curious bystanders stood in the street blocking our progress. We would have to go the rest of the way on foot. As we climbed from the pickup I could tell that Millie was upset. If the books weren't damaged by the fire, the water would probably finish them off. I wasn't holding out much hope.

I had the uneasy feeling that we were being watched as we got as close to the library as we possibly could. While we waited for the firefighters to do their job, I scanned the crowd. Finally, I spotted Marybeth Collingsworth standing near the back of the crowd. She was staring at me with a haughty expression. I squeezed Brock's hand. "Stay with Millie and see if you can find out how the fire started. I see someone I wanna talk to."

Brock looked around as though trying to see to whom I was referring. There was no way he would figure that I was wanting to talk to Marybeth—she just wasn't on his radar. "Don't be long."

I smiled. "I'll be back as quickly as I can."

Turning from my friends I found Marybeth still standing near the back of the gathered crowd of onlookers. Her eyes were still on me. I saw her lips moving as though she were speaking with someone. I tried to see who she was talking to, but there were too many people in the way.

As I stopped in front of Marybeth Collingsworth I saw two women standing on either side of her; no doubt they were members of her Coven. Witches. Marybeth gave me an amused look. "Shouldn't you be home in bed? It's a little late for children to be out and about."

I glared at her. "I'm *not* a child."

Marybeth laughed. "Is that so? I suppose next you'll tell me you can take care of yourself."

I put my hands on my hips and glanced at her two companions briefly. I met her gaze with a raised chin. "I'm not afraid of the Coven."

Marybeth took an unexpected step toward me, her glare was menacing. I couldn't help but take a step backwards. I slammed into something hard. A body. I turned to apologize but I was stopped short. Two strong hands gripped my arms. The hands of a man. Sebastian Barrister chuckled in my ear. "It's not *just* the Coven you should fear my dear. It is me as well."

I tried to free myself from his powerful grip but I couldn't. He was much too strong. His fingernails were starting to dig into my biceps painfully. He licked the side of my face with his overly moist tongue, causing me to cringe, but even that wasn't easy. "After I have dealt with you and the rest of your dog friends, I will rip your auntie's throat out. And then there will be your brother, all alone." He chuckled again. "I have big plans for him!"

I could feel the wolf struggle against the power of the Talisman, but it was useless. No matter how badly I wanted to give in to the wolf's desires, I couldn't. With Barrister's vice-like grip on my arms I couldn't pull the chain from my neck. I could feel the tears spring from my eyes. I growled in anger, but it wasn't the snarl of the wolf I heard; it was that of a frightened and helpless girl. I could feel the vampire's hot breath upon the pulse at my neck. To my surprise he didn't bite me. But he did throw me to the ground. I sprang up from my tumble, clutching my Talisman, ready to rip it off, but Barrister and the witches were gone...

Brock appeared beside me, a look of concern in his eyes. "Are you okay Kat? You look like you're about ready to attack."

I searched the thinning crowd but I could see no trace of Barrister or the witches. *How had they managed to disappear so quickly?* I relaxed my stance and turned to face Brock. I could see that the firefighters had gotten the fire out and were beginning to pack up their hoses. "It was Barrister. He was here with members of the Coven."

As I wiped the tears from my face, Brock touched my arm. "Did they hurt you?"

I could see his gaze move to my neck. Annoyed, I said, "I'm fine. He wouldn't risk biting me in public. He did warn me though. He isn't going to stop until he has destroyed us all." I gave him a worried look. "He said after he has killed the Wolf Pack he'd rip out Aunt Abby's throat. He said he had plans for Bobbybear."

Brock squeezed my arm. "We won't let him harm your brother, I promise."

We were joined by Silas. "They think faulty wiring was the cause. Millie's inside. She's pretty torn up about the whole thing."

"I'll go to her. You guys see if you can find where Barrister and those witches went." I left them and stepped toward the library entrance. The firefighters had taken axes to the front door to gain access. The door was in splinters and barely hung from its hinges.

Millie turned to me as I entered. She had smudges of soot on her chin and her cheeks. She had been crying. "Everything's ruined," she said through her tears. "They said it was the wiring, but I don't believe it."

I hugged her close. "It was the Coven. I'm sure of it. I saw Marybeth and two of her cohorts in the crowd. They seemed to be gloating." I looked to the back of the library where the fire had hit hardest. "Let me guess, that's the section that had the books about the vampires."

Millie nodded. "You got it."

Silas stuck his head in the doorway. "No sign of Barrister or the others."

Millie squeezed my arm. "He was here?"

I nodded. "I'll tell you all about it on the way back to the cottage."

CHAPTER 41

FRIENDS

By the time we got back to the cottage the morning sunlight was breaking through the trees causing the dew-covered ground to sparkle brightly. Millie and I both yawned as we climbed out of the pickup. It had been a long night. As we entered the cottage Aunt Abigail was softly closing the bedroom door behind her. "How's Grandmother?" I asked.

Aunt Abby shook her head. "Her fever has been returning off and on. I'm doing all I can to keep her comfortable, but I... I just don't know." She was exhausted. Obviously she had stayed awake all night. "Did you find what you were looking for?"

I shook my head. "No, there was a fire at the library. I think the Coven set it on purpose so that we couldn't find anything useful. The investigators claim it was faulty wiring but I don't buy it. It started in the section containing the very books we were going to look through. Everything was destroyed."

She frowned. "Sounds a little too convenient."

"Tell me about it," I said.

Aunt Abby yawned. "I need coffee." She stepped around me and headed into the kitchen where a fresh pot was waiting. She opened a cupboard and pulled out a clear bottle with a dark red powder. She opened a drawer and took out a teaspoon. She measured two spoonfuls of the powder and dropped it into a coffee cup and gave it a stir. She smiled as she took a sip. She closed her eyes for a moment and sighed dreamily. When she opened her eyes, they seemed brighter, more alert. She seemed wide awake.

I picked up the bottle of red powder and stared at it. "What *is* this stuff?"

She snatched it out of my hands and put it back into the cupboard. "Don't you worry about it."

I chuckled softly. "Well okay, then."

Aunt Abby smiled "It's harmless really, it only enhances the caffeine."

After she finished the cup of coffee she handed me the empty cup. "Would you be so kind, I need to get back to your grandmother."

I placed the cup on the counter with the rest of the dirty dishes. I began to fill the sink with hot, soapy water. "Sure. I've got clean up duty."

Aunt Abby kissed the side of my head and went back into the bedroom where Grandmother was resting. She closed the door behind her.

After washing the dishes and putting them away I looked around, wondering where Bobbybear was. I hadn't seen him since we got back from The Hollows. I went outside on the front porch where Cho and Tucker were talking. "Have either of you seen my brother?"

Tucker shrugged. "He was playing with a toy soldier over by the well. But that was about an hour ago."

Cho nodded. "I last saw Bobby heading toward the manor. He said he wanted to get something out of his bedroom." He looked around. "Surely he's back by now."

I felt a surge of panic rush through me. *There wasn't anything in Bobbybear's bedroom at Wellington House!* I took off running as fast as I could, hoping I was wrong. *Surely Bobbybear wouldn't go back in time to try and save Sara again...* I took off running. "Oh no! No, no, no!" I had that sinking feeling in the pit of my stomach, I knew Bobby had gone back in time to try and save his friend. If he had, I wasn't sure I could save him this time; I had come so close to losing him before.

I threw open the front door to Wellington House and called out frantically. *"Bobby!"* I wasn't expecting to get an answer, so I didn't wait as I raced for the stairs. I climbed them as fast as I possibly could, not sure if I was taking them two or even three at a time.

By the time I got to the second floor I was completely out of breath. I turned to the left and had to gasp for breath, placing my hands on my knees. The hallway seemed to be longer than I remembered. *"Bobby?"* I yelled out as loud as I could.

He didn't answer; but I hadn't been expecting a reply. I took off running toward the stairs leading up to the attic storage room. I paused at the foot of the narrow staircase. I could feel—*and almost hear*—my heart pounding in my chest. Tears started forming in my eyes, blurring my vision. *Was I too late?*

For the first time I felt the wolf inside me urging me forward. She wasn't demanding to be set free; I sensed she was insisting that I not stop, that I continue to push myself to my absolute limit. I heeded her call. This time I *did* take the steps three at a time. Reaching the landing at the top I took a deep breath. The door was closed. *"Bobbybear?"* I called out as I reached for the icy doorknob.

He didn't answer.

I pushed the door open and saw both Bobby and Sara standing in front of the portrait. They looked at me as I entered, their eyes wide and expectant. As I took a step toward them Sara Robinson smiled for the first time. The girl had such a pretty smile, her whole face lit up. I swallowed, uncertainty flooding me. *What was going on?*

Bobby looked at me as he took Sara's hand. "She's my friend."

"You can't go back with her, Bobbybear." I felt the tears running down my cheeks. "I *need* you here with me."

To my surprise, Sara reached out and took my hand in hers. Her skin was cold to the touch. Her voice was soft. "We just want to play together." She squeezed my hand. "He's my only friend. I promise I won't take him from you."

Bobby looked at me with pleading eyes. "Please, can we still play together?"

She had saved my brother's life by sacrificing herself. Had she not, I wouldn't have gotten to Bobbybear quick enough. The black wolf—*Grandpa!*—would've taken him from me; he would be dead now. I squeezed her ghostly hand in acceptance. *How could I be responsible for destroying their friendship?* I couldn't.

CHAPTER 42
A CREATURE OF THE NIGHT

Bobby and Sara had played for several hours. He fell asleep on the sofa with a happy little smile curving his lips. Millie stood at my side as we watched Aunt Abby tend to Grandmother's wound for what seemed like the hundredth time. You could feel the tension in the air as we looked on apprehensively.

Aunt Abby nodded as she carefully peeled back the bandage on Grandmother's neck, taking the utmost care. "It's looking better," she said softly. Her brows creased. Something was troubling her. Tiny beads of perspiration coated Grandmother's forehead and temples. It was clearly evident that the fever had returned. My aunt sighed as she placed her hand against Grandmother's skin. "I was really hoping her fever would break. She's still burning up," my aunt spoke in a whisper, her voice sounding worried.

"Does she need more yarrow paste?" Millie asked. "I can mix some up."

Aunt Abby shook her head. "The wound is no longer in danger of infection, so the yarrow has already done its job. What we need now is for this damned fever to break."

She stood. "I am going to leave her in your care."

"What!? You *can't* be serious!" I protested. "You can't just leave us."

Aunt Abby gave me a cold stare. "Marybeth Collingsworth and the Coven are responsible for this," she pointed at Grandmother. "No doubt they had something to do with what happened to the library as well."

I reached out and grasped her arm as she started to walk by me. I was beginning to feel uneasy. "Shouldn't we at least wait until Grandpa returns? One of you should be here!"

She pulled her arm from my grasp. "Kat, we can't afford to just sit around and do nothing. Sam might not even be able to locate Rourke. And if by some small chance that he does, they'll probably just kill one another in the process. The Coven may be our only other chance to stop Barrister. Someone has to know how to locate his lair. I'm betting that Marybeth knows where it is."

"Do you really think she'll tell you anything?"

Aunt Abby gave me a familiar smile; I had seen it on Grandpa's face several times already. "*I'll* make her talk." She placed both hands on my shoulders, giving me a little shake. "But I need you and Millie to watch over Mother. Can you do that for me?"

I nodded. "Do we have a choice?"

"The Wolf Pack will still be here if you need anything," she said. "I'll be back as quickly as I can."

I followed Aunt Abby to the front door of the cottage. I was still hoping that she would change her mind and stay with us; it was dangerous out there with Sebastian Barrister still on the loose, not to mention Harrison Beckett with his rifle. But I just couldn't come up with *anything* to say that would convince her to remain with us. Her mind was made up. She was stubborn—obviously a Wellington trait.

I closed the door as quietly as I could and turned to check on Bobbybear. He was still soundly sleeping—a soft snore escaped him as he lay snuggling against a throw pillow on the sofa. *I wondered what had happened to Mr. Grizzle?* I didn't want to disturb him, so I went back into the bedroom to check on Millie's progress tending to Grandmother.

Millie had just finished placing a cool, wet cloth over Grandmother's forehead. "How's she doing?" I asked.

Millie sighed wearily. "She's still feverish, but she seems to be resting peacefully. I don't know what else I can do for her at the moment." She put a hand to her mouth and yawned.

I draped my arms around her shoulders and pulled her close. "Aww Millie, you're exhausted! You should go into the other bedroom and get some sleep. You've certainly earned it."

I could feel her yawn against me. It actually tickled my neck and caused goosebumps to rise on my arms and legs. Great—just what I needed on top of everything else.

"Sorry," she said, pushing her glasses back into place with a giggle. "I *am* exhausted!"

I pointed her to the door and gave her a little shove. "Off you go."

Millie made a beeline for the sofa. "I'm not sleeping alone," she said over her shoulder. "I'm taking Bobbybear with me."

I could only smile. I wasn't about to object. Bobby *is* a great snuggler. She scooped him up, holding him against her chest and he flung his arms around her neck, still holding onto the small pillow. "Wake me if you need anything."

I nodded.

Silence descended upon the cottage. Everything seemed peaceful and serene. I went to Grandmother and removed the washcloth from her forehead. She was burning up. I dipped the nearly dry cloth into the bowl of water that sat upon the nightstand and dabbed it against her temples, and face, before returning it to her forehead. I wished that I had a thermometer so I could get a reading on her temperature. But one wasn't available to me, and I hadn't a clue where one might be.

I sat down on the chair that had been pulled into the room from the kitchen, for the bedside vigil. I reached out and took my grandmother's hand and held it gently. I caressed the back of her hand with my thumb. "Get well, Grandmother. We need you."

I must have drifted off to sleep without realizing it. I awoke to find Grandmother thrashing restlessly. She was literally dripping sweat, and the bed sheets were soaked. I pulled the washcloth from the pillow where it had fallen and soaked it again. I tried my best to cool her down but I wasn't having much luck.

Dark rings surrounded her eyes. Though she had been

unconscious she hadn't gotten any rest. Her eyes sprang open and I gasped, unexpectedly jumping backwards in the chair. The whites of her eyes were bloodshot. "Abby?" She whispered hoarsely. "Abby, I am so sorry! I... *I only wanted my family back!*"

Gathering myself, I squeezed her hand tightly. "It's me, Grandmother. It's me, Kat." I leaned close trying to hear her as best I could.

She licked her lips, but her mouth was dry from the fever. She tried to focus on my face. *"Katherine?"*

I nodded. "Yes. It's me, Katherine." I said. I couldn't keep the fear out of my voice. But hopefully she wouldn't notice how afraid for her I was.

"Katherine... tell Robert... tell Bobby... that I... I'm sorry!" She shook her head in anguish. "I... I didn't mean for any of this to... to happen! I... I *do* love him!"

She took one last, ragged breath and slowly blew it out.

"He knows, Grandmother. He knows!" Tears fell from my eyes. I laid my head upon her breast and sobbed. She was gone. We had lost the battle to save her.

I gently touched Millie's arm and she sprang awake. I quickly pressed a finger to my lips and she nodded in understanding. She studied my face and immediately knew everything. She placed a wavering hand over her mouth and said, "I'm *so* sorry."

"I need to get word to Aunt Abby. She'll want to know." I said.

Millie eased off the bed. "How?" She took her glasses from the nightstand and put them on. "How are we going to find her?"

I shrugged. I had no idea.

"Wait!" Millie said quickly. "She said that the guys were going to be sticking close by. Maybe one of them knows how to find her."

"Maybe."

She patted me on the arm. "Stay here. I'll see if I can't get a hold of one of them."Millie left the room and headed for the front door of the cottage. I heard her go out, closing the door behind her.

I lay down upon the bed and snuggled up against Bobbybear, gently wrapping my arms around him. He didn't resist as he wiggled, pressing himself up against me. I was glad of the close contact. I *needed* to feel his warmth against me; I felt so cold and numb. I didn't know how much more loss I could endure. I breathed in the scent of Bobbybear's hair, as my tears began to fall.

It seemed an eternity passed before Millie finally returned. She had Tucker Morrison in tow. Millie glanced nervously at him as they stood at the foot of the bed. He was carrying a small black doctor's satchel; his eyes were wide, his ever-present smile was gone. Millie swallowed. "Uh... Kat..."

I eased up off the bed, careful not to awaken Bobby. Poor kid was out! "You making house calls?" I asked Tucker.

He shot Millie a nervous glance as he frowned.

I indicated the bag in his hand with a nod.

"Oh!" he said giving me a quick smile before it faded. He swallowed. "Abby said that if it became necessary... then... I'd have to... uh... " He raised the bag. "Use this." He looked at Millie and then inclined his head toward the door. "I'll just wait out here."

"What's in the bag?" I demanded.

Millie jumped. She could tell I was getting upset. "Kat... your grandmother was bitten by a vampire. In all likelihood—"

"*No!*" I said, pushing past her.

She grabbed my arm. "Kat stop! We can't allow your grandmother to turn into a vampire! Think of Bobby!"

I stopped in the doorway, my eyesight blurring through the tears that suddenly welled up. I stared at Tucker. He gave me a steady look. He had already taken the wooden stake and the mallet out of the bag. "I can do this; you don't have to be there."

Millie came up to me and rubbed my back. "You know it has to be done, right?" she asked.

I could only nod. Finally, I straightened up and wiped the tears from my eyes. I looked at Tucker and shrugged. "Let's get this over with."

He nodded. "Okay."

I glanced quickly at Millie. "Stay with Bobbybear. I don't want him seeing this."

I closed the door behind us and leaned against it as I watched

Tucker approach the bed. He held the stake in his right hand, the mallet in the other. I had never realized it until this moment that he was left-handed. Grandmother seemed so peaceful, finally, truly at rest. I dreaded what was about to happen—she deserved far better—but I knew it had to be done. I refused to allow Bobbybear to see this, but I *had* to, as hard as it was. The tears continued to well up in my eyes, blurring my vision.

Tucker's hands were trembling. I wasn't sure he'd even be able to strike the top of the stake once he had it in position. I swallowed. "If you can't do this..."

He took a deep breath. "Nah. I got this."

Tucker hovered over my grandmother for a moment as he took another long breath, steadying his nerves. He placed the stake over Grandmother's heart.

I felt the hairs on my arm stiffen.

He raised the mallet in the air.

I couldn't breathe.

I saw his arm swing downward.

The mallet never struck the head of the stake. Grandmother's hand shot up and grabbed Tucker's wrist in a vice-like grip that made him gasp at the sudden, unexpected pain.

"Come to finish me off, have you?" Grandmother hissed. She jerked on Tucker's arm, slamming him against her breast.

I couldn't move. I couldn't *say* or *do* anything. I was frozen in place.

I watched in horror as Grandmother opened her mouth wide, exposing her fangs. Her eyes sparkled lustily as she bent her mouth to him, sinking her teeth into his neck. Tucker screamed, his arms flailing out to his sides.

"No!" I tried to shout, but it came out only as a whispered whimper. I slid helplessly down the length of the door plopping onto the hardwood floor, the tears rolled down my cheeks; I could literally feel them flying out of my eyes.

Tucker stopped flapping his arms in the air. He no longer struggled. His arms dropped down upon the bed. The only sounds I heard were those of my grandmother, drinking deeply.

I heard the deep sated sigh escape my grandmother's lips as she finished drinking. I squeezed my eyes tightly closed as I heard Grandmother release Tucker and allow him to fall, lifelessly to the floor like unwanted garbage. I heard her cast the sheets aside, the sound of her bare feet walking—almost gliding—across the hardwood flooring. She stopped in front of me, hovering over me. I was terrified, unable to summon the wolf to save me.

I knew I was next...

But the attack didn't come. She was sparing me.

I opened my eyes and cringed as I stared into the dead, wide open eyes of Tucker Morrison. Swallowing, I looked up at the woman standing in front of me. The dark splotches under Grandmother's eyes were gone now; her eyes sparkled brightly. She looked absolutely radiant, beautiful.

But blood covered her chin.

I looked away. Repulsed.

It was almost as if Grandmother could sense my thoughts. She knelt before me and wiped her chin with the back of her hand. I felt *compelled* somehow, to look at her. She lightly shook her head. "I had no idea that *dog* could taste so good!" She laughed at her own joke as she inclined her head toward Tucker. "He got what he deserved."

"No one deserves this!" I hissed.

Grandmother had a sad look in the dark pools of her eyes. "I couldn't agree with you more."

I could feel my pulse pounding in my neck. Grandmother's eyes seemed drawn to the throbbing beneath my skin. She rose quickly, slapping her thighs in the process. She stared at the window. "I should get going. The sun will rise soon."

"Where will you go?" I asked softly. "They destroyed the coffin that they found in your room."

"There are caves where I can seek shelter nearby. I can go there." She glanced back at me. "But Wellington House *is* my home. I will be back."

I nodded. "I know."

"Kat!?" I heard Brock call out as he entered the cottage. He sounded worried, but it made my heart skip a beat nonetheless. *Was he actually concerned about me?* I was flattered to say the very least. I hadn't expected this from him; we'd hardly even spoken since returning from The Hollows when he and Silas had driven Millie and I to the library. Maybe he did care about me more than I realized.

I got up off the floor and wiped a sleeve across my face. I knew I had to be a mess; but I was eager to get out of Aunt Abby's bedroom. I took a deep breath, and stepped out of the room, closing the door behind me. I didn't want Bobbybear to accidentally see Tucker's body just lying there on the floor where he had fallen.

Brock, Silas and Cho were standing in the kitchen with Millie. She was obviously pretty shaken. She had probably heard Tucker's scream when Grandmother attacked him. Heck, I was still unnerved by the whole ordeal!

Seeing me, Brock quickly moved to my side. "Are you alright? Millie said she heard a scream." He glanced toward the door. "Where's Tuck?"

I could see that Millie was leaning against Silas, and he was hugging her close, rubbing her arm soothingly. I glanced back at Brock. "It... it was Tucker. When he went to drive the stake through my grandmother's heart, she attacked him. She bit him on the neck. I think she drained him. I... I think he's dead."

Brock stiffened. "Where is your grandmother now? Is she still in the room?"

I shook my head. "No. She left. She went out of the window."

Brock looked over at Cho and inclined his head toward the bedroom door. Cho nodded as he hefted a baseball bat in the air. "I'm on it," he said.

We all watched as he opened the door and went inside. All was silent for a moment or two. Then he stood in the doorway, the bat resting on his shoulder. He shook his head, "Uh, man, there's no one in here."

I slipped out of Brock's embrace and ran to the bedroom. I squeezed past Cho and stared down at the hardwood floor where I had left Tucker. He was gone. Realization hit me like an icy gust of wind smack in the face. He had risen to become like Grandmother, like Sebastian Barrister, a creature of the night.

This just kept getting better all the time.

CHAPTER 43
ASSURANCES IN THE DARK

The mouth of the cave was dark. The wolf approached it slowly, ears prickled forward, listening intently. Wary. The wolf sniffed the air and let out a whine of uncertainty. The stench of death was thick in the air, mixing with the fragrance of pine. It was strongest near the dark cavity of the rocky slope. But there was a familiar scent too. Traces of jasmine and lilac...

Grandmother.

I shed the wolf form as I entered the cave. Looking down I discovered the source of the foul odor. A dead rabbit—several of them—lay upon the ground, at the edge of the light outside and the darkness within. I could see two round puncture holes in the necks of the dead animals. I swallowed. I couldn't keep the thought from my mind. *At least she's not starving!*

As I left the sunlight behind I walked slowly, the fingertips of my right hand gliding upon the rock wall, smoothed by wind and rain. My left hand was outstretched before me so that I wouldn't bump into the rocky surfaces. My vision was nowhere as keen as the wolf's. I regretted taking human form for that reason. Perhaps I would have been better off had I stayed transformed...

"Why have you come, Katherine?" The darkness whispered in

my grandmother's voice.

"Grandmother?" I swallowed the fear that was lodged in my throat. I was naked and cold. *Vulnerable...*

"Have you come to end me?" she said, there was no hint of emotion in the disembodied voice. I couldn't tell where it came from, it seemed to be coming from every direction all at once. Perhaps it was my fear playing tricks with my mind. I couldn't be sure.

"Honestly?" I asked, taking another step into the void.

She chuckled softly. "Of course, Katherine. Let there be no lies between us."

My throat felt tight, my mouth dry; my tongue too heavy and thick. I swallowed. "I need to know what your intentions are. With Bobbybear. And me."

Her eyes seemed to glow as she stepped in front of me, appearing out of nowhere. I could see the curve of her lips. They seemed pushed out a bit, perhaps from teeth that were unnaturally large. *Fangs!* "I mean to bring you no harm," she said.

She reached out and exposed my neck by pushing my hair behind my left ear. Her eyes seemed to flicker at the sight of my pulse. She licked her lips longingly and I could see her pointed fangs glistening in the darkness. Instinctively I put my hand to my neck as if to block her attack. I couldn't help but notice how my fingers were trembling.

"Are you frightened of me, Katherine?" she asked, sounding amused.

"No." I said, swallowing.

"Liar!" She laughed. "I can *smell* your fear."

I bit my lip and nodded. "Okay. All right. So I'm scared. Terrified if you must know. But who wouldn't be?"

"I told you that I will not harm you. Or your brother. Don't you believe me?"

"I want to."

"Then *do*. I give you my word. I will not harm either of you and I will make certain that no harm ever comes to you."

"What about my friends?"

She laughed. "Well, let's not get carried away... After all, a girl's gotta eat."

"I won't let you hurt them."

Her eyes narrowed. "Relax sweetheart. I was only teasing. You can have your friends."

"Then I guess I'll let you live." I said, allowing a nervous smile to appear.

She laughed. "That is so very gracious of you."

"What can you tell me about Sebastian Barrister?" I pressed, feeling my confidence returning.

She studied me for a moment. "He is one of the *Old Ones*. He is far too strong for you to confront."

"Can you maybe speak to him, get him to leave us alone?"

Grandmother laughed. "I can speak with him, but I doubt that it will do any good. He seems to have a bitter feud with Samuel St. Claire. He'll likely not stop until he has triumphed over him. He intends to destroy the Wolf Pack."

She licked her lips again, her eyes no longer locked with my own; they seemed to have drifted back down to my neck. "If you were to *offer up* your grandfather to him, he might be persuaded to leave you and Robert alone..."

I took a step back, appalled at the thought. "I *can't* do that!"

She shrugged. "Then there is little else I can do for you. I will speak to him on your behest, but I wouldn't hold out much hope." She met my gaze. "My dear friend Marybeth Collingsworth runs the Coven now. She wants to see your grandfather and his ilk perish as well. As long as the wolves protect The Hollows she remains less powerful. She desires a return to the *old ways*." Her eyes flickered to my throat. "You should go. I haven't eaten in a while."

I nodded, taking another step backwards.

"Oh," Grandmother said, "give Abigail a message for me, if you will."

"Of course." I said.

"Tell her that she should take you and your brother back to the city. The three of you should leave The Hollows for good."

CHAPTER 44

VALEN'S RIDGE

Aunt Abby glared at me angrily as she leaned against the kitchen counter. "Kat, you have to *stop* paying these visits to your grandmother—*especially now!* She's a vampire, for crying out loud! She didn't like werewolves before, she certainly won't now!"

I crossed my arms over my chest and glared at her defiantly. "Well what was I supposed to do? You and Grandpa just ran off and left us here alone, I needed to do whatever I could to keep Bobbybear safe."

She nodded, and then spoke more calmly. "I appreciate your need to protect him, but waltzing up to a vampire is *not* the way to do it. What if she were to attack you? You of all people know what she is capable of, you *saw* what she did to Tucker Morrison."

"Okay. First of all, I *didn't* just waltz up to Grandmother. And secondly, she *didn't* attack me."

"Kat, you have to understand that she *isn't* your grandmother anymore. She's changed."

"*No!* She's *still* Grandmother. She may have been physically altered, but inside, where it counts, she's still herself." I shook my head. "We can debate this all day, but we won't really get anywhere. We need to push on. What did you find out from the Coven?"

"I couldn't find Marybeth. No one else knows where she's gone. She and her closest cronies seem to have simply vanished. The others had no idea where Sebastian Barrister hides during the day."

"You trust they were telling you the truth? Why would they?"

"Oh they were telling the truth."

"How do you know?" I asked crossing my arms.

She smirked and arched a brow. "Do you *really* want me to tell you?"

I felt suddenly cold. I swallowed. "No. I guess I'd rather you didn't."

"That's probably best," she said.

"What about Grandpa? Have you heard anything from him?"

Aunt Abby shook her head. I could see the concern in her eyes; she couldn't disguise it. "Nothing. But I didn't really expect to hear anything so soon. Keegan Rourke doesn't like to stay in one place too long. It might take him some time to find him."

"And then," I added, "they have to get over their differences long enough to talk about our problems."

She nodded. "Exactly. The trouble is, according to Sam they always opt to fight first."

"Well, for our sake I hope this time it'll be different."

We heard Grandpa's truck pull up to the cottage. I watched as Cho Ming vaulted out of the bed of the pickup while Silas, Brock and Millie slid out of the cab. Millie had a *huge* smile on her face. They had all gone into town to see if they could find an address for Sebastian Barrister in the public records. By the grin on her face, she clearly had found *something* promising.

We gathered around the kitchen table to hear the news. "Well," Millie said pushing her glasses up her nose, "I had to pull some strings, but I was able to find a residence belonging to an *S.O. Barr* tucked deep in the woods near Valen's Ridge."

Cho Ming snapped his fingers together. "S.O. Barr—that's *got* to be him! He really *is* an S.O.B.!"

Silas slapped his shoulder, rolling his eyes. "Boo!" he chuckled.

Aunt Abby frowned as she tapped the piece of paper with the address that Millie had found. "Valen's Ridge. That makes *perfect* sense." She pushed the paper aside and looked up at Brock, who was standing beside me. "Have you guys had any luck searching for Tucker?"

Brock shook his head, sighing. "No sign whatsoever. We've continued to stakeout his house, but he hasn't gone there since your mother attacked and killed him. His family doesn't seem to know anything, they're getting pretty worried about him."

"Understandable," Aunt Abby said. She pointed at the address. "You never know, he might be there with Barrister."

Brock nodded. "That's a possibility."

"I think you guys ought to check it out. It's the only lead we've got," she said.

"I'm going too!" I said quickly.

Aunt Abby shook her head. "No, you're not. You're staying here, where it's safe."

I shook my head. "No, I'm not. The Wolf Pack is already down two members. They *need* me. I am going. Besides, both Brock and Silas already anointed me as Pack leader. And you know as well as I do, if we don't destroy Barrister then there won't be a safe place anywhere!"

Aunt Abby sighed heavily. "I guess you're right."

I reached across the table and squeezed her hand. "I will be careful."

She looked at Brock and Silas with narrowed eyes. "You really think making Kat the Alpha is a wise decision?"

Brock spread his hands wide. "Hey, she's a direct descendant of our leader. The position is hers by right."

Cho grinned. "I'm down with that!" He glanced at me. "I'll happily follow you and Shakira *anywhere!*"

Millie groaned. "Really? A *She Wolf* reference?"

Cho chuckled. "Hey, her hips don't lie!"

To be honest, the thought of being the leader was exciting. For one thing, the view was always guaranteed to change—sorry, but I just couldn't resist *that* one. So, lacking any other viable options it fell on the remaining members of the Wolf Pack and I to investigate the property out on Valen's Ridge.

Aunt Abby pulled me aside. "You do realize that when you

revert back to human form you will all be totally nude. You, and the three of them. Are you sure you're okay with that?"

I arched my brow and smiled. "It's not like we haven't ran together before."

Her eyes went wide. "Is that so?"

I shrugged. "It's not a big deal."

Aunt Abby gave us all a concerned look. "I suggest you try and get some sleep. If you plan on getting to Valen's Ridge by dawn, you'll need to leave fairly early."

I found it impossible to sleep. A myriad of thoughts came and went, chasing any thoughts of slumber away. I was thinking about Mom and Dad—the four of us, really—and our life in the City. It seemed a lifetime ago, and perhaps it was. But it was a whole *other life*. Nothing like what I'd had since coming to The Hollows. Back then, werewolves, vampires, witches and ghosts were the things of fantasy; simply make-believe. Now I knew better. So much had happened to Bobby and I that I knew we were forever changed. The supernatural was now our norm.

School would start sooner than I was really ready for. And *that* would be an entirely new experience for both Bobbybear and I. We had thus far been home-schooled and that was all we had ever known. But that was going to change. We were about to join the public school system. For Bobby that probably wouldn't be so bad—unless he started telling everyone that his best friend was a ghost of a girl who had died in 1884. He would be teased relentlessly. At least I already had a small circle of friends that would make my transition into public education easier. But still, I would already have enemies—the girls that were daughters of Coven members...

Grandmother was another story altogether. She was a creature of the night, and though she had assured me that my friends would all be safe, was that enough? She would *have* to feed. How long would she be content with rabbits and other forest creatures? How long before she craved human blood? Could I really allow that to happen? Would I be alright with her taking another's life? If not, sooner or later she would have to be dealt with. *Was I capable of dealing with her myself? I wasn't certain.*

Before long Aunt Abby came into the room where I was lying with Bobbybear and Millie. She put a hand on my shoulder and said, "It's time. The guys are waiting outside."

I sat up as quietly as I could, not wanting to disturb either Millie or my brother. The day had been a long one for us all, and though I couldn't, I knew they needed their sleep. I stripped down and Aunt Abby wrapped a blanket around my shoulders. "This will keep you covered until you transform." I started to say something, to object, but she shook her head, giving me a knowing look. "They are teenage boys, after all."

I chuckled as I kissed her cheek. "I love you Aunt Abby."

I had been carrying the black satchel that contained the wooden stake and rubber mallet in my teeth while in wolf form. I placed it on the ground and looked up at the others. They had already cast their wolf personas away and were standing naked in front of me. Waiting. I growled a warning and then I too, transformed. Now was not the time for modesty.

Cho Ming's whistle caused me to blush a deep crimson. Silas slugged him hard upon the bicep. "Dude! That's our *sister*!" he said pointedly.

Cho rubbed his arm and blushed. "Sorry," he said glancing at me one last time.

"Eyes on the task, people!" Brock said, moving forward.

We could see the cabin tucked near a grove of thick silver maples and a smattering of tall northern white pine. The place looked deserted, but that didn't mean that it was. We had come this far, taking great care to be vigilant; there was no sense in getting reckless now. *We were so close!*

I touched Cho's arm and pointed to the left, and then indicated that Silas go to the right. Brock and I made our way to the front porch. The door was open a crack enabling us to see inside. The golden rays of the sun filtered through the trees and shown through the windows. The cabin wasn't much bigger than the one my grandpa called home. It had two rooms and a small kitchen. The place was pretty much empty. The back bedroom had the only furnishing—a pine bier that had once supported a coffin. The casket was noticeably absent.

Sebastian Barrister was gone.

Evidence proved that he had been here. It also showed that he hadn't been here alone. Cho and Silas had found the prints of a wolf behind the cabin. Tucker's scent was all over the place, but he too was gone.

EPILOGUE

HOMECOMING

"So now what?" Millie asked. She had been coming over a lot, learning as much about *Healing* as she could from Aunt Abby. It wouldn't hurt to have another couple of hands tending wounds. Besides, she was a quick study.

Aunt Abby arched her brows. "We stay vigilant. Sebastian Barrister will eventually seek his revenge. When he does, we must be ready to strike."

I stepped outside, needing time to be alone and to think. I really believed that what Aunt Abby said was true. Sebastian Barrister would come. He wouldn't be content to just be satisfied with the victories he had already won. He would want to destroy us all. And then there was still Marybeth Collingsworth and the Coven. They too wanted to put an end to the Wolf Pack.

War was coming to The Hollows.

And sooner or later we were going to have to deal with my Grandmother and Tucker Morrison.

Standing on the porch of the cottage I listened to the sounds of the night. The chirp of crickets, the hoot of an owl high up in a pine and the lonesome howl of a wolf in mourning, somewhere far off in the woods. I could see thousands of stars shining above the pines. It was a cloudless night. The moon just beginning to claim its place in the heavens.

Closer to home, I saw the two wolves, one white and one gray, surrounded by their ghostly aura. They were on the path leading up to Wellington House. I stepped off the porch and started walking in their direction. They continued to stay just ahead of me, finally disappearing around the front of the manor.

I walked along, at my own pace and when I reached the front of the house, they were gone. I felt as though I was being watched. The feeling was overwhelming, almost disconcerting. I glanced up at the front of Wellington House and saw Grandmother watching me from a second-floor window.

She had come home.

ABOUT THE AUTHOR

Born in Kermit, Texas in 1960 and raised all over the Great American Southwest. He graduated High School from an American boarding school in Mallorca, Spain in 1978. He spent the next twelve years serving in the Navy.

Diagnosed as an insulin-dependent diabetic, he was forced to change careers and begin work in the construction industry as a Union Pipefitter where he often worked at the Kennedy Space Center.

He dreamed of being an author from a very young age and was always scribbling away in a notepad that he carried in his pocket. The Chosen, his first published novel is proof that 'Dreams don't have to stay that way.'

He currently lives in Satellite Beach, Florida with his wife, daughter, and granddaughter, along with two precious Maltipoo pups; Bandit and Patches.

The Hollows is his second novel; the first in a brand new Horror series. "My interests in writing are varied—just as the books I choose to read."

http://www.tomhornauthor.com

9 781912 677580